Books of Merit

The **MASTER** *of* HAPPY ENDINGS

Spit Delaney's Island (stories)

The Invention of the World (novel)

The Resurrection of Joseph Bourne (novel)

The Barclay Family Theatre (stories)

Left Behind in Squabble Bay (for children)

The Honorary Patron (novel)

Over Forty in Broken Hill (travel)

Innocent Cities (novel)

A Passion for Narrative (a guide for writing fiction)

The Macken Charm (novel)

Broken Ground (novel)

Distance (novel)

Damage Done by the Storm (stories)

The
MASTER
of HAPPY ENDINGS

Jack
HODGINS
A NOVEL

THOMAS ALLEN PUBLISHERS

TORONTO

Library and Archives Canada Cataloguing in Publication

Hodgins, Jack, 1938–
    The master of happy endings : a novel / Jack Hodgins.

ISBN 978-0-88762-523-7

I. Title.

PS8565.03M37   2010   C2009-907210-6

Editor: Patrick Crean
Jacket design: Black Eye Design

Published by Thomas Allen Publishers,
a division of Thomas Allen & Son Limited,
145 Front Street East, Suite 209,
Toronto, Ontario M5A 1E3 Canada

www.thomas-allen.com

 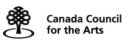

ONTARIO ARTS COUNCIL
CONSEIL DES ARTS DE L'ONTARIO

Canada Council
for the Arts

The publisher gratefully acknowledges the support of
The Ontario Arts Council for its publishing program.

We acknowledge the support of the Canada Council for the Arts, which
last year invested $20.1 million in writing and publishing throughout Canada.

We acknowledge the Government of Ontario through the
Ontario Media Development Corporation's Ontario Book Initiative.

We acknowledge the financial support of the Government of Canada
through the Book Publishing Industry Development Program (BPIDP)
for our publishing activities.

10 11 12 13 14 15   5 4 3 2 1

Printed and bound in Canada

for the family, with love

and in memory of our friend
Ian Smith

The **MASTER** *of* HAPPY ENDINGS

1

Axel Thorstad was not yet so old that he might at any moment forget where he was or why he still lived on this small island. Whole weeks went by in which seventy-seven was not as ancient as he'd been led to expect. Though he'd been long retired, he saw himself as a man of sound mind and healthy curiosity, a reader still of poetry and novels and, in order to keep himself informed, his monthly *Teacher* magazine.

He was a physically active man as well, taller than everyone else and fiercely unbent, a daily swimmer and frequent rescuer of flotsam off the salty beach, where his size 13 soles left water-filled depressions in the sand. Often those footprints were all that anyone might see of him for days on end—which was fine with him. He had chosen to make a solitary figure of himself, but with a decent man's habit of keeping a hermit's wariness in check, masked by a public courtesy.

In the privacy of his cedar-shaded cabin overlooking the beach, Thorstad was a widower still in mourning after seven years, a retired teacher dreaming up lessons he would never teach. He prepared his meals and scrubbed the floor and took the water pump apart for repairs. Sometimes in afternoons he stretched out, with his long feet propped on the rusted bedstead, to reread a little Joseph Conrad or a few lines from *Troilus and Cressida*. If he dozed

off now and then, it was never for long. He wakened to the crash
and spray of an incoming tide, the scream of circling gulls in the
wind, or a blurred exchange of conversation off a passing fish
boat. Until today he had usually wakened with renewed energy
for cutting firewood or setting out along the beach in search of
treasures washed in from the sea. Until today he had never wakened in a state of panic.

With heart pounding, he leapt to his feet and snatched his
shotgun down off the wall. After rushing out through the doorway and around the side of his shack, he steadied the barrel
against the building's corner to keep the intruder centred in his
sights. The heavyset young woman came thumping down the
trail through the woods with her head lowered, her gaze alert for
surface roots, apparently unaware of him or his gun until they
were fewer than twenty metres apart. She stopped abruptly in
mid-stride, with one foot barely touching earth.

"Mr. Thorstad? It's only me." The postmistress threw out
her arms as though she were casting a disguise from her shoulders.

But she'd worn no disguise. It was he who was not himself.

Even so, his arms refused to lower the gun, his mouth failed
to find the right words in the confusion that overwhelmed his
brain. How was he to explain that he'd dozed off and wakened
from a dream of invading barbarians? He hadn't imagined that
the footsteps might be the postmistress bringing him the mail
he had not picked up in more than a month. He'd expected—he
did not know what he'd expected: a cataclysmic assault? Panic still
fluttered in his throat.

Lisa Svetic stiffened her broad shoulders and retreated a few
cautious steps, placing one large gumboot carefully behind the
other. "Is there something wrong?"

There must be, there had to be something wrong, but he
could do nothing but stand like an absurd lanky statue incapable
of speech, his gun barrel tight to the corner post, its sighting
notch a steady V at the toe of the woman's boot. The deep chilled

silence of the forest was underlined by the murmurs of the retreating tide at his back.

"It's mostly junk mail," she said, holding out the colourful papers as though to display their innocence, "which may justify shooting *someone*, but it doesn't have to be me!"

"I'm sorry!" he said. "I was asleep. Your heavy footsteps . . ."

"My footsteps?" she said.

But she did not wait for an explanation. "If my footsteps are too heavy you can damn well remember to collect your stupid mail yourself!" She tossed flyers and envelopes out amongst the Oregon grape and giant sprays of sword fern, then turned her back on him and strode off.

By the time she had disappeared into the forest shadows, a trembling had travelled up his legs and torso and into his arms. He'd broken out in such a sweat that his shirt was clinging to his back.

He carried the shotgun inside and returned it to its rack of antlers above the window. He should have got rid of it long ago but had allowed it to remain on the wall where the previous owner had left it—its presence, like the beach-stone fireplace and the floor's oiled planks, giving his cabin a comfortable rustic touch. Now he would have to go after the young woman and explain. Try to explain. Try to prevent her from feeding the island's appetite for gossip.

He could imagine some of the residents up at the Store and down around the pier and the Free Exchange claiming to have seen warning signs: tall old Axel Thorstad, a figure descended from gaunt Norwegian giants, muttering to himself as he examined the shelves in Lisa Svetic's Store, or carrying home the door off an abandoned Ford for his root-cellar entrance, or becoming so lost in a book that he almost missed the ferry for a visit to the dentist across the strait. No doubt these local experts on human nature would see today's behaviour as a sign that he was cracking up, just as they'd expected of an old man living alone for years.

Well, he had never cared much for what they thought. And he certainly wasn't ready yet to apologize. What he needed now was time to collect himself, to allow his racing heart to calm and this chill to drain from his bones—time to think how he might go about handling this calamity.

To begin with, he needed a mug of good strong coffee. While standing over the sink to spoon the fragrant grains of Kicking Horse into his dented percolator, he avoided the little shaving mirror for fear of what it might tell him. While he waited for the coffee to perk and its smell to improve the world, he stripped off his grey wool socks—bristly now with fir needles, moss, and tiny twigs—then brought his cello over to the wooden chair in the centre of the room, planted his bare feet apart, cradled the instrument between his long thighs, and then instructed his hands to stop trembling so he could soothe his nerves with music—the one thing he could do on late-winter days when dark clouds rested their bellies on the tips of the Douglas firs. He drew the bow out long and slow across a deep rich lower D, inviting the Sinfonica to a gentle awakening. And now, E flat, with a tremor for the morning's disaster. And, after a pause, the opening phrase to the saddest movement of Dvořák's Cello Concerto in B Minor, Opus 104.

Faces observed from every side. Over the years he'd found these knee-high stumps and log ends washed in to shore and painted red circle eyes and a variety of mouths according to the shapes of knot-holes and the peculiarities of the grain. With levers, wedges, and a makeshift block-and-tackle, he'd wrestled each of these up the slope and inside to set it on end amongst the others, where they might have been an audience listening to the homesick anguish of Antonin Dvořák. Of course they might also have been a class awaiting instruction or a silent army of children standing guard. In any case they added the clean salty smell of sand and beach stones to the crowded room.

The black-and-white photos on the shiplap wall were as indifferent to the sounds from his cello as they were to everything else.

In a framed lobby card for the movie *Desperate Trails*, the great Cliff Lyons, doubling for Johnny Mack Brown, rode beside the driver of a U.S. Mail coach, no doubt expecting to be ambushed any moment. In the second, Lyons appeared with John Wayne and Susan Hayward, both on horseback for a scene in *Genghis Khan*. And in the third—a blown-up reproduction from a single frame of a 35-millimetre movie film—a man in a police uniform chased a shadowy figure across the rooftop of a square brick building. These long-dead Hollywood figures were too intent on their duties to be irritated by Axel Thorstad's recital.

He knew that Elena would have been surprised to see how little he'd needed for life without her in their holiday shack—its mismatched windows, rough walls, and driftwood corner posts making it look as old as the forest itself, an ancient playhouse beneath the towering firs. Inside, it could all be seen at once: his fireplace wall of books, his high plank desk at the window, the wooden chairs she'd painted red, the sharply angled rafters above the ceiling joists, and their bed in the lean-to with his poster of Chaucer's pilgrims on the wall above it, faded from its years in his classroom.

Ordinarily, he made an effort to limit the number of times he played the one brief melody his cello would still agree to, so sad that sometimes even he could barely stand to hear it. Last fall, a hunter in a red mackinaw had stepped out of the woods to accuse him of driving the deer population into hiding. "You're jeopardizing my winter supply of venison!" she'd shouted. "Play something else for a change!"

But it was too late to play something else. The instrument that had often accompanied Elena's piano had, since her death, gone into an extended mourning period of its own, refusing every piece of music but this one. Elena had claimed that music was a way God had of speaking to us, but if this was the case it seemed He'd had little to say to her widower for some time.

Lisa Svetic was bound to see his behaviour this morning as a form of betrayal—confronting her with his shotgun like some

crazed hillbilly guarding his moonshine still. She was easily offended at the best of times, often complaining that the number
of customers at her general store had declined, as though from
some conspiracy. Old people had been dying off, young people
were moving away, and there were all those suicides he'd been told
about, Lisa's young husband amongst them. She had been born
here, the granddaughter of pioneering farmers who'd arrived
when several families were moving to this island to start a new
life. "But they grew old and died, and most of the next generation
moved away—including my parents, who send me stupid postcards from Arizona. If I didn't have this store to run I wouldn't
see nobody from one end of the year to the next. Wouldn't see
anybody."

She was probably the largest young woman he had ever
known, broad of forehead and wide across the shoulders, with a
great roll of flesh between her chin and imposing bosom. She
kept her thin, nearly colourless hair twisted into a knot on the top
of her head, with escaped or overlooked strands floating messily
around it. He had made a practice of staying in her store no
longer than he had to, since knowing he'd been a teacher made
her a little defensive about the gaps in her education. And now,
in his state of confusion and panic, he had offended her today in a
way that could only make things worse. For all he knew, charges
could soon be laid. She might have broken with island policy and
telephoned the police.

For a moment he thought the sound of a boat scraping onto
the gravel beach might be the Mounties materializing out of his
imagination. But when he'd leaned the cello against the wall and
went out onto his step, the stocky figure of Bo Hammond was
stepping out of his small wooden skiff, followed by that always-
smiling friend from Cuba who sometimes visited Hammond at
the abandoned commune. Together they dragged the little boat
up the slope just far enough to keep it from floating away.

Shouting "Hello this house!" Hammond stepped up onto the winter-ravaged retaining wall. "My friend from *Cooba*," he said.

Because he introduced the friend in this manner every time, Thorstad was tempted to wonder which part was untrue—the *Cooba* or the friendship. This friend from Cuba was chubby, round-shouldered, dark-skinned, barefoot even in the coldest weather. He said nothing, now or ever, but merely nodded, smiling his toothy smile. "My friend from *Cooba* here, his ears picked up your music way out in the strait. I told him you're trying to drive us crazy—same notes over and over until we're so desperate we drown ourselves in the chuck."

Relieved to see only amusement in Hammond's face, Axel Thorstad folded down to sit on the rough plank step. "You came ashore just to tell me that?"

Hammond laughed. The Cuban lifted a foot to pry something from between his toes.

"Truth is," Hammond said, "I'm afraid you'll upset the fish and they'll take off for somewhere else."

"On the other hand," Thorstad said, thrusting his chin forward, "they may stay and learn to sing."

Again his visitors laughed, but Hammond quickly sobered. "Move deeper into the bush why don'tcha. Sound travels too far on the water. Anyways, something so sad can't be good for an old guy like you."

The friend smelled his fingers and wiped them on his khaki shorts.

"I'll tell you what's not good for me," Thorstad said, leaning forward to cradle his face in his hands. Who better than genial Hammond to confide in? "Being wakened too suddenly from sleep. Turns out, this old fool can be something of a savage when he's surprised."

Once Hammond had lowered himself to sit beside him on the step, Thorstad briefly recounted his unfortunate confrontation with Lisa Svetic. "Turned her back on me and nearly *ran*. I'm working up my courage to apologize."

"I'd give 'er a little time to cool down," Hammond said, placing a callused hand on Thorstad's shoulder. "There's no end of things that woman could do to punish you. If she barred you from the Store you'd have to cross the strait for every bottle of milk or pound of coffee." He cleared his throat and tilted to spit off his side of the step. "Right there's the reason you won't catch me in any one place for long. A change of scenery could do you good—especially if you look for scenery that don't include our Lisa."

Thorstad felt the fluttery wings of anxiety astir in his chest. This was not what he'd hoped to hear. When he'd come here seven years ago, he'd intended to *stay*.

Hammond studied him now, as though to judge his mood. "D'you suppose you could hold off your concert while we dig some clams? I'm scared they'll bury themselves too deep for shovels, escaping your gloomy sound." He laughed, and stood up, and started away, raising both arms high as though surrendering to the world's absurdities as he headed down to collect buckets and shovels from his little wooden boat. He would have been welcome company if he'd spent a little less time on his travels and more time here on the island.

While the two men spread out to dig up the exposed ocean floor, Thorstad went inside to rescue the frantic coffee pot from the stove, and brought his steaming mug out to the step. The long blue facing island had completely disappeared today behind a wall of mist or slanted rain, as though its scatter of coastline houses and backbone chain of mountains had drifted into the vast Pacific, leaving him to inhabit another dimension outside the normal world.

Where his land was about to fall away to beach, the upper limbs of a double-trunked arbutus were noisy with small black birds he couldn't identify, getting drunk and accident-prone on what was left of last fall's fermented berries. High on a skeletal snag, a bald eagle tilted its head to consider the man at the door, hoping perhaps to make some sense of this elongated figure of sharp angles dressed in a long-sleeved cotton shirt and corduroy pants worn thin and pale at the knees. Beside the step, the snow-drops in Elena's little patch of garden were in bloom.

Elena would not have permitted his shotgun behaviour to go as far as it had. Her laughter or her alarm would have stopped him in his tracks before he'd got outside. But of course the beautiful Elena was no longer here, or anywhere.

So aungellyk was hir natyf beautee.
That lyk a thing immortal semed she,
As doth an hevenish parfit creature,
That doun were sent in scorning of nature.

His *parfit creature* had deserted him by dying without any warning while he was changing the oil in their ancient Mazda, violating their agreement to expire in one another's arms well beyond his ninetieth birthday. He had reacted like a man robbed of a reason for living, left with nothing but his own despised involuntary breathing. He couldn't eat, refused to leave the house, locked the doors against friends who came to offer comfort, and lay for days in his bed, their bed, until the sheets had begun to stink. Firemen smashed their way in through a door on a Friday morning, to drag him off to a hospital bed and an intravenous drip.

What followed was a noisy life of too many people burdening him with advice, all of it interfering with his inconsolable grief at the loss of the woman who had been the essential centre of his life. He'd endured that clamorous hell of living without her for several months before selling their house and moving up here to tiny Estevan Island and their getaway cabin, dwarfed by the forest at its back, its windows facing the water and the sometimes visible mountains of the larger island that had been home for most of his life. On days like today, the sky sent down a window blind of grey-blue cotton, obscuring the rest of the world.

"It's all very well to hide out in that place in order to recover from the cruellest blow of a lifetime, my darling, but a man like you—used to many years of the classroom's lively flights of discovery and the staff room's essential gossip, accustomed to the stimulation of good movies and the pleasure of symphony concerts featuring cellos that remember how to play the most exquisite music, and addicted to the laughter of beautiful women and reckless young people as well—it's clear that this unnatural life of a hermit will eventually propel you into something rash like the suicides they've told you about. Pointing a shotgun at Lisa is just the beginning, and surely you can see that this means it's time you did something about those plans that have invaded your sleep night after night. Seven years in exile is quite enough."

He had no doubt that this was Elena's voice because he had never met anyone else who could speak in such long sentences. Still, he resisted the painful memories that would elbow their way into his head at a time like this—the young dark-eyed beauty flirting on the dance floor, the graceful white-haired woman striding like a confident duchess into a room—because it took only one or two moments of recalling the mysterious coquette just arrived from Europe, or the regal hostess in their own home, or the serious musician dedicated to mastering a difficult passage on the piano, to bring his day's activity to a sudden halt and fill his head with the tumult of too many memories all at once.

Of course he knew what she meant. Why had he always assumed that those who'd become "bushed" from excessive isolation were unaware of their state? The question was not whether you were aware but whether you'd seen it coming and had done something about it in time. He had no excuse because he had the poet's words for it—

But the moon carved unknown totems
Out of the lakeshore
Owls in the beardusky woods derided him

Long decades ago he'd brought the Earle Birney poem into the classroom as a *project*, so that a reluctant all-boys class might use his small movie camera to make a three-minute film based on a poem they might choose for themselves. He'd known it would not necessarily create a love of poetry, but it would require them to read more closely than usual. They might even learn how to work together without using shouted obscenities, threats, and their fists in order to express an opinion. He'd chosen this poem to demonstrate what the students were to do with those they would choose for themselves: moving pictures to accompany the words.

He may have selected this poem about a hermit because he had noticed, beside the gravel road to the town's landfill dump, a plywood shack and an elderly man on the doorstep—looking, it seemed, at nothing but the woods that had him surrounded. He would ask the man's permission to film him doing his chores, so that he might later match the footage to a taped reading of the poem, a model for his students.

On a Saturday morning, he and their nine-year-old foster child had driven up that road to the old man's property. Stuart remained in the car outside the sagging barbed-wire fence while Axel Thorstad went up the trail through the dense salal and knocked on the slab-wood door. The old man threw open the door and came out swinging a double-bitted axe that he brought down too close to Thorstad's right foot. There'd been no temptation to explain. He'd run for the car. By the time he'd got through the gate the car door was open and the boy was running down the road—convinced, he'd later explained, that once the hermit had chopped Thorstad to pieces he would then do the same to him. The wide-eyed terrified look in Stuart's face was something he'd not forgotten. It was probably much like his own.

And now he could only
bar himself in and wait
for the great flint to come singing into his heart

This was a thought too chilling to ignore. He must not let this sort of thing happen to him. Hammond had advised that he wait till Lisa had had the time to cool down, but Hammond wasn't the guilty one here. Surely, if she was to be prevented from thinking he'd begun to lose it altogether, he must walk out to the Store as soon as possible, to face the postmistress and put this morning's whole unpleasant business behind them both.

After passing through a stand of stunted hemlock, the trail returned to the coastline beyond Sogawa Point and became a path of pebbles and crushed shells where he could keep an eye open for anything worth rescuing from the clutter of washed-in tree roots and golden heaps of uprooted kelp wedged between the logs. Along the bay of volcanic rock with its ancient embedded oyster shells, he had once found a Michelin tire for Alvin White, and a wicker doll carriage for Gwendolyn Something's girls, as well as any number of golf balls, plastic ropes, and colourful Lego blocks he'd taken to the Free Exchange.

Up the wooded slope to his right, a half-dozen of the island's feral goats and sheep nibbled at weeds and lower branches amongst the boulders. These descendants of domestic animals abandoned when the commune dispersed in a hurry were without pen or shed for a home, or any master to answer to. They wandered the island for food and entertainment, respecting neither the fences, the ditches, nor the sentimental boundaries of humans. You never knew when a belligerent goat might burst from the woods with lowered head, in order to remind you of this. It was one of the miracles of Axel Thorstad's life that they showed no interest in Elena's flowers. He believed she must have had a word with them, and thanked her now as he passed.

Eventually he came to the tiny cedar-shake cabin that had been the summer home of Herb and Esther Townsend before they'd got too old for such primitive holidays and began to sign up for ocean cruises instead. One of the giant firs had rested its lowest boughs on the sagging roof as though it understood there was no one below to complain. Important as it was that he apologize to the storekeeper, he would surely benefit from spending a few moments in the silence of the Townsends' screened-in porch.

The door squealed on rusty hinges. The floorboards groaned beneath his step. But the nearest of the four unpainted Adirondack chairs did not complain when Thorstad lowered himself into the deeply angled seat. Perhaps it recognized his bony rear end, his long back and pointed elbows, recalling the hundreds of times he had sat here—as they had all four sat every time in the same chairs, facing out to the water with cold drinks on the wooden arms, catching up on the details of their lives and exchanging opinions before going inside to play a hand of bridge, or to solve, noisily and with much invention, a crossword that had been driving Esther Townsend crazy.

Elena had always been the first to become restless towards the end of August, missing her piano, beginning to fear that her fingers may have seized up during the summer, starting to anticipate a concert booked for the fall, which she was convinced she would not be ready for. "I'll be hissed off the stage!" she'd say, and then laugh. "But I will punish them, I will play something by one of those German composers who're never played any more, something that goes on and on until all of them are soaked in sweat and suffering from a psychosomatic deafness that won't go away for a week."

Elena might have been Esther's exotic cousin, eager to shock with tales of her childhood in Madrid during the Franco regime, holidays in mercurial Barcelona, her early piano lessons down a narrow back street past beggars and thieves and snarling dogs, and her brief disastrous romances with concert pianists from Czecho-slovakia and France. "It was because of those horrid men I decided to cross the Atlantic and never go back."

Esther Townsend knew better. "Come now! You crossed the Atlantic for a cousin's wedding, then stayed because of a certain person you'd met at the reception."

"A certain person yes!" Elena had taken Thorstad's hand in hers. "My darling giant—what did I know of his depths? Who was this man with his too-long legs and arms, all he wants to do is *teach*—nothing else! Can he play Chopin, has he ever con-fronted a Spanish bull, does he deserve the love of a beautiful woman from Madrid—of course not! But still, I could see that he needed me, that he could possibly learn to play something one day, though clumsily, and that he had eyes nearly as beautiful as my own, and such long powerful hands. So I stayed!"

This was not exactly the truth. After the marriage of her cousin, Thorstad's friend and colleague Andrzej Topolski, she had gone home to Europe for several months before deciding to return. Perhaps she intended to break up the marriage and have her handsome cousin for herself. Perhaps she wanted to find out whether this Axel Thorstad, who'd danced three times with her while she flirted with everyone else but him, deserved the most sought-after woman in Europe.

"So I stayed!" she told Esther Townsend, "and you see how crazy he is for me still, that he has practised the cello through excruciating periods of failure until he became just barely good enough to be my rehearsal partner, and brings me every sum-mer to this nowhere little island, which I love, and where I can visit every day with the most wonderful friends in the world!" At this she leapt from her chair and kissed Esther Townsend on both cheeks, and then Herbert Townsend as well, and finally drew Thorstad up from his chair so they could dance a few turns before kissing him, too, on the lips.

Amongst the confusion of marks in the raw floorboards he believed there must be some that suggested Elena's dancing feet, but no other sign indicated that she had ever been here. He'd occasionally visited the two bare rooms inside, smelling of wood rot and mice, before deciding again that neither Elena nor the Townsends could be found in the peeling wallpaper or the water-stained ceilings, just as they could no longer be found anywhere else on the island. No doubt the same would be true of others as well, if he were to visit all the island's forsaken buildings—cedar cottages, tarpaper shacks, rusted trailer-homes, and tall farmhouses, few of them visible from the main road and most nearly unreachable within a jungle of alder and brambles grown up around them since their owners had left.

Obviously it had been a mistake to stop at the Townsends' cottage if all it could do was remind him of the vanished past. None of the bramble-hidden shacks or trailer-homes was any more forsaken than he felt today himself. He brought his large hands to his face and breathed deeply into the dark while he tried to think of what to do next. An apology was necessary, but would an apology be enough?

From down the trail of oyster shells came the sound of energetic humming—Beethoven's Ninth—Eugen von Schiller-Holst imitating an entire orchestra while conducting his weekly "circumnavigation" of the island on his stumpy legs. Keeping time to the music with the thrusts of his hiking staff, he had almost passed by the Townsend cabin before stopping to peer through the rusty screen: "Who's there?"

This annoying man had a knack for showing up when he was most unwelcome. A former conductor of symphony orchestras in Vancouver, Graz, and Cincinnati, he preferred to be addressed as *Maestro*, since few on the island could remember *von Schiller-Holst* and fewer still could pronounce *Eugen* to his satisfaction. Though his short round figure passed by Axel Thorstad's cabin every week on his way around the island's perimeter, he had made it clear he would terminate his walks altogether rather than subject himself to the frustrating sounds from the reluctant cello.

"That's you, Thorstad? *Mein Gott*!" He shook his large head, disgusted or perhaps amused, the short grey ponytail slapping at his neck. "If you're wondering why your house is empty it's because that isn't your house! Yours is farther up the beach!"

Thorstad stayed behind the screen. "Don't jump to conclusions. I still know where I am."

"Trying to get away from yourself—that, I can understand. Up at the Store there is talk of a shooting!" The *maestro* spread his short thick legs and spent a moment observing Thorstad in silence. He prided himself in speaking what he called "hard truths," however unwelcome they might be. "So you made a fool of yourself. So what? You make a fool of yourself every time you pick up your bow. I told that woman to blame your behaviour on your height—the blood takes too long to reach your head." He wore the usual costume of younger men here—plaid shirt and wide suspenders to keep the waistband of his baggy jeans just below his considerable belly. Beside him, a wild-rose bush shifted gently in the breeze.

He put his head down and started away, but turned back after a few steps. "There are mutterings at the Free Exchange as well," he added. "Some have suggested the time has come to find you an old-folks home where someone can keep an eye on you."

Old-folks home was ice water poured on Axel Thorstad's flesh, the sound of doors clanging shut, a sudden rush of panic through his every cell. He could imagine the rules: no wandering, no chopping firewood, no Kicking Horse coffee, no scavenging parts for old machines. "I'd rather walk into the sea and trust my life to the killer whales."

The *maestro* laughed—derisively, it seemed—then gave the wild-rose bush a whack with his staff and strode on.

Old-folks home!

Lisa Svetic could wait for her apology. It was high time he put into effect the plan he had considered for this sort of situation but had delayed for too long, hoping it might be unnecessary—a strategy to save himself from the sort of arrangements other people might plan for him.

Once he'd returned to his shack he pulled a chair up to his plank desk beneath the window and opened his box of writing paper with his initials in gold at the top of each page, a retirement gift from a student whose parents owned a stationery shop. He removed his wire-rimmed reading glasses from his pocket and put them on, then uncapped a uni-ball pen, *deluxe FINE*, removed the top sheet of paper from the box, and set it down where his hands had long ago worn the raw wood smooth. His driftwood honour guard waited on every side to see what might come of this.

Editor,
Dear Sir or Madam:
   Please run the enclosed advertisement in your Classified section, weekends only, for as many weekends as the accompanying cheque will cover.

It was almost disappointing to discover that this was all that was needed in a covering letter. The page might have looked more impressive if he'd arranged to have his ancient computer repaired, but of course it was the words themselves that mattered.

An Adoption Request

He could not recall seeing an Adoption category in the papers, so the word would have to be mentioned within his advertisement, to attract attention. The editors could then decide the appropriate place for it amongst the Classifieds. This would be somewhere in the Personals, he supposed, amongst the appeals for romance and the desperate pleas for runaway teens to come home.

> *Widowed gentleman in his late seventies, a former high school teacher of English—healthy, responsible, and easy to please—wishes to be "adopted" by a family in exchange for tutoring.*

How pleasant it was to imagine a family reading this and recognizing that he was offering precisely what they'd been looking for—a youngster worried about exams perhaps, parents concerned for their child's future, a large house with bedrooms left empty by older children who'd gone on to university. Possibly a family of musicians, one of them fond of the cello.

Yet, how uninteresting his life would seem to those who read this advertisement, most people having little idea of the challenges and rewards of the classroom. Why not let it be known that he'd developed additional skills during school holidays?

> *Widowed gentleman in his seventies, a former high school teacher of English (with some experience as carpenter, newspaper reporter, cellist, and tour operator) wishes to be "adopted" by a family in exchange for tutoring.*

Unfortunately, this might suggest he was a man who hadn't been able to keep a job, and yet it was hardly appropriate to explain the details in an advertisement of this sort. Since it was impossible to know what other people might think, the safest thing was to stick to the point as he had in the first version.

And that was it. That was all the advertisement required. It was important not to sound desperate, like those pleading for the return of their lost children. But now that he saw it on the page, it seemed too little. Additional matters could be discussed once an interested party had contacted him, of course, a correspondence taking place before anything was decided, their letters crossing the strait in a mailbag guarded by Chief Danny Joseph, the captain of the little passenger ferry.

That it was necessary to add the postal code and box number where he could be reached was a compelling reason to make peace as fast as possible with Lisa Svetic, since she would have the power to sabotage his chances simply by tossing responses into the fire when they arrived. And naturally it would not be good enough to send only this one letter. He would have to send the same to every newspaper in the province, and so he must get their addresses. If he really hoped to be working again amongst the familiar and agreeable sounds of adolescent voices, he would have to convince Normie Fenton to remove, secretly, the giant directory from under Lisa's counter.

2

Although she'd accepted his clumsy apology, he was not entirely convinced that Lisa Svetic would put his letters into the canvas bag rather than drop the whole lot down the tilted privy behind the Store. "What's this?" she said, looking at the stack of envelopes he'd placed on her counter. "Ordering more firearms, are we? To scare off dangerous women?" She flipped through the pile, reading the occasional address. "Newspapers! Letters to the editor? Telling the world how little you think of us, I bet."

Apparently he was to be treated with suspicion. In her large flowered "tent dress" she reigned as the queen of her cinnamon-scented old store, with its rain-warped ceiling, corner cobwebs, and broken window covered over with a large cigarette ad. Until now, she had treated him with respect, or at least civility.

He had no intention of explaining the letters, but it was important to be sure she would send them. "They're strictly personal." He was a little breathless suddenly—anxious that he not be turned away as though he'd been planning something shameful.

She sighed and gathered up the envelopes and tapped them repeatedly against her linoleum-covered counter as though considering whether to do her job despite other possibilities that occurred. This set her throat and the loose flesh of her arms into a shivering dance, and loosened a few more strands of hair from the knot on her head. Behind her, the gaping canvas mailbag waited indifferently for a verdict. "They don't say nothing to scare away the summer people that come here, do they? *Anything*, I mean."

"They have nothing to do with the summer people."

She narrowed her eyes to study his face, presumably for clues to the truth. "You're not advertising for a mail-order bride?"

From uncertainty and guilt he'd gone to indignation in a moment. Did postal employees not sign an oath to mind their own business? Clearly she was confident he would not complain to Canada Post. His only immediate defence was to pretend not to hear the question—to frown fiercely at her *No cheques* notice as though there were something about the two words he didn't understand.

She eventually let him pay for the stamps and stood watching while he put them carefully in place, but by the time he'd left the Store he was convinced he ought to have taken the ferry and mailed them on the other side. Why would she turn down this chance to punish him? Living alone in this place was making him stupid.

But he could hardly ask for them back. She would delight in quoting some federal law that made this illegal.

He was in such a hurry to put Lisa Svetic behind him that he only nodded to Alvin White in his mechanics shed next door. Alvin looked up from beneath the hood of the '53 Fargo flatbed he was bringing back to life—adding one more set of wheels to this retirement home for vehicles rescued from junkyards across the strait. As usual, Alvin wore one of the baby-blue smocks he'd smuggled out of a hospital and somehow managed to keep free of grease. He'd gathered up his long white beard into an inverted hairnet while he worked.

Once Thorstad had walked the half-hour trail through the woods and along the coastline, he did not go immediately into his shack but went down onto the gravel beach where he shed his clothing and walked his long bones and ivory flesh into the chilling water—down over gravel and barnacle-crusted rocks and into patches of sand and orange starfish until the water had risen to his hips. Then he set off in an underwater glide before surfacing to strike out in earnest in the direction of the opposite shore. The Australian crawl. Those who knew of this daily 200-metre habit occasionally asked if he was practising for the "Geriatric Olympics" or merely out of his mind. But he was the son of an athletic stuntman for the movies and had been, himself, a competitive swimmer in his youth, and had always made the effort to keep fit with a daily swim. Keeping in shape had made it possible, last summer, to swim out beyond good sense in order to save the life of Normie Fenton, who'd fallen overboard from his skiff and had no knowledge of how to save himself.

Aside from keeping him in shape, his energetic ploughing through the waves was also an opportunity to think, away from the distractions of the human world. That he'd been a medal-winning swimmer long ago was just one of the facts he knew these islanders were aware of, despite his attempts to protect his privacy. At six foot eight he was the object of natural curiosity, the subject of invention as well. Apparently someone not content with his medals had reported that a statue had been erected in the town where he'd spent his career, a vaguely human shape constructed from twisted rods of steel—though no one ever claimed to have seen it. Not everything said about him was true.

Not all of it was invented either. He knew that everyone was aware—probably because of Elena's boasts during their summers here—that amongst the swimming medals at the bottom of his trunk were several "teacher of the year" awards, describing Axel Thorstad as "imaginative, innovative, courageous, and fiercely loyal to his students"—words that caused Elena to roll her eyes, though she'd quoted them accurately to anyone she decided should hear.

Because of Elena, people also knew that hardly a year had gone by without his being reprimanded for overstepping the boundaries of normal teaching practices in a conservative school district. Yet the student who'd fallen from the cafeteria roof while acting out his own example of Absurdist Drama had convinced her parents not to press charges once the scrapes and fractures had begun to mend. And the student who'd disappeared into a crowd on a Vancouver street while Thorstad was taking a class to interview a poet had not been murdered or captured into a life of crime, but had shown up just in time to catch the ferry home, having on his own initiative found and interviewed a former neighbour of Malcolm Lowry.

He'd faced a brief ripple of civic outrage when he allowed his students to write and perform a play lampooning the jingoistic leading citizens of their pulp-mill town, though he'd known a number of dignitaries and councillors would be sitting in the audience. At the end of the performance the mayor had mounted the stage to announce that he would be having a word with the Board of School Trustees in the morning. And indeed, a warning had later been issued, though allowances were once again made for the student-chosen "teacher of the year."

It was on that same stage, in that gymnasium smelling of old running shoes and adolescent sweat, that Thorstad had directed the now-famous Oonagh Farrell in her first starring role. That no one on Estevan Island had mentioned this fact suggested that no one here believed it—though this occurrence was as true as the medals at the bottom of his trunk and as easily verified as the mayor's indignant speech. He could imagine the disbelief if they were told of the offstage role that Oonagh Farrell had played, long ago, in his life.

Walking up the stony beach with water streaming off his body was perhaps the only time he was conscious of his exceptional height, of the long limbs and broad shoulders that had once inspired astonishment in strangers, curiosity in students, admiration in some women, and envy in competing swimmers. Though his habit of swimming naked here was considered eccentric, he knew the islanders attributed this to his having married a Spaniard, since Europeans were known for immodesty. That he swam during even the year's coldest months was not so easily explained.

When a week had gone by since he'd mailed his letters, he began to walk up to Svetic's Store once a day, though he behaved as though this was only for butter or salted peanuts or some other item from the shelves. He'd begun to wonder whether he really wanted to see what his advertisement might bring. Often Lisa was sitting in her large red-leather chair to study the weekend coloured comics, and sometimes worried aloud about family members in "For Better or For Worse." "I wish she hadn't killed off the grandma. It's getting too damn sad." Eventually she made a great show of hauling herself up out of the chair to take his money. "No letters today. You've got me so curious I'm tempted to open the first one that comes, just to see what you're up to."

It had never occurred to him that she might read his mail, but of course she was perfectly capable of it. He'd been a fool not to have crossed the strait with those letters!

Rather than give her the opportunity to witness his impatience, he adopted the habit of arriving at the dock in time for the ferry that brought the mailbag across, but the ferry was so often late that he was sometimes forced to wait amongst the rusty pickups and mud-caked old sedans parked chaotically on the gravel, some with doors left open by last-minute drivers who'd been almost left behind. Sometimes he waited down on the floating pier, breathing the sharp smells of creosote and rotting seaweed. He knew enough to bring a book with him to reread. *Heart of Darkness, As I Lay Dying, The Good Soldier*.

When the clouds opened up and sent down rain he moved inside to wait amongst the crowded rows of tools, dishes, machine parts, and cast-off clothing in the Free Exchange, a converted

boathouse of faded cedar planks and patched-up shingles, resting
at a tilt beside the government dock. Here the smells were of old
gumboots, sweat-soaked mackinaws, and fishing nets, sometimes
a kerosene lamp or a half-used can of paint. Framed pictures
were stacked against a window coated with mud and salt spray.
An entire shelf was devoted to discarded trophies—statuettes of
human figures holding basketballs or showing off a large fish.
Above the heap of old boots, a sign offered a bargain:

TAKE A PAIR OF GUMBOOTS OFF OUR HANDS AND WE'LL
THROW IN ONE OF MURIEL PARKER'S VELVET PAINTINGS!

No money was ever exchanged here. If you found something
you wanted or needed, you took it home. If you had something
at home you didn't want, you brought it with you and left it for
someone who did. There was seldom anything Thorstad needed.
He hadn't broken a dish in seven years, and he was still wearing
the three good shirts Elena had bought, the only man on the
island who wore his shirts buttoned to the throat. But occasionally
there was something he took away in case it came in handy one
day, adding it to the pyramid beneath the blue tarpaulin behind
his shack.

Since retiring to the island, he no longer purchased something
new if something old could be repaired. He rummaged amongst
people's tossed-out equipment and useless machine parts abandoned beside the road, and whatever he couldn't use himself he
brought here for a possible second life. He was aware of the figure he sometimes made—a lank Goliath wading through the
underbrush in order to rescue a discarded basin, a long-backed
Ichabod with a card table on his head, bringing it in to the Free
Exchange.

As a place to wait for the mail, this building was at least dry. It
was sometimes interesting as well. He'd once witnessed the surprised laughter of a woman realizing the pink silk dress she'd just

decided to take home was the one she'd deposited here herself. Another young woman recognized a turtleneck sweater she'd given as a present to a friend. "It's the last gift she'll ever get from me! I'll just give it to myself."

The volunteers who supervised the place occasionally viewed him with suspicion. Since the concept of shoplifting was irrelevant here, this could only mean that Lisa Svetic had told them about his letters—perhaps even that he'd advertised for a mail-order bride. If so, they saved their laughter until he was no longer there to hear it.

It was probably one of these volunteers who'd mentioned an "old-folks home" within the *maestro's* hearing—possibly Gwendolyn Something. He'd been told this attractive mother of six young daughters took turns with another woman, living in a motel across the strait so their offspring could get the education they could not get here. Gwendolyn Something was, according to Lisa Svetic, a calming influence in that motel life. "As placid as Elsie the Cow. You couldn't stir her into a panic if you set a hive of wasps loose under her skirt."

The easygoing nature of this woman in full skirts might explain the fact that all six of her daughters had different fathers. All were named after local flora: Ladyslipper, Rosy Pussytoes, Spring-gold, Fireweed, Solomon's-seal (which of course should have been "False Solomon's-seal"). The sixth was, Lisa Svetic had told him, Hooker's Willow. What could the future hold for a girl named Hooker's Willow? You had to hope the woman didn't intend to exhaust the catalogue of local flowers. Skunk cabbage bloomed in swampy ditches every spring! And hairy arnica could be found beside his trail through the woods. Of course, if you had to be named for a flower there could be some pleasure in answering to Hairy Arnica.

He was aware that she and her girls were in the habit of moving now and then into one or another of the island's abandoned houses or trailers, a form of expropriation that was not uncommon here. Someone else's roof could be sturdier than your own, a wallpaper pattern more attractive, a wood stove in better shape. He supposed that for Gwendolyn Something, changing houses was not too different from changing partners, allowing each of her girls to have both a roof and an unidentified father to call her own.

One morning while he was examining a pair of cast-off gaucho boots with elaborate patterns tooled into the leather, Gwendolyn snapped out of her reverie when Bo Hammond came in carrying a heavy cardboard carton against his chest. He nodded and crouched to place the carton against the nearest wall.

Then, noticing Thorstad amongst the second-hand boots, he sat on the box and rested his elbows on his knees. "So, Axel-my-man. You planning to donate your stubborn cello to this tidy pavilion of junk?"

Startled, Thorstad was quick to reject the notion. "You think I'd give up so easily? I've a little patience left and even a bit of hope."

Hammond's grin was a white gash in his dark whiskers. "I'll take 'er off your hands if you want—haul 'er out in the strait and give 'er a proper burial. If I fill 'er with rocks she'll sink to the bottom and stay there." He opened his eyes too wide and rubbed a palm over his jaw as though seriously awaiting permission.

"You'd probably do the same with annoying old men! My cello may be stubborn and forgetful but it isn't dead."

Hammond laughed and stood up, and nodded to Gwendolyn Something. Then, before leaving, he cupped a hand beneath Axel Thorstad's elbow. "Help yourself if there's anything you want in that box."

The box, Thorstad saw, was filled with books. He put on his reading glasses and sat on his heels to examine Hammond's titles. *Year of the Goat. The Sorrow of Belgium. Prose and Poetry of the Eighteenth Century.* He had taken his copy of *Prose and Poetry of the Eighteenth Century* to a second-hand shop before his move.

Though perhaps . . . He picked it up and turned a few pages. Defoe. Bishop Berkeley. Swift. Addison and Steele. Alexander Pope. *What dire offence from amorous causes springs, / What mighty contests rise from trivial things.* He could continue without looking at the words. If Gwendolyn Something was frowning at him now it was probably because he was smiling. He missed the large library he'd left behind after choosing only his favourites to bring to Estevan. He was thinking, too, of the numerous students for whom he'd read this poem aloud.

When he'd returned the book to its box and was about to reacquaint himself with the opening words of *The Old Man and the Sea*, Lisa Svetic put her head in the doorway and beckoned with a finger, half singing her words as though from a childhood taunt. "I've got something you been waiting for." She held an envelope high and forced him to follow her through the mud to the post office and wait while she went behind the counter. "I can't just go around handing out Her Majesty's mail in the *street*!" She probably thought she was amusing, but Thorstad was long familiar with the playground bully's notion of humour.

The return address was a street in Prince Rupert, hundreds of kilometres up the coast. At once he saw himself boarding a plane: Comox to Vancouver, Vancouver to Prince Rupert, stepping out into their ocean-scented rain. He tore open the envelope and turned away in order to read the tight handwritten script in the light from the window.

> *Dear Sir,*
>
> *Though you gave only a post-office address in your adver-tisement and could be a cold-blooded murderer for all I know, I am sending my telephone number because I can tell from the way you described yourself that you could easily be my dear hus-band who disappeared while on a fishing trip with some friends fifteen years ago, and must be suffering, I think, from amnesia. I am sure there are people now who can help a person recover his*

memory. If you call me and tell me where you are I will come
and identify you. Does the name "Sebastian" sound familiar? I
have waited so long for this.

"Well," said Lisa Svetic, coming out from behind her counter.
"Is she rich enough?" She used a broom to scoop a cobweb from
the ceiling. "You have to watch out for gold diggers when you
advertise for a wife." This set off a low satisfied chuckle in her
throat. "Let me see," she said, leaning the broom against the
canned-goods shelf. "Maybe I can tell if you've got yourself a
crank."

But he left the Store without showing her. How could he
expose this poor woman's desperate hope to Lisa Svetic's eyes?
Was this what he had done—invited the world to seize on his ad
as a solution to their lives? Now he would have to decide how to
assure the woman that he was not her husband. *I am sorry to tell*
you that I have never been to Prince Rupert, and my memory is still
reliable enough to remember my wife, who passed away several years ago.

A second letter arrived a few days later, along with his *Harper's*,
this one from a Nora Stockton (Mrs.) with a Vancouver address.
He waited to open the square pink envelope until he was deep
into the woods, passing through a swampy area where the trail
was lined on either side with the rust-coloured skeletons of last
year's cow-parsnips, nearly as tall as he was. Inside the envelope
was what appeared to be a homemade card, a watercolour of a
fawn drinking from a shallow stream choked with water lilies.

I believe you are the answer to my prayers. My son has just been
released from jail and banned from the nearest schools for the
time being and I am looking for someone to teach him at home
for I can't myself, having little education. His offence was not a
serious one, only a playground scrap where the other poor fellow
lost an eye. I hope that . . .

Without reading more, he returned the card to its envelope. As soon as he'd reached his shack he slipped it between *Under the Volcano* and *Death in Venice* on his wall of books. Then he dropped into his chair, exhausted. He was too old for this. If this was the sort of response he was to receive, there was little point in opening any more letters, or even in walking out to collect them. For several days he stayed home to read books borrowed from Hammond's box—thick histories of the Second World War, a set of mysteries by Reginald Hill.

According to Lisa Svetic, Bo Hammond had come up from California as a draft dodger during the Vietnam War. He'd taken up residence within a community of other transplants from below the border, on the property owned by Dave and Evelyn Edwards. This couple had opened up their extensive property for the purpose of creating a commune where like-minded folk could argue philosophy and smoke the marijuana they'd grown in the woods. Lisa's aunt had filled her in on this. Nobody minded them at first, apparently. They put on great parties. Some of them had brought skills the locals could use. Police raids were only a small inconvenience, and helicopters thrashing back and forth overhead were just something to laugh at. But then Ben Morrison began to notice some of his beef cattle missing and traced them to the commune, where he discovered they were being butchered and cut up to sell across the water. Even that was not enough to turn the island against the members of the commune, but they weren't satisfied just to steal their neighbours' cattle, they started to steal the neighbours' daughters as well. "I mean, they started turning the daughters of farmers and fishermen into hippies like themselves, smoking dope and dragging around in long skirts and having babies whose fathers they couldn't name." Because Hammond was the good-looking one, there was a time when three different girls all told their fathers that he was the one who'd got them pregnant, hoping this would end with a wedding. What it

ended with was most of the commune people taking off, including Hammond. "At the time, nobody knew where he went, but
now we know he went to South America and got mixed up in
politics. Soon afterwards, most of the commune was chased off
the island altogether, with a lot of island girls following close
behind."

In recent years, Hammond had returned now and then to take
up residence on the nearly deserted commune, where he built
furniture he sold to dealers across the strait. Apparently none of
the smitten girls had followed him for long enough to return full
circle to the island. Instead, there was often a mysterious male
companion from some foreign country. "Political agitators," Lisa
claimed. "He sends money back for their Causes and lives on
almost nothing."

Though he may live on almost nothing, it appeared he did read
books, and seemed to read them with remarkable speed before
leaving them at the Free Exchange. The volunteers were unable
to tell him where the books had come from. They knew for a fact
there wasn't a single volume in the abandoned commune. Since
no one had witnessed them arriving on the ferry they must be
brought in by someone down one of the narrow pot-holed roads
into the woods—one of those mysterious figures Thorstad sometimes glimpsed loping along at a distance, disappearing suddenly
into the disorderly bush. It was common knowledge that boats
came and went in some of those hidden bays, discharging or taking on mysterious cargo, so it was not entirely impossible that
some of the traffic should be in books—though it was hard to
imagine why.

"Obviously there are secret messages left in them," Lisa Svetic
explained when he'd wondered aloud about the books. "Some
sort of political stuff going on that's dangerous for you to know
about."

No more letters arrived until the snowdrops had faded in the
small garden outside his door and daffodils had begun to open.

The skeletal bushes of ocean spray had acquired their countless green knots of incipient leaves. By this time, the Sinfonica had begun to allow him an isolated bar from a familiar concerto, then a phrase from a familiar sonata—hints of the pleasant arrival of spring followed by a melancholy glimpse of uncertainty and indecision, tantalizing fragments of music whose entirety had been lost to him. It was as though his lovely cello had turned traitor and decided to torment him with chaos.

The next response to his advertisement had no return address on the envelope. Inside, there was a short note on a 3x5 card and, as well, a smaller re-used envelope with a previous address crossed out. On the card, someone had written:

Saw your advertisement in the paper. If you are looking for something to do with your life I'm sending this sad note I received but cannot afford to do anything about.

The letter was clumsily hand-printed in blue ballpoint on a page of foolscap, a red line providing a margin down the left side.

I greet you in God's name and thank the good Lord that I have learned of your address from a friend. I am a fourteen-year-old girl living with my blind father in our village in Cameroon. My mother was massacred in a rebel raid a short time ago, and my father, who is unable to work, is failing his health. I am writing to request for your kind assistance in God's name to help me with a gift of money. I will pray to God Almighty to let you hear my cry for help. God bless you now and forever.

So his advertisement had been read as a plea for "something to do" with his life? Stunned by what it had brought him this time, Thorstad gave in to Lisa Svetic's clumsy hints and allowed her to read the hand-printed letter. She opened the foolscap out on her counter and planted a hand to either side. As she read the immature printing she shook her head, setting off a cataclysm of competing tremors in her throat. "Now you've gone and done it," she said. "You'll be hounded for money till you give in." She read the letter a second time, the colour rising in her cheeks. "Unless you plan to catch a plane for Africa and carry a machete everywhere you go, you better stay right here, away from the horrors of the world." Since he'd last seen her she'd acquired a small tattoo on the side of her neck—a purple thistle.

It seemed she'd given herself the opening she must have been seeking. "Here you are, welcoming messages from strangers who would drag you into the middle of their messes when you haven't even got to know the folks right under your nose. I never heard of you paying anyone here a visit."

Of course he needn't remind her that when he and Elena had come here during school holidays they had made friends with other summer couples along the shoreline, since she would already know that three of those friends had since died, and a fourth gone into a nursing home in Vancouver.

When the next response arrived a week later, he did not open it immediately but wandered down to the pier and stood for a while to watch the herring boats pass by, a scattered parade of seiners and flat-bottomed scows and small trawlers heading south, all at different speeds, like individuals setting off for a large meeting they were confident would wait for them to get there. They would congregate at a designated area and mill about while they waited for a bureaucrat's starter gun—perhaps tomorrow, perhaps not—to begin this year's frantic season, possibly only two days long. Not a fish could be caught until a certain number had had the opportunity to lay their eggs and turn the water into a milky substance with their fertilizing milt. Only then would a government official declare it time to drop the nets.

While walking home through the woods he could still hear the throbbing engines of the assembling boats. From his doorstep he could see that several of them had chosen to gather not far out from his shack, as though to lay plans or simply indulge in gossip. As the light faded from the sky, he sat on his step to watch them mill about, no doubt impatient for that starter gun. Half a dozen trawlers remained close together, motionless, perhaps to visit, perhaps to avoid associating with the others. One long graceful boat with a series of white Christmas lights the length of its upraised rods broke away from the others and slowly cut a circle around the group of more than twenty boats, as though patrolling for danger.

Despite the throbbing engines, Thorstad was aware of the gentle slapping of the evening high-tide waves against the berms of gravel and scattered logs from his winter-damaged retaining wall. He remained on his front step until the damp chill and the falling dark drove him inside. Then, at his desk, he turned on only one low-wattage light so that he could still observe the floating city of milling boats even after he'd opened the long white business envelope.

> *Dear Sir,*
>   *It is clear from your newspaper advertisement that you are a man who has overlooked the countless opportunities available for doing good for your fellow humans. We at the Sacred Heart Charity for Homeless Men of Vancouver are always in need of additional volunteers at our east-side drop-in centre, where the homeless men of our city . . .*

If he finished reading this one he knew he would be nagged for weeks by pangs of guilt. All those homeless men would be happy to have his health and this shack to live in, while he was free to devote his life to improving theirs but had chosen not to. If the person who'd written this had hoped he'd be disappointed in himself, he had succeeded.

Of course this could be their careful way of asking if he himself might be destitute, in need of their services, so long as he was willing to move to Vancouver.

It appeared the effort of writing to the newspapers had been a waste of time. When he had folded this letter back into its envelope, he slipped it into the tight gap between *The Spoon River Anthology* and Chekhov's plays, tapping it into place so that it would not destroy the tidy uniformity of the row.

Out on the invisible strait, all of the boats had now turned on their lights, every one outlined in strings of white bulbs, some of them with small spotlights running up and down their own masts and splayed rods—a floating, throbbing, shifting city of lights. Those lights would be on all night, he knew, the men and women awake and waiting, chatting over coffee or beer, their engines thumping through his sleep, so that even in his dreams he would be aware of the restless and impatient population waiting for the signal that would allow them to move into position and let out their nets for the catch that would enrich their future. Of course the seals and seabirds and other creatures that knew nothing of government regulations would already have travelled unseen and silent beneath the surface or overhead in the dark to wherever it was the herring had congregated, and would already have started to feast.

3

On the second day of herring season he learned at the Free Exchange that Bo Hammond's overturned boat had been discovered floating just beneath the water's surface. Hammond himself had not been found—probably carried with the currents into the colder, deeper waters of Georgia Strait. To Thorstad this was shocking news, but it was discussed rather matter-of-factly amongst islanders who'd lived through too many herring seasons to be surprised. "Some of them guys, they can't stop filling their nets even long enough to deliver to the cannery boat. A little skiff like his, gets so low in the water the first decent wave just swamps 'er."

He knew that bigger boats than Hammond's had gone down before now from the weight of too many fish, their owners made reckless by the vision of countless herring enriching their bank accounts. This was greed, he supposed, doing its ugly work. Yet the news about Hammond caused him the same sense of loss now as he'd experienced whenever he'd heard unhappy news about former students.

Well, it was more than just a sense of loss. He was surprised by a heated rush of anger—the stupidity of it. Unlike Lisa Svetic with her sarcasm and von Schiller-Holst with his criticisms, Bo Hammond was one person here whose company, however fleeting, he'd enjoyed. He'd had a new tale to tell after each excursion away—close calls with pirates at sea, dangerous journeys up South American rivers, beautiful women left weeping in forgotten villages—all a little preposterous but, you suspected, probably true. They'd been welcome reports from a dangerous left-behind world.

When he stepped inside Lisa Svetic's store still reeling from this news, the postmistress roused herself reluctantly from her red-leather chair to stand large and stern and important behind her counter wearing a pair of faded bib overalls. "Do you think anyone ever found Blondie and Dagwood funny?"

She showed too little distress at Hammond's drowning. Her uncle, she said, had drowned in a similar manner. "Why they gave that fool a fishing licence I'll never know. Uncle Geoff I mean." She used a ribbed undershirt to dust her ancient cash register and the full length of the counter. "Hammond wasn't exactly a fool but he must've got carried away, thinking of all the revolutions he could finance with the money he'd make if he didn't stop pulling in fish."

"This is a terrible thing," Thorstad said, indignant that Hammond could be so casually dismissed. "A good man has been lost!"

She tossed the undershirt under the counter and bent to scribble something in the little notebook she kept beside the till. "The problem with a two-day season is it turns the whole damn business into a cutthroat competition." The thistle tattoo bristled with her disapproval. "They'll risk their stupid lives rather than leave a few fish for someone else's net."

Thorstad felt an unfamiliar brand of sadness to think of all the secret messages that had entered Bo Hammond's brain from those books—now lost, or dissolved in the cold grey sea along with his self-image as a saviour of the downtrodden, while all the fish he'd hauled in were free to swim away or spawn as they'd originally planned.

"Somebody over in Nairobi was probably counting on him," Lisa said, "or them poor suffering souls in Haiti. *Those* poor souls in Haiti."

He wished he'd never let her know he'd been a teacher.

"Of course it could be suicide," she added, standing back to fold her arms. "Or murder. I thought that Cuban fellow looked suspicious but Hammond always claimed they were friends. That's the sort of person they would send, isn't it?"

Was this what came of reading the coloured comics? "Why would anyone want to kill Hammond?"

"The usual reason." She looked off into the distance and tapped two fingers on her counter. "It's the risk you take when you get involved with drugs." Sharing this information seemed to cheer her up.

Thorstad made no effort to disguise his shock. This was enough to make him believe he'd been asleep for years. He'd liked Hammond, though of course he hadn't known him well. How had he got himself involved in a business like that? Of course Thorstad had no experience with illegal drugs himself, beyond catching the occasional student with a joint in his pocket.

"I figure he was collecting their money—large bills tucked behind the flaps of them books. *Those* books." She pulled a sour face and came out from behind the counter to roll a twenty-litre container of water over beside the others near the door. "Paying the local growers—you know—and sending the rest off to who-knows-where. Laundering it, I guess you could say. They must've caught him cheating someone big."

He crossed his arms, to hide his agitated hands. "And you knew this all along?"

Behind her counter again and panting a little, Lisa Svetic shrugged. "I thought you educated people could see right through the rest of us, ha-ha." She slid two envelopes out from his pigeon-hole and slapped them down on the counter. "Hammond knew the risks. He would've gone nuts if he'd stayed too long where it's safe, with nothing to do but building chairs."

Pushing the letters inside a pocket of his corduroys, Thorstad left the Store and started across the muddy road—confused, uncertain what he'd intended to do next. Though Alvin White stood up from under the hood of the blue Henry J he'd rescued from across the water, Axel Thorstad did not stop.

Lisa had followed him to the door. "If all them letters are offers of marriage you must be pretty damn fussy. You holding out for Penelope Cruz? Scared some old witch will get you in her clutches?"

"You knew Elena," he said without turning back. He meant: Do you think there's anyone could replace a woman like her?

"It was lovely of you to say that, my darling," Elena said, once he had started down the forest path, "but don't you think you ought to explain to poor Lisa what you really want, because I'm sure some part of her thinks that even having a man like you around is preferable to living alone in that house behind the Store and hoping every day that someone new will come in through her door and offer to make her life more interesting, since whatever you think of her she is a good-hearted woman who has treated you well and probably looks out for your well-being more than you realize—which reminds me that there is bound to be some sort of memorial service for your friend Hammond and it would be just like you to refuse to attend even though you know perfectly well that you ought to be there even if you don't speak to a soul, just so you will be seen supporting the only neighbours you have in your shrunken world, so please make sure Lisa drives you to the service in that old Ford pickup she parks behind the Store."

Elena was the only woman he'd ever known who was convinced the Ford Motor Company had manufactured every pickup on earth. Lisa's truck was an ancient Chev without doors, decorated with rusted-out holes, running on three cylinders and four bald tires, just barely capable of taking her down the narrow muddy roads into the hidden parts of the island when she needed to deliver a shut-in's groceries or mail. Like the few other vehicles seen on these roads, her Chev had been brought across the strait on a barge, since the little ferry was capable of carrying only pets, mailbags, vegetables, caged chickens, foot passengers, replacement parts for water pumps, and hardware purchased from Canadian Tire.

"Get you in her clutches," Lisa had said. To be in someone's clutches suggested strong fingers around your neck. His mother had used the phrase when she'd warned him against the excessive interest displayed by one of his students, a young woman determined to be a poet and embarrassingly grateful for every drop of encouragement. It had got so that it was impossible not to see what was between her lines, requiring him to respond as though he were too stupid to understand. "Watch out, my dear," his mother had warned. "You're so naive, that girl will have you in her clutches before you know what hit you."

Would a father have taught him how to handle the situation? Thorstad didn't know. He'd never had a father, except in a few frames of a Hollywood film and the photo he'd lifted from the celluloid to hang on his wall. His father had died after a leap from the roof of a four-storey building at Centurion Pictures, though only the first few seconds of his jump would appear in the film. His face could not be seen as he hurtled himself from the edge, and of course he'd been dressed to look like the actor Derek Morris, who was playing the role of a policeman attempting to apprehend the man who'd killed the woman he loved. The rest of the cop's dangerous feats were performed by a second double, who brought the original jump to a happier conclusion by landing safely on a lower roof to continue the chase. Why they hadn't re-shot the beginning of the jump with the replacement was a mystery, but Axel Thorstad was grateful the possibility had been overlooked.

The accident had occurred two weeks before Thorstad was born, which was the sort of thing he might expect in a Dickens

novel but not in his own real life. He had never seen his father's
face, he had never heard his father's voice, but he had watched his
copy of that black-and-white film starring Derek Morris and the
beautiful Marisa Gale, and so had witnessed those final seconds
of his father's life, anguished at his inability to alter the outcome.
Anyone who looked closely enough could see that the policeman
who lands on the lower roof is not the policeman who leapt from
the top of the four-storey building. His mother had pointed this
out when he was a boy.

His mother had explained that as a stunt double his father
had known his face would never be captured by the camera. Having failed as an actor himself, he'd chosen to devote his life to the
same dangerous career as the famous Cliff Lyons so that artists
with real talent could be free to do their work without fear of
harm. But he had lost the opportunity to live out this noble purpose when he fell from that roof on his first day before an actual
rolling camera.

Derek Morris may have been grateful for the sacrifice. For
thirty years Thorstad's mother had received an annual Christmas
card from the actor, though of course he might have been sending cards to any number of widows whose husbands had made it
possible for him to live on, unscarred, to old age and international fame. If it had been guilt that inspired those cards, Thorstad
would never know.

Rather than remain in Los Angeles after his father's death, his
mother had moved north to the place of her childhood, a mid-
size harbour town, a coal-mining centre in those years before it
was rescued from decline by the construction of a pulp mill
whose smokestacks pumped foul billows into the sky. Here the
new mother lived with her parents in the family home and did not
remarry.

No doubt his mother's account of his father's accident
explained his early fascination with movies. He'd been the only
boy at Saturday matinees who sat silent and unmoving, hypno-

tized by the activity on the screen—the movies somehow imply-
ing a link between his world and his father's, a direct connection
between his town and the mysterious place of his father's death, a
city as magical as it was dangerous.

As a young man, Axel Thorstad had aspired to something
like his father's dedication to the lives of others, though not in
any aspect of the movie business. It was in the classroom that
he'd eventually pursued his goals, exploring with adolescents the
power of Mark Twain's humour, the glories of Shakespeare's dra-
mas, and the heartbreaking beauty of Synge's *Riders to the Sea*. Of
course the great works of literature needed little assistance from
him, but they could sometimes supply the key that would open
the doors to those mysterious teenage lives.

And what had he ever been but a servant of love? For more
than thirty years he'd explored with teens not only the wise com-
passionate powers of the masters but also the more recent won-
ders and insights of contemporary writers. He had supervised
dances, and organized weekend conferences with living poets. He
could think of former students whose love of poetry had led them
to take up the teaching of Literature themselves; he knew of computer programmers who were writing plays in their evenings.
And of course there were young people in the world today who
would not be in the world at all if he hadn't encouraged their shy-
and-awkward fathers to invite their pretty-but-overlooked mothers to the graduation dance.

In later years he had needed to do far less of this gentle sort
of matchmaking, since somewhere along the way young women
seemed to have taken matters into their own hands. Such gestures—even where needed—were far less welcome than they had
been. Perhaps this was due to the widening gap between his age
and their own. Year after year students continued to be seven-
teen, while he'd advanced steadily through birthdays towards his
inevitable exit into the dark obscurity of retirement. Amongst the
latest students were the youngest children of those shy boys and

girls—middle-aged couples who'd turned out on parents' night to make sure he knew their gratitude had not worn thin. Grey hairs had begun to show up on their heads, while they could not help but notice the deepening lines in his face, the spots on his hands.

By the time he'd emerged from the woods behind his shack, a dark cloud had moved in above the strait, obscuring most of the sky and all of the facing island's mountains. Insects flew past. An owl hooted somewhere in the woods, perhaps thinking night had fallen. The waves slapped weakly onto the beach and then hissed and gurgled while sliding back through the gravel.

Normie Fenton's little wooden rowboat had been pulled up onto the rocks, and Normie himself was at work doing what Thorstad had once done for himself every year—rebuilding the retaining wall damaged by the winter tides, its logs and buttresses washed away or left in disarray along the beach. Normie raised a hand in greeting but continued hauling solid lengths of driftwood up the beach, seldom looking up long enough to notice anything outside the world immediately around his boots. If he needed help he would holler for it, but otherwise he worked alone to shore up the crib so the sea would not steal more than it already had of Axel Thorstad's soil.

Normie was as awkward and shy as a thirteen-year-old boy, but as strong as a labouring man in his thirties. When the commune disbanded he'd been left behind by his parents, who had handcrafted the willow-twig cradle they'd left him in. Since they hadn't bothered or remembered or perhaps cared enough to come back for him, he'd been watched over by the few who'd remained in the commune's sprawling log house. Though he was considered "simple" by some of those who employed him for odd jobs, he had acquired a practical knowledge that allowed him to know the secret of discouraging moss from overwhelming a roof, the proper dates for planting vegetables, and the best angle for stacking a bank of mismatched logs so that neither rain nor waves could seriously undermine them, at least for another year.

Thorstad had tried to do more for Normie than just hiring him for the occasional labouring job. Since the young man was afraid to leave the island, Thorstad had offered to help with correspondence courses, but courses and help had both been refused. He had tried to get Normie interested in books, but had failed at this as well. It seemed there was nothing he could do except insist on paying him for physical work he was willing to do without pay for the man who'd saved him from drowning. Nothing further was asked except that Thorstad listen occasionally to the plot of the latest *Star Wars* movie that Normie had seen on the commune's television set.

While Normie hammered spikes into logs, Thorstad brought the Sinfonica over to the chair and encouraged it through the first few tentative bars of the Adagio finale to Schubert's Piano Trio in E flat, almost unbearably beautiful. But the instrument refused to go beyond the moment where Elena's piano accompaniment was intended to take dominance over cello and violin. When several more attempts led him no further into the piece, he put the cello back in its case—a child sent to its bedroom for refusing to behave—and sat on his doorstep to read one of today's letters, a single typed page signed by an "Alan Doyle."

He had known an Alan Doyle—a Math teacher down the hall, beginning somewhere back in the seventies, or maybe the early eighties. He'd been an affable man whose bald head and long body were so exceptionally narrow that he appeared to have been squeezed in a full-length vise. He'd retired a few years before Thorstad, and would—if this were the same man—be eighty years old by now, or more. Perhaps a grandson was in need of a tutor.

Axel Thorstad!

Apparently when Alan Doyle began a letter he saw himself leaping from behind a curtain.

I was so sure it was you the minute I saw your anonymous ad (and address) in the paper that I won't even bother with "If you are not Axel Thorstad please ignore the following."

I suspected you would go downhill when they deprived you of a classroom full of adolescents you could charm and inspire and make ambitious with your antics. Maybe you should have stayed and volunteered as a teacher's aide. I take that back. You would drive the teacher crazy with your enthusiasm.

But I think I have to warn you that your ad campaign is bound to fail. Nobody is going to want an old geezer for a tutor, not when the world is full of over-educated and unemployed teachers right out of university and waiting for the old ones to die off and make room.

Travel, why don't you? You and Elena used to take off for exotic parts, if I remember. New Zealand. Spain. Argentina! Why not retrace your steps? When old men fall off their rockers they're expected to do outrageous things. Why not rob a bank? Why not kidnap an heiress if it's excitement you want? If all you want is an excuse to get off Estevan Island—and I can imagine any number of reasons to get off it fast—why not sign up to spend a winter on a Greenland ice floe, or take up deep-sea diving? Better still, find yourself a lonely widow (as I did) and move to Florida (which I didn't—this letter is being written in North Vancouver).

Good for you, for making the effort to get back into life with that advertisement, but you shouldn't put all your hope in that alone. Minna and I are planning a trip to Iceland this summer. You could be doing something like it yourself.
Yours,
Alan Doyle

"I suppose that is one of your famous letters—hah?"

He hadn't noticed von Schiller-Holst approaching along the beach. He came up the slope, planting his long staff in the grass and leaning into it just a little at each step, his stomach straining the buttons on his shirt.

Instantly annoyed, as he was whenever the *maestro* intruded, Thorstad also felt a sudden need to defend himself. It was ridiculous, of course, but he held up the sheet of paper and hoped he did not look sheepish. "A former colleague, suggesting I find myself a widow and move to Florida."

"Don't ask me in for coffee," the *maestro* said, though Thorstad had never invited him inside in the three years the man had lived here. "I'll sit just long enough to catch my breath." He lowered himself with a grunt to the step beside Thorstad and held his staff in both hands between his spread knees. It was an almost perfectly straight pole, ocean washed nearly white, with the suggestion of a sea serpent carved into the top. Like most men here, the *maestro* wore a ponytail at his neck though he was completely bald on top. "I decided to circle the island in the opposite direction for a change and it's taken me nearly an hour longer then usual. I suppose there is some explanation for that, but I don't know what it is. I just thank Gott-in-himmel you're not torturing that poor cello at this moment. The world needs fewer musicians and many more good listeners."

And fewer bullies as well, Thorstad did not say, but saw no harm in explaining the letter in his hands. "This man has written to suggest I put some adventure into my life."

The *maestro* stabbed the ground with his pole. "You were a teacher, for heaven's sake! He doesn't think teaching is an adventure? What a fool! It would be easier to climb the Matterhorn! Safer too!"

"He also suggests travel, but he fell short of inviting me to join him in Iceland."

Von Schiller-Holst spoke to the ground between his feet. "Once in a while—maybe twice a year—some small orchestra invites me to be a guest conductor for a concert or two. That's enough adventure for me. Enough travel as well. I have my CDs.

Music provides me with everything I need." He stood up, again with a grunt. "Off I go before the light begins to fail. To fall and break my neck is not the sort of adventure that appeals to me. Nor is a helicopter trip to the hospital my favourite form of travel."

Once the *maestro* had set off to continue his reversed circumnavigation of the island, Thorstad went inside to spoon coffee into the pot: Kicking Horse brand, Kick Ass quality, certified organic. Just the scent of it could lift his spirits, though Lisa warned him against the habit every time he brought a new package to her counter.

Doyle had suggested travel and adventure. Well, there'd been more than enough adventure travelling with Elena, who had a tendency to make scenes that Thorstad had to smooth over. On their final day in Barcelona a beggar woman had tossed her bundled-up baby at Elena, who instinctively dropped her purse in order to catch the child. Naturally the woman had snatched up the purse and run, which meant they'd had little choice but to carry the woman's doll to the police station to report the theft. Elena berated herself for her stupidity—she who ought to have known the habits of Barcelona beggars! The police were so incensed by her elaborate criticism of their failure to rid the streets of crime that they'd put her behind bars, though only until she'd calmed down and even, to Thorstad's astonishment, apologized. At least she claimed it had been an apology. He did not know enough Spanish—either Catalan or Castilian—to be sure.

He could not imagine travelling now without her, just as he could not imagine actually writing, without her encouragement, his planned biography of Jack Jones, the "Pocatella Kid," whose career as a stunt double ended when he was thrown from his wagon during the filming of *The Dawn Ride*. To write the biography now would feel like an unhealthy disappearance into daydream, a retreat to a world more dangerously narrow even than his current life.

The return address on today's second envelope included some sort of embossed logo created from an entanglement of initials, followed by the name of a street in the provincial capital. Inside, the handwriting was steady, and slanted uniformly to the right.

Dear Sir,

I did not see your advertisement myself, but my mother-in-law in Prince Rupert sent it to me as a clipping, along with some sentences praising the kindness she detected in the letter she received in response to her query. I am afraid the dear woman cannot accept the fact that her husband was drowned, along with his friends, when their small charter plane fell into the sea several years ago.

We may be able to help one another, you and I. Of course, I know nothing about you, except for what you've said in the newspaper along with the sympathetic nature my mother-in-law detected in your letter, but I wish to encourage you to telephone me at the number below so that we may speak of this "adoption" matter—by which I assume you mean a sort of barter relationship whereby you would apply yourself to helping our son with his high school courses in exchange for comfortable (and private) room and board.

I shall tell you briefly of our situation here. My husband is a dentist. We live in a pleasant neighbourhood of large lots with plenty of trees. There is a small self-contained cottage at the back of our property where you may cook your own meals if you wish. Or, if you prefer, you could cross the yard to eat with us. This is something we can discuss. Our son is a fine soccer player and a keen budding actor whose dedication to both sport and drama has resulted in unsatisfactory grades at school. He has promised to co-operate with a private tutor so long as we don't require him to quit the soccer team. We seem to have come to a firm agreement on this—that he will not be required to drop soccer so long as his work with a tutor results in improved grades.

I suspect I will be too late, having received your advertise-
ment only now, and that you will already have found a good
home and position elsewhere. If this is the situation, I can only
hope that it works out well for you, and that you will be happy
there.
Sincerely,
Audrey L. Montana

This was precisely the response he had imagined when he sent
out his advertisement! Upon reading the letter a second time he
saw that it was a real offer, that in its incomprehensible generosity
the world out there had sent him a reply he might have invented
for himself.

But this happy recognition was joined too quickly by a dis-
quiet that was almost dread, raising cold goosebumps down his
arms. Here was an opportunity to do what he needed to do—
escape from the dangerous isolation of this place on the very
terms he had hoped for—but he knew already that he would not
respond to this woman's offer. He must have been mistaken, he
must have been hoping for something he hadn't identified. Perhaps he shouldn't have used the word "tutor." Preparing someone for government exams was not teaching so much as nagging,
drilling, anticipating, and of course pretending that the exam had
something to do with education. He could think of any number
of reasons to stay clear of this Audrey Montana. As he replaced
the sheet of paper to its envelope and tapped it gently along with
Alan Doyle's letter into the space between his mother's Bible and
I'm Not Stiller, he told himself that even in his seventies a man
could wish for a future that offered more than what he had briefly
devised for himself.

4

Since he could not bring himself to accept even the perfect response to his ad, he saw no harm in allowing Lisa Svetic to know the nature of the advertisement that had resulted in all those letters crossing her counter. She was, or said she was, appalled. "This is far more dangerous than a mail-order bride! A family of lunatics could've decided to get themselves a servant for the dirty jobs they don't want to do for themselves. They'd lock you up at night so you couldn't escape." While tidying up a shelf of canned soup, she outlined a situation where he would be walking into a house filled with young monsters who would make his life a misery by playing tricks on him. "They'll hide your books, bust your cello strings, and mock you in public when you're forced to walk them to school."

This had been, indeed, a possibility. "But I expected an interview first, of course. And I've had some experience with mischievous youngsters—some holy terrors in fact."

But even after an interview, she insisted, the person he might have chosen from all those letters could turn out to be a former student who'd been waiting for the opportunity to take revenge for humiliations he'd suffered—because of his poor grammar, for instance, or the graduation ceremony he'd been denied because of Mr. Thorstad. "And there's always the chance you'd fall into the hands of a homicidal maniac who likes to murder old men who remind him of his father."

Since it must have been obvious that he was not especially alarmed by her imagined scenarios, she informed him, as she rang up his cheese and eggs on her ancient machine, that if he fell for one of those job offers he would find the world much changed since he'd said goodbye to civilization. "Haven't you been reading the papers?" For instance, if he thought wearing a fur coat was still the worst of crimes a person might commit in public, always punished with a hostile splash of thrown paint, he should be prepared for an endless list of newer crimes. "Suppose you lit up a cigarette in a restaurant! Prepare to see your picture in the paper. *'Old Man Endangers Public Health.'*"

"But," Thorstad said, aware that he was grinning, "I haven't smoked for forty years. It's not likely I'll start again now."

Although his letters obviously represented a failed attempt to change his life, he opened the next to arrive because it was addressed to a Mr. Axel Thorstad in quotation marks, as though he might not any longer be himself. He read it while sitting on a bench outside the Free Exchange. The long blue coastline across the strait had reappeared with this morning's light. Ragged columns of mist rose like white smoke from behind each successive hill as though from hundreds of secret bonfires, gradually revealing the chain of blue mountains down the island's centre—some rising to snowy peaks and others to scalped plateaus and isolated Mohawk cuts of timber left to drop their seeds for future growth. The world was still there and getting along without him.

> *Dear Sir,*
>
> *The other day I was told, by someone who was only partly sure of his facts, that my Grade Twelve English teacher now lived on Estevan Island. I am writing in care of the island's post office in case this is true.*

I was in the same class as Ivan Norris (I know you'll remember him and the red hat he refused to remove because he was already going bald—at sixteen!) and graduated thirty years ago before going on to the University of Saskatchewan and marrying a cattle rancher. I have not been back to the Coast since leaving, but I have kept in touch with Muriel Willis. I have no doubt you remember the day Muriel accidentally set my hair on fire while we were sneaking a smoke in the girls' washroom.

Now that my children have flown the coop, I've enrolled in university again to complete my degree. My Shakespeare professor reminds me so much of you that I feel compelled to write, if only to say hello. Like you, he towers above the class, his long arms flailing like an animated scarecrow. Like you, he is so much in love with his subject that it's sometimes comical—like a small wide-eyed boy excited to tell about the treasure he dug up in the garden. Like you, he is even more *interested in his students' welfare than he is in his beloved subject, somehow making you realize that what he appears to be teaching is only the tools he uses for teaching something else. I haven't yet figured out what this is, but I know it is something subversive. I may not have thought too often of* Paradise Lost *while helping my husband brand the cattle, but I know that whatever happened in your classroom expanded my life somehow, and may even have made me a better wife and mother and rancher, and community member as well.*

I didn't intend to write a sappy letter. Maybe I've reached an age where high school has begun to take on a rosy glow. I hope you are enjoying a happy retirement—fishing probably, and beachcombing, (and still practising your famous Australian crawl?) and re-reading Paradise Lost *for the hundredth time!*
Tammy (Adams) Hermann

Tammy Adams and Muriel Willis were two freckled girls who'd sat along the wall farthest from the windows and written messages to one another above the chalkboard ledge beside them, sometimes forgetting to erase them later.

Ernie Grant keeps a French safe in his wallet.
How do you know?
Never mind.
　　　Do you think everyone does?

He wished Elena could read this letter. She had often tried to convince him to give up teaching. On the Townsends' cool veranda she had even attempted to enrol Esther's sympathy in this matter. "I have begged him—*begged* him!—to quit and find something more creative and *important*! But the man is obsessed with his job, with his students, with becoming the best teacher in the stupid world!"

But Esther and Herbert had a son-in-law who taught high school science in North Vancouver. "Curtis loves his work. We wouldn't want him to give it up. Maybe Axel feels the same?"

"Oh, for heaven's sake!" Elena said. "He *throws away* his life! Listen, he thinks he's a servant of love—I've heard him say so! In fact, he is the servant of selfish adolescents and their demanding parents, and the stubborn school board, and the ignorant taxpayers. 'And what are you doing for your own happiness?' I say to him. Good God—I call him 'The Master of Happy Endings.' He is never happy himself unless he's slaving over lesson plans, trying to make his students' lives turn out like a Hollywood movie!"

"I can't imagine how I will survive retirement," he'd once confessed to Elena. He'd probably been in his fifties at the time. "Life will be almost as empty as it would be if I were to lose my fiery, too-opinionated beauty from Madrid."

She had not come to him from Madrid, of course, though that was how they'd always spoken. She had been born in Madrid, but her family had fled the fascist dictatorship and lived as refugees in various cities of France. Perhaps this was why, though she'd loved this getaway island, she was determined never to stay very long. "As everyone knows, if you stay too long beneath trees you will forget how to move. You'll be stuck here forever with your roots in the ground!"

His commitment to teaching was not Elena's only disappointment. That they had not had children was, at first, because children would have interfered with a heavy schedule of performances taking her away from home. And then, when she was willing to begin a family, they had discovered the miracle was not possible. This had been so distressing that eventually they'd applied to become foster parents, as an experiment before considering adoption. Stuart had come into their lives for most of his tenth year, but before they had fully comprehended what was happening he was taken from them and adopted by someone on the mainland. "Never again," Elena said, when she had grown exhausted from blaming him for not warning her of this. When he'd suggested they might adopt a child one day in the future, she made it clear she could never look at an adopted child without weeping for their lost Stuart.

Though Thorstad had been happy to work with a new crop of students every year, he had now and then wondered if he might one day encounter a young man who would offer his hand and say, "I don't suppose you remember me."

When the people still living on the remains of the disbanded commune announced that instead of a funeral service for Bo Hammond they would hold their first spring market of the year "in his honour," Lisa Svetic drew to his attention that this was his opportunity to act like someone intending to become part of the community. She kept his *Teacher* magazine pinned to the counter with her fist to make sure he heard her out. "Since none of your letters rescued you from the horrors of our company, you might as well force yourself to be friendly. Who knows—it might not even hurt."

She warned him, though, that because he'd never been anywhere near the old commune in all the years he'd lived here, he should brace himself for a shock. "It's a disgusting, filthy, run-down pigsty mess, but you shouldn't judge by first impressions."

Although Thorstad had no desire to go anywhere near the commune, he knew it wouldn't hurt to put out a little effort to honour poor drowned Hammond. Even so, when the day came, before climbing into Lisa's ancient pickup without doors—shuddering and emitting foul blue exhaust—he insisted on a promise that he wouldn't have to stay for more than an hour.

While he clung in rigid alarm to the edge of his seat in order to avoid being thrown into the roadside bushes, she hurtled them up the twisting road through the woods with little attention to protruding rocks or exposed roots, and only minimum regard for corners. At one sharp bend he believed his end had come when the truck swerved off the road altogether, carving a wide swath through patches of waist-high salal and barely missing a stand of sturdy pines. Some of the deeper potholes tossed them both off the seat.

This road took them speeding through a part of the island Thorstad had never seen, past deserted farmhouses dangerously aslant, their doors and windows removed to be used somewhere else. Deer grazed in an abandoned orchard. In the front yard of a house painted green, a white-haired woman sat on a kitchen chair to read a book while her sheets dried on a clothesline attached to a leaning birch.

Eventually they pulled to an abrupt stop at the edge of a clearing grown over with alder saplings and overlooking a cluster of log buildings and sagging sheds finished with slab-wood still attached to its bark. The postmistress yanked on the emergency brake and slid out to stand waiting for him to join her for the walk down to the buildings, but as soon as his feet touched the ground he discovered the reckless journey had left his legs a little shaky. By taking hold of a nearby limb he was able to swing down to sit on the fallen cottonwood it belonged to. "Go ahead without me," he said. "I need a few minutes to recover from the Ride-of-Death."

She narrowed her eyes. "You chickening out?"

He saw no reason to hide his smile. "Nothing in that *market* could be as frightening as what I've just been through. I'll be along as soon as these legs remember how to walk."

Great piles of dry brush sat here and there waiting to be burned, and fallen trees had been left, it seemed, where they'd landed. A filthy, run-down pigsty mess, Lisa Svetic had said. He'd overheard at the Free Exchange that the proceeds from this market would be used for converting the largest of these old buildings into a bed-and-breakfast for visitors who wanted to stay overnight, but he could see no evidence that the work had begun on this ambitious task. Nor could he imagine why anyone would choose to stay there.

The buildings were dwarfed by a pyramid of logs and car tires and scraps of old lumber stacked up to possibly five or six metres and crowned at the peak with a large hand-lettered cardboard sign spelling "Bo" with red paint. If he hadn't known that Hammond's body was still somewhere in the sea he might have believed it was in that pile, awaiting the flames. He felt a surge of indignation on Hammond's behalf. What sort of people created a memorial out of the scraps and rubbish they'd been too lazy to burn or haul away?

In front of the sprawling main house, two canvas tents had been set up, and several tables, covered with what looked like the sort of items you found at yard sales. Boxes of magazines, he imagined, and machine parts. He'd been to enough sales of this sort with Elena to be fairly certain there would be plants, bottles, cakes, loaves of bread, leather belts, hand-painted cards, lamps make from twisted driftwood off the beach, velvet paintings, stacks of old *National Geographic*, and books dedicated to the art of seeing the future in crystals, tea leaves, palms, and lizards tossed into a campfire.

The booths appeared to have been set down at random, without any thought of creating rows. Since the forest floor was a natural mess it was not surprising that those who lived within the forest should follow suit. The few customers working their way through their hodgepodge of tables may have come off the ferry but they might also have walked up one or another of the trails from the shacks or trailers or houseboats few had ever seen— the invisible islanders rumoured to be living in hidden bays in order to write a screenplay, plan a takeover of a rival company, receive shipments of Colombian cocaine, or honeymoon far from paparazzi interested in minor royalty.

Someone approached him from behind, feet swishing through the young alder, twigs cracking underfoot. "You timed out for misbehaving?"

When she'd come up beside him he saw that this was Gwendolyn Something from the Free Exchange, the young mother of the six indigenous flowers.

"Just waiting till I see someone I recognize."

"Well, you should recognize me, after all the time you spent pawing through Hammond's books."

She had Susan Hayward's slightly turned-up nose and tiny waist. She may have been aware of this herself—she always wore dresses with tight waists and loose gathered skirts to the knees. And white high-heeled shoes, even here in the bush.

"What will they do with that pyramid, do you think?"

"Goodness knows," she said. "You can't expect this bunch to follow through with anything. They'll wake up tomorrow and wonder how the damn thing got there!" Her laugh had little humour in it. "Their brains went up in pot smoke long ago." She was so pleased with this that she put a hand on Axel Thorstad's shoulder while she wheezed. She had never even said hello in the Free Exchange.

"Well, I better get a move on," she said. "I was back in the bush for a pee. No way am I going anywhere near their toilet."

She paused after just a few steps through the tangled twigs and clumps of grass. "You're going to sit there like a bump on that log, aren't you?"

There was no point in getting indignant. Staying here was exactly what he'd prefer. "I can think about poor Hammond better here than down amongst the money-changers."

"Don't brood about *him*. At least he had a life. Travel? Adventure?" This was wistfully said. Gwendolyn Something was envious?

"But murdered."

She might not have heard this. "At least he did some good while he was out there in the world."

"Not everyone would think laundering drug money was doing good."

She shrugged, as though indifferent to such fine distinctions. "There are poor people out there grateful he risked his life skimming off the top for them while he could. That's what I heard, anyway. He wasn't sending it *all* to the bad guys."

"Which is probably why he's no longer alive," Thorstad said. There was no harm in letting his impatience show when what he felt was far too close to anger.

"At least he wasn't afraid. Me, I haven't made a single enemy but I worry myself sick every time I have to go across with the girls to that school! What kind of life is that?" She shuddered, hugging her arms to her chest, and started off through the young alder shoots and the mess of fallen twigs.

But she turned and came back a second time. "I thought you were supposed to be leaving us. If you've decided to stay, you may as well take over Hammond's job."

He laughed. She really was an innocent. "You want to see me murdered next?"

But it seemed she was serious. "Hammond risked his life for others. What use are you and me to the world, hiding out in this place?"

"If Hammond risked his life for others, doesn't he deserve something better than a funeral pyre made of junk they're too lazy to haul away? If I don't go down there now it might be because I don't trust myself not to start tearing it apart."

"Whoa there!" She held up both hands as though to resist an attack. "You can stay where you are till you turn to stone if that's what you want. We'll hang a sign around your neck: *'This man took too long to leave.'*" She chuckled to herself as she set off again through the young alder. Apparently Axel Thorstad was amusing.

The alarming thing was that he could easily imagine himself as that stone figure, solidly in place, with a warning for others hung around his neck.

At the same time, it wasn't difficult to imagine himself standing up to stride through the mess of fallen twigs and clumps of weed down to their ridiculous pyramid, and then to climb—he was strong enough for this—from one log to the next, up over tires and dead limbs (market-stall merchants and visitors rushing over to demand that he stop) and eventually getting close enough to the top to grab hold of Hammond's name and fling it into the woods, then beginning to dismantle the monstrous heap, dislodging one ridiculous piece of rotted lumber or rubber tire after another, rolling them down amongst the alarmed crowd of islanders and visitors from across the strait. Quite possibly, too, dislodging a linchpin log and causing the entire construction to dissolve and tumble down to crush and bury him.

But why would he do such a thing—or even imagine it? He would have accomplished nothing except to make an absurd spectacle of himself. If he survived, the police would be called, a certain incident with a gun reported, and any number of additional complaints hauled out to reinforce the charge. An "old-folks home" would be threatened once again. Doors would clang shut.

Of course they would not understand that for him the pyramid was as unsuccessful for its purpose as the stone on Elena's grave. Just as his "teacher of the year" awards were little compensation for the loss of his career, a heap of logs or a cold gravestone could never compensate for the loss of another human. Neither stone nor pyramid nor framed piece of paper could cancel an unwanted dispatch to an irretrievable past.

When he reached home, five of the feral sheep had come out of the woods to crop the grass between his shack and the retaining wall's drop to the beach, their unshorn wool long and ragged and decorated with twigs and moss and bits of blackberry vine. They paid no attention to him, a foolish old man who had, in a rage, imagined pulling down a pile of logs upon himself.

What did this mean? Had he left it too late? He was frantic, it seemed, with questions. Was he on his way to becoming that frightened old hermit who'd greeted him with his long-handled axe? That poor fellow had eventually done real damage, badly wounding a young father who'd poached a Christmas tree from his land. By the time the police arrived to investigate, the hermit was already dead by his own hand, the interior of his shack a bloody mess. Perhaps Axel Thorstad was in danger of becoming another of those mad loners known to be living invisibly in the timbered mountain valleys across the strait, men who'd fled the coastal houses to survive with a gun and maybe a dog beside some hidden lake, scurrying off to hide at the sound of a human's approach.

Beside his doorstep the yellow trumpets of Elena's daffodils had gone dry and papery, while hyacinths and tulips had shot up and bloomed more showily around them. Fawn lilies bloomed in the shade beneath the trees, and here and there throughout the woods the wild currant bushes were heavy with their red flowers. The thick upper branches of the double-trunked arbutus, stripped of berries by the boozy birds, had all but disappeared within its overcoat of full white blossoms. This had always been, for him, the year's most anticipated month.

Whan that Aprille with his shoures soote
The droght of March hath perced to the roote,
And bathed every veine in swich licour,
Of which vertu engendred is the flour;

April after April he'd begun a lesson by speaking those words aloud, rolling them so richly off his tongue that he could almost taste them, causing some alarm and confusion amongst the desks.

Whan Zephyrus eek with his swete breeth
Inspired hath in every holt and heeth
The tendre croppes, and the yonge sonne
Hath in the Ram his halfe cours yronne,
And smale fowles maken melodye,
That slepen al the night with open ye,
(So priketh him nature in hir corages);
Than longen folk to goon on pilgrimages . . .

Rows of startled adolescents, fearing at first that he meant to speak this way indefinitely, soon recognized his intent. Though indifferent themselves to the notion of religious pilgrimages, they had their own reasons for recognizing the effects of spring and indications of rising sap. Lights, so to speak, went on. Glances were exchanged. It seemed perhaps that Mr. Thorstad might have had some understanding of their restlessness, despite being an old man in his thirties, in his forties, eventually in his fifties and still not ready to retire. Every year, he'd leapt into April with Chaucer.

And so, for him there'd never been anything especially strange in the idea of *going* somewhere. Could it be called a pilgrimage if you simply returned to the world? He had nothing like a Becket shrine to visit. What had Mrs. Montana's letter promised? An opportunity again to *teach*, if only in the guise of tutoring. Though Elena had mocked him for thinking of himself as a "servant of love," believing that he was meant for "better things," he'd known there *were* no better things—though he could hardly claim to have demonstrated this while living here on this small island. Maybe you had to keep trying until you no longer could—whether because you'd passed away in your sleep on your hundredth birthday or fallen and broken your neck on your first day in front of the cameras.

5

He should not have trusted his life to this woman. Since leaving the walk-in clinic they had been racing south at a speed he had forgotten was possible—fleeing down a wide ribbon of highway through regions of second-growth timber, sometimes crossing deep canyons on slabs of concrete with little to prevent them from plummeting to the river below like the doomed travellers in *The Bridge of San Luis Rey*. Tendrils of anxiety crawled in the pit of his stomach, already unsettled by a rough crossing from his little island to this larger one. If death didn't claim him at the bottom of a ravine it was bound to arrive in the tangled wreckage of a terrible crash. Mrs. Montana's silver Jaguar grimly overtook all convertibles, sedans, minivans, SUVs, buses, pickup trucks, and motorcycles as though she considered them the detested opponents in a life-or-death race—a contest that could never be won, since every corner revealed more contestants ahead, additional challenges for a determined woman's right foot.

Not only determined, Thorstad observed, but confident as well, confident that this highway had been constructed in order that she could pass unhindered down its length as on her private road. Her strong hands on the leather-and-wood-grain steering wheel conveyed this. She was, as well, a handsome woman, her short dark hair slicked back behind her ears. Her buttoned vest almost suggested a uniform.

During their telephone interview she'd described herself as a businesswoman, which should have meant she could be trusted to arrive in time to meet his ferry. But she'd driven onto the parking lot just as he was being helped to his feet by the driver of a blue Toyota van, blood still running down his face.

While walking up the paved slope he'd inadvertently got in the way of a youth in a hurry—his face half hidden inside a hood, his hands in his jacket pockets and elbows out like broken wings. Apparently unwilling to step around a preoccupied, white-haired geezer dragging his luggage, he'd snarled, "You want to die, old man?" and shouldered Thorstad aside. The shifting cello case on his back threw him off balance and he fell against the van, bashing his forehead on its front bumper.

Convinced this was obvious proof that he'd made a stupid mistake, he'd placed his handkerchief against the bleeding wound and started back towards the boarding ramp. When the van driver shouted, "Your luggage?" and caught at his sleeve, he pulled free and quickened his pace, determined to take the next ferry home.

But no one was allowed to pre-board.

Mrs. Montana appeared at his elbow insisting she take him to a medical clinic in the nearest village. His shouted refusal was, in his own ears, the roar of a great wounded animal. What a fool he must have looked! But he hadn't cared. Why should he care? He'd hurried along the planks and turned beside a seagull-splattered post to make his stand against the bullies. Below, oil uncurled in rainbow colours across the shifting surface of water. He would dive in and swim away.

"Two strings broken," announced the van driver, who'd checked the cello for damage. The instrument itself appeared unharmed.

Mrs. Montana pleaded. "Otherwise I shall feel dreadful about this!"

By the time he'd emerged from the clinic, bandaged but still in pain, she again insisted he come with her as planned. "If you are still determined tomorrow, I promise to make sure you get home." She'd appeared to take pride in the doctor's acknowledgement of his strength and good health, as though she were somehow responsible for this as well.

So they'd set out again on the highway to participate in this futile race—his legs braced for disaster, the thinning top of his hair touching the roof, the Jaguar's speed increasing as though it were running out of control. Everything seemed out of control—trucks and vans and sports cars and crowded sedans. This sense of hurtling in helpless free fall down a long unpredictable ribbon of pavement should have distracted him from reliving the "accident," but the youth's words continued to run through his head, "You want to die, old man? You want to die?" The message was clearly "You ought to be dead by now, so why are you cluttering up my world?"

Lisa Svetic had warned him of this. According to her, the world was in a hurry to get rid of the old. Those who weren't in a hurry to get rid of the old felt they had the right to bully them. "It's what happens to the elderly when they're on their own." He'd known this himself; he'd read the newspapers. He'd seen elderly friends bullied by those who claimed to be family. But he'd expected to control his own life as he had maintained control for forty-three years in his classroom. The impatient youth could have been sent by Lisa to remind him of the need to stay alert.

Yet she had decided to be happy with his decision. "No more wondering if you might shoot me. Life'll improve while you're down amongst the politicians and other crooks in the city. For one thing, I won't have to watch my grammar."

The *maestro*, too, had been pleased. For him, the silence would be a welcome respite. "Only temporary, of course. I have spent my life with music so I know a journey is never finished until it has returned to where it began. Or tried to return, at least."

In order to distract himself from the Jaguar's terrifying speed, Thorstad withdrew from his pocket the envelope Lisa had handed him as he was about to step aboard. She'd come thumping down the cleated ramp to the pier—"Hold it! Hold it!"—her flesh in a chaos of contradictory movements. "This was in the—" she bent low to catch her breath "—in this morning's bag."

In a tight neat slanted hand, this woman writing from Fort St. James offered an excellent fishing lake *"if you are prepared to put up with black flies and no-see-ums."* If her son were to graduate next year and move south to a technical college in order to become a computer expert making big money he needed a tutor who could prepare him for life in the lower parts of the province.

> *I figure someone from down there could teach him the ways of the world so he don't ruin his chances by saying or doing the wrong thing at the worst time. What worries me is that he tends to get lost if he's anywhere there's more than a dozen buildings in a row. He disappeared three times last summer in Prince George, so you can imagine how it could be like in Vancouver. A response will be appreciated, even if you turn me down.*

This had little appeal, but it was something to keep, in case Mrs. Montana's aggressive driving was only the first of unwelcome surprises.

When she veered off onto a secondary road in search of a gas station, he assumed they were entering a brand-new town he had never seen, but she assured him that this was where he'd taught school for all of his working life, subdivisions having replaced seven or eight more miles of farms. "Recognize the little brown church? It used to sit out here by itself."

This meant that what they passed next had once been Mc-Quarry's dairy farm. The fields had disappeared beneath black-top and a collection of stores painted bright as children's toys. Thorstad shifted in his seat to identify them. Home Depot. Wal-

Mart. Toys "R" Us. Michaels Crafts. Eddie Bauer. Starbucks. Dairy Queen. All of this had been pasture for McQuarry's holsteins. He might almost believe they'd somehow crossed the international border.

"The McQuarrys fought long and hard to get their farm removed from the Agricultural Land Reserve," Mrs. Montana explained, "then sold it for several million!"

Thorstad laughed. It was preposterous—an old rundown farm. "Not millions, surely."

But Mrs. Montana assured him the McQuarrys had been handed a cheque for several million dollars. "Now they're living in a waterfront penthouse and spend most of the year on cruises." She reduced their speed, perhaps so he could admire the transformation of McQuarry's dairy farm. "My partners and I developed this—despite protests from the usual lunatics." A sigh for the inconvenience. "If the McQuarrys had sold it as farmland it wouldn't have brought them a tenth of what they got."

And he would not, he supposed this meant, be riding in a top-model silver Jaguar. Platinum Jaguar, rather. She'd made sure he knew the colour was nothing as ordinary as silver.

As they pulled away from the gas station, Mrs. Montana offered to drive him past his former home before they returned to the highway. But Thorstad declined. He certainly didn't want to discover that Elena's sprawling villa had been demolished and replaced by an ugly condominium or a big-box store, as everything in just the past few miles had convinced him it would be. Neither did he want to see his mother's tall old Victorian house, which he knew had been converted to a restaurant long ago, with a suite of law offices upstairs and its backyard paved for parking.

While his former homes could be avoided easily enough, he knew his former place of work could not. Returning to the highway meant passing the high school he'd attended as a student and later taught in for the length of his career. As the Jaguar carried him into this part of town, he was not surprised by the sudden knot in his stomach, the sweat between his shoulder blades—identical to his reaction as he approached this building on his first day of teaching. The long two-storey structure with its flat roof and rows of tall identical windows appeared to be largely unchanged. He could count windows down the first floor to find the classroom he'd taught in the first few years he'd worked here.

"Ugly fifties architecture," Mrs. Montana said.

Thorstad felt a brief stab of resentment, though of course she was right. "It looked pretty good to us when it was new—while I was a student."

"And yet you returned a few years later to teach there, I understand?"

There was a hint of challenge to this, if not an accusation.

Of course it had looked rather dull and unimaginative when he'd returned from university—already a drab example of uninspired utilitarian architecture, as Mrs. Montana had suggested. But it was not for the building he had returned.

Lisa Svetic had advised him not to judge by first impressions, yet Thorstad knew that first impressions could overshadow and even erase all impressions that followed. How easily his first students could be recalled even now, despite the several hundred that succeeded them. Youthful faces, one behind the other down the rows just inside those windows. Freckled Andrea Thompson's nervous tic beside one eye. Eleanor Morrison's too-long curly hair, a hank of it always in her mouth. Rory Deakin's chin propped on a fist, eyes closed to listen hard. David Minnow's long nose following the passing traffic.

Amongst those in his first English class was the young Cindy Miller who sat in the front row and tended to hide her face behind a fall of long brown hair, fingers occasionally pushing open an inverted V through which she could keep one melancholy eye directed upwards upon the teacher. Whenever she was inspired to jot words that would eventually lead to a poem, she allowed this triangular doorway to fall closed and wrote with no need to see, apparently, except with an inner eye. Thorstad soon learned that, from her point of view, his purpose in life was to read, admire, and comment upon these poems, though he'd soon have reason not to read between the lines.

Like this homely building and those first students, his earliest colleagues had also made impressions that survived despite all that had happened since. To think of Andrzej Topolski now was to see him as he appeared in the doorway between Thorstad's classroom and his own that first morning: the expensive suit, the sharp blue eyes, the pencil-thin moustache, and the smile that could appear and disappear in an instant as though flicked on and off with an electric switch. "If they tie you up and gag you, stomp your feet and I'll come to the rescue." Behind his back he was known as the "Polish Prince," he said. "It happens that I'm in line for only a duchy—and only if the Russians retreat—but the local peasants are better behaved if they think you're royalty."

To think now of the beautiful Oonagh Farrell on that first week was to see her standing outside her classroom door to welcome her students with a musical rise and fall of words and hefty bursts of laughter—wearing a full-skirted dress, her sleek black hair pulled back to emphasize her cheekbones and long straight nose. "My mother's mother was a tinker on the roads of Connemara." She often kicked off her shoes and taught barefoot, her unique beauty made all the more remarkable by the unlikely surroundings. Not even her recent photographs on the covers of checkout magazines could fully replace the Oonagh of fifty years ago, three doors down the hall, welcoming students to her room, though he was not at all surprised at the direction her life had taken since.

As for Barry Foster, despite the newspaper photos of the man on his way to prison, it was enough to think of his long morose face in order to recall their first conversation, in which the man had expressed his hatred for the classroom, as well as his contempt for administrators, colleagues, and especially the students, all of whom he believed were stupid.

While he could summon up his first students and colleagues
at will, his classroom had been so familiar already as to be almost
outside his awareness. He had attended the school when desks
were still free of initials, its toilets innocent of obscenities. Seven
tall windows looked out across the front lawn to the Lombardy
poplars beside the street, the bottom sashes sliding up far enough
to climb through if this were necessary. By noon of his first day as
a teacher he had calculated how long it would take to throw up
the nearest window and race across the grass to the parking lot
where his green Pontiac stood waiting. Never, as they say, to be
seen again.

This fantasy had more to do with expectation than reality.
He'd been very young, after all. He was waiting for his students
to behave as some of his own classmates had behaved towards
teachers, many of whom had quit in despair. Miss Earley, it was
believed, had been committed to the provincial mental hospital
on the mainland. Mr. Barr had walked out halfway through
Pythagoras's theorem and found a job as a newspaper reporter
in Saskatoon. Mr. Woods had taken early retirement and withdrawn to a tiny lake in the mainland Interior, where apparently
he lived alone and welcomed no visitors. It seemed that every
year at least one teacher suffered from a form of classroom shell
shock and pulled out in what may have been the nick of time.

He'd wondered when he would turn to write on the board and
find a baseball bouncing off the surface just inches from his head.
Would he, like Miss Earley, fling it into the midst of the class
and rush out of the room in tears? When would he open his desk
drawer to find, as Mr. Barr had found, dog excrement smeared
through the pages of the attendance register? Would he explode
with rage, as Barr had done, and go up and down the aisles rip-
ping pages from student notebooks, tearing the pages into pieces
and tossing them over their heads? And when would someone
refuse to read the next stanza aloud and challenge him to a fist
fight, as Donnie London had done to Mr. Woods? Would he, like

Mr. Woods, be foolish enough to agree? Probably not, but what would he do instead?

To his own surprise, his most natural response to challenges, defiance, and distracting nonsense had defused most problems. He discovered that he was capable of a steady stare that somehow combined disappointment, disbelief, and disapproval with just a hint of sympathy for the impulse behind the behaviour. It was useful, he saw, to have a sense of humour even when there was little that could be considered funny. He suspected, too, that it was useful to be both young enough to identify with the students' need to resist and old enough to see this as just as endearing as it was foolish. "One day you'll remember today and your face will burn with embarrassment. Now take my attendance sheet to the office—it will give you time to think about what you just did."

He'd been only vaguely aware of rejoining the highway, the sprawling high school left behind. Mrs. Montana and her platinum Jaguar had not only achieved the posted speed limit but continued to accelerate in order to catch up to a large freight truck with *"ON THE MOVE WITH JOEY KEUVE"* announced across its rear. An additional surge of speed sent them flying past Joey Keuve, who was less aggressively "on the move" than Mrs. Montana. With Joey Keuve somewhere behind them, she informed him that something had recently come up that could lead to a change of plans. "But I will leave that to Travis to explain when we get there."

Though he'd become almost unconscious of his throbbing forehead, "a change of plans" gave it fierce new life. A change of plans had not been mentioned at the ferry dock or in the drop-in clinic. "You waited to tell me *now?*"

She laughed, her hand dismissing an old man's alarm. "An opportunity of a lifetime is how Travis will put it. For him, that is. I don't presume to know how it will look to you."

She would not tell him more. It would be up to Travis himself to explain.

An "opportunity of a lifetime" could be anything—a visit to the manned space station. He could be asked to chaperone a weekend camping trip with fifteen adolescents of both sexes, their vehicles loaded down with booze, their radios blaring long after midnight—bears raiding the tents, cougars dropping onto necks, and the police charging him with the corrupting of minors. Had he left his island for an encounter with the complex and confusing ethics of modern juvenile sex?

"I think," he said, as calmly as he knew how, "I would like you to stop."

"*Here*? I can't stop *here*."

"There is a wide enough shoulder. Unless you'd rather I threw myself out."

She laughed, but did not slow down. "I'm sure there'll be a public washroom ahead somewhere, if that is what you need."

"I don't need a washroom, Mrs. Montana. What I'm suggesting is that I can find my own way back to the ferry. I've hitchhiked before. I can do it again."

"Don't be foolish!" Her hand dismissed the foolish one's request. "Anyway, hitchhiking's illegal on this highway."

"An old man with a bandage on his forehead will not have long to wait. An accident victim, they will think."

She drove on without slowing. Joey Keuve would not be given the opportunity to catch up. "For heaven's sake, why would you go back now?"

"Because I've obviously made a mistake. You mentioned a change of plans."

"Oh *that*!" She seemed genuinely relieved. Her voice took on a reasonable tone. "Please trust me, Mr. Thorstad. You'll see a great improvement over what you'd expected. A privilege, really."

Since she obviously had no intention of stopping the car and he was not about to throw himself out onto the gravel shoulder at this speed, he folded his arms in a manner that suggested, if she should notice, resignation without pleasure.

While a world of strip malls and used-car lots and occasional stretches of lumber continued to flash by in a blur, he made an attempt to think of compensations. It was a city he was going to, with a university that would sponsor visiting speakers. Neighbourhood libraries could be within walking distance. There was bound to be a symphony orchestra, and a concert hall, an opera company as well. He would be living in a family home with comforts that were taken for granted by city people. And, most important, he would have someone looking to him for help with his studies—which was, after all, what he had hoped for, putting himself back into his own best notion of Life.

Mrs. Montana's right hand rooted around inside the red leather purse and eventually brought up a small cellphone that she unfolded and held up where she could see it while using her thumb to punch in numbers. Then she held it to her ear. At first there was only "Yes," and "Yes," and "Another hour or so," and then a good deal of listening before she spoke again, adopting an authoritative tone. "Tell him he's full of it. Nobody else will offer him that. Remind him of that swamp we'll have to drain." With her one free hand she manoeuvred the car around the flattened body of a racoon. "Tell him exactly how much it will cost to put in a proper road. Make sure he knows that his house will have to be demolished, in case he thinks it's an asset we might sell where it stands." Silence. "Unh . . . No, of course not." Silence again. "Well, tell him he's welcome to do that but it won't make any difference."

Elena would have been shocked to learn that he hadn't driven past the house they'd lived in for most of the marriage. She'd often claimed to have designed the building herself, he recalled, though in fact she had only pestered the architect into giving her everything she'd wanted—the sprawling villa of a Spanish aristocrat set down between temperate rainforest and the sea. She would see his refusal to drive by as a lack of courage, and would not of course be wrong.

His courage was something she had remarked on shortly after they'd met, at the reception that followed the Topolski-Farrell wedding. This was shortly after he'd completed his first year of teaching, and was already looking forward to more. The exotic dark-haired girl in a pale green dress had been pointed out to him and described as a wickedly flirtatious and talented pianist who'd flown from Paris (in exile from her home in Madrid) to attend her cousin Topolski's wedding. He'd watched her laughing as she danced, he'd seen how she flirted with one dance partner after another but refused to dance with any a second time. She was clever too, it seemed, and confident: he overheard her successfully argue a pair of History teachers down in a conversation about the causes of the Second World War, though they may have given in out of gentlemanly regard for her feelings and less-than-gentlemanly regard for her charms. Eventually he worked up the nerve to ask her to dance, then led her out onto the polished floor to whirl about the crowded room, where she laughed at every surprise turn, and shook her head (her dark eyes gleaming) when he tried out steps he had only seen executed by others. "You are a man of courage, I think," she said, "or simply reckless," and rewarded him later with a second dance. "I have been told you are a teacher but I see you have the hands of a musician."

"Be careful," Topolski warned him. "She is a famous coquette. She will capture your heart and then return to Europe and marry a banker."

Later in the evening, after Thorstad's third dance with the Spanish pianist, Topolski dropped into the empty chair beside him and said, "Jesus, Axel, I'd forgotten! I fell in love with her when I was thirteen—a distant cousin on my mother's side—and swore I would marry her one day or kill myself. How could I have forgotten?"

But Topolski had just that evening married Oonagh Farrell, who later left town with him and reappeared over time on theatre stages and television screens, and in the pages of celebrity maga-

zines. Axel Thorstad had married Elena Rivero, who after many
years had also vanished and could no longer be found on this
earth. He had been left behind by them all, to disappear from
the world in his own fashion—though he was returning now, too
fast, in a platinum Jaguar sedan.

Mrs. Montana continued to pass every car and truck that came
into sight until they'd reached the summit of the mountain pass,
and then was required to tailgate a cautious Camry down the long
winding single lane on the southern slope, sighing impatiently all
the way to the bottom. When level ground had been achieved and
the Camry overtaken, the lanes soon multiplied and they began
to pass scattered pockets of homes and new subdivisions still
under construction. Before long, they became part of converging
streams of bumper-to-bumper traffic about to enter the busy
streets of a city in mid-afternoon. Transport trucks groaned past.
Taxis recklessly shifted lanes. Traffic lights changed, cars sat idling,
drivers spoke into hand-held phones and then moved across intersections without interrupting their conversations.

Some distance ahead, a cluster of tall buildings rose above the
surrounding roofs. This tidy provincial capital was considered to
be a small city by modern standards, but it appeared to be a taller,
more crowded, and much busier version of what he remembered
visiting with Elena, to shop, or to visit the museums, or to attend
a movie where they would not be surrounded by his students.

But Mrs. Montana turned away from the main road and fol
lowed a street through block after block of residences occasionally interrupted by shopping malls and schools with fenced-in
playgrounds. "We're nearly there!" She called this out as though
it were a surprise even to herself. So they passed through the
city without fully entering it and came to something that looked
like the beginning of country again, or leafy suburbs at least. They
turned off a busy street and followed a paved road through woods,
passing beneath an archway formed by the leaning trunks of arbutus trees. Visible only from their driveway entrances, the houses

they passed were large, and far apart, some of them designed to look like Tudor mansions while others were surprisingly modern structures of cedar and glass. It seemed that most of the original trees had been kept but the forest floor had been tidied up and carpeted over with rich green lawns. A low stone wall ran along the side of the road, long driveways leading in past Garry oaks and blooming rhododendrons towards a *porte-cochère* or a three-door garage. The glittering strait could be glimpsed beyond the cinnamon-coloured trunks of arbutus trees. One of these estates had just recently sold for more than its listed price, Mrs. Montana said. "To some folks from Missouri."

Three old men walked slowly along the edge of pavement—on the wrong side. Obviously they'd lived their lives amongst sidewalks and hadn't been taught that where sidewalks did not exist they should keep to the left, facing traffic. The tall slim one was completely bald and walked with shoulders thrown back in military fashion, his gaze trained on some point far ahead. The white-haired one leaned forward over a pair of long aluminum props attached to his forearms to become a second pair of legs. In his old age he'd learned to walk like a giraffe. They did not appear to be talking, perhaps because the third man—who trailed a few metres behind at the end of a leash pulled tight by a sleek black dog determined to close the gap—was shouting out words from the rear.

"There are several assisted-living complexes nearby," Mrs. Montana said, "for *seniors*—that is, for *senior-seniors*." She swerved to go around the three *senior-seniors* without further comment, as though they were a regular feature at this spot in the road.

If there was much more talk of *senior-seniors* and assisted-living complexes, Axel Thorstad would take a taxi to the Coachlines depot tomorrow rather than stay for her mysterious altered plans.

They turned in between stone pillars and approached a large house of many gables and tall windows and french doors beyond an expanse of manicured grass that was interrupted here and there with islands of red rhododendrons and white bridal wreath. You might almost expect to see a Victorian Lady pensively crossing the lawn, the train of her long skirt whispering through the grass—though Thorstad supposed he was thinking of the movie rather than the E.M. Forster novel. Instead of Mrs. Wilcox or Vanessa Redgrave there was a slender youth in shorts and yellow T-shirt bouncing a basketball on the driveway. He stepped off the pavement to stand with one hand holding the ball against his hip and his free hand shading his eyes, watching his mother's platinum sedan bring this stranger into his home.

6

The boy stayed where he was, with the ball against his hip, as though the stranger getting out of his mother's car were merely an interruption to his basketball practice. A tutor may have been the last thing in the world he wanted, let alone a tutor with white hair and an old man's craggy face. This was how it looked, at least, to Axel Thorstad. Perhaps to demonstrate his indifference, the boy bounced the ball on the pavement again and tossed it against the backboard, then watched it circle the basket's rim. When it had fallen, he trapped it against his hip and waited, it seemed, for some signal, but paid no attention to the black Lexus SUV that pulled in off the road and quietly passed him to stop behind the Jaguar.

"My husband," said Mrs. Montana.

Apparently they had decided to surprise him with this dark-haired man, who obviously expected to be recognized. A graduation date was mentioned, a class with a reputation for impulsive enterprise. "A friend told Carl about your move," Mrs. Montana said. "He was convinced there couldn't be two of you on little Estevan."

When you'd taught for more than forty years on an island, even one this large, you got accustomed to this sort of coincidence. Thorstad knew this from experience. Former students showed up behind counters selling insurance, real estate, or shaving lotion. They materialized at street corners with their children, their wives, or members of their hockey team. They became your mechanic, your optometrist, or your financial adviser. The surprise was that he had not run into Carl Montana long before now.

"You could have had me kicked out of school any number of times," Carl admitted, with obvious amusement. "But instead you steered me into a corner and made me feel embarrassed for myself. I don't know to this day how you did it."

Axel Thorstad was surprised that Carl wanted to recall his high school days. The Carl he remembered was the clown who'd shot him in the chest with a water pistol during patrol duty in the cafeteria, the sort of situation where it seemed wise not to overreact while others were watching but to insist the boy step into the hall for a private talk. He'd known that Carl was not malicious, just fond of making people laugh. In the classroom, Thorstad had had to decide which of his comments to challenge and which to ignore.

He noticed a few white hairs had invaded the area above the ears of middle-aged Carl—a dentist, according to Mrs. Montana's letter. He'd come home from work in grey slacks and a pale blue shirt with sleeves rolled to the elbows. Now he examined the bandage on Thorstad's forehead. "She told me you'd agreed to this of your own free will, but I see a little force was needed."

The pain had all but faded away, but there it was again, as though it had been waiting for someone to notice.

Perhaps Mrs. Montana had signalled a warning. Carl changed the subject. "I'd forgotten how tall! Or maybe I thought you'd have shrunk." He stood up on his toes, perhaps to compare heights. "But . . . aha! Your forehead has made serious inroads into your hairline."

"Ridges of scar tissue now." Thorstad bent to display the evidence. "From coming up too fast from under things."

"Well, you've got a lot of body to manage—most of it far from your brain." He removed Thorstad's luggage from the Jaguar's trunk but made no move to carry it anywhere. "We used to watch you heading for the classroom door, convinced you'd eventually bash your head and fall back, cursing. We hoped for it, actually." He tilted his head in the direction of the boy with the basketball. "You can see we're a compact lot in this family—all bones and muscles close to Control Central."

Only now did the boy come forward to shake Thorstad's hand. Also, apparently, to conduct an interview with the ball still resting on his hip. "You play soccer?" He'd removed a small plug from his ear and allowed it to dangle on a black wire from the pocket in his shorts.

Presumably he meant "in the past." Hoping this would not lead to a cross-examination, Thorstad admitted that he'd been bullied into coaching a soccer team once when the school was desperate. "But I was not very good and wasn't asked again."

"He was a human torpedo in the pool," his father said. "Or so we heard."

The boy was slighter than his father, with a head of wheat-coloured hair, closely cut and lying forward to a sort of point on his forehead. No tattoos were visible, no ring penetrated his bottom lip or the dark, perfectly shaped eyebrows. The black-and-white chequered tops of his runners may have been his only eccentricity.

He made it clear that finding a tutor was not his idea. "I told my friends my grandfather's coming to live with us. You okay with that? Escaped from a village of cannibals and wandered for months in the jungles of Brazil." He bounced the ball between his feet, captured it with both hands, and looked up at Thorstad aslant. "If I'm forced to have a tutor I want one who's had a poison arrow in his back." This was an invitation to join a conspiracy perhaps, though possibly also a threat.

"Oh, for heaven's sake!" His mother clapped hands together. "Pay no attention to his nonsense, Mr. Thorstad. Carl?"

Appealed to for help, Carl looked down at his feet and smiled. The boy ran his free hand over his hair, pushing it upright and then letting it fall back into place.

"You'd better watch yourself with this one," Elena cautioned. "He's exactly the sort of student you had a soft spot for, imaginative and mischievous and likely to drag you into more trouble than you could have anticipated just because they know instinctively the minute they meet you that you will enjoy their hijinks and even find a way to accommodate them despite the rules of the school or family or even country—like your little escapade with the school newspaper, for instance, where that principal hauled you into his office and demanded you stop having the newspaper club meet at your mother's house at night where all sorts of things could be going on behind your back, which was exactly what happened if I remember you telling me about that girl who kept leaving you her poems under a vase or behind a book with barely disguised confessions of the crush she had on you, one in a long list of such would-be poets probably all dead by now of their own hand, so be careful with a young fellow who's only just met you a minute ago and already imagines an arrow sticking out of your back, cannibals at your heels, probably a veiled warning against trying to stop him from doing just about anything he wants to do, just as those parents have probably let him get away with for years."

Elena may have been the only person he'd ever told about discovering Cindy Miller's love poems behind the windshield wipers of his car, tucked between a corner of the daybook on his desk, and all over his mother's house after Thursday-evening meetings of the newspaper club. He hadn't told anyone else about the humiliation of being called to the principal's office and shouted at for risking the reputation of the school with his habit of thinking he could behave as if he weren't working for the district's taxpayers.

To Thorstad, the Montana family home appeared to be large enough for a dozen people to live in, though Mrs. Montana hadn't mentioned children other than Travis, or a tribe of in-laws living beneath her roof. But it seemed none of its rooms were meant for him. Travis took the suitcases from his father and led Thorstad across the lawn to a cottage he called "the guest house"—cedar-shake walls and a border guard of blooming rhododendrons. Even if he decided to stay, he was obviously not to think of himself as family.

"Sorry about the poison arrow," Travis said, when he'd set the luggage down on the beige carpet. "I don't want my mother to think I take her seriously."

"Then I'm not to masquerade as your wounded grandfather?"

Apparently this did not deserve an acknowledgement. "I wouldn't unpack if I was you. You aren't really needed. And I know you won't want to stay."

Was this a challenge or an outright rejection? It felt, rather unpleasantly, like a door slammed in his face. He was tempted to inform this young man that it was *he* and not the tutor who was on probation here. But he had returned the plug to his ear and set off, shaking one hand to a beat that only he could hear.

Though Thorstad was not to live in the family home, here in the guest house he was at least able to enjoy the forgotten smell of furniture polish, the tall pot of flowering plum branches in a corner, the comfortable furniture upholstered in leather—everything so immaculate the place might have been furnished yesterday. Framed black-and-white photos hung on the burgundy walls—half-lit faces, horses stampeding at night, unidentifiable fragments of naked flesh.

He discovered nothing quite so artistic in the bathroom, where a garishly coloured poster demonstrated the horrific fate of neglected gums. An array of toothbrushes, rubber picks, and

packages of dental floss had been set out along a shelf. The boy
with the water pistol had found new ways to give himself a laugh.

Axel Thorstad had arrived in a surprisingly tidy world. The
grass outside was as uniform as plush carpet, the driveway free
of leaves and coniferous needles; the inside of this guest house as
clean and polished and free of clutter as a furniture showroom.
Of course, this could be temporary. The boy was not keen that
he stay, and the "change in plans" could very well be unthinkable. He imagined a burst of applause from his honour guard of
red-eyed stumps when he appeared at his door, but did not look
forward to his first visit to Lisa Svetic's Store.

He stood his cello case in one corner of the sitting room.
Obviously, he should not have brought it with him, but it had
begun to surprise him lately with additional shards of melody
from the Dvořák Cello Concerto, and even a few splinters of
sound from within the score of Prokofiev's C major Sonata for
Cello & Piano—though only long enough to ignite a flame of
excitement and hope before sinking again beneath the dark cloak
of lost memory. However, there was little point in replacing the
broken strings until his future had been decided—if there was
any point in replacing them at all.

Until the telephone rang to invite him across for dinner it
hadn't occurred to him that he might not be dining alone, as he
had done for years—making his own meals and eating whenever
he pleased. He hoped that seven years of Estevan hadn't destroyed
his table manners.

But of course the Montanas knew how to make you relax in
their dining room, which looked out through a wall of glass
and across an expanse of lawn to a latticed gazebo, a drop to the
beach, and an expanse of water, islands, and mainland mountains
beyond. Despite the wafer-thin china, the fragile glasses, and the
pale carpet underfoot, they were so casual they might not have
noticed any of this luxury, and expected their guest not to notice

as well. Axel Thorstad could not recall when he'd last eaten at a table covered with a linen cloth, or with a bowl of yellow roses positioned beneath an elaborate chandelier.

Dinner had been prepared by someone named Marietta, who had since gone home to feed her own family. They helped themselves to bowls and passed them on. Apparently there were no other children living in this enormous house, no in-laws in the extra rooms, no other guests. There were just the four of them to work their way through a sequence of dishes—a crab-and-melon salad, the salmon en croute, and a lemon soufflé dessert. The conversation alighted briefly and almost distractedly on several topics: the rising costs of a university education, Carl's reasons for taking up dentistry, Mrs. Montana's successful colleagues, and Travis's admiration for the great basketball player Steve Nash, a local hero. Occasionally Travis paid attention to the small gadget he'd laid beside his plate, his thumb tapping at tiny keys. Once, he looked up to address Thorstad. "So, would you say you were a hotshot teacher or what?"

Mrs. Montana put down her fork. "Travis?"

Travis shrugged. "Just wondered."

"I apologize," Mrs. Montana said. "Our son isn't overjoyed at having a tutor—but he usually remembers his manners. And he doesn't need to *wonder*. He knows how his father has spoken of you."

"Centuries ago," Travis said.

Thorstad made an effort to smile at this, though he considered it reason enough to get up and walk out. Obviously this boy had little interest in winning him over.

Only when the coffee had been served and Thorstad had sat at this table longer than he'd remained in one spot at any time during his seven years on Estevan did Mrs. Montana sigh and place her china cup carefully in its saucer, and examine him for a few moments as she might once have examined McQuarry's farm for its commercial potential. Then, as though with confidence that he would measure up to expectations, she said, "Now Travis has something to tell you."

"Yes." Carl Montana addressed the edge of tablecloth he'd taken into his hands. "Time to tell the man how he's been misled."

"Carl," his wife warned.

Travis snapped his electronic gadget closed. "I have to go to L.A.," he said, though he looked to his mother while he said it. "My parents were afraid you might not agree if you'd known. I *told* them you aren't needed."

So this was it, the mysterious change, withheld from the old man till now. Thorstad had just arrived and the boy was planning to leave. He wasn't needed after all.

"We didn't know about this ourselves!" his mother protested. "*This* time!"

"I have a small role in a TV series." Pushing his shoulders back, Travis delivered this with something like defiance. "*Forgotten River*. This is its third season."

Perhaps it was a confused expression on Thorstad's face that prompted Mrs. Montana to help. "Travis has been in several school plays over the years. Last year this TV producer or whatever he is came up to visit the drama teacher, an old friend from school, and saw Travis perform in *Our Town*. He interviewed him the next day, and flew him down for auditions."

"Just a minute," Thorstad said, both hands flat on the table as though to keep things from shifting more than they already had. "Does this mean I'm to go home and cool my heels until he returns?"

"We thought it was just a lark," Carl said. "But he was offered a speaking role—a young fellow who appears only now and then on the series."

"He's gone down three times," Mrs. Montana said, "and one of us has always gone with him."

"We hadn't anticipated this one," said Carl Montana to the tablecloth in his hands. "Apparently they've added Travis's character to an episode where he didn't appear initially. The final one of the season. And neither of us is free to go with him."

"And anyway," his wife added, "this time he needs a tutor and not just a chaperone. He must do well on exams."

"It will be two weeks out of his life," said Carl.

Thorstad might have stood up to leave immediately but needed to be sure he understood. "You're planning to ship me off to California?" The anticipated comforts of home and the easy access to libraries and concerts had been, it seemed, illusory. "And this is before the exams?"

Mrs. Montana regretted to say that yes, it was indeed to take place before the exams. "Which is why we hope you will agree to go with him. At our expense of course. He has agreed to put in two or three hours of study every day, with your help." This was delivered with narrowed eyes, daring the young actor to contradict. "He has a room in a trailer where he can work between scenes, and there will be times when he isn't needed. It is crucial that he come home and ace the finals."

Carl Montana barely parted his teeth. "We realize this may not be what you'd expected, Mr. T. If you decline, Travis will have to turn them down."

Travis thumped the heels of both hands against his forehead. "I have a *contract!* I *have* to go! The studio can find me a tutor if you're going to, like, *force* me to have one!"

When Mrs. Montana asked if he had ever been to southern California, Thorstad was inclined to suggest this was irrelevant, but he was a guest here and admitted that he had visited Los Angeles once. "More than fifty years ago. It was a chance to see where I might have been raised if my father hadn't had a fatal accident."

"Fatal?" Both parents said it. Perhaps this was not a word for the dinner table.

He was sorry he'd given them this, but could not refuse to explain. "He was a stuntman for the movies."

Travis threw himself back in his chair, obviously impressed. Perhaps a stuntman's son was almost as exotic as a grandfather with an arrow in his back.

"Well," Carl Montana said. "It will be up to you to make sure our son does not get up to any *stunts* of his own. We want him back alive."

"Carl!" His wife had closed her eyes as though to escape the conversation.

Carl Montana held up both hands to surrender. "I'm a dentist. I poke and probe and cause occasional pain. What do you expect?"

"Very funny," Travis said. "What I want to know is *his* opinion, not yours. Of course he doesn't want to go. Why would he want to go where he isn't needed?"

If Thorstad had been standing rather than glued to this chair, his brain might have offered him something worth saying. He had a lifetime behind him of thinking on his feet, some of it surprising even to himself. Today, however, in this posture more appropriate for a job applicant, he could offer only to think about it. It wasn't something you would get to your feet to announce.

Travis looked rather pleased to hear this. The old guy was having second thoughts.

Mrs. Montana's body language was that of a chair about to adjourn a meeting. "You won't be leaving for a week, which gives us time to book a flight." Perhaps she believed an agreement had been reached. She stood to finish her coffee, "I must run— a meeting to attend," and returned her cup to its saucer before leaving the room.

Carl raised his eyebrows and smiled at his son. "It seems her pals have convinced the council to exempt their golf course from property tax—like a church or Legion Hall!"

Now Carl, too, pushed back from the table. "I'm afraid I have my own meeting to attend." There was a hint of apology in his voice. "Not as important as Audrey's, of course. We're planning to bring another dentist in to the clinic. You can see it's impossible for us to go with Travis ourselves."

Once Audrey Montana's platinum Jaguar had whispered past the window and Carl had gone off to some other part of the house, Travis pushed his dessert plate away and laid his folded arms down on the table to rest his chin on his wrists. Obviously he was not about to suggest they shoot baskets or stroll to the water's edge. With some dismay, Axel Thorstad wondered if he had given up a world of movement for a world of talk, with his rear end forever attached to a chair. As a teacher he had preferred to wander the room.

"So, were you really the hotshot my father says you were? Did they make you principal?" This time he seemed more curious than defiant, though possibly he was just being careful.

"You think being made principal is a reward for being a good teacher?"

Travis shrugged. "I've had some pretty rotten ones. Most of them were just lazy. My mother told me you had a bachelor's degree before you started, and then got a master's in your summers. Right?"

"I'm not sure that made me any smarter but it helped my paycheque. And, since you asked, it also meant I was eventually offered a vice-principalship I didn't want."

But this young man was concerned for his own immediate options. "I signed a contract. *They* signed it too. They have to let me go, whether they make me take you with me or not."

"Let's just suppose for a minute I agree to go. How could I know you wouldn't tie me up and drop me off a pier the minute we got there, and go out on the street to buy drugs?" Thorstad said this as though he were amused and only quoting someone who *might* suspect such a thing. "How could I be sure you wouldn't party the whole time and expect me to make your excuses?"

Travis sat up abruptly. "I won't have time! I want to be, you know, so *good* they will give my character a bigger role next year!" Again one hand went to the top of his head and pushed back through his hair, raising it on end. "By the time they try to bully me into law school I want to be, like, indispensable."

Though it seemed to Thorstad that Travis did not have the sort of good looks you associated with Hollywood actors, he did have long lashes and perfectly shaped eyebrows, and the sort of sharply defined features that were probably favoured by the people behind the cameras. Nothing about his dress or manner suggested the modern teens you saw milling about in their sloppy rags and earrings and hooded jackets outside the village dentist's across the strait. He appeared to be a type that endured despite the changing manners and costumes of successive times: the clean-cut "only-child" who identified to a certain extent with adults. Thorstad recognized something that triggered memories of certain students in his past—an eagerness to claim the attention of the teacher, an anxious need for either equality or intimacy. They were the easiest sort of pupil to work with if you responded as they wished, the quickest to turn against you if you did not.

These boys were sometimes convinced they didn't need you. They suspected you weren't qualified to teach them. The hooligans were easier to win over, and the class clowns, as well as the struggling D students just wanting to get out and find a job. None could be as difficult, at first, as the confident, the wealthy, the talented, or the notably intelligent. The question was, did you want to make the effort?

Evidently convinced that Thorstad had heard enough to know where he wasn't wanted, Travis pushed back his chair at last. "I gotta do some math. No help needed!" He started away but turned back in the doorway. "Leave the dishes. Marietta'll throw them in the dishwasher tomorrow morning. You got your own TV. *Bones* is on tonight."

Thorstad could not bring himself to leave the house without first clearing the table and stacking dishes on a kitchen counter, but eventually he walked out into the familiar evening scent of sea air, cool and a little damp, and passed between the gateway pillars with the intention of exploring this winding tree-shaded street. The declining sun sent striped shadows of the arbutus trunks across the pavement. A purple finch rested on a slender limb of mountain ash and sang its simple notes, throat repeatedly swelling and then subsiding, while it regarded the human below with indifference. Somewhere deep in the woods another responded. Amongst the long grass beside the pavement, bluebells and small white daisies bloomed.

Outside the stone pillars framing a neighbour's driveway, a cardboard *"HELP YOURSELF"* sign leaned against a stack of clay bricks—some broken, most with bits of mortar still attached. Beside the bricks was a roll of fencing wire that would keep the deer and goats from someone's garden if he were to ship it up to the Free Exchange. Or somehow arrange to take it with him when he returned.

From around the bend ahead, two of this afternoon's old men came into sight, again on the wrong side of the road. They made their slow way towards him, apparently investing all their keen attention in the pavement immediately before their feet, a continuous challenge to be conquered with every step. Again the third man appeared several metres behind the others, leaning back at the end of his dog's tight horizontal leash, and it was clear even at this distance that he was talking—words that might have been meant for the dog, or even for the two men ahead who might not have been aware that he was tailing them.

Mrs. Montana's talk of *senior-seniors'* homes was enough to make Thorstad look on these old fellows with alarm, the voice of that hooded youth still clear in his head. *You want to die, old man?* He felt obliged to be polite to these gentlemen, who had almost certainly heard that question themselves. "Pleasant evening," he said when the first two had got close enough. He'd stepped aside onto gravel, because of course he had been walking towards them on the same side of the road as they in their dangerous city-bred ignorance were walking towards him. The two men turned their startled attention his way, as though to question whether it was he or one of the mock-orange bushes that had spoken. They nodded but did not speak—two pale faces, all eyebrows and watery eyes and loose yellow flesh—before resuming their turtle progress. Both wore thick shoes with Velcro straps instead of laces. It was the man with the dog who spoke—having almost caught up to the others—continuing what appeared to be an ongoing narrative. "I told the lying bugger he wasn't going to get away with nothing just because he was married to my niece, I knew better than to think he'd ever bring the TV back once I let him get his hands on it. . . ." His words carried on past Axel Thorstad and the roadside bushes and faded eventually to a murmur as the little parade crept on towards the next bend.

7

There was nothing to keep him from relaxing on the guest-house couch to read from Travis's literature anthology—just an owl hooting softly in the trees, and the familiar sound of waves against the rocky shoreline. The throbbing in his forehead had faded to a dull untroubling ache. Yet even as he slid happily into the lines of Gerard Manley Hopkins, *For skies of couple-colour as a brinded cow*, he was aware of an annoying energy that would keep his limbs alert and restless, his brain unwilling to concentrate on printed words so long as there was a decision to be made. Hadn't he already struggled to make the decision that had brought him here? For a man who hadn't had to make a decision of any consequence in seven years, one was quite enough. Before he'd even got used to this place, he was expected to move on—this time to what was, after all, the city of his father's death.

"The city of your father's death" was how his mother had put it, seldom "Los Angeles" or even "L.A." As a child he had imagined it as a romantic sun-washed city capable of sudden betrayal. He had never wanted to see it for himself. His mother had been eight months pregnant and reading a library book beneath a green umbrella when the police informed her of his father's fall from that roof. He had heard her tell this a thousand times—a tall slim elegant woman in a housedress, often speaking with her back to

him while she prepared a meal at the kitchen sink. She was a nervous, high-strung woman who often spoke too fast and occasionally left the room in the middle of a sentence, leaving him to
imagine the rest.

His mother had loved the climate in Los Angeles, or claimed
that she had. He remembered her insisting that she hadn't missed
the rain she'd grown up with, or the subtle seasonal changes in
this mild corner of the continent. She could have spent the rest of
her life on the beach, she said. His father had been a superb swimmer, a fine athletic figure in his bathing trunks, invited by noisy
crowds to join in their games, but he'd chosen to spend his time
with her, walking hand in hand along the waterline. He had, she
believed, made her a gift of his place. To her young son, all of this
might have been the lovely-but-tragic plot of a Warner Brothers
movie.

Yet she'd never gone back. Once she'd moved north to her
hometown, she allowed California and perhaps his dead father
to become a lovely sun-washed memory—a happy episode that
came to an abrupt end while she was reading *David Copperfield* at
Venice Beach. Once the policeman had delivered his awful news,
she said, the beaches, the sunshine, and the brilliant exotic flowers ceased to belong to her.

So it was not surprising to Axel Thorstad that she'd shown
no interest in joining him and his friends on their Christmas trip
to Los Angeles during his first year of teaching. She would have
preferred that he and his friends stay home, or consider some
other location for their break.

But to him and his colleagues, it seemed important that they
put some distance between themselves and the school, to go
where there was little chance of meeting their students on the
street, and would not be tempted to plan lessons for the coming
month. And somewhere near Los Angeles Andrzej Topolski's sister had a home where they might stay. By Christmas break they
were exhausted from the strain of preparing lessons, dealing with

problem students, and marking tests and essays, as well as supervising extracurricular activities. Barry Foster had already decided to resign in June.

Andrzej Topolski had made the arrangements. They flew south on Boxing Day and moved into his sister's extravagant house above Laguna Beach. Though she and her husband were away on a holiday of their own, Topolski was confident they'd meant for them to have the run of the house. Naturally this included the liquor cabinet. He demonstrated his talent for mixing frosty margaritas, which they drank beneath umbrellas on a terrace overlooking the ocean. To local inhabitants this may have been winter but the teachers on holiday were determined to spend as much time on the sand or even in the water as the temperature would allow.

But the weather turned cool their second day. Since Topolski was certain his sister had intended to leave him the keys to the Cadillac, and because Barry Foster had known which wires to cross, they'd driven in to the city and cruised up and down the streets of Hollywood and Beverly Hills, counting, as they spotted them, four Gloria Swansons, three John Barrymores, and one small Mickey Rooney. A seventy-seven-year-old man cringed to recall such adolescent enthusiasm, though his body easily remembered the excitement that had buzzed in his twenty-two-year-old chest.

Oonagh came out of a gift shop with a "Homes of the Stars" map, and insisted on driving past Yvonne De Carlo's house. She had been told she resembled the actress, who had grown up as Peggy Middleton in Oonagh's Vancouver neighbourhood. Of course they had all seen Yvonne De Carlo as Moses' wife in *The Ten Commandments* and later as a gold-rush entertainer in the first episode of *Bonanza*. Thorstad could see the likeness but believed Yvonne De Carlo lacked Oonagh's surprise of *character*, especially Oonagh's husky laugh and her smile that bared her teeth out nearly to her ears.

Seeing Yvonne De Carlo's house inspired in Oonagh a need to *be* a star herself, at least temporarily. She insisted on returning to Hollywood Boulevard where she got out of the car in order to walk down the sidewalk alone. They were instructed to drive up behind and recognize her. Of course this would be a lark, and they were happy to humour her. Something to tell when they got home.

Topolski waited just long enough, then drove ahead until they were abreast, then proceeded slowly. "Hey!" he shouted. "Aren't you Yvonne De Carlo?" The name was probably lost in the traffic noise but the shout had turned a few heads. He honked the horn. Barry Foster and Axel Thorstad cheered. Oonagh raised a hand and gave them her widest smile, but kept on flouncing down the sidewalk. Though Thorstad had recognized her astonishing beauty from the first day they'd met, he had never witnessed such a provocative walk, her light cotton dress swishing around her legs at every step.

Satisfied that she had caused heads to turn, and even for two or three people to snap her picture, Oonagh continued to the end of the block before getting back into the car. Of course they congratulated her on her gutsy performance. Although they suspected that the real Yvonne De Carlo would probably make herself as inconspicuous as possible in public, this did not diminish their pleasure in knowing that Oonagh Farrell, even in Hollywood, had turned a number of heads.

After this success, Topolski had decided that they should find the house belonging to Derek Morris, the actor Thorstad's father had stunted for. "Let's see what sort of mansion the bastard lives in." He was contemptuous of those who handed life's risks to others—actors letting stunt doubles face the dangers while they took all the credit themselves, not to mention the money and fame.

The prospect of meeting Derek Morris had thrown Axel Thorstad into confusion. Did he want to discover whether Morris could remember his father, or his father's accident? But Topolski cared little for the ambivalence of others and Topolski was behind the wheel. With the aid of Oonagh's map, Barry Foster guided them up a canyon and along a winding road atop a narrow ridge until they came to the stuccoed wall and elaborate ironwork gate to Derek Morris's property. Between the bars of the gate they were able to see, at the head of an oyster-shell driveway, a mansion that belonged more properly on a Louisiana sugar plantation. "That's where your mother's ten-cent cards are coming from," Foster said.

"A guilty conscience," Topolski said. "Signed and stamped by a servant."

It was an encounter Thorstad would rather forget. Topolski got out of the car and insisted that blushing Axel Thorstad join him in admiring the garden that was visible through the bars. Almost immediately a figure appeared from behind the shrubbery—a groundskeeper, to judge by his faded overalls with dirty knees.

"Mr. Morris is out of town," he said. "There is no one here but staff."

Relieved, Thorstad turned away. But Topolski explained to the gardener that he was a relative, a cousin to Mr. Morris, in fact a member of the Polish royal family, as Derek must surely have mentioned. He flashed his on-off smile. "The last time we spoke, he went out of his way to invite me to visit. Along with my friends."

"Mr. Morris is not at home," repeated the gardener—if that was what he was.

"Pity," Topolski said. "And of course he did say this was a possibility. But he insisted that we come by and use his swimming pool anyway."

"I'm sorry," the servant said. "He left no such information with me."

As they drove away, this episode was a matter of some hilarity to the others, though Thorstad was certain his father would have disapproved of their intrusion upon the actor's privacy. Of course, if this were a movie, the gardener would turn out to be Derek

Morris himself, fully aware that Andrzej Topolski was lying and his red-faced friend was a fool.

He did not resist their determination to find Centurion Pictures, somewhere to the east of the city. The others seemed to think the fact that Axel Thorstad's father had been employed there would gain them easy entry to the studio, but again they were stopped at a gate, where a skinny youth in uniform turned them away. All they saw of Centurion Pictures was an avenue of leafy trees and a high stucco wall that extended the equivalent of several city blocks. He could imagine his father walking or driving in through the gate but had no way of knowing where he'd gone after that.

His father's Hollywood was long gone by the time he and his friends were turned away from Centurion Pictures. Behind that wall Centurion was making what would be one of their most successful Westerns, starring Paul Taylor and Elizabeth Robson, which Thorstad would later force himself to see on the screen of the Capitol Theatre, though it meant sitting amidst a hundred noisy students on a Saturday afternoon. At the same time, elsewhere in the city, Marilyn Monroe was in front of RKO cameras for one of her first roles, in *Clash by Night* with Barbara Stanwyck and Robert Ryan. If the travellers from the north had seen Marilyn Monroe on the street, they could not have guessed she was anything but just another shopper or, perhaps, a tourist, and would not have given her the sort of attention they had given Oonagh Farrell.

After they'd been turned away from Centurion Pictures they put aside their disappointment and attended a performance of *Returning to Troy*, a new play by Horace Feltham at the Canyon Playhouse. A rather simple story—a young wife searching for her husband, the husband determined to sabotage this reunion, and a shy fireman who helps the woman with her search and may or may not be rewarded for his efforts. By the time they'd got back to Topolski's sister's home and talked about what they'd seen, they'd begun to suspect that Oonagh Farrell had discovered the life she believed she should be living. They did not imagine, then, that the lives of all four were about to make a drastic change in direction.

"Which of course they did, my darling! And now maybe you will realize what is going on that you may have become too confused to notice—how you have been led into exactly the situation you haven't even recognized is one of your most compelling aspirations, because it's time you woke up at last and faced the fact that something you have left incomplete and unacknowledged for most of your life is precisely what you have been led to confront without knowing it."

Axel Thorstad almost responded aloud—"What? What have I been led to confront?" Of course it was not Elena who had kept track of Oonagh's progress over the years, noticing the occasional photograph on the cover of some grocery-store magazine, the smallest news item in the Arts section of the newspaper—a role in some Broadway play, an award held high for the photographers determined to capture her incomparable smile—making it clear that she could not be found in any one place but belonged everywhere at once. Only recently had he noticed that she'd been photographed during a period of working in California.

When he mentioned Oonagh's name at breakfast, Mrs. Montana was able to tell him why she'd been photographed in L.A. "Retired from the stage years ago, I think." Travis and Carl had already left the breakfast room, and Mrs. Montana was about to leave for the office wearing a navy-blue skirt and jacket, though had yet to put on her shoes. "Now she has a regular role on TV. Are you telling me you knew her?"

"A colleague once, long ago," was all he would admit to. Mrs. Montana did not strike him as someone who would appreciate knowing more about the relationship, but it was clear that he had just acquired a little additional interest, perhaps a small amount of mystery as well.

Mrs. Montana recalled seeing Oonagh Farrell in a televised version of *The Glass Menagerie*. "I've heard she was magnificent on the stage. But then you've probably seen her yourself, if she was a friend."

"Once. Well, twice." This was long ago now, in New York City. "My wife and I attended a performance of *Saint Joan*." They had hoped to see Topolski as well, but apparently the Polish duke-in-waiting was on a business trip to Peru.

Oonagh had been a brilliant Joan, just as he'd expected. You wanted to rise up and follow her into war, and yet at the same time you wanted to take her away and save the poor child from herself. And, near the end of the play—Thorstad had waited for it—she had been able at last to say, legitimately, with a catch in her voice, the heart-wrenching line she had made her own on many occasions—usually during interminable and tedious staff meetings: "How long, oh Lord, how long?"—but provoking tightened throats this time, and possibly tears, rather than muffled laughter.

She had probably been smiling to herself, knowing that Axel Thorstad was in the audience recalling her staff-meeting mischief. She'd hinted at this when they met for lunch the next day, but made no reference to having been, though briefly, the centre of Axel Thorstad's life.

After lunch, Elena had chosen to shop for a black opal whose mix of colours was perfectly matched to her dark Castilian eyes, but he had returned to the theatre for the matinee performance of the same play, convinced that every word spoken by the inspired and headstrong girl from Domremy was intended just for him.

"Of course her *Saint Joan* was later shown on television," he informed Mrs. Montana. "You may have seen it yourself. As was her *Cherry Orchard*."

"Well! If you had told us she was an old friend we'd have watched *Another Life* last night. She plays a dotty old neighbour who claims to be Swedish royalty."

He could not allow Mrs. Montana to see how he felt about this. That Oonagh Farrell could be in Los Angeles, and Topolski possibly with her, might be good enough reason to refuse the Montanas' assignment. Oonagh Farrell might see his sudden appearance as the sort of harassment stars were sometimes subjected to from people claiming a long-ago friendship. Neither Oonagh nor Topolski had got in touch during all those years, though they certainly must have known where he could be found.

At any rate, this did not alter the fact that he wasn't sure he wanted to be responsible for a resistant seventeen-year-old in the noisy glamour of Los Angeles. How much did he know about today's youth once they were beyond the reach of their parents? He had heard that they had little in common with the students he'd taught, and might as well have been from another planet— inscrutable, unpredictable, and dangerous. Even a clean-cut boy without a nose ring could be waiting to cross the border in order to show his true colours. And, he mustn't forget, this one was reluctant to have him along.

Because the city's teachers were having some sort of professional workshop today, Thorstad assumed this would be an opportunity to discover how serious Travis was about his preparing for exams. But Travis had other plans. When he'd come thumping down the stairs from his room and paused to jam his feet into his runners inside the front door, he explained that this was his chance to put in some hours at the homeless centre downtown. "I volunteer." He yanked a jacket from the closet. "Research for my role!"

His role in the TV series, he explained, was that of a teen who'd run away from his family to live amongst a group of street people in some New England town. His companions were dope addicts, alcoholics, released convicts, the mentally ill, and the unemployed. "This is *vital*, man!"

Mrs. Montana's protest was cheerfully pushed aside. "He can come with me! They'll be happy to put him to work."

Axel Thorstad repressed an involuntary groan. He had no desire to go downtown, which he was sure would be a confusion of dangerous traffic and crowds of rude, impatient shoppers. Even less appealing was the spring rain that had worked itself up into a deluge during the night, the downpipes roaring at every corner of the Montanas' house. Travis was obviously determined to sabotage or at least delay his would-be tutor's opportunity to find out what it would be like to work with him.

Yet it could be useful to observe the boy when he was away from the family home.

Travis grabbed two umbrellas from a jardinière and led Thorstad out to his battered green Tercel in the three-car garage. The wheels were without hubcaps and the rear window had been replaced by a sheet of plastic duct-taped in place, but the engine roared into life at a turn of the key. Travis assured him that the rattling would not be noticed once they'd exceeded the speed limit.

They worked their way out of the neighbourhood past mansions Thorstad did not recall noticing on his way in. "That," Travis said, indicating a large pink-stucco house out near the water, "my mother sold to a couple from Arizona who come up to stay in it three weeks a year. Empty the rest of the year, except when gardeners or cleaners make their rounds." It wasn't clear whether he was criticizing the extravagance of foreigners with money or simply boasting of his mother's ability to attract wealthy clients.

"Now she's talking about investing in a residential cruise ship. She figures once the idea catches on there'll be big demand— retired people wanting to, you know, own a suite in a ship that never stops roaming the world!" Thorstad assumed he was speaking of luxury liners for the wealthy, but couldn't help imagining shiploads of *senior-seniors* sent out to sea and forbidden to return to land.

Once they'd turned onto a major thoroughfare and other cars were left behind in a rooster tail of rainwater, it was clear that

Travis had been taught to drive by his mother. Drivers shook their fists. Horns were honked, though Travis appeared not to hear. Axel Thorstad decided that this was one too many reckless drivers to suffer in silence. "Slow down, please. Or let me off at the next intersection."

"She hates me volunteering," Travis said, releasing the pressure on the accelerator just a little. "She's scared I'll, like, bring home a disease. Or, even worse, street people to camp in our basement. I wouldn't be surprised if bringing you here was, y'know, to keep the guest house occupied by someone she chose herself."

There was little about the downtown area that looked as Thorstad remembered it from occasions when he and Elena had driven down for a movie or a play. What interested him now was the number of tall cranes standing above holes in the ground. Giant billboards displayed colourful illustrations of the towers that would rise from these sites—glass and steel and lush roof gardens. "Homes for your homeless?" Thorstad asked.

"Very funny, haw haw! A one-bedroom suite in those will cost more than, you know, a four-bedroom house in Winnipeg." While they idled at an intersection, he added, "They're being built for rich outsiders to invest in and later sell to other rich outsiders planning to retire here." Then, as they started across the intersection, "Eventually local working families will have to camp outside the city limits in shack towns. You're looking at a future Rio." He turned a broad grin to Thorstad. "See how I drive my mother nuts?"

An astonishing number of vehicles had been reborn as moving billboards. The back ends of buses advertised new condominiums for sale. Pickup trucks were as colourful as the Saturday comics, with Action Heroes advertising bathroom fixtures and cartoon kittens promoting toilet tissue. One Toyota advertised the company that would paint advertisements on your vehicle, and—by way of example—displayed an image of its own decorated self on its door.

"My mother's company advertises on great long moving vans. It takes a lot of space to show a townhouse complex big enough to, you know, bury a produce farm."

Of course all of these vehicles were shedding rainwater. Rain poured off awnings in front of stores, ran in rivers along the curbs in search of drains, danced on the lake-like surface of intersections, and defeated the best efforts of the Tercel's windshield wipers. The interior of the car was loud with the wipers' thrashing and the steady drumming of water on the roof, increasing Thorstad's sense of having entered a city in the throes of a clamorous panic. He felt a touch of alarm himself.

They circled the block twice before finding a vacant parking space, then waited for a break in the traffic before dashing across the street to come up onto the sidewalk beneath an awning, stomping their feet and shaking rainwater from their umbrellas. Thorstad's stomach told him he was about to become an intruder in a foreign world.

In this covered space outside the squat green stucco building, they were amongst people who'd come outside and started off in one direction and then turned back, perhaps surprised by the rain. Smokers and lounging dogs formed a sort of hub around which others revolved. Shopping baskets piled high with garbage bags sat parked by the window. Thorstad watched a cyclist pedal past, pulling a trailer stacked with cardboard cartons. An elderly Chinese, adopting a custom of his ancestors, balanced a long slim pole on one shoulder, a bulging black garbage bag hanging from either end.

He hadn't thought to expect such noise inside, or so many people. Seen from the doorway, this was rather like the first glance at a crowded Breughel painting, where individual faces might belong to any of the overlapping dark-clothed bodies. Several round tables were occupied—some people chatting, some only staring into the table's surface. As he followed Travis through the crowd inside the door, he saw there were also clusters of people engaged in conversation while standing. On the floor along a side wall, several dressed in winter coats appeared to be sleeping against a pile of camping gear, while above them silent stock cars tried to demolish one another on a wall-mounted television screen.

There were too many people for the space, and yet more streamed in. Already his toes had been stepped on, his elbow pushed aside. It wasn't all that easy to breathe. He was aware of sweat breaking out on his forehead. How was it possible for there to be so many in need of this place? Some came to the counter where mugs were available while others pushed through to a side table where they could make toast. Travis explained that after a night of sleeping in cardboard boxes or under bridges this was the closest thing these people had to the comforts of home— though the bare plywood walls and marked-up flooring brought to Thorstad's mind a bingo hall or small-town community centre.

Wherever he stood he was between someone and something that person needed—the coffee urn, the small computer lab, the outside door, or the entrance to the pool table area. Fingers plucked at his sleeve. "Hey you—Stretch! Yeh, you! You know where Neil got to?" A woman who looked as though she hadn't slept in recent weeks put herself directly before him to demand attention: "I don't remember your name but I'm looking for the dumb shit who took my mug before I'd finished my drink."

Thorstad wasn't sure he could deal with so much evidence of *need* without betraying signs of pity, or an instinct to apologize— for what, he didn't know. But Travis seemed to be comfortable. He stopped to chat at a crowded table, then turned away laughing, calling back something as he walked away. While gathering mugs at another table, he appeared to be listening hard to a diminutive woman's earnest monologue, her hand clamped to his arm. When he'd been freed to turn away, he was confronted by an obviously distressed man who stood solidly before him, struggling hard to explain something. He walked this man to the back of

the room where he knocked on a closed door and waited for it
to open.

Eventually Travis showed him how he could help by gathering up used coffee mugs and taking them to the counter where
they would be washed, then carrying a plastic tub of clean mugs
back to the table of coffee urns. Thorstad was soon using paper
towels to wipe up spills, returning the knife to the peanut butter
jar, and tidying the sliced bread that seemed to get scattered
across the side table every time someone used the toaster. He
spotted his own crop of abandoned mugs to carry to the kitchen,
where a large man with a blue plaid shirt and wide suspenders
dumped them into a sink of soapy water. No one asked why Axel
Thorstad was here. He could have been just another of the regular volunteers, or a felon sentenced to community service. He
smiled, to think of Lisa Svetic reporting this to the others: "Old
fool left to become a rich boy's teacher and found himself cleaning up for the down-and-out!"

The dishwasher may have been the only one to be curious.
When he'd handed over Thorstad's fourth or fifth tub of washed
mugs, he cocked an eyebrow. "You came with young Travis?"

When Thorstad had explained his situation, the man bent to
rest his folded arms on the counter. "A good boy, him. 'Course he
makes no bones about his reasons. The Hollywood people told
him he had to do this." He was a large man with a good deal of
unruly facial hair. "A bit of a snot at first, he made it clear he
didn't want to be here. Made a few enemies. But eventually he got
into the right spirit and does a fine job."

"People seem pleased enough to see him."

"Oh, he can be a charmer when he wants to, when there's someone he wants to impress. Today I'd guess that's you." He shifted
his weight and chuckled. "Maybe he'll be a big movie star one day
and send us a few million bucks for a new building! Or give some
of these folks a job. What about you? You planning to volunteer?"

He should have expected this. "I'm supposed to help him pass exams but I'm probably just heading home."

"We need someone willing to do shower duty but you wouldn't like it." The dishwasher straightened up and stretched, pressing both hands into the small of his back. "Means you stand outside the shower door with a clipboard, check off a person's name when his turn comes up. Let him in. Bang on the door when his time's up. Then go in and clean everything before you let the next one in. There'll be needles—broken, some of them. Nobody's favourite job, but it has to be done."

The dishwasher wrung his nose with a red-and-white handkerchief, which he then returned to his jeans pocket. "Anyway, a man your age should be taking it easy. There's a hell of a lot of frustration in this and you've probably had more than your share already."

Thorstad became aware that a pair of eyes was trained on him from a lying-down position. Apparently the bulky person laid out on a pair of chairs needed to puzzle out something about the old fellow talking to the dishwasher. He raised his head and frowned, as though trying harder to see through a haze. "Sir?"

For most of his career Axel Thorstad had been "Sir." When he wasn't "Sir" he was simply "Mr. Thorstad." If other names were spoken behind his back he'd chosen not to hear them.

"Shee-it." This person put boots to the floor and sat up, then heaved himself to his feet. "Thorstad?" He was a middle-aged man with long matted hair shooting off in several directions, wearing layers of cardigans and shirts beneath a heavy overcoat gaping open—a sort of greatcoat with dark patches where the rain had not yet dried.

The dishwasher said, "You got a problem, Walker?"

The man named Walker closed his eyes and shifted unsteadily. Then he opened one eye and peered at Thorstad as though trying to decide why they were looking at one another.

"Not *Angus* Walker?" Thorstad said. The name had come to his lips of its own accord. There must have been some remnant of the seventeen-year-old in the rough features of that face. Since Walker's attempt to come closer unsettled his balance, Thorstad took the few necessary steps and held out his hand. He supposed they both would wish that he hadn't.

There was nothing to indicate this man was surprised to find Thorstad here, or embarrassed to have his English teacher catch him laid out to sleep on a pair of chairs. Thorstad was careful to show no surprise himself.

"Jesus!" Walker laughed. "Lookit you! You're fuckin' old!"

Thorstad laughed. What else could he do? "You're no more surprised than I am. A joke has been played on me, as you can see."

"On us both!" Walker threw out both arms to present himself for inspection. With the heavy coat opened wide, Thorstad was shown the washed-out flannel shirts and sweaters meant for someone larger, as well as the stained and sloppy jeans.

Walker was too shaky to hold the position long, and put a hand against the wall, then seemed to forget for a moment that he'd been involved in a conversation. Should Thorstad back away and behave as though the exchange had not taken place? He looked to the dishwasher for guidance, but the man had stepped up close to Walker. "You sleep last night?" No answer. "The cops hassle you?" The response was too quiet for Thorstad to hear. "Did you have something to eat, then? There's doughnuts somewhere."

Walker was not interested in doughnuts. He'd decided to return to his chairs, where he laid himself carefully down and curled up, perhaps for more sleep, having already forgotten or dismissed his encounter with his Grade Eleven past.

"Walker's a regular," the dishwasher said. "Has been for years."

"He was quite a good student," Thorstad said. Angus Walker had been a son of the town's optometrist. "I'm sure his plans did not include this."

"All I've been able to find out is, he got an education and started teaching somewhere up north. Spent a few years in a mostly Native school. A newspaper friend of mine tried to get his story but that's all he learned."

When the dishwasher went back to his soapy water, Thorstad carried a tub of washed mugs out to the coffee-urn table. Then he mopped spilled coffee from the floor, carried discarded newspapers to the recycling bin, and fetched paper serviettes or sugar packets for those who asked. He looked around for more used mugs to gather in his tub.

When Travis's shift had ended and they were outside and ready to dash across the street to the parked Tercel, Thorstad's name was called from behind. Of course it was Angus Walker, coming unsteadily up the wet pavement.

Travis took hold of Thorstad's sleeve. "Come on, man. It's wet!"

"To hell with teaching, Thorstad!"

Thorstad felt something turn in his stomach but of course he mustn't run.

"To hell with Shakespeare, Thorstad! What use was John Keats to me when it mattered, huh? What use was the subjunctive mood when the chips were down?"

But Walker was already turning back, one hand making the unmistakable gesture of dismissal, and Axel Thorstad was left feeling weakened and a little shaky, as though he'd just been pulled free from genuine peril.

After lunch at home, Travis was again able to avoid a study session by setting off to take part in a "compulsory" game of lacrosse with his friends. Thorstad went for a long walk along the coastline before returning to the guest house to read from Travis's textbooks. Later, over pre-dinner drinks in the living room, Carl apologized for not warning him about Walker. "I saw him when I went down with Travis the first time he volunteered—to see how

I felt about this so-called research. Angus played on the same hockey team as my brother. Lived two blocks down the street."

"There is a temptation to sympathize, of course," Mrs. Montana said, examining the vase of orange gerberas at her elbow, "but people make their choices."

"Audrey," Carl said.

Thorstad watched a grey squirrel run up the trunk of a Garry oak outside the window. "It seemed cruel just to walk away," he said.

"You've spent your life leaving students behind," Carl said. "They've left *you* behind. Forget him. He'd probably be the first to tell you that."

Thorstad had never imagined former students living on the streets. Now he wondered if Angus Walker was one of many. He knew little about their adult lives, except for those who wrote to thank him or request a reference letter. He had no idea whether his students slept in mansions or in a cardboard box under filthy back-alley steps.

"And Angus was a teacher?"

Carl nodded. "Somewhere up north."

Thorstad was aware that he must be frowning rather fiercely. "And Hollywood has turned this sort of thing into a television series."

Carl sighed, perhaps a little wearily. "When you get back from L.A. your head will be so filled with the Hollywood version you'll suspect Angus Walker and his pals of putting on their sadsack show while you're there to see it, and becoming activists and troublemakers as soon as your back is turned. Like so much else, *Forgotten River* is in the business of telling stories in order to pry you loose from your money."

8

After dinner, Travis offered to give their guest a tour of his second-floor quarters, beginning with his study at the head of the stairs. Here one wall of floor-to-ceiling shelves displayed children's books and several biographies of actors, *Laurence Olivier* and *Steve McQueen* amongst them, and a row of published movie scripts. *Closely Watched Trains. Cannery Row.* The remaining shelves were occupied by matchbox pickup trucks and miniature spaceships along with small figures Travis described as his childhood superheroes. A guitar leaned against his long black desk.

"He claims strumming on that thing helps him think," Carl said from the doorway. "I'll leave it to you to decide if it does any good."

He reminded Thorstad that he and his classmates had been influenced by the disco music of the seventies, and had considered the Bee Gees' songs the equal to any of the poems they studied in class. "We could hardly believe it when you agreed to let us write essays on the cultural importance of *Rolling Stone* magazine! Or—what was it?—the thematic undercurrents of "Stayin' Alive"! I defy you to find any meaning in the stuff *he* listens to up here."

According to Carl, the "stuff" Travis listened to was closer to shouting than to singing, short rhyming couplets delivered like quick jabs to the solar plexus. Apparently his friends listened to the same sort of thing, three of them sometimes coming home with him from school to do so—two with braces on their teeth and rigid mohawks on their heads. "But we won't let them get in your way."

Travis's study was remarkably tidy but no tidier than the rest of the house. Nowhere had Thorstad noticed stacks of CDs or books on a chair, or abandoned magazines left open on the carpet. But rather than give credit to his mother or a cleaning service, Travis explained that it was only because they hadn't lived here long. "We never stay *anywhere* long!" He threw up his arms as though this were a source of frustration or alarm. "I could come home from L.A. and be met at the door by strangers! It's happened before. Someone offers her more money than it's worth and she'll take it, then find an even better deal for an even better house. We won't be out on the street—just *moved*."

Apparently Travis had most of the upper storey to himself. Across the hall was what he referred to as the "viewing room" where they might later watch an episode of *Forgotten River*. From the doorway Thorstad saw rows of armchairs facing a screen almost as wide as the wall. "Me and my friends have marathons in here. Once we watched the whole *Lord of the Rings* trilogy—no breaks except for bathroom and food."

Beyond his small bedroom, the room at the end of the hallway had its own bathroom and had probably been meant for guests originally, but it had been furnished as an exercise room, with treadmill, weights, mat, and a pair of rings hanging from the ceiling. Fencing masks and two foils were displayed on one wall. "Here's where I keep my body in Hollywood shape."

When he'd stripped off his shirt to step onto the treadmill it was clear the "Hollywood shape" was meant as a joke. His upper body was mostly visible bones.

Of course this tour was meant to delay a study session. Would he be required to stand by and watch this youth walk on the spot until it was time for bed or the ten o'clock news? But Travis hadn't taken many steps before it was clear the boy meant to make this an interview. "Tell me about your father. I mean, what sort of film was he in?"

Thorstad wasn't sure how he might describe *Desperation*. A crime story? "I suppose it was a sort of film noir." He sat on a bench against the wall in case this eventually turned out to be worth staying for. Though Travis was literally walking "on the spot" he was obviously attempting to go somewhere else with his questions.

"He was murdered?"

No adult had ever asked this quite so bluntly. "He was simply jumping off the roof of one building onto a lower one. And missed." Obviously this boy had hoped for a crime. Maybe this was what working in television did to you. "The jump was being filmed. I've seen it. I own a copy of the movie."

Travis stepped off the treadmill and removed a towel from a wall rack to mop his face and skinny chest, though he hadn't walked far enough to break a sweat. "You bring it with you?"

"It's in a safety deposit box at my bank." Along with Elena's rings and his ancient teaching licence. Not that any of this had to do with why they were upstairs in this house but avoiding the "study."

Travis tossed the towel aside and reached for the phone on the wall. "Tell me the title and I can pick it up at Blockbuster."

But Blockbuster did not have a copy of *Desperation*. Nor did Pic-a-Flic have the movie, which Travis learned had never been released on video or DVD. It was possible that Thorstad's was one of very few surviving copies of the film.

Now a pair of barbells was taken from a rack and put to half-hearted use. "Did it make a difference, knowing you were the son of a stuntman? Did you throw yourself off horses when you were a kid? You can guess how exciting it is to be a dentist's son."

Of course, even as a boy Axel Thorstad had been as interested in the stunt doubles as he'd been in the stars. Even now, he remembered the names of Tom Steele, Dave Sharpe, Eddie Parker, Henry Wills, Fred Carson, and Yakima Canutt. Henry Wills had done twelve hundred falls in his career, mostly from horses. Fred Carson had done a "horse fall" as late as 1959 and lived into the twenty-first century. Canutt had become a "ramrod" or boss of stunt crews later, and introduced the safety standards that might have saved his father if they'd existed earlier. "My father might have known the great Cliff Lyons, who was in the original *Ben-Hur*. For all I know they could have been pals. The movie world was smaller then."

But it seemed there was still more Travis needed to know about this stranger who might become part of his life. "Dad told me you were a swimming champ—way back. A friend of mine's on a swim team, says they make him shave his body hair. They do that in your day?"

"The legs," Thorstad said. Shaving the legs had been common practice even in the distant days of his youth. "It was supposed to increase your feel for the water." He pulled up his pant leg a little to show how thick the hair was now. "I shaved my head as well, which was eccentric for the time. But my real advantage was these limbs—a wingspan wider than most." When he spread his arms to demonstrate, Travis said "Cool!" though Thorstad suspected he resembled a gliding pterodactyl.

Once Travis had returned the weights to their rack, he studied Thorstad for a few moments as though he was trying to think of more questions to ask, though of course he could be simply assigning a grade. After a few moments he said, "I'm gonna have a shower and put in a little study time before bed. Maybe you could give me a hand."

In his "study," Travis pulled up a second chair so that Thorstad could join him at his desk. It had been a long time since he had sat at any but his own custom-made desk, so joining Travis meant trying to find a place for his legs beneath this one. Books were toppled in the attempt, a lamp prevented from falling. In the end he sat at an angle.

He withdrew his reading glasses from his pocket, held them up to the light, wiped them on his shirt, and put them on. One ear and then the other. Travis had gone on the Internet and printed copies of the previous year's exams, and was less surprised than Thorstad to discover a large portion of the English final would be best-answer questions that could be marked by a computer. There were also short essays to be written, however, and because Travis admitted to a dread of writing essays, this gave Thorstad a topic for their first session: the importance of defining your terms before anything else. "Let them see you know what you're talking about." He folded back the page and laid the essay question out before them on the desk. "This asks you to discuss *Gulliver's Travels: The Voyage to Lilliput* as an allegory. Do you know what an allegory is?"

Travis shrugged, as he was probably required by the rules of adolescence to do.

Axel Thorstad cautioned himself to be patient. "You know it isn't a building. Or a tree. Or a lyric poem."

"Yeah-yeah. Right. Sure. Okay. I get it. It's like, you know, a story."

Thorstad was patient but not so easily satisfied. "It's a good idea to remember there are four aspects to a good definition. The second: What *kind* of story? What makes it different from, say, a Harlequin romance or a newspaper report? You've told me a category, but now we need to know how it's different from other stories—before we come up with an example—other than *Gulliver's Travels*—and finally an explanation of its function—what it *does*."

Travis cringed while pronouncing the word "symbolic." Since he could not follow it with an example, Thorstad was pleased to bring Geoffrey Chaucer into the conversation. "Isn't 'The Nun's Priest's Tale' still on the course? The story of a boastful rooster and his clucking hens sounds suspiciously like an allegory to me."

"Yes!" Travis jerked upright in his chair. "Listen—Old Man Struthers played . . . you got to hear this. A rap version!" He tapped at his keyboard, waited, and tapped again. "This is the one about the three greedy men who go looking for Death?"

A powerful thumping rhythm drove the voice of a young man through rhyming couplets like a series of jabs with a fist.

> *"They met this guy all wrapped in bandages,*
> *An old handicapped man, with disadvantages,*
> *And the three friends examined his bleeding flesh,*
> *And demanded he tell them how he was cheating Death.*
> *Seeming perplexed, the old man responded with soft words,*
> *And said, 'I walk the earth like a creature God has cursed!*
> *My lot is the worst and most desperate place to be;*
> *I pray faithfully every day for Death to take me,*
> *Waiting patiently, and someday he will arrive,*
> *But in the meantime, until I die, I'm still alive.'"*

Once the three greedy men had killed one another in "rap" language much as they had in Middle English, Travis explained that Old Man Struthers had invited the fellow who wrote this to visit the classroom but he'd been too busy with other gigs.

What Axel Thorstad experienced now was envy. This was the sort of the thing he would have done himself if he'd been in the classroom still—surprise his students with a visit from this young performer, hoping the "rap" version of *The Canterbury Tales* would send them to the original. But it was Old Man Struthers's turn, and Old Man Thorstad's only job today was to get Travis back to the essay question and discover what could be learned for the exam he was still to face.

If the boy—the lad? the youth? in today's newspapers boys his age were often referred to as "men" whether they'd earned it or not—if Travis had wanted to drive him off he should probably not have invited him into a discussion of *The Canterbury Tales*, even reborn as contemporary rap. "Good. Fine. Now back to this essay question. Identifying terms: general type, then specific differences, then an example, and finally its function."

Some time during the night he dreamed again the sort of nightmare that had often invaded his sleep while he was teaching but had gradually faded since retirement. He was always a teacher in these dreams—one night dealing with an uprising of students determined to eliminate him with weapons pulled from their desks, another night suffering a series of detours between home and school forcing him farther and farther away from his classroom where he knew an impatient superintendent waited to watch him in action before writing a crucial report. This time he'd driven all over town in search of a film projector essential to the day's lessons, then entered his classroom without the faintest idea what he was going to teach, discovering he was naked and badly in need of the toilet, which was in the very centre of the crowded classroom. Nothing like these situations had actually happened, yet in sleep he was forced to experience them as though some secret part of him wished to taste the excruciating humiliations of inverted reality. Always, he woke in the hot soup of his own sweat.

This time the seventeen-year-old Angus Walker was in the dream—sitting in the window row, fourth desk from the front. Someone was reading "Ode to the West Wind" aloud. Angus looked up, waited for a pause in the reading, and said, "You think it was Byron's club foot that turned the women on, or did he have some other deformity they don't mention in books?" This was more or less what had occurred. The classroom had erupted with laughter. A lad at the back stood up to demonstrate with his hand where and what this deformity might have been. But then in the dream the clean-cut Angus, clever son of the town's optometrist, stood up and limped across the front of the classroom dressed in rags and a huge overcoat, his feet in unlaced boots with rundown heels, his face disfigured with blackheads and scarlet boils. He dragged one foot behind him out through the classroom doorway and, when Thorstad went out to call him back, disappeared into the chaos of students trying to get out of the building as fast as possible.

At the breakfast table Audrey Montana presented Thorstad with his plane reservation. Perhaps she feared he might never make a decision. His "e-ticket," she called it, a term he'd never heard before. Apparently it wasn't really a ticket at all, but something to help the person at the check-in counter find him on the airline's computer.

Of course this explanation was meant to give him time to get used to this development. Well, a person did not so easily get used to bullies. "I'm afraid you'll have wasted your money. I haven't made a decision."

Carl, obviously amused, wanted to know how long he'd been away from the world, to have forgotten how things are done. "I think it's called the pre-emptive strike. In Audrey's work it is a matter of having the papers ready for the undecided buyer to sign—a nudge, so to speak, in the preferred direction." He placed his large pale hand over his wife's much smaller one, perhaps a pre-emptive strike of his own. "A plane reservation can be cancelled, of course." A brief pause for a possible protest from the one who had purchased the ticket, but she had chosen to bite her tongue and look away. "I hope, though, that you've kept your passport up to date."

"Otherwise," Travis said, "you're off the hook. Unless they hire smugglers to take you over at night, hidden beneath a shipment of crystal meth."

The sun had risen from behind the mainland mountains high enough to shine in Thorstad's eyes through the little breakfast room's wall of glass. Thirty minutes earlier he'd been out in that choppy water for his morning swim, giving all the long muscles of his restless limbs a workout. The familiar taste of the salt water was with him still, in spite of the good hot shower. He wasn't sure he possessed a valid passport.

Seeing his hesitation, Mrs. Montana sat forward and clasped her hands together on the glass table, obviously putting effort into maintaining her calm. Everyone's knees were visible beneath the floating coffee cups and plates of toast.

"Just a minute," Thorstad said. "Let me think." Naturally he'd allowed his passport to expire soon after moving to the island, foreseeing no reason to renew it, but when his driver's licence expired as well, he'd begun to feel as though he was relinquishing a little too much of his identity. Since he'd seen little point in renewing his driver's licence, he'd applied for a new passport on the slim chance that he might decide to revisit Madrid one day, to look up Elena's birthplace. That must have been three or four years ago now.

Mrs. Montana closed her eyes while he explained this, her fingers pressed to her temples. No doubt a headache was coming on.

"But I saw no reason to bring it with me." He had not been warned, he meant, that a plot had been hatched requiring international travel.

"Then we must *get* it!" Mrs. Montana was working hard for restraint. "Do they have phones up there? Could you tell someone where to find it?"

Carl drained his third cup of breakfast coffee. "If you don't want Audrey to drive up and look for your passport herself—and probably sell your house to a consortium of Texas oilmen while she's there—you'd better phone someone and get this business started."

Whenever he and Elena had flown to Europe a passport had been required, but when he and his friends had flown to California during his first year of teaching, just having a ticket was enough to get you a boarding pass, and having a boarding pass was enough to get you on the plane. A driver's licence had been enough to prove you were who you said you were. It would never occur to you that the fellow beside you might have a bomb in his shoe. Why would he?

But his dream of Angus Walker had not entirely faded. He pushed his chair back from the table, preparing to stand. "I'll phone about the passport later, in case it's needed. But first, if you'll tell me where to catch a bus I'll go downtown while Travis is in school. Angus Walker might be more approachable early in the day."

Mrs. Montana drew air through her teeth.

Carl put a hand on Thorstad's shoulder. "Please don't. There's nothing you can do for him. Chances are, having you see him yesterday will have embarrassed him. You could make him feel even worse."

"My Lord!" Mrs. Montana stood up and left the room, carrying her coffee but leaving her plate and cutlery behind.

Travis, too, was on his feet. "I'll drive you to a bus stop on my way to school."

But he should have listened to Carl. When he joined them late that afternoon for a glass of wine before dinner, he could report only that Walker had not been found. He hadn't been at the drop-in centre, and the dishwasher had advised against looking. He'd even suggested that Thorstad could be sorry if he found Walker. "He has a history of making life hell for anyone who tries to help."

Apparently Walker sometimes camped in one of the parks, or down on the beach. But the dishwasher had warned him to be careful, explaining that some of these people had been turned out of institutions, thanks to a government that considered addiction, mental health, and unemployment to be none of their business. "Their business," he'd added, "is making sure the Profit-god keeps smiling on the rich. What you see here, my friend, is the future— anyone who isn't wealthy will be destitute."

So with a tray of doughnuts and steaming coffees he had set off through the city's largest park where there were bodies behind the occasional bush, most of them snoring. Amongst the few who opened their eyes, no one was able to tell him where Walker could be found. Park gardeners planting red-leafed begonias were as indifferent to his search as they were to the peacocks' screams for help. Beyond the duck pond and the petting zoo he'd followed a dirt path down into the woods, where he came upon five or six people sleeping on a king-size four-poster bed, its canopy decorated with ribbons, miniature flags, and dead bunches of flowers, along with items ransacked from a child's toy box—racing cars and dolls and skipping ropes. Nobody stirred.

At the foot of the wooden staircase to the beach he set out along the uneven bed of boulders, careful not to slip and break his neck. Here, the mountains to the south and east seemed surprisingly near, perhaps because of the morning sunlight. He'd forgotten this city faced the coastline of a foreign country—a nation that liked to call itself "America" as though a dozen other nations sharing these continents were of little consequence, as though Spain were to refer to itself as "Europe," for instance, making Juan Carlos the King of Europe, whatever the Poles or Portuguese might think.

But Walker had not been down on the beach, though several others were. At the sound of Walker's name, a red-bearded fellow stepped out of a construction of driftwood to accuse Walker of stealing his sleeping bag. Farther down the beach a man in a logger's woollen undershirt and wide braces rose to his feet on a plywood-surfaced raft flying what appeared to be a high school football pennant. The raft was furnished with cot and camp stove and an ancient traveller's trunk. The *Globe and Mail* lay neatly on a wooden crate, magazines stacked beside it with the *New Yorker* on top. This man's face seemed to have been boiled for a while and then attacked by giant mosquitoes. He reported that there'd been a big fight last night. Walker must've got into some bad dope or something. The cops had come down and taken him away before he could do more damage.

"But he was no longer in jail when I stopped in at the police station," Thorstad reported to the Montanas. "No one had any idea where he might be."

"So what would you have said to Walker if you'd found him?" Carl said.

He had to admit that he didn't know, he knew only that it seemed important they exchange more than the words he'd fled from yesterday.

Mrs. Montana returned her glass to the coffee table and frowned. She sat beneath a wide fabric hanging that suggested the contorted arbutus trunks that framed the view beyond the windows. "Is that the jacket you were wearing when you left this morning?" Perhaps she feared he'd stolen it off a sleeping pauper.

"I found it in the Thrift Shop. I was asking for Angus amongst some folks milling around outside and it occurred to me I'd need something lighter for the cool evenings if I decide to go to L.A."

"Oh." She looked at Carl. "And this morning's jacket?"

"Left it behind for someone else. It was already second-hand when I got it from the Free Exchange."

There was pleasure in saying this. She may not have been aware that she often spoke as though to an irritating child. He did not tell her that he had stopped at a men's clothing store as well, in order to purchase new dress pants and shirts and shoes suitable for life in a city, just in case. All stored in a guest-house drawer.

She closed her eyes. "The Thrift Shop is not really intended for us." After a few moments of awkward silence, she again suggested he phone to have his passport sent down. "I'd hoped you would do it this morning, but of course . . ."

There was probably no point in mentioning, now, that on the bus ride home he had wondered about staying on to take Travis's place at the drop-in centre while keeping an eye open for Angus Walker. Once he was back in the guest house, he dialed the number for Svetic's Store.

"Yeah?" The familiar voice was on guard.

Thorstad took the portable phone to the chair by the window where he could look out at the familiar sea. "Is this a bad time?"

"What's the matter? They tossed you out on your ear?"

"Not yet. You sound like someone too busy to take a call."

"I *am* too busy to take a call. I'm trying to make the money in my till match the receipts. Unless you snuck back on the island without me knowing, I guess I can't accuse you of theft."

"Do you think you could ask Normie to go into my shack and find my passport, have it couriered down? I'm sure I kept it in the cupboard above the sink, with my receipts." He should have put the passport in his bank deposit box, of course, but had tossed it into the cupboard and hadn't thought of it again.

"Why would you need a passport all of a sudden?" There was suspicion in her voice. Indignation as well.

"They want to send me to Los Angeles. If I decide to go I'll call again to have my trunks sent down as we planned—for when we're back. In the meantime I should have that passport, just to make sure I've got it with me if I need it."

A small sailboat glided past not far from shore, its mast and bright red sail tilting it sharply to starboard, a young woman leaning in the opposite direction in order to keep it in balance. The man sprawled against the stern appeared to be laughing.

His news had clearly offended Lisa Svetic. "Well, haven't you just plunked your skinny butt on a velvet cushion! They taking you down for a wine-tasting tour or what?"

"If I go I'll be doing the same in L.A. as I'd be doing here—preparing the boy for exams."

"That's what they want you to think. They'll put you to work in the fields with them illegals. While you're down on your knees weeding their crunchy white-in-the-middle strawberries, think about Normie Fenton brooding around up here like a kitten thrown from a car. He goes down to your shack every day."

"Just checking his retaining wall, I imagine."

"They've bullied you into this, haven't they? They've got you down there where you don't know nobody and put the pressure on." The sailboat was upright now, the woman more relaxed. The laughing man stood against the stern as though threatening to throw himself backwards into the water. "Why didn't you tell us you were knocked flying the minute you stepped off the ferry? Everybody heard about it but you never sent a word to say you *lived*." She paused, possibly to let him consider his oversight. "I suppose you'll be flying first class."

"Maybe. Maybe not. One way or the other this could be a shock to my system."

"It's a shock to my system just thinking about you lying around on the beaches amongst the movie stars. I never heard of nobody—anybody—keeping their wits about them once they get down in that place. Keep in mind, you're a little old to hope they'll make you a star. Paul Newman got discovered *young!*"

He imagined her entire body participating in the laugh. With the phone to her ear, she would be leaning with one elbow on her counter, beside the stack of daily newspapers from across the strait. This week's coloured comics wouldn't be far away. The blue-tinged plastic containers of water would be stacked beside the door. "I've sent on a couple more of your stupid letters," she said. "So, keep your options open, eh? From what I've heard, Los Angeles sends their oldies out to perish in the desert, to keep them from cluttering up the beach and spoiling the scenery."

He would not be sent out to perish in the desert with the other "oldies." He'd been given a job to do. In many ways, Travis was the chance of a lifetime—perhaps his last—though he knew there were certain risks. He liked the boy, but he was also aware that if Travis Montana had decided to win him over it could be only because this suited some purpose of his own.

"Don't forget to get your hair cut before you go down amongst the stars," Lisa added. "You were looking a little scruffy when you left here."

9

After three days of evening study sessions, it seemed that Thorstad may have proved himself worthy of a glimpse into Travis's other life. Carl led the way up the carpeted stairs and stood just inside the closed door of the "viewing room," but Thorstad chose to sit in one of the upholstered chairs. Heavy burgundy curtains concealed all four walls except where they'd been drawn to reveal the large wall-mounted television screen. You could easily imagine a red exit light and the smell of popcorn—though it was impossible to believe that Audrey Montana would allow melted butter near her furniture.

When he had dimmed the lights, Travis explained that what they were about to see was an episode from early in this current season. "The main plot is really a soap opera type of thing," he said. "This rich family with its stupid rivalries and, you know, romances and scandals and stuff. The old lady owns this empty building downtown she doesn't want to do anything with, but she doesn't like us homeless guys in it either. So we're just a sort of subplot now and then. The cops come in to drag us out and throw some of us in jail."

"Tell him your backstory," Carl said. "Short version."

"I'm the son of a real estate developer!" Both father and son laughed. "My old man kicked me out of the house for mocking his lifestyle and, like, refusing to follow in his footsteps. As if!"

Having lived for years without a television set, Axel Thorstad found it necessary to concentrate in order to make sense of the rapidly shifting series of short scenes. Someone stood on a bridge, obviously planning to jump. In fact he did jump, and had begun to float downstream when someone else leapt in to save him, or try to save him. But suddenly the cameras were no longer interested in the rescue effort. A dinner party was in progress in what appeared to be a luxurious mansion, the conversation scornful of someone who'd betrayed the family. Even so, there was a good deal of laughter around the table, and glasses were raised, toasts made to a successful business venture. The voice of the short round matron at the head of the table seemed familiar, but Thorstad did not know the face.

"Dolores Williams," Carl said.

Of course. Dolores Williams had been a young beauty in long-ago movies. Jean Simmons came to mind. In *Tiberius* Dolores Williams had been the emperor's mistress, addicted to blood sports in the Coliseum. You could not have imagined her planning to become this plump elderly woman.

Soon they were back with the bridge-jumper, who had been dragged inside what looked like an empty barn or warehouse, where a number of others in layers of mismatched clothing tried to discover why he had done such a stupid thing. Weren't they all in this together? Weren't they really brothers? The nearly drowned one weakly agreed that they were.

He didn't notice Travis in this crowd until Carl had pointed him out. "On the right, behind the fat guy's shoulder." Travis looked out from under a dark uncombed wig.

Though the hostess of the dinner party continued to suffer the petty battles amongst family members determined to destroy one another, the would-be suicide still dominated the subplot. It seemed that Travis had been chosen to befriend him, assuring him he could rely on "the guys" to support him when he despaired.

Eventually, after an excursion out into the city to eat at a shelter, the suicide promised that rather than cause his friends any more worry he would never kill himself again—a tentative happy ending to this adventure. The wealthy matron's battles with her family, however, promised to become even more contentious in the following episode.

"Television may never look the same after you've been down there," Carl said, when Travis had turned up the lights. Then he added, "If you decide to go, that is."

"I'm not likely to see any television afterwards," Thorstad said. "I gave my set to the Goodwill before moving up to Estevan."

"Well, the set in the guest house will still be there when you get back." When Thorstad did not respond to this, Carl narrowed his eyes. "We'd rather you didn't wait till the last minute to make your decision."

But Thorstad, unwilling to commit himself, turned to Travis. "Have you always wanted to act, or is this just a big adventure for you?"

"He was acting from the time he could walk," Carl said. "We thought there was something odd about him. He'd get up in front of the TV and mimic the people on the screen when he was no more than two years old. And you?" He followed Thorstad out into the hall. "You never acted yourself? Never got involved in one of those local theatre groups they have up there?"

"Just once. But not as an actor." This was before Carl's time, of course—his first year of teaching. "One of my friends decided she'd missed her calling and dragged us all into a drama club for the rest of the term. Not wanting to act myself, I agreed to direct."

Carl stopped in the foyer at the foot of the stairs, perhaps to suggest it was time the family had the house to themselves. "And the friend who missed her calling—is she the one you mentioned to Audrey?"

It was Oonagh who'd insisted on seeing *Returning to Troy* a second time. It was Oonagh who'd later convinced the others to form a drama club once they'd returned home. "I haven't seen her for years."

"Oonagh Farrell," Carl explained to Travis, who did not appear to recognize the name.

Instead of returning immediately to the guest house, Thorstad followed the gravel pathway past a row of blooming rhododendrons to the latticed gazebo above the stairway to the beach, and sat on the slatted bench to look out at the darkening islands. A white yacht cut a line in the water, heading south. He wondered if Oonagh mentioned *Returning to Troy* when interviewers asked how she'd got her start. Did she explain that her success could be traced all the way back to that Christmas holiday and the play they had produced in the spring?

Oonagh Farrell. Elizabeth Currie. Allison Beech. Andrzej Topolski. Their little theatre troupe, he remembered, had included a number of fellow teachers, a few students, and several survivors of an earlier club that had dissolved after a set designer's near-fatal attack on a director. The disbanded club had a long tradition of performing British comedies involving mistaken identities, cross-dressing, and bathroom jokes, but Oonagh suggested they tackle something meatier for their first production, something like *Saint Joan* perhaps, or *The House of Bernarda Alba*, plays with a strong woman in a principal role. But as a novice director, Thorstad believed it would be wise to have someone else's production fresh in memory, for inspiration if not for outright imitation. They would mount the play they'd seen during their winter holiday, a story in which, as he'd drawn to Oonagh's attention, the principal character was a woman, with men in the two supporting roles.

Even now, the story remained vivid in his memory. In *Returning to Troy*, a young woman arrives in town with her little girl to join her husband, who'd been released from prison after serving a sentence for knifing a friend in a brawl. Because one of the town's firemen does all he can to bring about the reunion, by the time the hot-headed husband blows his chance to save his mar-riage, it is obvious the fireman's kindness has earned him the gratitude and possibly even the love of the young woman.

He'd suggested the simple plot might have been inspired by the story of the abandoned Lena Grove in a William Faulkner novel, though the three main roles could have been modelled on characters in Chaucer's *Troilus and Cressida*. The title encour-aged this, though the story was set in modern-day Nebraska. It was as though Cressida had returned to Troy after the end of the poem and discovered that Troilus was not dead after all, as he was in the Chaucer, but was no longer interested in the woman who'd betrayed him. Naturally, Pandarus, who had assisted the love affair in spite of his own interest in Cressida, would be will-ing to act on her behalf again, though with better hopes this time for himself.

To take on the role of the jailbird husband, Topolski was will-ing to put aside his daily role as the expensively dressed future duke temporarily teaching high school French. But he was crit-ical of Thorstad's casting of the minor characters—convinced he'd assigned the role of Clarissa Alvarez to the school secretary, for instance, simply because he felt sorry for her after the breakup with a boyfriend. He accused Thorstad of trying to make every-one happy. "This will drive you crazy, It isn't in your *power* to make everyone's life turn out the way they want."

He'd expressed this opinion over a dinner prepared by Thor-stad's mother, who explained that her son was like his father in this regard. "A happy man himself, he had a compulsion to make others happy as well." According to her, he would stop for every flat tire or car-in-trouble, and wouldn't give up until he'd helped to make things right. Once, when he was about to fly east to visit his folks, he'd given up his seat to a young man who would other-wise miss his girlfriend's birthday.

"Your son," Topolski said, flashing his on-off smile, "confuses teaching with sainthood. What he needs is a dose of Barry Foster's cynicism to keep him in balance. Like an inoculation, before it's too late." It had probably not occurred to his mother to wonder what Topolski meant by "too late."

He could remember Oonagh raising her glass and showing every tooth to the world. "It's neither too late nor too early to toast ourselves, my darlings." She was wearing a black silk dress with a low neck, a white rose tucked into the left side of her gleaming dark hair. And large silver earrings. Half a century had gone by since then and yet he could still hear her voice. "Here's to a production that makes stars of us all! Either that, or scandalizes the population so profoundly that we're run out of town!"

Directly below, at the foot of these wooden steps, was the little cove where he set out each morning for his swim. Shallow waves raced shoreward into the narrowing wedge of bay until they were confused into a turmoil by earlier waves thrown back by impact with the worn-smooth embankment of stone. Ropes of seaweed swirled in winking foam. At this time of year you had to be grateful for the lengthening daylight. No doubt the longer days and improved weather would be welcomed by the people sleeping in parks and alleys and down on the rocky beach as well— a small, temporary mercy in lives of discomfort and hunger.

You had to wonder how tutoring a wealthy family's son in Los Angeles measured up against staying to volunteer in Travis's stead, helping to bring a little comfort and companionship to some of those difficult lives. An ordinary heart could possibly break from the effort. How many of those desperate souls could expect or even hope to be rescued one day from their need for that shelter? Of course you had to wonder, too, how many had, like Angus Walker, fled from jobs that would at least have kept a roof over their heads.

The world had destroyed any number of young teachers before they'd managed to find their feet. Yet, miraculously, it seemed, young Axel Thorstad had known by January of that first year that

he would be one of those who survived. Parents had begun to
stop him in shops and on the streets of town to tell him how
pleased they were with what they were hearing at home. Students,
too, were friendly outside of school, some of them offering assistance if he should need it—"I work at my dad's service station, so
any time you want a cheap oil change!"

Though Oonagh seemed capable of walking into a classroom
without a moment's preparation and pulling off a raucous but
unforgettable lesson, at one of their earliest play readings she'd
expressed her admiration for what she was hearing about Axel
Thorstad's classes: the city mayor involved in a rehearsal for a
student-written scene, a school board member participating in a
debate on dress codes ("Should jeans be allowed in school?"); the
newspaper editor listening while a bunch of sixteen-year-olds
told him how to improve his paper. "Good lord, Thorstad! If you
insist on being so innovative you may find yourself promoted to
administration and forbidden to do anything innovative at all!"

How eagerly he'd absorbed her praise! In the company of
Topolski and Oonagh Farrell he had almost believed he might
become, one day, as unique and amusing and perhaps even as
attractive as they.

Once the air had begun to cool he returned to the guest house
where he kicked off his shoes and went about in his long blue socks
to turn on some lights. Because of the tall firs and arbutus trees,
the lowering evening sun barely entered these rooms. He boiled
water in the electric kettle and poured it over a tea bag dropped
into a mug. He found a classical music station on the little radio
and, sitting sideways on the thickly upholstered couch, stretched
out his legs and crossed his feet on the armrest, and sipped his tea
while a British orchestra played Sibelius's lively *Karelia Suite*.
His cello, no doubt glaring at him from within its case, wondered
when he intended to replace those strings. Travis's history text was
within reach though not a serious temptation.

Would he have met with Oonagh Farrell and Topolski by the time he returned from California? He could not recall seeing Topolski mentioned in the magazines. If Andrzej Topolski was there with Oonagh he would take control of their itinerary, perhaps arrange for a camping trip into the southern California mountains. Of course, Topolski would have to be into his eighties by now, and probably no longer up for strenuous hikes.

It was Topolski who'd taken command of their weekends during the early spring, before the play rehearsals took over their after-school lives. He'd driven them out of town to canoe around Cameron Lake, to climb partway up Mount Arrowsmith, and to walk the beaches south of Port Renfrew. Oonagh, Barry Foster, and Thorstad. He had a way of making even a hike in an old-growth forest as civilized as an excursion of aristocrats in pastoral Europe. He brought silver cutlery, a set of china dishes, and wine, as well as a tablecloth to lay out on the ground once it had been swept clear of fir cones and fallen branches. There was no "roughing it" with him, who gave the impression he had been sent into this rugged world to teach the locals how to live a life of "quality."

But when their duke-in-waiting began to spend his weekends with a wealthy widow in Vancouver and Barry Foster started working Saturdays for a car sales company, Oonagh and Thorstad had been left to spend their days off on their own. They dined at Nicolino's and sometimes went to a movie afterwards. They drove to the Cowichan Valley to buy fresh vegetables for a meal in either Oonagh's kitchen or his mother's. They fell into the habit of holding hands while exploring the markets, possibly to keep from losing one another in the crowds.

He'd spent so much of his growing-up years in the local pool that he'd had little experience with romance. During high school he'd had crushes on certain girls, and had later dated Lorraine Wooldridge from White Rock for much of his fourth year at university, but nothing had prepared him for either the frightening attentions of Cindy Miller or the extraordinary magnetism of Oonagh Farrell.

He remembered her now as clever, beautiful, unpredictable, and of course loud. He had never before met anyone so confident of her charms and at the same time so casual about them. When she'd sashayed down that Hollywood street waving to the strangers who believed she was Yvonne De Carlo, he'd known that he was in danger of falling in love with someone who would belong in a foreign world.

He wondered now, as he'd wondered then, how it was that he had her company so often to himself. Why would such a vivacious beauty not be surrounded by men competing for her attention? Possibly, there was something about her that conveyed a sense of the extraordinary future she would eventually achieve in a world that would not include any man she might meet in this one.

During the Easter break, the two of them set off with tents and ice chests and sleeping bags in the trunk of his Pontiac, to zigzag on dusty switchbacks up the side of one mountain after another and then to descend several hours later upon the long sandy beaches of the central west coast. For several days they would have an entire world of ocean, tide pools, driftwood, and wilderness to themselves.

Before going down onto the sand to set up their tents, Oonagh was distracted by the row of summer cabins overlooking the beach, separated from one another by stands of stunted spruce. She was especially intrigued by a birdcage sort of structure painted red, with a wraparound veranda and a glassed-in second storey with a look-out gallery cut into the veranda roof. "Test the lock, Thorstad. Let's have a look inside."

He had never knowingly done anything illegal in his life. Still, when the door would not give way, he found an unlocked window and pried it open, then crawled through to open the door from the inside. They held hands as they might if they'd been children

exploring the home of a dangerous witch. They climbed the staircase to the second floor to admire the ocean view, and peered
through a powerful telescope set up to observe whatever ships
might pass on the endless sea, or, he supposed, to admire summer
visitors out on this wide expanse of sand.

When they'd returned to the main floor they'd visited the
bedrooms—one and then the other—both with unpainted walls,
thumb-tacked marine maps, chests of drawers, and tattered mat-
tresses stripped of sheets and blankets. "It would be a helluva lot
more comfortable in here than out in our tents," she said. "There's
a cold wind in off that sea."

Of course he'd believed she was joking.

"Well, why not?" she said. "Live dangerously for once!"

She could not have imagined the danger there was in this for
him.

Because she had not moved away when he'd inadvertently
pressed closer than he'd intended, it seemed natural to put a hand
to her chin, turn her towards him, and, since she had still not
stepped away, to lean down and kiss her. A tentative kiss, he supposed it was now, and a little timid. But apparently it was not unwelcome.

"Axel Thorstad," she said, stepping back and taking hold of
both his hands. "A man of surprises." She beamed up at him, all
her perfect teeth displayed.

He bent to kiss her again, much longer this time, while she
murmured something amused against his mouth but did not pull
away. He was aware of the mysterious scent she always wore, the
strawberry taste of her mouth, the sleek shine of her dark Irish
hair, and his own body responding in its involuntary way. Raising
a hand to either side of her face, he walked her backward to the
couch where she stumbled and pulled him down with her so that
they both collapsed along its length, the rough upholstery emitting a gust of musty-smelling air. But the couch could not accom-

modate his long body, and he found himself with one leg wedged in beside her and the other kneeling on the linoleum floor. When his attempt to straighten himself out caused her to bump her head on the wooden arm of the couch, she yelped, and struggled out from beneath him. Laughing. "My God! Where has this wild man *been?*"

"Don't move," he eventually said, and ran back through the woods to his car and brought the ice chest and their camp stove to the cabin while she laughed at his frantic industry. He went out again and came back with their sleeping bags and tossed his own rolled-up bag onto the bare mattress of the front bedroom. Then, light-headed at his own daring, he unrolled her bag and prepared to toss it onto the bed as well, but stood holding his breath instead—probably the clumsiest invitation in the history of the sexes.

Had he been, at twenty-two, as mindlessly ravenous as the adolescents reeking of hormones in the back-row desks? Was this how she had seen him? If she had, she was kind enough not to show it. "Oh hell." She stood up from the couch and put a hand on his arm. "Axel Axel Axel! Shoot! I can be so *thick!* I wouldn't have suggested breaking in if I'd imagined—"

He was quick to prevent an end to that sentence. "That's okay." Though of course it hadn't been okay at all.

Still, she'd put her face against his chest and wrapped her arms around his ribs and held him tight. "Ummmmm," she said. "A good man smell. Come back to the couch. We don't have to go whole hog just because of a little smooching! I was rather enjoying myself till you tried to give me a concussion on that stupid arm!" The little beach house threw back echoes of her wonderful laugh.

Amazingly, they had not been caught by the owners during their six days in the house. When the weather was fine they'd spent hours exploring the beach, and occasionally ran into the water for a difficult swim in the giant waves. They'd built bonfires and cooked their meals over the flames, and then had returned to their bedrooms with the marine maps on the unpainted walls, where he lay awake imagining that she was waiting beyond the wall for him to get up and go to her, and yet knew that she was not.

He could still recall Andrzej Topolski's reaction when he learned of their holiday. The Polish Prince became the disapproving older brother. Thorstad ought to have known better, he said, than to behave like a teenager sneaking off for a dirty weekend. He should not have exposed Oonagh to the kind of gossip she would be subjected to if certain people found out. In this small town, they could both be stripped of their jobs. He knew this had happened to others.

Oonagh made certain that Topolski knew she needed no protection from an arrogant Polack who didn't see anything wrong in *him* spending weekends with his moneybags widow. She would do whatever the hell she wanted.

Whatever she wanted did not include more overnight excursions with Axel Thorstad. "You of all people should know what it's like around here. You grew *up* in this town! We want to keep our jobs. Especially you. No more overnight trips. And we don't want Opening Night to be ruined, do we, with good citizens walking out when the scarlet woman makes her entrance—the shameless Jezebel suspected of leading their swimming champ and favourite English teacher astray!"

Would his students in 1954 have been shocked if they'd known about this? Cindy Miller certainly would have been shocked. There'd been something about Cindy Miller and her poems that filled him with alarm, aware that he must watch his step—must tread the fine line between professional compassion and dangerous sympathy. Of course, later he could see that his tiptoeing through the minefield of Cindy's poems served as basic training for treating carefully all the fragile too-needy Cindy Millers he would meet in the decades ahead. He'd have preferred that she have nothing to do with their spring production of *Returning to Troy* but did not refuse her request to be prompter once she understood that she was not, during rehearsals, to ask anyone to read her poems.

Though Oonagh had come to the second rehearsal in his mother's living room with her lines already learned, most of the others needed to keep their scripts in hand or to rely on Cindy's prompting for much longer than he'd hoped. Yet despite forgotten lines and occasional outbursts of hostility amongst old rivals, by the time they'd moved to the school auditorium he'd begun to believe they might pull off something fine.

At rehearsals Oonagh had been even more vividly *present* than at her energetic best in real life. Yet somehow she'd also been able to transform herself into that modest small-town woman who was not at all like Oonagh Farrell. Standing beside the coffee urn she'd been the familiar Oonagh, laughing large, acting out with wide gestures the movements and facial expressions needed in all sides of her anecdotes, placing the palm of her hand on the top of her head as if trying in vain to keep a lid on her personality. Yet the second she'd stepped onstage she seemed to have shed a good deal of her physical presence and become a rather dainty, shy, and genteel young woman. You were tempted to check the coffee urn, to see whether Gillian Tripp had left Oonagh Farrell standing off to one side of the room.

Barry Foster complained. "She'll make the rest of us look like amateurs."

"We *are* amateurs," Thorstad reminded him. "Be grateful. If they can't take their eyes off her this makes things easier for you."

Of course he would not have been able to take his eyes off her himself if he hadn't been obliged to pay attention to the other cast members as well. Even so, he was never for a moment unaware of the subtle energy in her every move and every spoken line as genteel Gillian Tripp, of the radiant beauty and unreserved femaleness that issued from her whether she was her exuberant self on the sidelines or the dainty central character on stage. He was never for a moment without an almost sickening sense of both desire and defeat.

When Topolski said "You're not bad at this directing business!" Thorstad had not been able to compliment him in return. Even now, he could recall how awkward he'd felt about this. The sophisticated duke-in-waiting seemed incapable of slipping into the skin of a violent small-town convict. He'd been saying Henry Tripp's lines without much help from the prompter, yet his eyes, you could see, kept returning to Oonagh, offstage or on, as though he hoped to see her raise a placard with a news bulletin setting something right.

"We should never have done this," Topolski said. "She's *loving* it!"

He was afraid. But he was more than just afraid. Whether he was offstage waiting his turn to go on, or onstage playing the role of her self-destructive husband, he behaved as though Oonagh had cast some sort of spell over him. At first this appeared, to Thorstad, to be simply the overacting of a first-timer. But of course it was more than that. Based on nothing more than what he was seeing in Topolski's face, it appeared that a separate story had been unfolding somewhere, and that whether this "somewhere" were solely in Topolski's head or in his outward life it had obviously not included Axel Thorstad. Something had shifted just beyond his field of vision.

He'd called an early halt to that evening's rehearsal and driven down to the nearest beach to walk along the gravel in the weak moonlight, trying to understand what was happening. Of course there was something he had to face immediately, as the director of this play. Who would believe that Andrzej Topolski was a husband so terrified of being reunited with his wife that he would deliberately undermine the opportunity even though it meant going back to jail? Anyone could see at a glance that Topolski would do almost anything—threaten, kidnap, kill the fireman if necessary—rather than give this woman up. This was not something he could teach the man to disguise.

Looking back on this now, Thorstad could see that he'd been saturated still with his university literature courses where protagonists were inclined towards large gestures and personal sacrifices. Topolski had been the first to offer friendship when Thorstad arrived on the scene, had pledged his support in the presence of his first students, had invited him to join Oonagh and Barry Foster and himself for Friday-afternoon drinks. There was no way of measuring—then or now—how responsible Topolski had been for the successful start to Axel Thorstad's career. A sacrifice of some sort had become a necessity.

The production of *Returning to Troy* had been only one of Thorstad's successes recalled in speeches during his retirement dinner forty-three years later, but it was given special attention for being the first public indication of two successful careers that lay ahead, his own as a teacher and Oonagh Farrell's as an actor. He knew that no one speaking at the retirement banquet could have been aware that while he'd been staring out across the water after that crucial rehearsal it had occurred to him that the thing to do was to have Topolski and Foster exchange roles, even this close to the opening performance. If Topolski was having to camouflage the effect Oonagh had upon him, he should be playing the role of the shy firefighter doing everything he could to help Gillian reunite with her husband while trying to keep his own growing infatuation out of sight. Let Topolski be the man struggling to hide his feelings, as he was struggling to do in real life. Of course no one at the retirement dinner could have known that he'd spent the next morning on the phone cancelling that evening's rehearsal and instructing Topolski to meet with Oonagh somewhere alone, to get accustomed to their new onstage relationship.

To ease his own real pain, he'd told himself that like the humble firefighter in the play he could possibly be rewarded one day for this—a romantic delusion that even half a century later could make an old man cringe.

Timid knocking startled Thorstad into the present world. He padded across the carpet and opened the door to Travis Montana, who hadn't been to the guest house since delivering Thorstad's luggage the day he'd arrived—looking awkward now, perhaps embarrassed, even ready to flee if he discovered he wasn't welcome. He removed the plug from his ear and let it dangle. "I saw the light so I figured you hadn't gone to bed."

Thorstad glanced at his watch. "It's only nine-thirty," he said. "I probably won't go to bed until I've drifted off a few more times on the couch."

Travis came in only far enough for Thorstad to close the door behind him. He held up both hands as though he was contemplating surrender. "So?"

Thorstad turned an ear towards an expected explanation. "Yes? So . . . ?"

Travis's hand pushed back through his hair. "Well." He looked about the room as though searching for some clue to what he'd hoped to hear. "Are you coming with me willingly, or under protest, or has seeing the show decided you against coming with me at all? You walked off and didn't say."

It hadn't occurred to Thorstad that the special showing of *Forgotten River* might have been a sales pitch, rather like the vacuum cleaner salesman dragging his demonstrator model across your carpet.

Travis seemed to think he was waiting for more. "Nobody's gonna, like, put it on a university course for great moments in television or stuff, but I love being in it. And I want to keep on being in it!"

"You're still wondering if I've made up my mind?"

"Well, you haven't said! I thought maybe you're planning to, you know, wait till the last minute and then go back to your island, to hell with me and exams."

"You'd better come in, then." He waited until Travis had perched on one arm of the couch. He perched on the other arm himself. Both, it seemed, were prepared for sudden flight. "It appears I've got a little out of practice at reporting what I think. And you're probably too young to be good at reading minds."

His passport arrived a day before their flight. In the same courier package Lisa Svetic had included three more envelopes addressed to him. It was unlikely that any of these could make an offer that would tempt him to change his mind at this late date. He could not imagine letting Travis down. He put the envelopes in a pocket of his new second-hand lightweight jacket, in case he was curious enough to read them later—on the plane perhaps, or when Travis was before the cameras.

But he brought them out again. On one, his Estevan Island address had been written on a separate piece of paper and then taped in place, presumably over some other name and address. There were fingerprints in several places. The top had been slit open and then taped closed. This was someone who'd rather waste a good deal of tape than throw away a single used envelope. He brought his reading glasses out from his pocket and put them on.

It had come from a post-office box in some place called Horsefly Creek, British Columbia. He imagined Horsefly Creek would be as different from Los Angeles as it was possible to be. Sagebrush, dusty streets, cowboys lounging in the sun, horses running madly to escape the giant flies sipping at their eyes. There would be no television industry there. Instead, it was probably a place where good, hard-working people grew their own vegetables, shot their own meat, fixed their own vehicles, helped their neighbours, and on Saturday nights played bridge in a church

hall or got roaring drunk at the community dance. Anyone looking for a tutor would probably have children desperate to leave
and willing to work as hard as necessary in order to make sure it
happened.

> *Dear Retired Teacher,*
>   *If you'd given an email address instead of a post office box I*
> *would've been the first to answer your ad, but I don't know how*
> *long it is since I wrote on paper. What I need is someone who*
> *works miracles. I don't mean water-into-wine, I mean dunce-*
> *into-student. I'd like my kid to learn how to read good enough to*
> *know which toilet to use when there aren't any pictures painted*
> *on the doors or when they put pants on the woman figure so she*
> *looks like a man in a tunic. Also how to read a recipe in case she*
> *ever accidentally finds herself a husband.*
>   *Just kidding! Everyone that knows me takes me with a grain*
> *of salt. The plain fact is, I have a thirteen-year-old daughter who*
> *thinks those marks on the page have no more meaning than*
> *chicken scratch.*

He should probably consider handing the letter over to Social
Services.

> *The school system being what it is these days, they don't risk*
> *harming her self-esteem by making her repeat a grade so they*
> *keep promoting her along with her so-called peers. Also, they*
> *don't want to hurt her feelings by telling her if she don't learn to*
> *read properly people will treat her like a dummy and she'll never*
> *get a job. As a result of this she has plenty of self-esteem—too*
> *much, as far as I'm concerned, and I'm the one that has to live*
> *with her—but she don't know beans about nothing she hasn't*
> *learned from listening. She memorizes what the teachers tell her*
> *(she's got a good brain) and they let her get away with doing "oral*
> *tests." I talk to them till I'm blue in the face about this—Are*

they prepared to read the newspaper to her every day when she's grown? Is she going to find a job where the boss reads out the orders she's expected to fill? Will they give her a driver's licence if someone has to read out the road signs every darn block?

The good thing is she's scared of men, especially old men— her grandfather was a corker. So when I seen your ad in the paper I figured this guy has got to be old if he's wanting to be "adopted" instead of just looking for a job, and he's probably a little mean if he's survived a lifetime as a schoolteacher. So that's why I'm answering your ad. The kid's old man left us years ago and wouldn't have been any good in this situation anyway. I ran for the school board once, thinking I could agitate for change from within, but I came in last when the votes were counted. Where else have I got to turn?

I asked her what she thought of me answering your ad and she said "Whatever," which is an enthusiastic endorsement coming from her. Otherwise I would've been treated to a screaming hissy fit full of accusations that I hate her, I want to drive her crazy, I want to f—— with her brain, etc. etc. So I figure, as long as I warn you what to expect I might have a chance. (I'm a totally adequate cook. And the empty bedroom I have in mind for you is at the farthest end of the house from Barbara's, so you won't have to listen to her godawful music all night.)

Don't keep me in suspense. I've alienated everybody I know, thanks to my campaign for a seat on the school board, my arguments with the teachers, my fights with my daughter, and my tendency to lip off whenever people give me free advice on how to raise my own kid. So where else have I got to turn?
(Mrs.) Joan Luxton

Not even learning that Mrs. Luxton was a "totally adequate cook" could tempt him to take on the task of tutoring a daughter with too-high self-esteem and a taste for godawful music. Though he had always been a strong and determined competitor in the face of difficulties, as his swim coach had discovered, he could not imagine lasting long in Horsefly Creek with Mrs. Luxton or her daughter. He returned the two other envelopes to his pocket unopened, in case he found himself one day in Los Angeles with nothing to read.

10

Because the hotel's breakfast area was in the centre of the ground-floor atrium, he had only to look up in order to see Travis leaning over the fifth-floor railing, his script held out as though he intended to toss it down. Of course he would not let go, knowing it could fly apart over four tiers of open galleries, or land intact on someone's scrambled eggs, adding one more element of absurdity to their disrupted journey. This was all it would take—Travis must know this was all it would take for his tutor to throw up his hands and go home.

Moments later, Travis slid onto the upholstered bench across from Thorstad and placed the manuscript on the table between them. He wore jeans this morning, and a white T-shirt with *Forgotten River* scrawled across the chest. "Elliot's furious! He has to re-schedule everything." There was alarm in his voice but excitement in his shining eyes. "He wanted to know why we didn't find some other way to get there last night! As if I'm the one who put a bomb on the plane."

"You told him there was a bomb?"

"Naw!" Travis laughed—a welcome change from his angry disappointment when their flight last night had been cancelled. He placed his cellphone on the table and slid off the bench to head for the hot-and-cold buffet.

Axel Thorstad was content with his coffee and crumbling blueberry muffin, all he could imagine swallowing in this state of suspension. They'd been neither left behind at their point of departure nor delivered safely to their destination, but were frustratingly stalled in between. In terms of their intended journey they had been shelved in the nowhere world of a large hotel near a large airport and a large city that had nothing to do with the reason they'd left home.

Voices were briefly raised at the check-in counter. An elevator chimed to announce its arrival on the second floor and a conversation spilled out to travel along the gallery. In a hotel you had the impression that everything was being taken care of without fuss, all turmoil kept well out of sight. Still, a night here had not been part of the plan. They had flown to Seattle yesterday and passed through Customs without incident. After taking the underground train from one terminal to the other without going astray they had survived the security check with only temporary trauma, and buckled themselves into their seats on the plane. But the wait for a missing passenger had gone on for half an hour before an announcement was made that all checked luggage would have to be taken off in order to find and remove a bag belonging to someone who had not shown up. Eventually everyone had been de-planed to wait in the departure lounge for further instructions, and after an additional hour they were informed that the flight had been cancelled and some passengers re-booked on a later flight. Like others put off until morning, Thorstad and Travis were given vouchers for rooms in this hotel.

The unsettling sense of being somewhere he did not belong was not all that had kept him awake for much of the night. Was Travis asleep in his own room? While checking in at the front desk, he'd smiled at an attractive young woman waiting her turn, and then engaged her in an obviously flirtatious conversation, suggesting they go for a walk once he'd got settled. Thorstad did not consider it his job to sit in the coffee shop and wait, like an anxious parent, for their return. The Montanas had instructed him to watch out for Travis's welfare as they might have done themselves, yet they hadn't explained how far this should extend. Surely Travis knew the importance of a quiet night before arriving for work in the morning.

When he returned to the booth with a plate of stacked pancakes, he vibrated with youthful energy and obvious excitement. Though his complexion was pale this morning, in contrast to his dark lashes and eyebrows, Thorstad suspected that if he had spent a night as a successful Lothario he would not resist the temptation to drop hints, if only to see how his ancient tutor might react. But there were no winks, no raised eyebrows, and no sign of the girl arriving to join them for breakfast. Apparently Travis's only concern was eating fast. "If we miss that plane we'll both be shot on sight."

A middle-aged man and woman, both of them stoutly encased in embroidered denim shirts and studded jeans, formed a careful parade transporting heaped plates in all four hands to the booth across the aisle. Catching Thorstad's eye, the woman shook her head in a manner that suggested she was disappointed in herself. "Everything looked so *good*!" Her husband immediately set about excavating his mountain of hash browns. Once his mouth was full, he upended the ketchup bottle and gave it a hefty shake, then picked up his knife to saw half a dozen sausages into halves.

Thorstad lowered his eyes to his muffin, surprised at his own rude interest in these happy strangers eagerly defying public warnings of disaster. Travis studied his cellphone for a moment, then snapped it shut, pushed it aside, and placed an open hand on his script. "I want to go over my lines but I'm going back for juice. Elliot said we'd be shooting Scene 4 as soon as we get there." He pushed the script towards Thorstad—the first time he'd been allowed to touch it.

Although the cover page named Elliot Evans as executive producer, he was only the first in a list of four executive producers, two co-executive producers, three producers, and one director.

Nine producers in, presumably, descending order of importance or power. There were more producers, he noticed, than speaking members of the cast, at least in this episode. Travis was Cody McCutcheon, bottom of the list.

Travis had explained that the yellow and green pages represented different revisions and additions. Apparently more colours awaited their arrival. A "pronunciation guide" was apparently for actors who could not be counted on to pronounce "hematoma" or "exacerbation" correctly. Thorstad wondered if Travis, being a foreigner, would have to be told to say "bin" instead of "been" and "sawry" where the script said "sorry" though these were not amongst the words in this guide.

Axel Thorstad had seen scripts before, though not for television. Stage plays usually contained directions for actors. *Mrs. Roberts continues stuffing chocolates into her mouth.* Playing Mrs. Roberts in *Returning to Troy*, Muriel Hanson had insisted on sugarless candy at rehearsals. "Six weeks of gorging on chocolates will have me busting out of my clothes." Apparently writers for television left it to the director to decide whether an actor should be stuffing chocolates into her mouth.

It was all he could do to resist making notes in the margins of Travis's script: *"Long pause here." "Turn away while speaking?"* But of course this was none of his business. His business was Travis's preparation for exams, and Travis's safety, but Travis's spoken lines and actions before the camera were not. Anything more would reveal itself in time.

When Travis returned with his tall glass of orange juice his grin suggested mischief. "Okay. This actress you told my mother about, will she be there to meet you at the airport?"

Surprised by this, Thorstad laughed. He supposed it was a laugh. He returned the blueberry muffin to his plate. "We can be confident she will not."

Travis was incredulous, or pretended to be. "You didn't write and tell her?"

"Travis, I don't know that she's in L.A. now. And even if she is, she may not even remember me."

There was no opportunity to say more. A young man had suddenly appeared beside their booth, wearing a black baseball cap turned backwards and the huge moustache of a Victorian major general. He seemed absurdly pleased with himself, perhaps for having materialized out of thin air. "Travis Montana?" Without asking permission, he slid in beside Thorstad and placed a camera on the table. Though his interest was obviously in Travis alone, he did a quick involuntary double take to check out the man beside him—in particular, his height. Thorstad was accustomed to this. Even while sitting he could be a surprise.

"Evans told me what plane you'd be on this morning so I made sure I had a seat on it too." He held out a hand, which Travis, though obviously puzzled, briefly grasped. "Ivan Lewis? I write for *Teen TeeVee*? The e-zine?" He slid a green business card across the table. "They're doing a series on 'stars-of-the-future'? Maybe Evans told you. He said his publicity folks would, like, arrange for me to follow you around for a while and stuff like that?"

Travis appeared uncertain. Small ruddy stains bloomed high on his cheeks. Pleased no doubt, yet afraid to believe.

This fellow was probably no more than a few years older than Travis, the moustache failing to make him look as mature as he probably wished. His small dark eyes—the eyes of a sea otter, Thorstad thought—shone like wet beads with pleasure, or possibly satisfaction. Axel Thorstad was almost disappointed to discover himself becoming the boring old teacher to set the fellow straight. "When he isn't in front of a camera he'll be studying for exams."

"I'll look in on the study sessions then." This young man was too interested in examining Travis to look at the ancient spoilsport at his elbow. "It's a long time since I wrote a test. Our readers will identify with you, cramming for math between scenes."

"You take your own pictures?" There was a little disappointment in Travis's voice.

"Yeah-yeah. You'll be just one of maybe a dozen bit-part actors in the TV world. This is strictly for the teens who notice sexy young guys in minor roles. If the editor likes what he sees he may send a staff photographer around."

"I've had mail from teens," Travis said, though didn't say how much there had been. He seemed too eager, perhaps, as though the reporter needed to be convinced. Then, suddenly remembering his manners, he attempted an introduction. "This is Mr., uh, Thorstad? My, um, assistant?"

Thorstad said "Unnh!" as though from a finger-poke in the chest. Were they to speak a different language now, where you had an *assistant* to take care of all your needs, in the manner of movie stars? This would have to be discussed before they boarded another plane.

The reporter had no interest in the *assistant*. Having been dropped from the conversation, Thorstad was free of any responsibility except to observe. And wonder, perhaps. Something useful might be learned from this exchange, some hint of what he might expect when they were fully immersed in the television world, maybe some new insight into this young actor who believed he'd acquired a private assistant.

"I've checked the website for *Forgotten River*," the journalist said. "You did an interview with Silas Post. Pretty shallow questions, I thought. Mostly just a gushy ad for the show. I'd like something with a little more meat. People who read *Teen TeeVee* want to see into your soul. Well, they'd like to see into your pants but we aren't allowed to go there. I did a piece on Andy Shell last month. You see it?"

Travis admitted that he hadn't seen a recent *Teen TeeVee*.

If this was an unwise admission, the journalist didn't seem to care. Perhaps he hadn't listened. "He's an asshole, that kid. He didn't even mind that I'd have to make him look like a dick-head. Y'know? He knew the girls'd pin his photo up on their bedroom walls whatever nonsense he babbled."

"Elliot said you could follow me around?"

The writer pumped his head up and down. "Is that cool? Of course he threatened me with castration if I step out of line." If this was a significant turning point in Travis's career, it was probably not a moment Mrs. Montana would care to know about.

After frowning for a moment at the framed bowl-of-roses print on the wall, the journalist jerked into action as though suddenly inspired. "I'll take a couple now. Eating your breakfast."

He took four or five shots before glancing at the oversized watch on his wrist. "That's cool for now. I'll see you at the airport!" He spoke exclusively to Travis. "You got a regular button-up shirt? Something with a little colour in it? Leave a couple buttons undone at the top—okay? Consider yourself to be in the spotlight from now on."

So a journalist for teens assumed the right to tell Travis what to wear? Travis's face was flushed as he watched the young man leave, presumably aware that a magazine aimed at teens would mean a significant boost to his reputation. "Elliot should have warned me," he said, fingers plucking at his T-shirt. "Now I have to buy a shirt with buttons."

"There's a huge shopping mall a block to the north." This was offered by the denim-clad woman across the aisle, obviously glad of an excuse to enter the conversation. As soon as she'd caught Thorstad's eye she added, "We spent half of yesterday in it!" One of her plates had been cleaned off and set aside, the second still in progress. "Our first visit to this part of the world," she said, pushing blonde strands from her forehead. "From Arkansas. Herb here is retired." *Re-tarred.* She tugged at her vest, smoothing it over her bosom.

"Soft drinks," Herb proudly explained. "Gave me a hefty buyout, so we decided to see the world."

"San Francisco's next," the woman said. And shivered. "I've always wanted to see that Golden Gate."

"And you," Herb said to Thorstad. "Wha'd you do before re-tarring?"

This was a rather sudden leap to such intimacy, but Thorstad had crossed to a foreign world where some things were bound to be different. At least this fellow wasn't yelling for him to take off his belt and shoes. "High school teacher," he said. "For more than forty years."

The big man thought about this. "What would top salary be for a teacher?"

Since Thorstad was not about to say "None of your business," he could think only of feigning stupidity. "I've been retired so long I can't remember."

A server came by with a steaming pot of coffee, refilling cups without bothering to look at the people who would drink from them. "Thanks," Thorstad automatically said, and "Sure" she said as she moved on, though it was impossible to know if "Sure" meant "You're welcome," or "I hear you but I couldn't care less."

Throughout this conversation the stout blonde had been smiling at Travis. "You're an actor?" she said. "We couldn't help overhearing."

She might have offered him a best-actor award. "You seen *Forgotten River*?"

"We haven't seen nothin' lately," she said. "We been on the road! If Herb turns on the TV it's only sports or killings."

Her husband studied Travis for a moment. "If the magazines are after you, you must be pretty good."

"They haven't killed my character off," Travis said. "That's something."

"You the hero, then? You get the girl?"

"Just a friend of one of the main guys is all." He was sorry, perhaps, to disappoint.

"How much they pay a young fella like you doin' a job like that?"

Thorstad could see that Travis was tempted to answer this

question with actual figures, but after pausing a moment he revealed only that he was paid by the episode. "Every episode I'm in gives me enough for a year of university—all expenses. At least that's how my parents see it."

"Poor folk, are they then?"

"Not really." He said this without looking at Axel Thorstad, who knew what "not really" meant in this case. If it weren't for the *assistant* across the table, Travis might have given this Arkansas gentleman his father's annual income from dentistry and his mother's average share of the profits from the company that bought up farms for condos and big-box stores. If they sat here much longer he could be exchanging all sorts of private matters with soft-drink strangers from Arkansas.

"You in the same show?" the woman said to Thorstad. She spoke carefully, as though to an unpredictable child.

"Backstage only—to see that he passes exams."

"How nice," the woman said with a noticeable loss of interest. "I'm sure you'll be a big help."

Before her husband could ask how much a backstage tutor was paid, she gathered her purse to her chest and began sliding in stages towards the end of her upholstered bench. "Well, it's been lovely meeting you-all." She grasped one leg of her jeans to keep it from riding up her calf, and put a foot blindly out as a feeler searching for floor. "But if we don't get moving soon," she found the floor and trusted it to hold her—"we'll never get to San Francisco." To her husband, who looked as though he had questions he hadn't yet asked, she said, "C'mon, Hon, let's go."

Hon wasn't quite ready yet to leave, but stood in the aisle for a moment shoving his wallet into his back pocket. "We give you folks a lift?"

"Thanks," Thorstad said, "but we've ordered a ride to the airport."

"Of course," the woman said to her disappointed husband. Perhaps he'd offered to pick up strangers at every stop. "These folks are tee-vee stars. There'll be a long white limo waiting at the door." To Travis she said, "I never thought I'd want to see L.A. but now I'm not so sure." Before moving on, she touched fingertips to Travis's bare forearm—but waited, Thorstad saw, until she had moved a few steps beyond Travis's field of vision before putting the fingers to her lips.

The woman's husband followed reluctantly, but not before he'd raised a hand to his forehead in a farewell salute.

"You didn't suggest she read the next issue of *Teen TeeVee*," Thorstad said.

"I didn't need to." Travis had opened the cellphone again and frowned at the screen. "She was all ears while that reporter was here. Maybe I'll get fan mail from 'Alice in Arkansas.'" He held the little phone up and turned to aim it across the atrium towards the retreating tourists.

"What are you doing?"

"A picture to send the guys."

Thorstad tried to make this casual. "So suddenly, just by crossing that border, I've become your *assistant*?"

"Sorry," Travis said, smiling sheepishly. "I didn't know what to say." He ran his left hand back over his head, a sort of thoughtful caress. "The shirt stores won't be open this early."

Axel Thorstad hadn't realized they would be crossing much more than a mere dividing line between nations. He'd known he would be responsible for the only child of wealthy parents but not for a "star in waiting" who had caught the attention of the teen media. He was not at all sure his life so far had prepared him for this.

"There'll be shirt stores in the airport," he said. Since airports had recently turned themselves into shopping malls, they were bound to find shirts Travis could leave undone for the readers of *Teen TeeVee*. "But maybe we should consider how I'm to be introduced in the future."

11

That Elliot Evans was not only the executive producer but creator, head writer, and show-runner for his series as well meant little to Axel Thorstad, but when they drove onto the studio lot in Evans's BMW, his position obviously meant something to the uniformed man in the little gatehouse, who barely glanced at the security card. "Morning, Mr. Evans. Good day ahead, I hope?"

"Mostly arguing with stupid people. You?"

"Mandelson drove in a minute ago, looking savage. Thought you'd like to know."

"Well there you are, just as I said."

The magazine writer was not with them now, though he had sat across the aisle from Travis during the flight. At the airport, Evans had suggested he wait and join them tomorrow. "A publicist will call. The kid has a few surprises to adjust to first."

Without explaining what the surprises were, he'd driven them on a series of streets lined with tired-looking shops and shopping malls and drab private homes, the air thick with exhaust fumes. A tense, impatient driver, he'd shifted from lane to lane to take advantage of gaps in the traffic, cursing drivers who seemed determined to block him. At red traffic lights, he'd filled his passengers in on why he was so "pissed" when they hadn't arrived last night, and why he hadn't sent his assistant to pick them up today. Because of a stupid decision by "that idiot Geoffrey Burns," certain changes had had to be made to the script, affecting Travis's role—but he hadn't got around to explaining these changes by the time they reached the studio.

So they had achieved their destination, these several hectares of Travis's other world—once the property of a movie company in the early days of film but now a television network's studio. Thorstad understood that the flutter in his gut had something to do with the movies he'd seen as a boy from the seats of the Capitol Theatre. Like everyone else on the continent, he felt he had been up this avenue of palms before, or another much like it. Any number of stars had come in past the little booth where the security pass must be shown—Lana Turner maybe, or Montgomery Clift—and then driven up this paved avenue past the office buildings where decisions were made by powerful executives, noticing pedestrians who might be actors or cinematographers, or even stunt doubles like Cliff Lyons and Fred Carson on their way to work. Little electric go-karts zipped this way and that. All of this had been just out of sight or perhaps disguised in any number of movies he had seen in the cinema, or later on the television screen.

"Man, I love this place!" Travis said—too enthusiastically, Thorstad thought, for a high school boy whose parents expected to add a lawyer to the family.

But he felt, himself, rather like a boy invited into a world where magic was created. A boy's excitement vibrated in his solar plexus. Spencer Tracy and Katharine Hepburn might have worked in these buildings. Marlon Brando might have slouched against that lamppost, smoking a cigarette. Or James Dean. How many times had he taken classes through *Rebel Without a Cause*?

They moved up past buildings the size of warehouses with giant paintings of movie scenes on the walls—oxen pulling a covered wagon, a police shoot-out—and trucks disgorging black cables that disappeared through doorways into white stucco buildings. They passed down a row of what might have been units of an "auto court" of the fifties, the sort of motel the lonely Joan Crawford character lived in before taking up with a man who was interested only in her money. And eventually they parked in front of a tall old Tudor-style building Evans referred to as the Writers' Roost, the exclusive headquarters for *Forgotten River* and "home" to writers, producers, Evans himself, and any number of *assistants*.

Axel Thorstad carried his old leather bag of books and teaching materials inside, hoping it would be more useful in his hand than in Elliot Evans's car.

The executive producer's office was a large room with desks and computer screens and leather couches that faced one another across a coffee table. A framed poster dominated one wall, the title *Forgotten River* floating above a white mansion with well-dressed people gathered on a lawn to raise glasses while a border of threatening figures suggested a band of hostility. A dreadlocked assistant came out of a glassed-in side room to present Evans with a list of appointments and telephone messages. "Mandelson's furious about something—wants you in his office at eleven." Evans cursed through gritted teeth, slammed a fist on his desk, and quickly spun about as though checking the room for insurgents. A large bearded man appeared in an interior doorway with coffee mug in hand. "You'd better come have a look at this. I've just watched Klassen's rough cut and the idiot's ruined our cemetery scene!"

Evans checked a schedule on his desk and suggested that Travis take Mr. Thorstad with him to his trailer. "They'll want you on set right away. Charlie has your copy of the rewrite." Before they left, he warned that the "B plot" had been seriously altered and Travis's role expanded. "Here's where we find out what you're made of!"

An obviously overwrought Charlie waited on the pavement outside one of the huge white buildings. "Thank God. Thank *God*! We've got to get you ready fast, you can go over the scene while they're fussing." He handed Travis a thick multicoloured manuscript—"New draft"—as well as a thin sheaf of stapled half-size pages. "I'll let them know you're here!" He set off with arms up high—"Oh! Oh! Oh!"—and disappeared through a doorway to the building.

"Look behind you," Travis said. "Ryan O'Neal."

Three middle-aged men in jeans walked past, deep in conversation, but none looked familiar to Thorstad.

Travis prompted. "Got his start in—"

"*Peyton Place*. Yes, I know." Elena had watched it every week and insisted he watch it too, believing that a high school teacher had an obligation to know what went on in the lives of adolescents when they were not in his classroom. It had not been reassuring. Though none of these three men triggered a memory of "Rodney Harrington," he supposed Travis had reasons for being so sure.

But Travis was already absorbed in the pages of the new script. "Jeez!" He read a few lines on the yellow pages, and flipped ahead again through blue. "I've never been on screen so much!" Then he pulled his face into an obviously false suggestion of dismay. "This'll keep me too busy for anything else!"

Of course it was not good enough for Travis to feign dismay. Thorstad with his bag of books followed him down the side of the long white trailer past an open door where a young woman shrieked and bounded down the steps to throw her arms around Travis's neck. The embrace was brief. Travis laughed. The young woman was alarmingly thin, with nearly transparent skin and hints of fading bruises on her arms. Her nearly colourless hair had been hacked off in an amateur manner that suggested violence. Flesh could be glimpsed through several small tears in her jeans. Stepping back from Travis, she let her gaze drift indifferently down the length of Axel Thorstad, then went back up the steps and inside and closed the door.

"That was Rosie," Travis said, climbing the three metal steps to his own door.

"One of your homeless?"

Thorstad ducked to go in through Travis's doorway but came up too soon and grazed his skull.

"Rosie? Naw. She was just being herself! In the show she dresses *up*—the rich old woman's granddaughter."

This room was far too small and crowded for a man of Thorstad's height. It contained a leather couch, a desk, a small refrigerator, a television screen, and a door to a bathroom. Its walls were decorated with photographs of singing groups and long-legged women, and another poster with the happy family group surrounded by angry faces.

Travis was clearly excited. "I've never had so many lines. Us homeless guys usually get, like, only a few short scenes—mostly as a *crowd*! But look!" He turned an open page in Thorstad's direction.

It was not as though Thorstad hadn't been thrown plenty of curveballs in his day—by principals, colleagues, students, secretaries, parents, school boards, and temperamental audiovisual aids. Though the flight had tired him more than he'd anticipated, he was confident he would think of something to bring Travis's attention to exams. At least he didn't have to compete with the journalist today.

When Travis had gone off to the makeup trailer, Thorstad made the mistake of sitting on the couch and closing his eyes while he considered a study schedule, if such a thing were possible. He took the elevator down to the foyer of last night's hotel and went outside where he tried to cross the busy road without being killed, yet stood frozen before a gigantic freight truck bearing down. In the nick of time he wakened to the rustle of Travis changing his clothes.

He was barefoot, in a pair of jeans torn at the knees and a striped shirt far too large for him, its tail irregularly scalloped and charred as though flames had been extinguished on their way up his back. The tidy head of fair hair had disappeared beneath a shaggy wig. Dark hollows had been painted beneath his eyes. "There are viewers who find me sexy, believe it or not."

He explained that for this afternoon's short scene his fellow squatters had sent him to the home of the old woman who owned the derelict building. "All we want is, you know, to convince her to make it a legitimate shelter before winter kills more of us off."

"You think it would help to tuck in your shirt?"

"I'm ahead of you." He shoved the charred shirttail down behind his belt.

Thorstad left his bag in the trailer and followed Travis past a row of small bushes trimmed to resemble grazing deer, and entered a massive building with STAGE 5 printed in large gold letters above the door. They followed a cluster of cables duct-taped to the concrete floor, past stacks of furniture and partial walls, and down a narrow passage to an open space where a group of men and women in jeans and T-shirts appeared to be in a state of passive and indifferent waiting.

"The maid let me in," Travis said. "She said . . ." He consulted his script. "She said she'd get Mrs. Bradshaw but she didn't come back."

Two of the men shook Travis's hand and welcomed him back. "We heard you had a brush with bin Laden's friends." Laughter followed this.

The director was a young man named Paolo who gave up reading a newspaper behind a monitor to shake Thorstad's hand and invite him to sit on one of the canvas chairs where he too could see the screen. Once a makeup woman had touched up his forehead, Travis handed Thorstad today's small script and followed the director through a narrow entrance to a room visible only in the monitor. Though the walls were rough plywood with two-by-four studs on the outside, the interior appeared in the monitor as professionally finished as a room in Mrs. Montana's house. White walls with gold trim. Behind the couch where Travis and the director settled into conversation hung an abstract painting as wide as the couch itself.

Lit by powerful standing lights, the living room was a small intense arena of brilliant colours—the painting bright with powerful reds and yellows, the couch a dazzling white, the leafy plants a garish tropical green. Travis's fire-damaged shirt was a far more vivid blue than it had been in the trailer, his face and hands a much healthier colour than they were in real life. The world outside the lighted set was now a drab cluttered storage barn on a chill concrete pad, a rough workshop where just behind that plywood wall you might find stacks of lumber and half-built sets waiting for the workers to return.

Men and women paced back and forth outside the set, or stood to chat, while one man with a heavy tool belt at his waist sat engrossed in a Harry Potter hardcover. Whatever their jobs, they obviously weren't needed yet, but neither were they free to disappear. They nodded to Thorstad, if they noticed him looking their way, but seemed preoccupied with actively waiting. The director came out and looked into his monitor, and then talked briefly with a woman holding a clipboard, who drew his attention to something in the script. He explained to Axel Thorstad that they had set everything up with the stand-ins while waiting for Travis to arrive. "So we're ready to go."

Thorstad put on his glasses to read the half-size stapled-together sheaf of pages Travis had given him. This was the script for today's scenes only, but the front page listed the names of the numerous producers, the writer, and even the address of the nearest hospital—presumably for emergencies. The scheduled rehearsal time for Scene 4 had passed while they were travelling in from the airport. Apparently this was the second of eight days of shooting.

The dialogue was surprisingly sparse. What was an actor supposed to do with *Ella's not a maid. She's a nurse.* Of course it was realistic enough. Glancing through the scene that would follow he came upon *He was layin' on the road like he was dead.* Also realistic, of course, but it caused an involuntary cringe in a lifelong teacher of English.

A young woman appeared suddenly and hurried in to the set where she sat on the couch Travis had just vacated, brought her legs up under her, and lifted a magazine from the coffee table. "Oh hell," said Paolo, and hurried back in, steering his lithe body around a passing crew member and in through the entrance to the set—all with the elasticity of an eel. Thorstad could see their images engaged in a conversation he could not hear. A man with a brush smoothed the woman's hair into place, tucking strands behind the ear nearer the camera, himself made bright and more vitally alive by the intensity of light.

Thorstad might not have realized who this young woman was if the camera hadn't zoomed in on her face as she gave the retreating hairdresser the same almost-contemptuous look she'd given Thorstad outside the trailer. Makeup had given the transparent skin a healthy glow, and the hacked-off hair had disappeared beneath a carefully shaped blonde wig. As the camera moved back, he saw that the smart tight-waisted dress had been designed to give the impression of a womanly figure inside.

Once Paolo had returned to his seat behind the monitor and examined the image in his screen—the young woman glancing through a magazine, an open door beyond her, a glimpse of leafy conservatory beyond the door—a stocky young man passed by shouting "All right. Here we go! Positions please! Quiet now! Quiet!" Then someone else, unseen, shouted, "Background!" Another: "Rolling!" Then Paolo: "*Aaaand action!*" After a moment in which the young woman turned pages, Travis appeared in the open doorway, obviously nervous and uncertain. She looked up, apparently alarmed, but he quickly explained: "The maid let me in. She said she'd get Mrs. Bradshaw but didn't come back." His voice, coming to Thorstad from the headphones, was distant and thin.

"Ella's not a maid, she's a nurse. And she's probably calling the police." She got to her feet. "If you've come to bully my grandmother, I can tell you she won't be threatened."

Travis did not retreat. For a moment the two looked at one

another as though neither knew what to say next. Had someone forgotten the next line?

"I didn't know," Travis eventually said, though what he didn't know remained unspoken. "Your surname . . ."

"She's my mother's mother," the girl said. "Are you going to threaten me? You probably told your folks you were off to make something of yourself. Wouldn't they love to see where your plans have brought you? At least I have a roof over my head."

Travis did not move, his character evidently uncertain how to react to this. Then, after a few seconds, he turned away without speaking and disappeared into the shadowed leaves of the conservatory. "Okay," the director shouted. "*Cut!*"

Again, Paolo left his seat at the monitor and navigated his way around others and into the set. The camera people had not come out. The man with the tool belt perched on a stack of wooden blocks and took up his book. Of course Thorstad should have known that once would not be enough. As the first-time director of a stage play he'd needed six weeks of rehearsals before deciding it was "ready." For a television director, perhaps there was always a possibility something might be salvaged from even the worst of the takes.

Once the scene had been shot three more times and Paolo had reminded everyone that they'd be shooting Scene 13 in an hour, Travis walked with Thorstad back along the cables to the exit. Before going up the three metal steps to the trailer door, he stopped, and asked to be left alone for a while. Already a Greta Garbo. "This is a tough scene. I've got to get it right!"

Thorstad could not recall having a door shut in his face before. Still, he'd learned long ago not to be insulted by the words or gestures of a preoccupied adolescent. He'd known better than to imagine himself the centre of his students' world.

"A word?" Elliot Evans was at Thorstad's side, indicating with a tilt to his head that they step around behind the trailer to have their "word" in private.

"I have the impression you expect to come onto the lot every day."

Because he recognized the impatience in this man's voice, Thorstad determined to be calm and reasonable and, if possible, unimpressed. He'd had plenty of practice at this. "He expects me to be here. His parents expect me to be here so we can take advantage of the times he isn't working."

Evans's fleshy face was surrounded by a halo of wild and nearly colourless curls. Brown eyes blinked behind dark-rimmed rectangular glasses. "Look. In case you've been misled, I'd rather you weren't here. We need the boy's undivided attention."

"I understand." Despite an immediate flush of alarm, Thorstad made sure he sounded unperturbed by the hostility of someone with so much power. "But his parents would be here if I weren't."

"His parents would not expect to be on the lot every day."

"I'm sure they would when there are exams on the horizon." Alarm had become indignation. This man had decided to be an obstruction.

Because Evans had begun to walk, Thorstad had little choice but to walk with him if he was to state his case. "It is important to them, and to him, that he graduate. It is up to me to make sure he studies every available minute, on the lot or off." He had raised his voice a little, and paused to take a deep breath.

"I understand." Evans stopped again and turned to confront his pursuer. "But I'm telling you that in expanding his role we've made it more difficult." They were face to face now, standing amongst the pedestrians—people with clipboards, briefcases, and folders. A white electric cart whizzed by, its tires hissing on pavement. "If he doesn't measure up, there won't be more. Just so you know."

Just so you know that Travis's future was at stake and Axel Thorstad was the one who could ruin it.

Thorstad had little doubt this young man in faded jeans and dirty tennis shoes regarded him as a nuisance, an inconvenient old man who ought to be resting in an easy chair somewhere,

reading the newspaper and drinking mugs of tea. He was probably one of those short men who resented having to look up while
speaking to someone tall. Right now he'd like to cut Thorstad off
at the knees. To poke him in the chest at least. "I know *this*," Axel
Thorstad said. "He's a minor, and expected to finish his school-
ing. I have the impression the parents would prefer he not be
down here at all."

Evans's smile suggested pity for the misinformed. "Don't kid
yourself. If you think they'll be furious if he doesn't pass his exams,
just wait till you see how they react if he's written out of the show.
There are others I could replace him with if I have to." He turned
away to leave, then turned back, his eyes blinking rapidly behind
his glasses. "Look. I get it. You want to cram in a bit of study whenever he's got the time. But you need to understand he won't have
much." He looked to either side, as though hoping for someone
to support him in this. "I intend to put the pressure on, to make
sure he doesn't take anything for granted. If I decide you're in the
way you won't get past the gate." His voice had gradually grown
louder, his tone more impatient. "I don't have the time to argue!
There's an actor waiting in my office who's about to hear that I
won't renew his contract if he doesn't get his shit together soon.
Then I have to meet with a bloody network Suit with both the
power and the will to chop my budget."

He started off again but again turned back. "Every day eats up
another three hundred thousand bucks. Understand?" Then he
strode off again, the back of his neck a dangerous red. Perhaps
he resented being forced to admit that it all came down to money.

Travis hadn't wanted a tutor—he'd made that clear the day
they met. But then, in the days that followed, he seemed to have
decided he could handle this one. Perhaps he'd simply assumed
that Old Man Thorstad would be powerless once he came up
against the strong-willed Elliot Evans.

He had been left in an alley between glaring white buildings
where he recognized nothing. There were no street signs—the

"streets" were not named, were not even strictly speaking streets but simply paved gaps between buildings, some of them wide enough for vehicles to pass by, and for trucks and trailers to park, while others were barely wide enough for a person to walk. This "lot" appeared to be a collection of buildings in the way Alvin White's field was a collection of wrecked cars, arranged in rows but with a lack of uniformity in size or shape that made it impossible for the rows to look ordered.

Couples strolled past, deep in conversations. Individuals rushed from one building to another, though one woman paused long enough to tell him she'd enjoyed his performance during last week's episode. She did not say which show he'd been in. A cyclist in white shirt and tie tilted a head in a sort of friendly nod, and wished him a good afternoon. A man in overalls was down on hands and knees yanking weeds from beneath the animal-shaped bushes against a white wall. Outside a portable snack canteen two men, dressed in jeans and short-sleeved shirts and runners, interrupted their conversation to watch him pass. Perhaps it was clear, even to them, that he didn't know where he was.

Nothing looked familiar. Or rather, everything looked familiar—another "stage" the size of a warehouse, another row of identical white trailers, another truck attached by thick black cables to something beyond an open door. His bag of books was still in Travis's trailer. Would Travis think to bring it with him later?

A small delivery van pulled up and stopped, and the driver stepped out—a dark-skinned young man in a brown uniform. He turned a slow full circle with lowered brow before approaching Thorstad. "You know Building 46?"

Thorstad turned, himself, to look at the nearest buildings, all of them beaming sunlight off white stucco. There were numbers on some, in no discernible order, but not a 46. "I don't know where I am myself."

The driver bounced the parcel in both hands. "I been all over this place looking for Building 46. Nobody knows where it is."

"And I'm looking for the building where they're shooting *Forgotten River*."

The delivery man grinned. "A fine pair, us. Should turn ourselves in to Lost and Found." He came closer, a deep crease dividing his forehead in half down the middle. "You somebody's missing grandpa?"

"I turned a wrong corner somewhere is all. It makes me think I might be getting old!"

The delivery man threw back his head and closed his eyes for a silent laugh. "The mirror got news you're gonna hate." The eyes opened again; the laugh abruptly stopped. "But, man, you are *tall!* Old men supposed to shrink!"

A long-legged blonde towered above them on the wall of the nearest building, her red high-heeled shoe larger than a person's head. "I remember passing by that shoe—coming, I think, from over there somewhere. Maybe I'm closer than I thought."

But he wasn't closer than he'd thought. When he got to the other end of this alley nothing looked familiar: a deserted city street of brick walls and large storefront windows, some of them papered over on the inside. These appeared as substantial as the sound stages and office buildings, though they were clearly no deeper than their front walls. All of this was waiting, he supposed, to become Main Street in a small town, or a back street in a city. At the moment it appeared as though its population had fled a spate of killings, or a plague. You expected to hear wind howling, a scrap of paper travelling erratically over the pavement. He probably *had* seen it, at some time, from his seat in a movie theatre.

Yet, when he'd moved beyond the first bend, a bar and grill appeared in full colour in the midst of all this drab neglect. Where a long wall of windows slanted off to a side street, the bricks and windows had been scrubbed clean and a neon sign lighted overhead. Behind the glass, workers pushed furniture into place—a long bar with stools, booths beneath the windows, shelves and mirrors across the back wall.

If he hadn't looked up at the neon sign—*"Casey's All-Nite"*—he might have overlooked the tall brick building next door: a storefront window and DELI sign, three rows of uniform windows above—it could become an office building, he supposed, or a tenement, but at the moment it was only a wall with a fire escape attached outside the three upper rows of windows, each window topped with a solid brow. He could be looking at the wall his father had scaled before leaping to his death.

But of course every movie and television studio must have a row of false fronts like these—solid facades of concrete or brick that could be used repeatedly for any number of cities or towns in almost any country on earth, as insubstantial and illusory as the surviving walls of a bombed wartime street—though he was certain, now, that there was not a DELI sign in the fatal chase sequence of his father's film.

And here was the delivery man again, this time on foot with the parcel in the crook of his arm. "Building 46?" His voice betrayed disappointment-in-advance. When he recognized Thorstad he briefly mimed an exaggerated state of shock. "You still Lost, or are you Found?"

"That actress with the high-heeled shoe misled me."

"That is her way. Probably didn't invite you home for dinner neither." The world was determined to disappoint them both. "Me, I'm making the rounds by foot this time. Maybe my truck can't fit where they hidden Number 46." He turned away as though to leave, but turned back again. "You come across it down some alley, now, you find me let me know."

12

If Evans was displeased about having Travis's tutor at the studio, he must surely be unhappy about having him in his home. The man had more or less suggested to Thorstad that he get lost, speaking with the patient restraint of someone addressing a confused *senior-senior* who'd strayed beyond his care-home walls to intrude upon other people's turf.

But the arrangements had been made by Travis's parents—another testament to Mrs. Montana's powers of persuasion, though the drama-teacher friend may have had something to do with it, or the executive producer's wife. This tanned, athletic-looking young woman met them at her door with a welcoming smile and introduced herself to Thorstad as "Camilla." She insisted they join her guests for dinner as soon as they'd settled in. "Very informal. Just a few old friends. Arriving in an hour."

Thorstad had not been to a dinner party in a decade and had no interest in attending one now. "I'm sure your friends would rather have you to themselves."

She laughed, "They'll be relieved to meet someone new," and sent them off to the guest house. Another guest house! To get to this one Travis led them through a garden of fragrant herbs and the sort of mysterious succulents you saw in photographs of deserts, and past the shallow end of a swimming pool whose water reflected the unclouded evening sky.

Inside, Thorstad could see it all at once—a large room with a fridge and small electric stove, and two sleeping alcoves behind curtains, with a bathroom door in between. A few books had been laid out on a large table in the centre of the room. The cover photo of *A House on the Water* was of a building spread wide beneath a swooping roof, its veranda posts blurrily reflected in the dark water below. At the centre of the table, a tall blue vase was crammed with a spray of eucalyptus twigs, perhaps from the tree outside the door.

They were above the Pacific Coast Highway and looking out upon the ocean from high on a hill so steep as to be almost a cliff face. The Evanses' sprawling white house was a comfortable distance from other homes with their own terraces and towering palm trees and walls of glass, each perched on a narrow shelf of earth shored up with retaining walls of concrete and shaded by clusters of feathery eucalyptus trees. Like the private boxes in an opera house, they looked out from various levels in the one direction, as though waiting for a drama to unfold on that apparently endless sea. There was nothing operatic out there now—only a barely moving tanker and its spreading wake. Perhaps when these people came home from running corporations or directing movies or capping the teeth of celebrities, they preferred to look out on an empty world and the blur of an indefinite horizon.

"All of this"—Travis spread his arms to indicate both directions—"all this twenty-seven miles of coastline used to be owned by a married couple who kept the world out with chained gates and, like, armed guards on horseback." Since he hadn't confessed to tour guide ambitions, he must be practising for the day he welcomed visitors to his own Malibu home. "After the old guy died, the widow sold a row of lots to celebrities who built their homes along the beach, shoulder to shoulder with their backs to the road. From down on the highway you can't see the water—just blank walls and doors."

"And a few parked Audis." Thorstad could see five immediately below.

"You see that house with a tower?" Travis pointed to the right along the slope. "Sold for twenty-eight million last year. My mother nearly peed her pants when she calculated the commission!" It was impossible to know whether he intended to mock his mother or was impressed with the sum himself.

"How would your mother know what people pay for their houses?"

"They tell you. It's in their papers. They can tell you how much Richard Gere paid for his estate, they know how much it cost Cher to build her fenced-in compound up the coast, they can even tell you how much she paid for the, you know, palm trees she imported from Europe or somewhere." He stood back from the railing and turned to Thorstad with a mischievous smile. "Guess how far their teachers drive to get to their jobs. They have to cross the mountain range every day, like the maids who clean these houses."

Thorstad would prefer to avoid a dinner party with people whose maids and teachers were restricted to the back side of the mountains, but some things could not be avoided. Once they had showered and shaved and changed out of their travel clothes— Thorstad wearing his new dress pants for the first time, and a pale green shirt—they crossed the garden to the house where Camilla Evans again met them at the door, wearing gold earrings and a dress of cornflower blue. She led them through to a flagstone terrace off the dining room and introduced them to two guests who had arrived, she said, only moments before. The slender bespectacled man with ginger hair was a cosmetic surgeon named "Larry" whose patients were "high profile and highly confidential." She explained that Larry had given a certain actress "now starring in *The Brigadier's Lady*" the upper lip that had made her famous, and now was swamped with demands from others wanting the same. "Larry tends to size you up, imagining how he'd alter your appearance if you'd let him."

"I'll keep my distance then," Thorstad said, shaking a hand that was undoubtedly insured for millions. "A face as old as mine could be a temptation."

The surgeon's thin smile appeared to cause him pain. No doubt he'd heard such things before.

His diminutive wife Louise had piled her dark hair on the top of her head—perhaps to acquire a little more height, something her husband's profession was not equipped to do. She wore a bright red shawl around her shoulders and a patterned skirt that fell to just above the painted toenails in her spike-heeled shoes. "Louise is an interior decorator," Camilla said. "She recommended the realtor who found us this house—which explains why I adore her."

The adored one's glasses were too large for her small round head. Surely a husband accustomed to studying faces must have informed her of this.

"That will be Harold's car we hear," Camilla Evans said, offering a platter of mushrooms—stuffed, she said, with crab. To Thorstad, who watched the red Ford sedan zigzag its way up the hill, she explained that Harold had written a long-running series back in the eighties but was living in Texas now. "He's in town to pitch a couple of story ideas. Also, I imagine, to show off his new friend."

The new friend, introduced as "Lyle," was only a little older than Travis and possibly thirty years younger than white-haired leathery Harold. He wore a cobalt shirt with tight denim jeans and electric-blue runners, and stood with arms crossed and hands clamped to his own shoulders while old friends greeted one another. He may have felt as foreign here as Axel Thorstad.

"A Norwegian name?" he said, when they'd been introduced. He ran his glance down Thorstad's length and answered himself. "Well, of course! Ten feet tall and brooding forehead! Legs for striding over mountains. You make movies where everyone commits suicide in the dark of winter. Am I right?"

He was disappointed to learn that Thorstad was not in the business.

Harold wanted to know where their host was hiding. "Not called to the studio, I hope."

"We may wish he was," Camilla said. "He's just had a call from Morrison. The network's moving *Forgotten River* to Fridays."

"On no!" Lyle said. "Isn't Friday night supposed to be certain death?"

"Except for those who survive it," Camilla said. "Don't bring it up unless he does. I expect he'll join us once he's simmered down."

Harold seemed determined to outline the route they had taken to get here—a dizzying list of street names and sharp turns and shortcuts through unfamiliar territory—while one hand explored his considerable paunch. "We outsmarted ourselves and had to come over the ridge from behind, risking our lives on those hairpin downhill bends."

Elliot Evans had come out onto the terrace while Harold was taking them through the back roads of Greater Los Angeles. "God bless the PCH," he said, slipping his cellphone into a pocket. "Life would be impossible here without it." No longer in the faded jeans he'd worn at work, he was dressed in wide-legged cotton slacks and a blue shirt with a pattern of silver diamonds.

To Thorstad, Camilla said, "In L.A. it's always 'How did you get here?' before anything else—in case someone has found a route without traffic jams or streets blocked off by film crews. I'm told that where you're from all party conversations begin with the weather."

Harold would not agree to Louise's suggestion that he practise pitching his story proposals to the present company, but he was interested in hearing how *Forgotten River* was doing at the end of its third season. "Still no temper tantrums from Dolores?"

Evans made a show of gritting his teeth. "Until today, the biggest problem I've had is the studio's newest series. This guy waltzes in with nothing behind him but two mildly successful procedurals and they give him his own show and my best writer! I'm still fighting to get her back."

"I heard your biggest problem was Tom Morrison," Harold said. Apparently he believed that Camilla's warning had not been meant for him.

Evans's face coloured up. "The bastard says he's convinced we can handle Friday but I bet he hopes we die!"

"He's an idiot," Harold said. "It probably means his days are numbered and he wants to do as much damage as possible while he can. Did he give you a reason?"

"He gave me a shitload of reasons but he didn't need to. It was only a few weeks ago I told him I'd seen his new girlfriend's audition and wouldn't hire her for a two-second spot if all the *real* actors in town were on strike. I guess he holds a grudge."

"Elliot!" Camilla's shock appeared to be genuine.

Evans grinned. "Morrison's idea of talent is a baby-doll voice and a rack of hooters out to here."

"Don't get him started," Camilla cautioned, putting a hand on her husband's shoulder while glaring at traitorous Harold. "Bring your glasses to the table."

A small spinach salad waited at each setting. Apparently the idea was to sit wherever you wished, except for Camilla and Elliot Evans who would sit at either end of the table. Evans stood behind his chair until everyone else had chosen a place. Louise was to Thorstad's left, Travis directly across. Behind Travis, a painting thick with oils and nearly as long as the room suggested the expanse of empty waves it faced beyond the glass, a sort of stylized reflection. It was meant, he supposed, as compensation for those who sat with their back to the sea. If Thorstad were to hang it in his cabin he would have to saw it in half and place it on two separate walls.

Camilla explained that the children had been fed and placed in front of the television at the farthest end of the house. "They are not to bother us unless there's blood."

When Evans mentioned that their guests were "down from Canada," the cosmetic surgeon put down his fork and clasped hands together beneath his chin, both elbows on the table. "I saw Dave Thomas last week, having coffee with someone at the Hideaway. At least I think it was him. He seemed to be into a long involved outrageous routine that had his pal laughing so hard he was doubled over wiping his eyes and had to run for the washroom clutching himself like a kid!"

"I was born a few miles from Dave Thomas," Evans said.

"Where?" Louise said—a challenge, as though she might catch Evans in a lie.

Evans waited until he had swallowed his spinach. "Small-town Ontario."

"But moved to Saskatchewan," Camilla reminded him.

Lyle gasped. "I saw *Saskatchewan*! Marilyn Monroe and the Rockies."

"The Rockies are not in Saskatchewan," Camilla gently said. She dabbed at the corner of her mouth with her serviette.

"Neither is Marilyn Monroe," Harold said.

"And," Evans added, "you were thinking of *River of No Return*. Shelley Winters was in *Saskatchewan*. And Alan Ladd."

Beneath this crowded table, Thorstad's long thighs seemed incapable of finding a place of their own. His left knee touched what he assumed was Louise-the-decorator's leg, but quickly retreated. He must concentrate on keeping his legs together.

From experiencing far too many long-ago dinner parties, he knew that as an outsider favoured with a place at the table it was necessary to look interested in what the others had to say, even if the context was not explained. Sooner or later a sensitive hostess would steer the conversation to a place where she would force you into the fray. Even knowing this, you might say things you would later realize were foolish.

Travis, too, had been quiet since they'd come to the table, looking from speaker to speaker with a neutral expression on his face. Was he worried by the news about "Friday night" and how this might affect his career? Or had he, like his elderly "assistant," been brought up to speak in a crowd of adults only when directly addressed?

Evans stood up and circled the table, collecting the salad plates. "We moved to Saskatoon when I was twelve." When he'd returned to the room with a large blue bowl he added, "I dreamed of becoming another Tarkovsky, or maybe a Bergman, making serious art films—even though I'd only read about them. Dammit, this is hot!" He placed the bowl of paella in front of Louise and returned to his chair. Camilla left for the kitchen and came back with a loaf of bread on a board. "But, since I wasn't born in Quebec I knew there was little hope of doing that in North America, so I headed south to make TV shows for the masses."

"Money is reasonable compensation for abandoned dreams," the plastic surgeon said, examining his own expensive fingers.

"Help yourselves to what's in front of you," Camilla suggested. "And pass it on."

"Wanting to make Bergman movies in English Canada," Evans said, now back in his place, "was rather like wanting to become an Olympic athlete while growing up in poorest Chechnya, say, with a serious case of rickets."

Lyle laughed. Travis grinned. Most of the others groaned.

"And even if you did achieve this remarkable feat, the Giant Next Door, represented by a certain 'Jack Valentovich,' would make sure it was never distributed."

"Elliot," Camilla cautioned from the opposite end of the table.

"Mr. Thorstad has movies in his blood as well," Travis said, suddenly leaning forward to address the whole table. Thorstad had been brought to class for show and tell.

"I knew it!" Lyle exclaimed. He scowled at Thorstad. "You lied."

When all eyes had turned to startled Thorstad, Travis explained. "His father was a stuntman here." To Thorstad he looked far too pleased with himself.

Eyebrows were raised. Perhaps until now they'd wondered if he was a bodyguard allowed at table only on condition that he keep his silence. "That was back in 1930," he said, attempting to make the few words sound like an intelligent contribution to the discussion.

"Killed," Travis announced—so enthusiastically, he might have done the killing himself.

"Killed?" Several said this. Lyle added, "That's *terrible*!" Axel Thorstad was now more interesting than a bodyguard, but wished it were otherwise.

"An accident," he corrected.

"Oh dear," was said here and there around the table.

This was followed by an awkward silence until Camilla, perhaps to avoid keeping Thorstad any longer on the spot, turned to the interior decorator. "I read in the paper that Louise and her realtor friend have been squiring that singer from England around, showing houses in Beverly Hills."

"In Bel Air actually," Louise said. She'd been caught fishing out her chained turquoise pendant from inside the low neck of her dress. "They're looking for something in the thirty-to-forty range, but haven't found one yet they liked. Apparently his wife wants tennis courts and a putting green and a four-car garage."

Evans tended to wave his fork around like a baton—their own Eugen von Schiller-Holst. "How do these prices sound to someone from your part of the world, uh . . . Axel?" Perhaps he was simply being the good host. "What's your opinion of clients who insist on four-car garages and a putting green?"

Thorstad slammed his thighs together. His left knee had wandered off again to nudge his neighbour. He didn't want to think of the legs beneath this table—a forest of them, everyone's but his maintaining discipline. "Sorry," he muttered to the diminutive woman, who pretended not to hear.

Dare he express, here in this company, his wish that people with thirty million dollars to spend would use it to save a few dairy farms from Mrs. Montana and her pals? This was not the sort of thing you said to hosts who'd welcomed you to their table.

"He lives in a two-room shack," Travis said, perhaps to explain an old man's silence. They could now imagine the shock of arriving here directly from a two-room shack.

Possibly out of pity for the man who lived in a shack, Harold changed the subject. Since the price of real estate was being discussed, he was able to report the latest trends in Dallas. Houston as well.

Every bone and muscle in Thorstad's body begged to get up off this chair and move about, though he knew that even if this were not unthinkable during a dinner party there was nowhere here a person could roam—certainly not on the vertical world that separated this house from the highway.

Of course he recognized that what he was feeling was not just restlessness. After a day already filled with frustration, even a casual dinner party could seem like one more attempt to thwart him. A young man in training, whether for a swim meet or a final exam, had little time for casual conversation. Of course he had been too single-minded all his life and ought to relax tonight, since they would both be working hard tomorrow.

Real estate prices were still on their minds. "I don't know what the Robertsons paid for the house next door," Camilla Evans said, "but they seem determined to get their money back from renting it to the movies. Our street is constantly being clogged with trucks and film crews and we're being told to keep quiet."

"They don't pay for the inconvenience?" The plastic surgeon was prepared to dislike the movie companies.

"They don't want to," Evans said, "but once we get our noisy lawn mowers out they come around."

"The Robertsons are related to Someone," Louise said. "Eastwood? Coppola? One of those guys throws business their way. Maybe they like living in hotels."

"Could be hard on their children," Harold said.

"I thank our lucky stars we don't have any of those," Louise-the-decorator said. "Has anyone at this table had children? Aside from brave Camilla."

"Not me!" said Lyle, denying responsibility for the world's worst crime. He shook the very possibility from his fingers.

Harold had four sons living with their mother in Connecticut. "Grown up now. I see them two or three times a year."

"Mr. Thorstad?" Camilla Evans had turned attention to him. "Axel? A grandfather, I would guess."

Thorstad was tempted to say "No children"—the literal truth—and leave it at that, but found himself naming Stuart. "A foster child. But of course it was long ago and we didn't have him for long."

Travis reacted to this revelation with too much pleasure. "Man, that's weird! I mean, him and you could, you know, meet somewhere and never know it." This scenario inspired another. "You could get into an argument with him, or punch him out. He could be, like, somewhere in this city right now. Or sitting at this table."

Startling himself with this last possibility, he fell back in his chair looking a little confused.

"He could be your Prime Minister," Harold said, "or a 'promising' abstract painter living like a parasite off an old fool like me."

Lyle glared. "Or the cute little man who cleans our pool."

"Or, since we have plummeted so quickly down the ranks," the cosmetic surgeon said, "he could be a murderer languishing on death row."

"They don't have a death row up there," Harold said. "Or so I've heard. No hangman, no electric chair, no lethal injections, no machete, no firing squad. They're a strange primitive bunch. They think they live in Oregon!"

"We're a little suspicious of you folks," the cosmetic surgeon said. "Wondering why you're even *there*."

"Maybe," Axel Thorstad said, flushed out at last, "you find it hard to believe that more than thirty million people who want to live in North America would rather not live in your country— with its death rows and Jack Valentoviches." It was possibly not a polite thing to say, but the conversation had begun to irritate.

The worried plastic surgeon leaned forward. "You do put killers behind bars?"

"They chain them to an ice floe," Evans said, "preferably an ice floe occupied by a hungry polar bear."

"The ice is melting fast," Harold said, "and I hear the polar bears are moving into your cities and eating your children. It serves you right for snubbing The Greatest Country on Earth." He reached for the bowl of paella for a second helping.

"What I want to know," said Louise, "is when Elliot is going to come through with his promise." She explained to the table at large: "I've always wanted to be an Extra in a television series and Elliot said he'd call me the next time he needed a crowd."

"This is your lucky day," Evans said. "Or, your lucky week, I should say. We need a crowd on Friday. For a riot."

Louise slapped her tiny hands together. "I'd love to be in a riot. I want to carry a double-bitted axe and behave like a drunken Viking."

"No axes this time," Evans said, holding his loaded fork halfway to his mouth. "I'm sorry to tell you it's the regulars who'll riot. The homeless bunch. What I'll need is a few dozen people dressed for a costume ball."

"While the riot is going on without me?" Indignation raised the interior decorator halfway out of her chair.

"The ball will be invaded."

Louise sat again and bowed her head to accept what was offered. "I'll be allowed to strike a few blows, I hope?"

"But a costume ball?" Camilla asked, evidently not aware of this event.

"A society costume ball," said Travis, who had read the script.

"To raise money for the homeless," Evans explained. "That's its advertised purpose. Louise will be one of the society matrons, though her clients may not recognize her as Little Bo Peep."

"Little Bo Peep my ass," Louise said. "I'd rather be the Wicked Witch of the West. Or the North—whichever's worse."

"Louise will not be alone," Camilla informed her husband. "We will all be there in costume, signed up as Extras. Everyone at this table. Even Harold and Lyle if they're still in town. We will not be left out of this."

Louise did not look pleased.

"Except Travis," Evans said. "Who will be one of the invaders."

For the benefit of the confused, Travis explained that the homeless would see the fundraiser as an offensively empty gesture. "Most of the money will disappear into paperwork and newspaper ads broadcasting their generosity."

"And here is Mr., uh, Axel's big chance to be Discovered." The plastic surgeon seemed pleased to offer this. "What will your costume be?" There might have been a hint of malice in the question.

"Yes yes." Camilla Evans seemed delighted to insist. "A wise magistrate? Something tall and important."

Thorstad looked into the white tablecloth where his plate had been before it was swept away by Evans, wondering if these people would really go to such lengths to make a fool of him.

"We will be using stuntmen in the battle," Evans said. "A chance for you to see the sort of work your father must have done."

"He doesn't need a costume," Travis said. "Just an open book. He can be the Oxford scholar."

"What's that?" Louise suspected forces moving against her. "What am I missing here?"

But Travis, grinning, said only, *"And gladly would he learn and gladly teach."*

"Explain! Explain!" Louise demanded of Thorstad, thumping her tiny fist on the table.

Rather than let this become a case of *having to be coaxed*, and perhaps to make up for his earlier silences, Thorstad sat up straight and cleared his throat and looked down at his hands while quoting as he might if this were his classroom—adopting, as near as he knew how, appropriate pronunciation:

> *"Nought oo word spak he more than was neede,*
> *And that was said in forme and reverence. . . ."*

Perhaps it was their silence that encouraged him, perhaps it was the look of expectation on Travis's face, but more likely it was the recognition of some familiar sensation in his gut. He pushed back his chair.

> *"Nought oo word spak he more than was neede,*
> *And that was said in forme and reverence,*
> *And short and quik, and ful of heigh sentence:*
> *Souning in moral vertu was his speeche,*
> *And gladly wolde he lerne, and gladly teche."*

This was rewarded with a burst of applause, probably more for the surprise than for his performance. Lyle enlightened the puzzled ones. "*The Canterbury Tales*! I saw the musical! Well—I read the book. It is a book? Maybe I read the libretto."

More surprising than the applause was Thorstad's discovery that he had risen to his feet during his recital. Of course he could not remain standing now, though he found it easier to breathe up here. But even once he was sitting again it appeared that he still had their attention. "I hadn't intended to become the evening's Entertainment!" There were smiles on both sides of the table now. "My ideals may be as high as the Oxford scholar's but I am less humble about them, I'm afraid. We live in a time when almost everything will claim precedence over learning—ambition, the battle for profit, and competition for the limelight."

The smiles had become a little strained. Elliot Evans, who'd kept his gaze on his plate from the beginning, closed his eyes.

"So it's settled!" his wife said. "You shall come as an Oxford scholar." At least she hadn't proclaimed him a pompous fool.

He hadn't meant to make a speech. Nor had he intended to give the impression he would go to this thing as the humble Oxford scholar. Of course he would not go at all. But if he were to go he would prefer to dress as the Oxford scholar's wise creator himself—a friend to princes, a diplomat to foreign lands, and a beneficiary of countless honours and gifts from the crown, a man who managed to achieve old age without retiring from his work. Also without losing his life to the plague, the sword, the noose, the rioting commons, or the King's scheming magnates.

"We'll take our dessert and coffee into the living room," Camilla said. "Harold promised to bring his mandolin, so I assume he has it in his car."

Dessert was a crème caramel, but Thorstad had little interest in eating anything more. He would head for bed as soon as heading for bed was no longer impolite. He was sure that the adored Louise resented the manner in which her request had been granted not just to herself but to everyone at the table, including Axel Thorstad, who did not belong here and had no business receiving a round of applause for showing off. During the applause, she had turned away, though not before distaste appeared on her face.

She would laugh, when she and the plastic surgeon reached home, perhaps while they undressed for bed, about the burr she'd put under the old man's saddle with nothing more than a glance. "Disgusting old fool, nudging me with his knee! Standing to *lecture* us! Why do the Evanses always invite some boring old stray to their dinners?"

He was in need of a good deep sleep to help him shake off this sense of having become irrelevant. Thanks to Travis, he had known before sitting down at the table that if he had been a teacher to one of their children he would not be at the table at all, but eating his dinner in some hot interior valley on the back side of this mountain, far from the view of the sea.

13

Carl and Audrey Montana had probably imagined his insular life expanding with exposure to life in Greater Los Angeles, but in fact his world had been shrinking steadily since he'd left their home. How else could he have seen it? One night confined to a hotel room, more than two hours strapped into an airline seat, and several hours restricted to a chair amongst strangers at a dinner party. After being released from dinner, and while Travis telephoned a friend for results of his team's soccer game, he lay in the prison of his bed, his restless limbs refusing to let him sleep. He longed to go for a walk, but imagined tumbling into one of their canyons and impaling himself on a giant cactus. Eventually, unable to endure the sheets any longer, he got up and looked out from the cantilevered deck upon an ocean lit by moonlight, the moon itself reflected in the surface of the Evanses' pool.

Far off to his left, the city towers were a blur of smoky-red. He hadn't asked anyone where in the city Oonagh Farrell might be found. But there was little point in pursuing old friends until he and Travis had found some way of working together. He had advertised for room and board in exchange for tutoring and should not have to lay down the law as well. He should not be expected to nag.

He walked cautiously down the steps and crossed the concrete patio to the pool where he stood for a few minutes studying the subtle movements of the winking surface before dropping his pyjama bottoms and lowering himself into the water—almost warm, certainly warmer than the sea at home, and a welcome comfort to his grateful flesh. The breaststroke was the quietest way to travel, so long as he kept his feet from breaking the surface and allowed his limbs and body to glide through the silky reassurance of this underwater world. Even after all these years his instinct was to strike out with all his strength and leave his imagined competition behind—but this was a small pool with more tranquil pleasures.

He had completed only three slow laps when a floodlight slashed down from somewhere and Elliot Evans stepped out of the nearest door in a pair of striped boxer shorts. "Good lord, man, why aren't you asleep?" He crouched to sit on his heels, with one hand on the ladder's top rail. He had not put on his glasses. "I often forget to close the cover before going to bed. Camilla's convinced she'll find a dead coyote floating here one morning, or a human corpse and a lawsuit. If you don't mind, I'll close it now."

Trapping you beneath it if necessary, Thorstad supposed he meant. The naked intruder could only apologize, while dripping water up the flight of concrete stairs.

In the morning he saw that it was impossible to predict the amount of time he would be allowed to spend with Travis this day. Before breakfast, Travis set off with Evans for their "daily run" on the trails along the ridge above. And later, once they'd been driven to the studio, the day became more uncertain still when they were joined, as they stepped out of the BMW, by the journalist from *Teen TeeVee*, wearing his backwards baseball cap again, a pair of dark glasses, and of course his stupid moustache.

Evans introduced a stern grey-haired woman as a studio publicist—capable, Thorstad hoped, of exercising control over the writer vibrating with excitement beside her. "Yes! Here he is! Candidate for next month's heart-throb, wearing a maroon silk shirt!" This young man was probably as much a beginner as the "future stars" he interviewed. "Don't change—I've seen the sort of rags you wear in the show."

While the publicist and the journalist led Travis off across the pavement, Evans placed a restraining hand on Axel Thorstad's upper arm. "Too much depends on that magazine. Come, I'll ask Zeena to find you a room to work in." The hand guided an irritated Thorstad in through the door to the Writers' Roost. "I've got to hole up and rewrite—*completely rewrite* a godawful script by someone who seems to think I hired him for his poetry."

Inside, the dreadlocked Zeena informed Evans that Morrison had called. "He's bringing Mandelson with him this morning to 'reach an understanding' with you." She used fingers to make quotation marks in the air.

Evans shouted, "Christ!" and tossed papers from his desk into the air. "Did he mention bringing pliers or electric prods?" He crossed the office floor to the washroom, slammed the door behind him, and yelled through the wall. "If you poison their coffee I'll support you in court!"

At the top of the stairs, as Zeena was about to open the second door on the left, it opened by itself—or seemed to. A bald slightly built young man wearing pink cotton pyjamas rushed out, stopping himself in time to avoid crashing into Thorstad. "I'm going! I'm going! You're welcome to the room!" Having blundered past them towards the staircase, he shouted, "An emergency meeting! The other writers think my script for *Man in the Shaft* sucks!" And went thundering down the steps. "Whoopee! This oughta be fun."

If this was the fellow who thought he'd been hired for his poetry, he had more to worry about than the opinion of his fellow writers. "Pyjamas?" Thorstad said. "His way of protesting something?" Perhaps he felt enslaved in a work camp here.

Zeena did not appear surprised by this encounter. "You could see others in sleepwear as well," she said, encouraging Thorstad to go before her into the small office. "It means only that they're writing today. It's their way of saying Do Not Disturb."

Once she had closed the door, Thorstad was alone in a room smelling of burnt coffee. It had been furnished with shelves of books and family photos and framed wall posters of Coen Brothers movies, as well as a photo of Clint Eastwood. A copy of *Daily Variety* lay on the desk. A second magazine was open to a page of unfamiliar faces: "Leading Ladies of Leading Series." He put on his glasses to read that an actress named Claire Adams was required by law to pay 8.3 million dollars for backing out of an oral agreement. Apparently you had to watch what you said in this city.

Against the facing wall a whiteboard had been divided by red vertical lines into six columns. Someone named Bert "appeared" for the first time in *Act II*, while someone named Carrie was "found dead" in *Act IV*. It seemed that little else had been decided.

He took a deep breath and sat at the desk, trying to swallow his resentment. He'd been detoured by a jealous overseer, and hoodwinked, it seemed, by an experienced manipulator. Evans was obvious about it, but Travis . . . There'd been a time when Thorstad could quickly size up someone like Travis—intelligent, talented, and determined, with possibly a sense of his own superiority to teachers. They usually acknowledged that you'd earned their respect—once you had—but Travis must have seen that the old man from Estevan Island had rather liked him, and assumed he'd got himself a pushover, easy to ignore once they were far from home.

But this old man was not so easily defeated. He brought the sample History exam out of his bag in order to see what lay ahead, and sat at the writer's desk to organize his attack on the twentieth century. The parade of important events was fairly easy to outline.

The First World War
The Russian Civil War
The League of Nations
The Spanish Civil War

India's rebellion against British Rule
U.S. isolationism
The Battle of Britain
The United Nations
The Korean War
The Suez Crisis
The Cold War
The Vietnam War
The Fall of the Berlin Wall

Travis and his friends were probably relieved they hadn't been born any sooner than they had been in that bloody century. But shockingly, all of these events would be reduced to best-answer questions. *Which of the following was the result of the Suez Crisis? Which two of the following groups fought one another during the Spanish Civil War?*

The building was alive with footsteps and excited voices. Maybe this had become a meeting place for an impromptu seminar. Had Chaucer composed his verses with human discourse all around him in his Aldgate mansion, or had he gone back at night to work in his government office on the docks? Herman Melville locked the door to his writing room but it was not known whether he stuffed cotton in his ears. Perhaps the writers of television scripts required less silence than poets and novelists who wished to hear only the sounds inside their heads. At any rate, it seemed the pyjamas' message did not go so far as to insist on silence.

After more than two hours in this borrowed room he found it impossible to concentrate any longer while voices rose and fell around him, sometimes with bursts of laughter. There were benches outside he might sit on, and sunlight to enjoy. With the books back in his bag he went down the stairs and past a coffee urn where a woman in orange shorty pyjamas chatted with a grey-haired gentleman in a blue striped nightshirt. Both looked down at their bedroom slippers and stepped back to let him pass.

Since Elliot Evans was not in his office, the instruments of torture must be at work in some other room. Outside the front door, sun glared off white stucco on every side. The shadows of leaves from a single tree were playing so prettily over a slatted bench near the door that he sat in order to feel the coming and going of the sun on his face, and to watch the constant movement of the leaf-shadows on his hands. His bag of books gaped at his feet, waiting to be put to use. Failure spoke from every tilted volume.

From his bag he withdrew one of the letters that had arrived as they were about to leave for the airport. The return address was a post office box in some place called Bald Rock, North Carolina. He imagined green hills and pretty university towns, though he knew nothing about the state except what he'd read in the disproportionate number of novels it produced. The writer had included a telephone number, perhaps in case he was desperate to secure a position in North Carolina as fast as possible.

Dear Sir,

I may have come upon your advertisement too late to do either of us any good. My attention was drawn to your ad by an acquaintance who knows I once lived on Estevan myself, a very long time ago, but have never returned. Several of us young women and men left about the same time, and found ourselves drifting south to very different lives. I have kept up a correspondence with an old friend in that part of the world—and she has sent the newspaper on to me with a pencilled circle around your advertisement.

I have an elderly neighbor who remains illiterate despite my occasional efforts to help her. She is a dear old soul, and was so good to me in the earliest years of my widowhood that I am prepared to return her kindnesses in any way I can—and that would include putting you up in my spare room and cooking your meals if you were to move here and dedicate yourself to her education.

It is very beautiful here in the gentle shaded coves amongst the blue hills. I have referred to Eleanor Sweet as my neighbor ("neighbour," I suppose, to you), though her house is a little more than two miles from my own. There has been no serious crime hereabouts since my husband, eighteen years ago, was murdered on our front doorstep by two drunken men from just beyond the first hill to the south, and they, thank goodness, have been put away. Their wives do not speak to me when we meet in the nearest town—as though my husband had invited their men to attack him with their axes—but their attitude is of no importance to me now, and I am quite self-sufficient, even to the matter of growing my own food and shooting my own meat.

Of course there are times when I am homesick for the lovely island of my childhood. How innocent are the young, so easily convinced that an infatuation with a forceful man is reason enough to abandon all that is familiar and dear and follow him off to foreign locations. I am prepared to contribute what I can to your travel expenses and, as I've said, supply room and board, if you are inclined to consider this opportunity to make not one but two women happy who are marooned, so to speak, amongst these quiet hills. I have one of the few telephones up this valley, if you are inclined to respond in that manner.

Yours truly,

Isobel Cleary (nee Hammond)

Might he have been more effective as a tutor to an old mountain woman in North Carolina? He might, at least, have exchanged memories of tiny Estevan Island with the woman whose husband had been murdered on her doorstep—since this Isobel Cleary must have been one of the young islanders who'd fled soon after the cattle-rustling had been discovered and the hippie draft dodgers sent packing. Because she'd included the *Hammond* in her signature, she may have been related to Bo. Had anyone informed her of his death? Axe murderers aside, he could imagine that life in a remote North Carolina valley should offer fewer distractions than Los Angeles.

He might have reread the letter if the little courier truck hadn't appeared from behind a squat white building and pulled to a stop in the shade. Yesterday's delivery man stepped out, holding a large flat envelope. He nodded to Thorstad before going past him up the steps and in through the door to the Writers' Roost. Within moments he came out again without the envelope. Before getting back into the little truck he turned a worried face to Thorstad. "You still Lost?" A perfect crease had been ironed down the length of his brown trousers.

"What about your Building 46?"

The courier scratched rigorously at a bushy sideburn. "It don't exist!" His eyes bulged. "I walked into one of their offices and said, You tell me where you hid Building 46 or I leave this parcel on your desk! They said there aint no 46! Number 46 was *retarred*. So I took the parcel back where it came from and tol' them Try again!" He sat on the bench beside Thorstad and draped his forearms over his long thighs. "No one's gonna shoot me if I rest a minute."

"You're not from here? Your accent—"

"Nobody's from here. I'm from N'Orleans, me. You heard of it? I'm one of Katrina's orphans, scattered farther than most."

"Your home was wrecked in the storm?"

"Busloads of black people hauled out of there fast—sent as far as they could send us. Hoping they send us far enough we won't come back. I heard some ended up in Utah! Lord! My bus come all the way to California before it let me off in desert. They're not getting *me* to stay in no desert." He looked this way and that, as though to reassure himself that he wasn't in desert now. "So I put out my thumb and kept moving till I got to here. My Momma's cousin works for this courier company, gave me a job when somebody quit. Studios only! How you like that? Messages to beautiful actresses. Parcels to famous directors. The gossip I hear, oh my!"

Noticing the bag at Thorstad's feet, he reached down and pulled out a book—Travis's modern poetry anthology. "What y'all do with *these*?" He laid the textbook on his lap and opened it carefully, like someone nervous of what he might find inside. "You goin' to old-folks school or what?"

"I'm supposed to be a teacher for a busy actor."

The courier bent forward to peer hard at the open page and sounded out the words at the top. "Lucinda . . . Matlock. Hmmm. Who she?"

"A woman speaking from her grave. She raised twelve children, lost eight, enjoyed her marriage, died at ninety-six. No complaints." Thorstad took the book and ran a finger down the page. "Listen—her last few lines:

"What is this I hear of sorrow and weariness,
Anger, discontent and drooping hopes?
Degenerate sons and daughters,
Life is too strong for you—
It takes life to love Life."

"She sound fierce, that one. Dead and still speaks her mind?"

"There's a whole graveyard full of people speaking their minds in the book she came from. Most complain, but not her."

"Somebody ought to tell us what Katrina victims say from their graves—*Whooo!* My granny's tongue would blister the son-bitch *she* decide to blame." He reached into the bag again. "These other books got poems?"

"Geography. Composition. History. The boy has exams to write."

"Exams!" The courier abandoned the books and stood up to flee exams. "I missed as many them things I could. 'Course, I am one damn ignorant fool."

Thorstad also stood, once he'd returned the poetry book to his bag. He would go up and see whether he could interest Travis in the twentieth century's list of horrors and the abundance of best-answer questions they might spawn. Assuming, of course, that he was free of the journalist and not acting before the cameras.

The delivery man returned to his truck and concentrated on his clipboard. Thorstad had got ten or fifteen metres past him up the paved slope before the little truck caught up—enough time to be struck with the thought that this was one person who might know the whereabouts of people in this business. He held out an arm. "Hold it, please?"

"No room for passengers. Anyway, it's 'gainst the rules."

"You ever deliver something to *Another Life*?"

"What studio's that?"

"I don't know. An old friend sometimes appears on that show. Oonagh Farrell?"

The courier closed his eyes and thought.

"Plays an elderly Swedish princess," Thorstad said, to help him think.

"Lady with a big laugh?" The courier's grin was wide. "I seen her name on a door, yes sir. Heard big laughing behind it, then it opened and out she come to read something on the paper in her hand. She had the whole place roarin' in a minute."

"Next time you see her, maybe you could tell her an old friend from her teaching days says hello."

"Put yourself in a box and I'll take you to her. You can tell her hello to her face."

"I directed her in her first stage role. She'll remember that."

"You a director?" He slapped a knee. "Hell, I thought you was a granddaddy brought to work because your caregiver sick!"

Thorstad hoped this was meant as a joke. "You want to say hello on paper I'll put it in my pocket and remember it next time I hear that laugh."

That imagined piece of paper was suddenly dangerous. What did he think he was doing? He felt, suddenly, as though he'd come too close to slipping off a cliff. "I think you should forget I mentioned her."

"Fine with me." The delivery man put his truck in motion. "That woman just gone off to Nowhere with Building 46. Now I got my job to do. You do yours but don't get lost! *Ha, ha!*"

His job? His job was to drag Travis back into the bloodshed of the twentieth century and his obligations now in the twenty-first as soon as the journalist, the publicist, and the director had all had their share of him.

When he'd crossed most of the distance to Stage 5, the writer in pink pyjamas was suddenly beside him, his beaded moccasins silent on the pavement. "I hope you left a few good ideas in my office, man. I'm about run out of my own!"

Thorstad saw no signs of distress in the man's face, though there were beads of sweat on his shiny scalp. "You survived your meeting?"

"What do I care what they think?" He flung his arms wide, as though to throw off what he'd heard from his fellow writers. "They think we're a *team*. They think they're auditioning for *The Closer* or something. Hell, I don't care what they think. I won't be back next season anyway."

"You know this?"

"I've *decided* this. My brother-in-law's working on a movie script for Brad Pitt and needs me." Before going in through the door to the sound stage he said, "Apparently Paolo wants to talk with me now—something about my stupid script." He tilted back his head and shouted fiercely to sky. "Probably wants to tell me how brilliant it is!" Then, chuckling, he quickened his pace and left Thorstad behind.

Apparently a scene had just been completed. The powerful lamps had been extinguished and crew members were securing or shifting equipment amongst the temporary walls and stacks of unpainted plywood in the grey depleted light. The excitable Charlie, rushing off to an emergency elsewhere, informed him that Travis had already left the building. "Only one little line, but he'll be back for his big scene later!"

It appeared the actress who played the wealthy matriarch was still in the building. At least Thorstad assumed this woman sur-rounded by a group of admirers was the actress. She was famil-iar from the episode he'd seen in the Montanas' viewing room, though he could not at the moment recall her name—once a glamorous star in the era of Jean Simmons and Susan Hayward, now something of an elderly matron in a moss-green sweater set and tweed skirt. She appeared to be holding court, with several of the crew clustered around to overhear what was being said between her and the director. Evidently she was hearing only compliments from Paolo and Paolo was hearing only compli-ments in return, while her eyes checked the faces of her admirers. She seemed pleased with whatever it was she saw.

Dolores Williams. You could see traces of the lovely Dolores Williams despite the added girth. Tiberius's bloodthirsty mis-tress. As a young man he had seen her swooning in the arms of Gregory Peck. And, if he remembered correctly, shooting the hat off Gary Cooper's head. There was a time he might have asked for her autograph, but now he could only wonder why it was dis-appointing to see that certain people had allowed themselves to get old.

When Paolo led the writer off for a private conversation, the clipboard woman stepped up to the actress. "Always a pleasure to watch you work, Miss Williams."

"Thank you, sweetie. And *gracias* for not blowing the whistle on me." She glanced to either side but did not lower her voice. "I buggered up that one line pretty bad, but everyone was too polite to stop me so I kept on going. There are some advantages to being older than everyone else on the planet."

"This is Travis's friend," the clipboard woman said. Perhaps Thorstad had been gawking.

The actress put out a small round hand for Thorstad to shake. He assumed she did not expect him to raise it to his lips. "You thought this old dame had died off years ago—admit it. A few close calls but I'm still here!" Her laughter was low and warm. "You could probably say the same yourself." She patted his hand, perhaps with sympathy, then wiggled goodbye fingers and set off towards the outer door where a young man hurried forward to take her arm.

Her perfume remained in the air. He was surprised to discover himself confused and embarrassed. For a moment he'd been his seventeen-year-old self thrilled to be meeting the famous Dolores Williams and at the same time he was his seventy-seven-year-old self shocked to discover that the movie star, down off the screen, looked older than his remembered grandmother. Apparently sixty years, once behind you, were little more than an instant.

"You might want to check on Travis," the clipboard woman said. "Paolo was pretty hard on him."

Inside his trailer, Travis pounded a fist into the padded arm of his couch. He had removed the wig, but hadn't changed out of his clothes or removed his makeup. "As soon as he sees what we got he'll make Paolo do it again. They had to take me through my *single line* six or seven times before he used the cameras and still I sounded like a high school drama dork with stage fright! Wrecked the scene for everyone."

"Well, you didn't ask them to expand your role."

"They're giving me a chance to show what I can do!" His tone suggested that Thorstad was a fool not to have known this. "One of the other guys was dropped and they picked me to replace him."

He ran a hand back over his hair, once and then again. "There's others waiting for me to fail."

"You know this?"

"Rosie told me. A guy named Reynolds Green is waiting for me to screw up so they'll, you know, give him a chance."

"Well." Thorstad lowered himself onto a chair and laced his hands together and looked for a few minutes at his feet. "I suppose," he said as gently as he knew how, "this is not the time to consider the causes of the Spanish Civil War." If this were his son he would move to sit beside him on the cot and offer sympathy, but this was the son of Carl and Audrey Montana who were far away, fixing teeth and buying up farms for townhouses.

"I'm sorry." Travis closed his eyes. "Everything's, like, *crowding* me. That journalist kept reminding me how important it is to get in his stupid magazine. Sticking his camera in my face. No wonder I screwed up, with *him* watching!"

"But you're done with him now?"

"No such luck." Travis unbuttoned his fire-damaged shirt, shrugged out of it, and tossed it onto a wall hook. "Elliot told him he could meet us tomorrow at breakfast." He removed his Seattle airport shirt from a hanger, put it on, and began to button it up. "How much more of me does he fucking need?"

14

Before going on to a meeting farther up the coast, Camilla Evans dropped them off at the restaurant in Paradise Cove with instructions to order a hearty breakfast and put in some serious study before she returned. "I don't want to be blamed if you fail at your job."

He was already failing at his job. What else could you call it but failure when so little had been accomplished? Last night he'd telephoned Carl to explain what he was up against, but Carl had only suggested he employ his teacher-ingenuity to deal with the situation. "Remember how you outsmarted that music teacher who tried to borrow Selena Thompson whenever her pianist was sick?"

But that young music teacher hadn't possessed Elliot Evans's advantages.

Even the choice of this restaurant may have been a deliberate act of sabotage, when you considered the distractions. The walls were crowded with black-and-white photos of old-time movie stars. Cary Grant. Judy Garland. James Dean. Too many of the customers looked, to Travis, like contemporary movie stars he couldn't quite name. And there was the wide beach beyond the glass—golden sand traversed by scantily clad strollers. The long white pier extended well out over the water on picturesquely spindly legs, its nearer railing a roost for resting gulls.

Travis knew too much about this place. Apparently Barbra Streisand lived nearby. A movie named *Gidget* had been filmed here, a series called *Baywatch* as well. He could not believe that Thorstad had never heard of *Baywatch*.

Ignoring this apparently serious gap in his cultural background, Thorstad pushed his coffee mug aside and opened the textbook next to his seafood omelette. "We agreed we would talk about Shakespeare's tragedies this morning."

"And that other series was shot here too," Travis said. "A private investigator—had a sidekick named Angel. What was it called? Used to be my dad's favourite show." He opened his cellphone and pointed it at Thorstad. "Axel Thorstad amongst the stars." He frowned for a few moments at the little screen, then folded the gadget shut. "James Garner was the PI."

Thorstad did not know the series but he did know that if Travis was not familiar with Shakespearean tragedy both of them would be in trouble. Literature, History, and Geography were the courses most at risk. The Montanas would throw Thorstad's belongings out on the road for the *senior-seniors* who passed in their daily walks. Whatever was left would be shipped to the homeless shelter. Angus Walker would be wearing his socks.

"According to the course outline, your teacher could have chosen *The Tempest*, *Hamlet*, or *King Lear*. But yours chose *Hamlet*?"

Travis flopped back in his chair as though dealt a blow by Shakespeare himself. "*Hamlet* boring *Hamlet*!"

Thorstad had heard this quick dismissal too often. "Most of the world's great actors have played Hamlet. Half the actors in this room have probably tried it, even those with roles in *Baywatch*. What is it about the Danish prince that makes him tempting to every actor in the world but Travis Montana?"

"There isn't room in my brain for this." Travis closed his eyes as though to make Thorstad disappear. "I should be going over my lines."

"I'll help you with your lines as soon as we've dealt with the Danish prince. Look, we'll come at it another way." Thorstad drew a sheet of loose-leaf paper from his bag and sketched an isosceles triangle, then divided it with vertical slashes into five parts. "Look at the shape of his tragedies. Five acts. For half the play things go right, more or less." Here was something he'd always loved. If there were a chalkboard nearby he would be up on his feet drawing diagrams and explaining things to strangers, famous actors included. The geometry of literature! Eyes were supposed to widen now, the lights were supposed to go on. "For the second half, beyond this peak in the middle, they go steadily downhill, usually because of the hero's actions in the first half. Or inaction in this case." A pause for the beauty of it all to sink in. "What is it about Hamlet that causes his own destruction in the end?"

Before Travis had time to come up with an answer, the journalist from *Teen TeeVee* slipped into the booth beside Thorstad. "Morning!" he cried, loud enough to turn heads. A knapsack was placed on the seat between them. "I have a volleyball in my car," he said. "And a photographer. I want you out on the sand. Didn't Evans tell you to wear a swimsuit?"

"He didn't," Travis said.

"We'll have you take off your shirt, then. And roll up your pants. Let's go! The photographer's waiting outside."

The publicist was outside as well, frowning at the expanse of sand as though doubting its value as a backdrop. After convincing their waiter that he would return immediately, Thorstad followed Travis in order to register his protest. The journalist would be impervious but a grey-haired woman might understand—might hope to see her own children pass exams.

But when she turned to confront Thorstad he saw in her eyes that she made no sentimental distinction between an old man and an inconvenient post. "Lewis is on a tight schedule. We had no choice. We shouldn't be more than an hour."

Travis had already started out across the sand, but turned suddenly and jogged back. "Hey, look. I'm sorry. Be patient, eh? I don't have any choice here!" He started walking backwards now, away from Thorstad again. *"Hamlet!"* He raised his arm and pointed a finger. "We'll talk about *Hamlet* later. *To be or not to be—in Teen TeeVee.* Maybe this is the end." He turned again, and ran to catch up with his masters.

To Thorstad it was obvious that, for this only child, pleasing some adults was more important than pleasing others. His tutor had been demoted to some inessential post-adult state. Travis had made a choice, which was not to say he wouldn't suffer for it. Some only children of Thorstad's experience would make nervous wrecks of themselves if trying to please one adult meant displeasing another.

Of course he'd been an only child himself, and suffered from it still. If he was not more patient with this situation, it was at least partly because he wanted to avoid disappointing Carl Montana. And what were his chances of pleasing anyone? How could his desire to *teach* compete with Travis's drive to *act*, or Elliot Evans's determination to complete his episode within budget? Or, for that matter, the journalist's need to get a good story for his magazine? As though to drive home the point, by the time he had paid for their unfinished breakfasts and gone out to the small sand-strewn terrace, Rosie had also appeared. Was he to compete with her as well?

She was not alone. A dark-haired youth in knee-length shorts and red muscle shirt stood frowning beside her—impatient perhaps, or painfully self-conscious, or so intensely aware of his own good looks that he believed others were compelled to admire him. Apparently, to be this handsome was a serious burden.

The girl smiled at Thorstad in a manner that suggested she was pleased to think a sly trick had been played on him. Or perhaps she thought he was admiring her mostly naked figure. In fact he was thinking how emaciated she appeared in that tiny green swimsuit. Perhaps she had chosen this look to distinguish herself not only from the curvaceous bodies of Hollywood but from the anorexic starlets as well, outdoing all of them to the point of giving herself the perverse appeal of a child prostitute on the streets of a war-torn city.

"It is probably a good sign, my darling, that you notice such things even now—but really, to find something even a little attractive in a starving refugee is almost embarrassing, though I suppose we should be glad you're still alive enough to admire the female figure, but I think pity might be the more appropriate response in this case, a desire to send her away with money for a restaurant meal, except she would probably stuff herself full of the richest food on the menu and then throw it all up in the toilet, which is probably how your friend the photographer ought to be shooting her—so I think you should report the child to some agency that might investigate those bruises, or demand of that executive producer that he forbid his two young actors from seeing one another off the set, it will only lead to serious trouble for them both, and of course for you as well."

Determined not to react to Elena's voice this time, Thorstad chose a deck chair on the concrete pad between restaurant and sand, to keep a distanced eye on the photo shoot. Also, perhaps, to fight the temptation to indulge in self-pity. Was this sense of frustration and failure unique to him, he wondered, or was it something that came to everyone with retirement and age? Perhaps it occurred only to those who had tried to put themselves back into the world. Well, he couldn't afford to give in. He had better pull himself together and make an effort—put up a fight, if necessary.

No driftwood lay on this sand, no seaweed that he could see, no plastic bottles or wooden crates washed in by the tide. Armies of city employees must have come out at dawn to gather everything up and dispose of it somewhere else. This tidy stretch of sand should be photographed for those on Estevan who'd mocked an old man for rescuing tennis balls and wicker doll carriages from the beach.

The ocean breeze was pleasant but not so warm that he was about to take off his lightweight Thrift Shop jacket. Since he had been rendered irrelevant here, he might as well make use of the time to construct a more convincing lesson on *Hamlet*. Wasn't it widely believed that the young had little trouble identifying with the Dane? It seemed that Travis was not amongst them. But while digging around in his bag in search of the paperback Shakespeare, he came upon yet another of the letters that had arrived as they'd been leaving for the plane. Elena would have been appalled that he hadn't opened it. Good manners dictated that at least you have a look. And you couldn't know for sure that the solution to your life was not inside.

This time the return address was a street only a few kilometres from where he'd lived for most of his life. A former colleague, perhaps. Not, he hoped, a former student requesting a reference letter after all this time.

> Dear Mr. Thorstad,
>   I got in touch with the postmistress on Estevan Island to make sure you were still living up there. She assumed I was responding to an advertisement in the newspaper and was reluctant to talk to me at all until I explained that I was a student of yours many years ago and wanted simply to say "hello."

The name scribbled at the bottom was "Carter Stone." Carter had been in one of his very first classes and worked on the school newspaper, an intelligent boy but shy. His romance with Rona Quimby had caused parents to worry and Miss Mavis Hinds to demand he do something to stop it.

> I was in your English class the year you took us on a field trip to the Horne Lake Caves for something to write about and then got into trouble because you'd neglected to warn the School Board ahead of time—an uncharacteristic oversight for you. A friend

of mine worked for a while on that little ferry that goes back and forth between Vancouver Island and Estevan every day, and he told me you were living over there now. Apparently you aren't there any more, so I hope Canada Post still forwards things like they used to.

You may remember that you were the one who suggested I ask Rona Quimby to the school Christmas dance, assuring me you'd somehow found out she would not say No. While you and your wife were not able to attend our wedding, you may remember my approaching you long afterwards—in a department store I think it was—to tell you it was our fifteenth anniversary and to thank you again for giving me that little push. Ours was a very happy partnership, and she has left me with two wonderful children (both of them adults now, of course) who are a great consolation in my grief.

Why do I feel compelled to tell you this while I still hope for her return? Perhaps because I feel I've somehow let you down. Perhaps because I don't have to look you in the eye to tell you this, or witness your disappointment.

In fact, amongst the high school friends we kept in contact with we were just about the only couple still together after more than twenty-five years. Marriages were failing all around us. Maybe we were inclined to be a bit smug about our own, I'm not sure. At any rate, I became too involved in my business and didn't notice that something was wrong at home. Rona, mean-while, had got quite involved with the local drama group and announced, one day, that she was leaving town with the leading man (brought over from Vancouver for the role). Though I've always been leery of drama types I didn't see this coming.

I doubt that many teachers receive letters as intimate as this from former students, but I suspect you may receive more than you'd care to read, since there was always such an air of frankness, trust, and genuine affection in your every lesson. (Though not always in your exams, which were TOUGH!)

I might have lost the impulse to write you if the postmistress had not told me you were starting a new life elsewhere. If your travels bring you back to town (I'm just seven blocks from the house where I grew up!) I hope you'll consider looking me up. The blow to my happiness and pride has made me doubly aware of my gratitude for your generosity, inside the classroom and out.
Affectionately,
Carter Stone

He waited for the sound of Elena's voice reminding him again in one of her interminable sentences that he'd thrown his life away on a misguided faith in his ability to give people some sort of lasting happiness, or at least the tools to find it. A "servant of love," she had called him, but not in praise. "The master of happy endings" had been pronounced with a sarcastic edge. He had loved her without the smallest reservation, while she had loved him despite his faults-in-need-of-attention.

But it seemed she had nothing to say about the letter. Perhaps, after her comments about the skeletal actress, she had abandoned the complex crannies in his skull and gone off somewhere to join the lost memory of his wounded cello. Was he to believe that this was what it meant to get old—a series of quiet desertions? Obviously he was not supposed to be a teacher any more, he was supposed to fade away in front of a television set or behind a newspaper and keep himself at a distance from the actual world. None of his old colleagues would be surprised by Carter Stone's letter, though some might be surprised to learn of his ineffectiveness here in L.A.

What would the woman in North Carolina think of his situation? Would she suggest he abandon Travis in order to teach her friend how to read? By recording her telephone number she'd implied that a call would be welcome even if he had no intention of accepting her offer. Perhaps she'd simply hoped to hear news of her childhood home.

He became so absorbed in thinking of Mrs. Cleary that for a moment he believed the person he sensed settling into the deck chair next to his might be Mrs. Cleary herself, bringing with her the rustle of female clothing and the faint scent of a perfume that was familiar but until now forgotten. He was aware, as well, of a naked foot in a gold sandal, a slender ankle, the colourful corner of a long cotton skirt rippling from the breeze off the ocean.

There were several other deck chairs on this slab of concrete but she had chosen the one so close as to be almost intrusive. If he were to open one of his books, she would be able to read the words of Shakespeare or the decisions made at the Geneva Convention. Because it would be impolite to turn for a direct look, he went only so far as to peer off into the blue ocean just a little to his right so that his peripheral vision might examine her without causing offence. It seemed that he'd been joined by a woman whose left hand was placed on the crown of a broad hat, presumably to keep it from flying off.

"I swear this chair was farther away when I chose it," she said, "but the minute I sat, it practically threw me into your arms."

The laughter that followed this was all he needed—Oonagh Farrell's robust rumble. His entire body recognized it. He abandoned the horizon and turned in his chair to look.

"You can't be all that surprised, since I understand you've been asking all over the city for me."

For a moment he was without breath. He half rose from his seat, his heart hammering at his throat.

She stood and opened her arms and he walked into an embrace. The familiar scent was from some flower or mixture of flowers that no one had ever been able to identify. He recalled that if you guessed, she wouldn't help. She would smile as though she'd made it up herself, or smelled that way from birth. Perhaps she had.

When he'd stepped back, aware that his hot face had probably coloured up, she took hold of his right hand and looked him over. "Axel Thorstad, large as life!" She was a woman whose crow's

feet, like her too-broad smile, had been essential to her beauty.
The cheekbones, too, hadn't changed. His instinct was to hold
hard to both hands and gaze at that wonderful face indefinitely.
Until, perhaps, she protested, or turned away.

"I mentioned your name to one lost courier, but changed my
mind and asked him to forget it."

"You should have known better. A refugee from Katrina will
go to any length to win friends in this city."

"And he told you what show—"

"He told me whose doorstep you were sitting on." She obviously found this amusing. "So I called up Elliot Evans's assistant,
who called up Evans, who told me where his wife had parked you
for the morning, a sitting duck with no visible means of escape.
He told me not to interfere with his young actor's work, but I
could tell he wouldn't mind if I interfered with yours. So far the
only thing I've seen you do is shove a letter into your pocket and
stare at that skeleton-girl by the pier."

He laughed, delighted to see this woman—vivacious and loud
and still beautiful. But he was nervous as well—a chill had shot
up his back. In fact, he was alarmed. Confused. Perhaps he hadn't
believed this could happen, hadn't properly imagined it. When she
sat back in her deck chair without releasing his hand, he dragged
his own chair closer by hooking a foot behind its nearest leg,
hoping he didn't look too obviously flustered.

This was not simply the Oonagh of his remembered past,
grown older, but an Oonagh who'd acquired the special magic
of the admired, the famous, the successful artist. He'd seen her
described, in print, as one of the world's "genuine originals."

Yet, no assistants had arrived with her—none of the masseurs,
private secretaries, or makeup artists he'd seen swarming around
her in his imagination. For a moment she looked off towards the
water like someone who didn't know what to say or do next—like
someone who had made a wrong turn. He knew the pose: Amanda
Wingfield wondering where the gentleman callers had gone. It

was all he could do to keep from running a finger along the line of her jaw.

She seemed smaller than he remembered, more slender than she sometimes appeared on the screen. She had played large women as often as not. Her raw-boned farm women and busty suffragettes were as convincing as her fragile Amanda Wingfield and youthful Joan. Which was, he supposed, successful acting. Today she was dressed in an ivory shirt, with something like an elaborately decorated tablecloth wrapped around her waist to become a long skirt you might see in the South Pacific. When she dropped the broad hat on the concrete, he saw that her dark hair had been pinned behind her ears.

She may have dressed to avoid recognition on the street but any stranger could see a surviving beauty. It was in the eyes, he supposed, and those bones she attributed to a grandmother from the roads of Connemara. If they'd met unexpectedly somewhere and she had looked at him without recognition he would not have introduced himself. As a teacher, he'd known and even occasionally welcomed invisibility. Guest speakers invited to his classroom—authors, journalists, songwriters—had seen him first as a genial chauffeur, then as a pleasant but innocuous host, a generous introducer, and finally as a facilitator who did not, thank goodness, insist on being Somebody himself. Most were grateful for this, if they thought of it at all. That Oonagh Farrell had sought him out suggested she would not have him remain anonymous today.

She showed no hint that anything about him surprised her. He might have had this unruly white hair fifty years ago, and the extended forehead. Of course he had always had these hollow cheeks, these too-long bony limbs, these heavy brows. "God, Thorstad! Look at you!" The smile did not remain a smile but rumbled into laughter, as though this moment, like all twists and turns in life, was a great surprising joke. "What happened? Are we really not twenty-two any more?"

Out beside the pier, Travis and Rosie were tossing the photographer's volleyball at the water's edge. From this distance and low angle it was impossible to know whether they were on the sand or ankle deep in water. He expected it was water, and that eventually the journalist would toss the ball out to where Travis would have to wade in to retrieve it, getting soaked to the skin in the process, his wet jeans clinging to his hips and legs. Wasn't that how things were done in this place? The young man who leaned against a leg of the pier to watch could be the one who waited for Travis to fail.

He imagined taking Oonagh by the hand and leading her out to the water's edge where they might forget their age and run together into the ocean as they had done on that secluded Vancouver Island beach. Of course she would roar at the very idea, would think he was cracked. Instead, he attempted to explain his presence. The hand she held was warming up. "Unlike famous actors, teachers are forced to retire. At least my generation was. As a retiree I've been trying to help that young fellow prepare for exams. But unfortunately he is an actor being packaged for teenage girls who read *online* gossip magazines."

She squinted in the direction of the little group by the pier. "Has he decided how high a price he's willing to pay?"

"Any price that's asked, is my guess. He has two successful parents to outdo and, I suspect, a lust for fame and fortune."

Oonagh raised her eyebrows. "And you are supposed to keep him focused on humbler things?"

"Between Evans and that journalist—and that girl too, I think, and the boy himself—the job has been nearly impossible since we set foot in this city."

She let go of his hand in order to press her own together. "So! Is this your first time down here since that famous Christmas?" It seemed that she was not prepared to bestow any more of her attention on Travis.

"It is."

"Lord!" She smiled at the nearest beach umbrella. "Remember the fuss Topolski's sister made when she got home? She hadn't given the bastard permission after all." She took his nearer wrist in her hand as though to keep him anchored for this. "She had no idea we were living in her house and eating her food and using up the gas in her Cadillac. Of course we were far away by the time she returned, it was Topolski who had to take her phone calls."

"And Topolski is . . . ?" Too late, he wondered if he should not have asked.

"Old!" Her tone suggested she was disappointed in Topolski for this.

"Of course." Andrzcj Topolski had been a few years older than Axel Thorstad. "I was told I'd find no old people in Los Angeles and so far it has appeared they were right."

Oonagh laughed. "We *are* the old people here! You and I and a handful of others."

It seemed she'd misunderstood. "I don't know if this is true for women, but it always seemed important that there be those who were going before us—sometimes as teachers or coaches or self-appointed uncles, but mostly just *there*, running things, providing examples, and causing us to feel we're following in their footsteps."

"And now they've disappeared." Her voice was disappointed for him.

"Taking their footsteps with them." This seemed to have happened while he was hiding out on his island. "Of course I should have known, but it has caught me by surprise."

"I hate to be the one to break the news, my dear, but there's a reason for it!" Her tone suggested he could supply the reason himself—which of course he could. Now she released his wrist and sat back as though something had been accomplished here. "And so we have all been orphaned! Look at it this way—it means there's no one left to tell us how to behave. We can do anything we want." In the brief silence she appeared to be considering what this might be. "You can come and have lunch with me without asking anyone's permission."

He could see that she was serious. His heart should not be racing like this—an adolescent flurry. "I can't run off and leave Travis to those people out there. Evans would see it as giving up."

She laid her hand against one side of his face. "I didn't mean right now, my darling. That boy may need you any minute—he suspects he's in deeper water than he imagined and will be glad of a convenient spoilsport. I meant tomorrow, when your Elliot Evans assures me the child will be busy earning his pay." She stood up, and stomped sand from her sandals. "Meet me outside the studio gate. I'll pick you up at—shall we say one o'clock?"

Far too aware of his body's every agitated cell, he accompanied her around the side of the restaurant to where her car was parked, a silver-blue Mercedes convertible from an earlier decade. "You see how determined I was to find you? It cost me twenty-five dollars to park this thing for a fifteen-minute conversation!" She laughed again, and was still laughing as she slid into her car and shut the door. She started the engine, released the brake, and made the car leap forward to roar around behind Thorstad and along past the restaurant and uphill past the wooded trailer park towards the one wide highway that seemed to link everything in this world to everything else.

15

Nowhere on the studio lot could he find an indication that nature knew it was spring. No birds sang here. No squirrels courted, no flowers bloomed. Nor were there any trees capable of blooming. The only trees he could see in the area outside the Writers' Roost were evergreen shrubs trimmed to resemble animals. The pavement beneath his feet prevented the very idea of grass. Perhaps there'd been a decision to exclude the natural world and limit reality to the camera's eye.

His principals would have laughed to learn that Axel Thorstad could be sidelined so thoroughly. Administrators who'd suffered his campaigns against school rules, unjustified demands, unnecessary interruptions, and ridiculous schedules were aware of his ability to negotiate around foolish regulations that came between him and his students. But he had never before confronted the superior forces of a television producer.

"Be patient" was Evans's advice. "Go up and watch the morning scenes being shot. If you get bored, come back to the Roost for a nap. Don't men of a certain age need a daytime snooze, so they won't nod off and miss their supper later?"

Did it show that he hadn't slept well last night? The prospect of lunch with Oonagh had kept him awake. The woman had meant too much to him once, more than he should have allowed. Then she had gone out of his life and meant something else altogether, at a distance. There was something rather pitiful about keeping alive the memory of an ancient infatuation for someone who'd since succeeded in a world where she was admired and even adored by countless strangers.

He was surprised he hadn't been accosted by Elena's voice reminding him that it was *she* and not the actress who had found and drawn out the man in him, while the actress had had only the infatuated boy. Elena had always told him precisely what she thought, before laughing and kissing him, and walking him into a corner with her tongue in his mouth.

It would be a mistake to go to this lunch. He would discover they had already, yesterday, said everything they had to say to one another. He would be embarrassed and awkward, would make a fool of himself, accidentally betraying the confusion of a bewitched youth. But there was no escaping now. Because she hadn't given him a phone number or any other useful information, the only way to avoid the lunch would be to let her wait at the gate until she gave up, something he could not do.

Travis had insisted he dress for the occasion, ordering Thorstad to wear the "good clothes" he'd worn to the Evanses' dinner party—his dress pants, his pale green shirt, and his dress shoes, which Travis himself had insisted on polishing for him. "You've let yourself get out of practice! This woman is used to millionaires and movie stars."

Before walking down to join her at the gate, he'd hoped to introduce Travis to an article he'd come across, a review of a book in which an academic had drawn a straight line between the nineteenth-century poetry of Wordsworth and Coleridge and the twentieth-century songs of the Beatles. He wasn't even certain that Travis's generation listened to the Beatles, but if "The World Is Too Much With Us" were to show up on his exam, he could do worse than refer to the words of "Eleanor Rigby" or "Love."

But Travis was in his trailer preparing for this morning's shoot and did not want to be disturbed. It was Paolo who accompanied Thorstad in through the wide doorway to Sound Stage Number 5. "We'll be shooting a series of short scenes today," he said, "mostly out of order."

Inside, they passed by a good deal of clutter before coming to a tall set whose open front wall exposed staircases and naked beams and three storeys of rooms empty of furniture, all in dim shadow. "We'll have forty people crammed in there later, with half a dozen cops trying to get them out." Paolo's hands conducted the rhythm of his own speech. "People will get hurt. Shots will be fired. Eventually all of them will be cleared out, except for one who refuses to leave—and two others who'd been hiding in the cellar, including your Travis."

But when Paolo perched in his canvas chair, his monitor and the chairs behind him weren't facing this exposed interior but rather the separately constructed front exterior walls of several buildings in a row, the tallest of them rising three full storeys, a handsome red-brick structure with a column of bay windows, one above the other, each with elaborate trim, though some of the windows had been replaced with sheets of plywood. Its neighbour, a squat one-storey building, also had boarded-up windows, its walls and door and even the raised letters of a sign—"*Eastern Junk Co*"—painted over with a dull green. A sidewalk, complete with parking meters, had been built along the entire base of this two-dimensional city block.

"You'll recognize Craig Conroy," Paolo said. "Great actor. Made his reputation in *Season's End*."

Thorstad had not seen anything called *Season's End* and had never heard of Craig Conroy but assumed there would be pleasure in watching a "great actor" at work. From his canvas chair behind Paolo he could see in the monitor that the camera was trained on the window directly above the front entrance to the tallest building. Of course he didn't need to watch the monitor this time. A man in faded jeans and a too-large cotton shirt stepped into this window and turned to face inward, with feet apart and a hand clasped to the frame on either side. Both the building and the man were flooded with light from the tall powerful lamps, the red bricks and blue cotton more brightly coloured than even midday sun had ever managed in Thorstad's outdoor world. The air in the tenebrous non-world outside the range of the lamps was surprisingly cool, possibly because of the bare concrete under-foot and the high ceiling and storage space above.

Voices belonging to people he couldn't see shouted for quiet and "Background!" and, after a pause, "Rolling!" Then Paolo shouted *"A-a-and . . . action!"* Immediately a uniformed policeman grabbed the man in the window from inside and tried to wrestle him back into the building. The two men struggled until the man in jeans lost his footing, teetered for a moment with arms wind-milling about, then twisted about and leapt to the sidewalk, land-ing to roll forward on a mattress.

Once the mattress had been removed, the jumper—now splayed on the sidewalk—was leapt upon by a second policeman, who pulled his arm up behind his back and levered him to his feet, then thrust him ahead so violently that he fell to the side-walk again. The policeman kicked him repeatedly before drag-ging him again to his feet.

The stunt double stepped down off the sidewalk and came back to stand by Thorstad behind the monitor while another man in identical clothing took his place, face down, with hands and feet placed where the double's had been. This must be Craig Conroy. Paolo left his chair to shift the actor's right leg a little, but the actor got to his feet, apparently with questions he needed the director to answer. The conversation was conducted with voices lowered, both men looking down at the floor.

Though the stuntman watched this conversation intently, Axel Thorstad saw this as an opportunity that might not come again. "A pleasure to watch you work," he said.

The man grunted a throaty "Thanks."

"My father did your sort of work but I never got to see him on the job."

"Yeah?" The eyebrows went up but the eyes suggested he'd heard this sort of thing before. His face, this close, was broad, and marked with acne scars. "He work here, did he?" Axel Thorstad was being patronized. Perhaps it seemed absurd, a man his age speaking of his father.

"For Centurion Pictures. A movie called *Desperation* with Derek Morris. He died from a fall."

This was probably not the sort of thing you should mention to a stuntman while he was on the job. But at least this one responded sympathetically. "A real bugger, that. I'm sorry to hear it." He smiled, and tilted his head to one side. "He couldn't have been as tall as you. A man your size'd have precious few he could double for. Good movie, was it?"

"Not so good it was worth a man's life."

"Sorry." He looked down at his own boots. "My grandfather was in the business too. Lots of bruises but no serious wounds. He's in his nineties now. What year you say this was?"

"Nineteen thirty. Your grandfather might have heard of him. Tomas Thorstad."

"Could be." The man shrugged. "The world was smaller then."

"If you see him, maybe you could ask? Your grandfather. Just in case."

The stunt double considered his boots for a moment. "I suppose I could give it a try. The name again?"

But Paolo was back behind his monitor now, ready to shoot again. "Where's Travis?"

This stab of anxiety in Thorstad's stomach must be the sort of thing parents sometimes felt. He turned, in case it was necessary to fetch the missing one from his trailer. But Travis came up from behind, wearing yesterday's costume, and passed by, grim-faced, to walk in through the door to the building and disappear, with Rosie immediately behind him.

The window struggle and the leap was shot once again. This time, when Craig Conroy had taken his place on the sidewalk and the policeman had begun to yank the actor to his feet to march him out of camera range, Travis exploded from the open doorway shouting. "Stinking bloody fascists! Bastard cops!"

This was the sort of outburst that Thorstad knew would be met with audience laughter if this were a high school play and the moment had not been prepared for. Here, he supposed the job of preparing for this moment would belong to an editor, who had yet to cut and rearrange things in order to fit this moment into a larger context.

Rosie had appeared in the doorway as well. Apparently the old woman's granddaughter had also been hiding in the cellar. Travis went down on one knee with a hand to the sidewalk and raised a finger smeared with red liquid. "They'll kill him this time," he said, and showed the bloodied finger to Rosie, who was obviously unimpressed. When Travis had got to his feet he shouted, "You told me he wouldn't be one of them. You told me he would, uh . . ." He threw up both hands. "Sorry. I'll try it again."

"You told me he'd be out of town," the woman with the clip-board read.

The back of Thorstad's neck was hot. He had no idea if what he was witnessing was a common event, every actor's occasional bad moment, or if this was a sign of something going wrong. Ridiculously, he found himself thinking, *Take a minute to breathe, then try to relax. We're pulling for you.* Of course he didn't know if anyone was "pulling" for Travis. This wasn't a swim meet, with parents shouting encouragement from the stands.

Travis went down on his knee and again found blood on his finger and again stood up, apparently to chastise Rosie about something, but got only a little further into his speech than he had the first time. It may have been a long speech, or it may have had some awkward construction to stumble over. It may have been a last-minute addition. No one had given Thorstad a copy of today's script.

Paolo stood up from behind his monitor and drifted in for a private conference. Everyone turned away and tried to look as though merely wondering what might be happening on the concrete floor behind them. Those who raised their eyes, Thorstad noticed, were careful not to look at the others. Whatever Travis was hearing from Paolo was not praise. The girl hung on the door frame and watched as though class clowns were spoiling her opportunity to shine. The handsome Reynolds Green, who must have been standing back in the shadows, moved up closer now to watch, or perhaps to be seen.

Since it was Travis in trouble, and since he had certainly glanced in Thorstad's direction before walking away from the set, his instinct was to go after him. But he knew this would be a serious blunder. Paolo followed with his head low, one hand to his mouth, perhaps trying to think of something that might help. Evans had appeared from somewhere as well, and moved up to confer with Paolo for a moment, before letting him go after Travis and out of sight behind a stack of furniture.

Perhaps anticipating Thorstad's impulse to interfere, Evans was suddenly beside him with reassurance. "He just needs to remember he's not in a high school musical. Let's get you a coffee." He lowered his voice to add, "Maybe this is the result of trying to serve two masters." Then, to the crew member with the tool belt at his hip he said, "Show Mr. Thorstad to the canteen?"

The crew member almost certainly understood that he was to make sure the old guy was not only directed to the coffee but prevented from coming back. This was not the first time

Thorstad had noticed that more than forty years in charge of a classroom was inadequate training for being confined to the sidelines in other people's worlds. There was nothing he could do but accept the coffee, served from the back of a truck, and stand outside in the lane to drink it. The man with the tool belt had gone back inside but no doubt would keep an eye on the door.

Reason enough to wonder why he was here! Did he need to remind himself of the alternatives? He had been trying to save his life. He had not become just another of the misanthropic recluses down the various trails through the woods. There'd been the Birney poem to alert him, and the mad old fellow with the axe. And there'd been Lisa Svetic at the other end of his shotgun barrel. He had chosen this—to return to the world, to be a teacher again, to prepare Travis Montana for his exams.

"This is disappointing, my darling, to think that the great servant of love would be exiled on the pavement while his student is so obviously in trouble, especially since I know you have never been content to let anyone down, mainly because you seemed to feel responsible for the welfare of everyone who came near you, a trait that nearly drove you crazy at times, so that I constantly felt there must be something I could do to convince you that the whole world did not rest on your shoulders every minute . . . though of course this may be one situation where you are justified in feeling responsible, since the boy is far from his family with no one to protect him from the bullies who would pull him this way and that for their own purposes, getting away with it simply because they know how to make their own goals seem identical to his—all of which is to say, my beloved, that you have got yourself into a situation where you are in danger of failing yourself as well as everyone else."

It was Travis's "help me even though I can't be helped" look he had recognized. He'd seen it countless times in students. But here, cast out from the sound stage—banned from the false derelict buildings, the lair of the homeless, the scene of police harassment—it wasn't only Travis he found himself thinking of, or even Evans's casual accusation. Now that he had been left on the pavement with a bitter cup of coffee in his hand, he was thinking too of the people he'd seen sleeping under bushes and down along the water's edge. He was thinking of Angus Walker.

Help me even though I won't accept your help.

That day at the drop-in centre was not the first time Walker had reappeared in his life. Many students returned to the high school, some with problems to share, others with accomplishments to report. A knock at the staff-room door—one more student you hadn't seen for years had come back to say hello.

This was probably early June, the summer break just a few weeks away. Walker stood in the hall, his arms too long for his jacket. He'd come to tell his former English teacher that he'd graduated from university with a degree in education, but not, it turned out, in order to be congratulated. Walker—a young man now—was clearly upset. "Can I talk to you, sir? In private?"

It seemed that he had not only graduated but had been hired by a school board for September and was terrified at the prospect of facing a class of his own. That a new teacher was terrified seemed natural enough to Axel Thorstad, but this was the first time anyone had come back to confess it. Thorstad put a hand on Angus's elbow and walked him down the hallway to his classroom, where he asked the chess club to leave. If he'd been a university professor or a department store manager he'd have had an office for conducting private conversations, but as a high school teacher he'd had only his classroom with its dusty chalkboards and pale green plywood walls. When Thorstad wasn't teaching in it, the room belonged to the chess club on Mondays, the newspaper club on Tuesdays, the future teachers club on Wednesdays, the comic book club on Thursdays, and the grad planning group on Fridays. Chess club members had grumbled when they were asked to leave, but agreed to stand outside the door until they could return to their games. "Can we trust you not to touch?"

"You made it look so easy," Angus said. He sat on the slanted top of a front desk while Thorstad perched on a corner of his own. "All I had to do, I thought, was to act as enthusiastic about my subject as a ten-year-old explaining the features of his new bicycle. All I had to do was act as though I loved the students like a father, counselled them like an older brother, and disciplined them like a disappointed mother. You see, I paid attention. I watched you—how you did it."

Thorstad tried not to betray his shock. "You thought I was putting on an act?"

Angus was preoccupied with what he'd planned. "But it wasn't so easy after all. I tried hard through five years of university— weekly practice sessions in someone else's class. I was given barely passing grades but was encouraged to try harder. So I did. Every year." For his final "long practicum," however, the sponsoring teacher had given him a failing grade. "To save me from a barely-good-enough future, she said. She said that barely good enough may be fine for some jobs but isn't good enough for a teacher. But the university ignored her grade and I graduated with a degree that's useless for anything else. What could I do but apply for a job, hoping I wouldn't get one?"

Now he had the job and didn't know how he could face it.

How had Axel Thorstad responded to this? He could not remember now if he had given advice. To put the five years of education down to experience and start again with another career in mind? To speak to a lawyer about suing the Faculty of Education for misleading encouragement? He could hardly write out a script for Angus to memorize in order to survive his first week.

There may have been nothing he could say, beyond expressing the hope that an experienced colleague next door would take him under his wing, that a beauty down the hall would inspire him with her eccentric example, that the failure of another teacher on staff might prove the job was impossible if you didn't respect and truly care about the students you were supposed to serve.

There was no way of knowing, now, what advice he'd given then. He'd probably suggested that Angus would learn how to teach by teaching, like everyone else. Whatever he'd said, their recent encounter at the homeless shelter suggested it hadn't been enough.

Should he feel guilt for being a model that someone else believed could be duplicated with sheer willpower? Angus Walker had arrived in his classroom when Thorstad had had two decades of experience behind him, but this was probably not enough to know how to save the life of a frightened young man who'd been sadly misled. Perhaps Walker in his first year had had no Oonagh Farrell down the hall or Topolski next door to help him get started, no Barry Foster as a cautionary tale. Now, according to the dishwasher at the drop-in centre, Angus Walker had a reputation for making life hell for anyone who tried to help him.

One Angus was enough to have on your conscience—though of course there could be others he didn't know about. He supposed he'd never thought of this before. He wished he hadn't thought of it now. Whatever else might happen while he was here in Los Angeles, he could not allow himself to add another failure to the list.

16

The silver-blue convertible was waiting for him outside the gate but Oonagh was not alone in it. When Thorstad approached, a young man with sun-bleached hair and a toothy smile leapt out and held the door open for him. "Corbin is off to beg and plead with his agent today," Oonagh said. Corbin blew a kiss to Oonagh and lightly squeezed Thorstad's elbow, then turned on his heel to set off briskly up the sidewalk.

"I didn't keep you waiting?" Thorstad closed his door and buckled his seat belt. "Our courier friend cornered me just now, wanting to know if there were any books about hurricanes in my bag!"

Oonagh looked up to the pale blank sky. "He's expecting a *hurricane?*"

"He's been hearing news from home. New Orleans." It was necessary to sit at an angle in order to avoid propping his knees against the dashboard. "Crime everywhere, orphan babies playing in mud, his brother's house still without a roof. He wants to understand what made this mess."

She dropped her forehead to the top of the steering wheel. "And he thought your books would help?"

Thorstad admitted he'd had to disappoint. "A geography textbook won't explain what happened to his family. I suggested he visit a library, dig up newspapers and newsmagazines. He agreed, but still intends to corner me in his coffee breaks."

She recovered from her mock despair and placed the palm of her hand against his cheek. Involuntarily he caught the hand in his and kissed a fingertip. "I'm a lucky man today."

She laughed, and took back her hand, and steered them too quickly out into the impatient city traffic. "I should have guessed you'd still be teaching. I'd be in a loony bin by now if I hadn't quit."

"But you were a brilliant teacher." The students had loved her—adored her perhaps. Girls imitated, boys were beguiled. Those colleagues who weren't afraid of her were enchanted. He was himself bewitched—and hadn't, it seemed, entirely recovered. The long line of her thigh was enough to remind him of this. And her pale green eyes.

She laughed, and shifted into the left lane to pass a dawdling Buick. "I was a good entertainer, which may look like good teaching but isn't quite. I needed a different sort of audience, and grew tired of writing my own scripts—lesson plans! Are teachers still forced to make *lesson plans*?" Now, abruptly, they were in the right lane again, too close behind a black Volvo. "I thought we'd visit the Huntington Library after lunch." She turned onto another, narrower, but just as busy street. "If you're still a little loopy about English Literature, that is. The Ellesmere manuscript is there behind glass."

He should have welcomed the prospect of seeing the Chaucer manuscript, but he suspected that any pleasure in it would be undermined by his sense of being in the wrong place. He was beginning to feel it already. The buzz of anticipation in his limbs did not override this. Travis was scheduled to be working all afternoon, but things could change—a scene could be postponed. He imagined Rosie talking him into an afternoon of kayaking, experimenting with cocaine. He saw the kayak overturn and Travis disappear. How did parents stay sane?

Wind stirred up his hair. Not all convertibles were made for people his height. Topolski had had a convertible, he remembered—smaller than this. A playboy's sort of exotic car. Of course this Mercedes could belong to both Oonagh and Topolski if Topolski was still in the picture. But if Topolski was still in the picture, why she hadn't told him yesterday?

Her house was a white two-storey flat-roofed box in Venice Beach, not six feet from a neighbouring house on either side and apparently no wider than the one-car garage they drove into. He was finding it a little hard to breathe—anxiety or hope, he wasn't sure which. An unfamiliar shakiness had invaded. He followed her down a walkway on unsteady legs and in through a side door partially obscured by a cluster of tall bamboo. Inside, they were in an all-purpose room—to one side a small kitchen with white walls and wood-panel cupboards, to the other a lounge area that looked out through a wall of glass upon a small herb garden and a narrow canal with a red canoe roped to the concrete wall.

"No gondolas," Oonagh said. She tossed her wide-brimmed hat onto a chair and went behind the counter that divided the room. "It's small, but it's mine. I have an old farmhouse outside Toronto where I still do the occasional bit of stage work. *Another Life* is what you might call my pension." She held up a tall amber bottle. "Too early?"

"A coffee maybe."

"Coffee later. I need to check my messages. I'm waiting for something."

She carried her half-filled glass towards an open doorway but paused when a young man with wet hair and a freshly scrubbed look to his handsome face came bouncing happily down the narrow staircase from above. "You're up already?" she called, obviously sarcastic. "It's only noon!" When he'd reached the bottom of the stairs, she turned back to introduce him. "Skyler Shreve." He wore baggy surfer shorts and a bright red muscle shirt, and flip-flops on his large hairy feet. "He's camping here till he finds a place of his own."

"Just another bloody actor," the young man said, tilting his head apologetically. "Currently looking for work."

"Fresh from the Alberta oil patch," Oonagh called from another room. "God help us all!"

"I'm on my way!" shouted Skyler Shreve.

Through the glass wall Thorstad watched him set off alongside the canal, perhaps, like the other young man, to beg and plead with his agent.

She hadn't tidied up for company. Books lay open on the floor. Blouses and slacks had been draped over the counter stools. Unwashed dishes were stacked beside the sink. Thorstad could have predicted this—she had never had the time or patience for housework.

But no man's shoes had been kicked off inside the door. No shirts hung from a doorknob. Obviously Skyler Shreve was tidier than Oonagh, and Topolski was either meticulous about his own belongings still or did not share this house.

"So there really are canals in Venice Beach," he said, when Oonagh returned to the room. He'd never thought of this before. "You may have noticed how often men in novels go off to Venice and die. Professor Aschenbach was only one of many. In one, an elderly professor returns to his childhood home in Venice and gradually turns back into a wooden puppet—guess who!" It seemed he had got himself into something he didn't know how to get out of. He was more nervous than he'd anticipated. "Even Turgenev. I remember saying 'Oh no!' out loud when this fellow travelling south from Russia makes a sudden detour to visit Venice. He'd coughed—just once—early in the novel, and no one ever coughs in a novel unless . . . Long before he sees the Rialto Bridge you know the poor man's doomed."

Oonagh was barely suppressing her laughter. "If you're trying to tell me you're afraid of my cooking, relax. I've made a reservation—walking distance from here." She placed her emptied glass on the counter.

He couldn't seem to stop what he'd started. "It was a woman in the Henry James. A man, I think, in the Unsworth. I don't *think* anyone died in the McEwan but I seem to remember someone going crazy."

Now, grinning widely, she stepped close and gently took hold of his shirt front with both hands. "But my darling Axel, this is Venice *California* where no one ever dies. Not even if they cough! They find a yoga teacher and live forever." She stepped back. "There!" She'd undone his top shirt button. "Now we can breathe!"

She may have had little interest in housework but she had always showed interest in how others dressed. She dressed, herself, in clothes that were carefully chosen, flattering to her figure, immaculately clean and pressed. Today she'd draped a dark blue filmy scarf over her shoulders, its patterned ends lying down the front of a light blue linen top. Blue pointed shoes peeked out from below her white slacks. She had worn expensive shoes even then, had owned too many. They had teased her about this— would she go without food in order to spend her salary on shoes? He could imagine, now, that her closet overflowed with them.

A collection of vaguely human carvings had been arranged along a shelf inside the wall of glass. They were each about six inches tall, their outlines appearing to follow the natural grain of the wood, so that rather than attempting to imitate some standard human form they appeared to be solid representations of human attitudes. Horror, delight, and the shrinking violet were easily recognized. Hilarity as well, and despair.

"My family," she said, selecting one small figure to stand in the palm of her hand. "All mute." She laughed. "They don't yell at me like the directors when my acting stinks. Or write nasty things in reviews. Unlike the men in my life, they don't nag at me to retire and come live in South Dakota, or northern Quebec. And unlike my widowed sister, they don't remind me that I might have had children instead of making a public spectacle of myself."

After replacing the figure, she took up a multicoloured bag off a chair and looped it over her shoulder. "Now! Shall we eat?"

She led him out across her small patch of greenery and onto the canal-side walkway, which they followed past several small houses, some of them identical to hers, with windows through which you could see someone moving vaguely in the shadows. Thorstad reduced the length of his stride to match hers, conscious of her hip brushing lightly against him. He was again aware of the unnamed scent she must have worn all her life. Half a century had passed since they had walked together, or touched. His body hadn't forgotten. His body's instincts would have him run a hand lightly down her bare arm, if he dared. He'd known the feel of it once. He knew the feel of it even now, in his nerve ends. That he had loved this woman fiercely once was not an imagined thing, though he'd sometimes feared it might be. She had done her best, for his sake, to pretend she hadn't noticed.

Sooner or later the question had to be asked. He asked it now, while they weren't facing one another. "Is there a reason we haven't really talked about Topolski?"

"We haven't talked about what's-his-name either—Barry Foster. Did someone tell me once the man was in jail?"

"He wouldn't be in jail after all this time, surely—not for cooking the company books."

"What a grouch!" She paused to breathe in the scent of a scarlet hibiscus alongside the path. "Think what damage he could have done if he'd stayed!"

Eventually they came out from between two buildings onto the broad walkway bordering a pale expanse of sand that stretched to the sea and off in either direction along the city's edge. Tall palms grew up from both sand and grass like long-handled feather dusters, some of whose trunks had been decorated with blue and red graffiti. The lower fronds of the closer palms hung grey and ragged as ostrich tails, possibly dead.

"Sometimes you'd see a fellow juggling three running chainsaws down here," Oonagh said, "while standing in a ring of fire."

"Much as I felt at the beginning of every September."

"Your whole career?" She turned abruptly to him, obviously surprised. A stage actress should have understood first-day jitters. "You proved yourself a fine chainsaw juggler in your very first month—that was my impression."

"It took most of September every year to get it back. I feel a little like that even now. Dealing with Elliot Evans is much like facing a class of future mechanics who resent the fact they're forced to read *Elegy in a Country Churchyard*."

Oonagh stepped aside to avoid colliding with a cyclist in a head-down hurry.

To Thorstad, this walkway appeared to be an orderly sort of flea market, with painters sitting before their easels and craftspeople displaying their wares on a blanket. They passed a row of open-faced shops selling postcards and T-shirts, purses and belts and mugs. Rows of shoulder bags hung from hooks. Most of the tourists or shoppers wore flip-flops on their feet, with shorts and skimpy tops, or in the case of some young men no top at all. Elaborate tattoos crawled up muscular arms.

"Were we ever that young?" Oonagh said. She'd stopped to watch several tanned youths involved in a game of volleyball. Young males waiting for the ball to come their way explored their own bare chests with the palm of one hand. "We played our own games on a sandy beach, so I guess we must have been."

She, too, remembered. Or remembered what she called "games." Certainly they'd been two young people at play, though Axel Thorstad hadn't thought at the time that they were merely playing games.

"Yvonne De Carlo was Miss Venice Beach," she said. "Did you know that? In 1938, while you and I were in—what?—Grade Two? You remember Yvonne De Carlo?"

"I do. I also remember a Yvonne De Carlo look-alike flouncing down Hollywood Boulevard."

"Oh Lord! Yes!"

Beyond the volleyball players and the outdoor cafés and children's playground the grass was available to the less energetic. Some lay on blankets to take in the sun while others chatted over a picnic lunch. A group that might have been a high school class sat discussing something in a remarkably low-key manner. At the foot of a palm tree a young woman in a straw hat and pale green dress sat with her knees pulled up to support the book she was reading.

"Somewhere along here is where my mother was given the news. While she was reading a library copy of *David Copperfield*. You may remember knowing this."

He supposed it was ridiculous for a seventy-seven-year-old man to be shaken by a surprise reminder of his mother as a young woman. Well, the world must think so anyway, but it felt natural enough to him. Your mother remained your mother, though she had long ago gone from your sight, and your father remained the man who leapt from the building as recently as yesterday. Sometimes what they called the "distant past" seemed as close behind you as your heels.

Oonagh placed a hand on his arm. "You seemed to think your father's accident was the most important thing about you. Surely you've left all that behind by now."

No doubt she could see that he hadn't. "Does anyone know where Centurion Pictures used to be?"

"Well, we found it once, didn't we? Long ago." She started walking again. "We could look again, I suppose, if it's important."

Three young men in skimpy swimsuits were suddenly upon them, throwing their arms around Oonagh. This was a noisy reunion—with male shrieks and explosions of laughter and much dancing about. No one seemed to listen to anyone else. The pleasure in this reunion seemed an end in itself. Oonagh stood unmoving, apparently accustomed to this, her smile wide and steady and patient.

Then, as suddenly as they'd appeared, they rushed off, the one in the middle holding a hand on either side, their flip-flops slapping the pavement. Oonagh was left behind to shake her head and smooth back her hair. "So many boys without mothers." She took hold of his hand and led him down a narrow alley between two buildings painted aquamarine. "Half the young hopefuls in L.A. have camped in my little house." She seemed to find this amusing. "Mother Courage or Mother McCree, I'm not sure which."

The air inside Roberto's smelled powerfully of seafood, though all the windows were open—were, in fact, without glass. Inside a tank of bubbling water several lobsters crept across the false sea floor, perhaps hoping for a tunnel that would lead to a safer ocean. The nearest of them might have been appealing to Axel Thorstad for help. A slight young man with dark eyes and a broad head of black hair turned away from the table he'd been serving and threw his arms out wide to welcome Oonagh with a grand embrace. He shook hands with Miss Farrell's "very much welcome guest."

"A friend of my youth," Oonagh said. "The amazing thing is that neither of us has aged a day." Her laughter rumbled just beneath her words.

Roberto smiled, and dipped a shallow bow. "But of course." He led them to a small table in the back corner. Some Spanish was exchanged, haltingly on Oonagh's part. Elena's widower understood little. Apparently Roberto's tooth was painfully *roto*. He pulled down his bottom lip to display. *"Debo ver un dentista."*

Once Roberto had received enough sympathy from Miss Farrell, as well as the name of a good dentist, he hurried away to disappear behind a beaded curtain.

Oonagh had taken the liberty to order ahead. "I hope you still like seafood. He has created his own Mexican seafood thing—a sort of crepe." She removed a handful of brochures from her bag. "The Huntington."

She had put a bookmark on the page describing the Ellesmere manuscript, which would be, he saw, displayed in the first glass tower inside the exhibition hall, setting off a tremorous thrill in the pit of his stomach. The opened-out first pages of the illuminated *Canterbury Tales* were presented here in a photograph, a flowering vine in blues and reds down the left side and across the bottom to serve as perch for a tiny winged dragon.

Apparently it was also possible to see a draft of the Magna Carta, the manuscript of *Piers Plowman* from the fifteenth century, and a first edition of Dante's *Divina Commedia*. "A first edition of *Pilgrim's Progress*. The first edition of *Gulliver's Travels*. The whole of my English Literature course has been down here all along. You could have invited me years ago. Thirty-five students sleeping on your floor!"

Why hadn't he known about the Huntington during that long-ago Christmas holiday? He might have organized a field trip. School bands earned money to take themselves to Seattle. He had taken students to a performance of *Death of a Salesman* in Vancouver but he hadn't known what was available down here.

Roberto came out from behind the beaded curtain to set down two glasses and a carafe of white wine before rushing off to welcome new customers at the door. Thorstad seized the opportunity to ask again about the invisible Andrzej Topolski. "If I knew where Topolski could be found I'd suggest he come to the Huntington with us."

"He would do his best to spoil it for you." She watched him pour wine for them both. "If you're asking where he *is* I can tell you. I know where he is because I write the cheques that keep him there." She tasted the wine and nodded. Her voice dropped to a whispery growl. "He suffered a series of small strokes. Now he's in an Assisted-Living Home—and not especially happy about it."

Thorstad shuddered. *Assisted Living.* Two simple words, but terrifying when put together. "Poor man! Sometimes I have this awful feeling that somewhere one of those places has an empty room with my name on it."

She laughed. "Not this place, I promise you! Only corporate crooks and celebrities can afford it. There won't be a single high school teacher there, unless there's a charity wing I don't know about."

When he asked if Topolski had inherited his promised duchy, she rolled her eyes. "The family mansion was a pile of rubble and the land beneath it radioactive swamp. But a wealthy brother died in France with no heirs, and darling Andrzej came into most of his fortune. Of course he used the money to make more money, then lost it all, several times." She paused, and looked out the nearest window at the deserted alley. "We divorced years ago, Thorstad. Axel." She'd dropped the tale-telling tone from her voice. This was something more intimate. "Obviously you don't read the tabloids, or didn't at the time. It was a disastrous marriage. Exciting, I suppose, if you think violent battles are fun!" She spoke to her glass. "After a while we gave up. Lived apart for years. Not long ago he showed up out of the blue, in terrible shape—financially, physically, the works."

Thorstad had always assumed the marriage had been a happy one, that he'd heard nothing about it simply because she'd kept Topolski out of the magazines. And Elena had not kept in touch with her cousin, who had been, it turned out, only a very distant relative, his wedding simply her excuse for a trip to North America. He'd seen Oonagh and Topolski as the perfect couple from the moment he acknowledged the failure of his own hopes—the extravagant beauty and the sophisticated older man from Europe and Montreal. Otherwise . . . well, otherwise. He did not want to think of otherwise.

"When he lost most of it in some stupid business scheme, he came back to Laguna Beach to live with his sister, but his sister died and left him her house. He suffered a series of strokes soon afterwards." She paused to examine her glass for a moment. "I visit him now and then, though I'm not sure he's pleased to see me. He seems to be more irritable by the time I leave than when I arrived." Again a rumble of laughter. "Which may explain the marriage." She raised her eyes to his. "The past few years I've been with a kind and patient architect outside of Toronto who keeps my feet firmly on the ground."

Had she decided he was anxious lest she might assume he'd come with higher hopes? Which perhaps he had, he wasn't sure. He was relieved that at least he hadn't allowed his imagination to initiate some foolish action. And yet he experienced something like indignation as well. Why had she felt it necessary to set his mind at ease? Why had she assumed he didn't want to be thought of as a man with a man's hopes? Did she think he had gone beyond such things?

Well, he supposed Oonagh Farrell had remained a certain boy-man's enduring fantasy, surviving somehow in a corner of his soul, even throughout his happy marriage. Oonagh was simply being kind to what remained of that young fellow. Maybe it wasn't easy for a well-known actress to be simply a friend to a man of any age.

Roberto burst out through the beaded curtain with a large red plate in either mittened hand. "*Caliente!*" he warned. He placed a plate before each of them and stood back, ready to accept their praise. "For the fabulous Miss Farrell and her guest."

The fabulous Miss Farrell breathed in the aroma. "Bravo, *señor!*"

"So," she said, once Roberto had turned to other customers and they had tasted the seafood dish, which was indeed very *caliente*, "you told me the television world has conspired to make sure you can't do your job. The first question that has to be answered is: What difference does it make if one more adolescent fails a few exams?"

Thorstad did not believe this deserved an answer. Instead, he explained that things had got even worse. "Now he's having trouble on the set. This morning I had to stand by while he kept forgetting his lines. If it happens again I'll be tempted to step in and help!"

She did not disguise her horror. "I wouldn't advise it—unless you want to be banned from the studio altogether!"

He knew this already, of course. He'd been a director, once, himself. "Evans says that Travis needs to remember he's not in a high school musical. That sounds pretty damning to me."

"It does indeed!" She briefly frowned, but closed her eyes to enjoy the Mexican seafood crepe.

Of course she could help him with this if she were willing. Instead of dwelling on his own questionable fantasy, he could act his age on Travis's behalf and simply *ask*. He had never been shy about soliciting aid from outside the classroom. If you were teaching *The Mayor of Casterbridge* you naturally invited in a former mayor of Dorchester if a former mayor of Dorchester were living two blocks from the school. Unlike Henshaw, he may not have sold his wife but he could talk about the town and other landmarks mentioned in the novel.

"If it weren't impertinent, I'd wonder if you could help me with this."

She looked up from her lunch, head tilted a little. Perhaps suspicious.

"I mean. Imagine how happy he'd be if you were to give him a few tips. Things you've learned. Advice from an experienced actor—a star?"

He saw how bold this was, and presumptuous—as though she were still that colleague down the hall. "I meant only if you're inclined, and have the time."

Eventually she put down her fork and reached across the table to lay a hand upon his. Something had been decided. Her hand remained on his while she looked inward. "We can't let this go on." She appeared to be a little amused by the situation, but he could think only of how familiar that hand was, the long fingers, her mother's sapphire ring, her lovely female skin. "I'll tell you what—we'll spirit your lad away. A picnic somewhere?"

Naturally he was pleased, but then immediately, alarmed. This could be a serious risk. "Only when he isn't needed at the studio. Otherwise Evans would have a fit."

"Evans won't object if this old warhorse gives his youngster some hard-won acting-for-television tips. But we'll drag him off to somewhere remote, just to be safe!" She laughed, perhaps foreseeing an adventure. "If the boy isn't grateful we'll tie him up and leave him to be eaten by the ants." She sat back, apparently satisfied, and looked at Thorstad as though to suggest they could be proud of themselves for this. "Now! Eat up. I've changed my mind about the Huntington. Today we'll have our dessert and coffee with you-know-who."

This time she drove in what he sensed was a southeasterly direction. For a while they passed through areas of drab apartment buildings and small garishly decorated shops until the world opened up on their right and they were following the coastline. Sunlight glittered off lazy waves.

"Ours was surely the worst marriage ever endured by two humans living on this planet!" She chuckled—wickedly, he thought. "While you, I've heard, have the perfect union. Topolski told me—in one of those rare moments when we were not only in the same room and sober but actually speaking. I don't know how he knew. He was *jealous*! He regretted not marrying her himself. Missed his chance. Or rather, he'd forgotten she existed until it was too late—our heads were so distracted by that stupid play!"

"Well, you couldn't have known this—Elena died some time ago."

"Oh my dear, I'm so sorry." She touched fingers to his arm. "I'm so bloody thick, I didn't think to ask."

Eventually they were travelling between the open beach and a high chain-link fence. A passenger jet rose up from somewhere and crossed over them so low that Thorstad felt he might have reached up and touched its broad white belly. He held on to his armrest, for fear of being sucked up after it.

Rows of palm trees lined streets of cracked and buckled pavement, but there were no houses, only broken concrete foundations and weeds. "The site of a disaster?"

"It is," Oonagh said. "All this was a beach community once, condemned and bought up for airport expansion. People were driven out—scattered. It's still a hot issue, after years." She turned inland now. "I nearly miss this damn turn-off every time. Jets rattle my brains. We'll take the 401."

He might be sorry later but he had to ask. "You thought *Returning to Troy* was stupid?"

"Well! It wasn't Eugene O'Neill, was it? Or Tennessee Williams." She chuckled, perhaps at some private memory. "Of course Tennessee would have scared us half to death back then."

"Audiences liked it!" He sounded, he knew, annoyed—but didn't mind. "I'd even imagined, once, gathering us together one day to re-mount it." He added, quickly: "For fun."

"With the original cast?" She threw up her hands. "Lord!" But then sobered. Frowned. "Surely most of the cast—the old ones—must be dead!"

He hadn't thought of this. Well, he supposed he'd never been completely serious about it. "We'd have to use students for the old people this time, and keep the principal roles for ourselves. For you and Topolski. And Foster if we could find him."

She was showing all her teeth again, her voice gone down a staircase to speak through gravel. "You'd be sued by the author, or his heirs." She honked her horn at a slowpoke, who raised a middle finger in response. "Topolski was terrible—wasn't he? Well, he did a decent-enough job once you'd switched him and

Foster. Not that he was especially good even then, but he was a hell of a lot better than he was as the husband. I should have taken note! Did you know what you were doing when you made the men exchange their roles?"

"I knew what I was doing, but I didn't know what it might lead to. For us all."

"You should never have read that damn *Troilus* thing. Chaucer isn't *safe*! At least he isn't safe for you."

Eventually they joined a freeway, heading south. She increased their speed, and changed lanes, causing horns to blare. Because of the wind in their faces, they gave up attempts at speech. At any rate, Thorstad did not want to distract her. He concentrated on watching the world fly by and hoped to be still alive when they reached their destination.

When she swung onto an off-lane at last, and onto a narrower road heading downhill to the west, he thought this would be the end of their private Grand Prix. But she turned off this road too, and the next one as well without slowing much, making a series of confusing moves to both left and right, and then raced up a steep hill and in through an archway entrance to what he assumed was their destination at last, both of them still alive.

Topolski's new home had the pillars and fountains and elaborate gardens of a major destination resort pictured in travel magazines. There seemed to be several wings, four storeys high. On each floor, rows of tall French doors opened onto cantilevered balconies with wrought-iron railings. Brilliant bougainvillea crawled up pillars and draped itself off shutters. In the parking lot, rows of too-large luxury sedans from a much earlier time sat radiating heat from the blazing sun—brought here, perhaps like family portraits and favourite chairs, by those who could not bear to part with them.

He was sure there would be no escaping this place without making several gaffes—leaving dirt from your shoes on a carpet, or making a remark that caused someone to cry. And of course somewhere in his brain was the suspicion he might not be allowed to leave at all.

They were told at the front desk that Topolski had been wheeled down to the dining room for lunch. "He'll have been fed by now, but there's entertainment." When Oonagh said, "Oh dear," the receptionist explained, "It's only music. A small local trio. You can ignore it if you talk softly. No one will mind."

Only music! Elena would have minded. The slightest disturbance would have resulted in an angry glare. If the glare was not enough to put a stop to the talking, however soft, she would crash down a chord and walk out.

"What can we expect from our hero today?"

The receptionist rolled her eyes. "He hasn't bitten anyone, I can say that much. He ate a little breakfast but complained about it. And Cathy said he threatened to sabotage the music if he didn't like what they played. He pinches her, you know."

The view from the large windows here, Thorstad noticed, was not unlike the wide expanse of Pacific seen from the Evans house, except for its division into equal segments by a row of eucalyptus trunks along the parking-lot border. A multipanelled image.

The view was much the same from the dining room, where the "small local trio" was situated in the farthest corner, perhaps to keep at a safe distance from those who hadn't yet finished their lunch. Piano, violin, and cello. The young musicians, perhaps still in their teens, were frowning their way through something that swelled and fell back and swelled again. Schubert. The adagio from the Piano Trio in E flat was at least recognizable.

What seemed like an acre of elaborately patterned carpet lay between the musicians and the new arrivals, with any number of wheelchairs pushed up to several round tables across the distance. Some diners had apparently gone to sleep after their lunch. Others nodded with open eyes. One or two were still patiently being fed by young women and men in uniform. These were the wealthy *senior-seniors* he'd imagined Audrey Montana sending off in a cruise ship to roam the oceans forever, leaving more property free for developers.

Off to one side a man sat at a table all his own, scowling stiffly into space. Perhaps he was preparing a critique of the music, which was surely more ponderous than the composer intended. Perhaps he wasn't welcome at the other tables.

Of course this was the "Polish Prince." The thin dark line of moustache was unchanged. Surely he must dye it, or have it dyed. His once-black hair had thinned out and faded and lost its shine. The blue eyes were rimmed with an unhealthy red, as though he had been reading far too long without glasses or neglecting to eat something important to his diet. His greeting, when he saw them, was an indifferent on-off smile. They might have been two workers from Maintenance come to oil his wheel bearings.

Thorstad turned away for a moment, to let a wave of dizziness pass. Perhaps Oonagh had grown used to this, and hadn't thought to warn him properly. Here was the very thing he'd dreaded, the *maestro*'s threatened "old-folks home" with *senior-seniors* breathing laboriously in their wheeled prisons. His own breathing had quickened, his chest tightening almost painfully, as though to crush his lungs. "Oh my," he said, though he hadn't intended to say it aloud. He fought an urge to bolt. He couldn't bolt. Oonagh would not forgive the cowardice. This *was* their friend Topolski, after all.

"What . . . doing here?" Topolski sounded annoyed, as though Oonagh had only just left and was not expected back for several weeks. Or perhaps he was annoyed at the extreme effort it took just to form those words.

"What kind of question is that?" She affected a cheerful tone she probably did not feel. She took possession of his table by flopping her large bag upon it and pulling out a chair for herself. "I'm here to let an old friend get a look at you. And you at him. We've come to have our dessert!"

Thorstad took the chair across from Topolski, though he wished with all his heart that he hadn't come. Topolski's expression suggested he felt the same. A young woman wearing a pale blue cotton top like Alvin White's placed a bowl of pudding before each of them. Cooked berries of some kind, and cake, with a dab of whipped cream. They were given spoons and sturdy mugs of coffee.

Topolski looked on this activity with suspicion but seemed to settle on Thorstad as the one who deserved his scowl. "Whozz-iss?"

"Think, my darling. Think! Axel Thorstad? High school teacher? Married your cousin?"

The old man who was just barely Topolski continued to stare at Thorstad as though he suspected an imposter. "What'zee . . . want?"

Apparently Oonagh had already exhausted her patience. "Oh, for Christ sake, Top. What does he want? He wants to see you tap dance! He wants us to remount *Returning to Troy*! What do you think he wants? He came to say hello." She scooped up a spoonful of dessert and tried to tempt the grim old mouth to open, but Topolski turned his face away, his lips clamped tight and thin.

Thorstad knew he should not have been surprised, but it was a shock now, as it had always been, to see what time had done to people you'd once known as young and strong and handsome. Somehow it was even worse that this victim of time had been that smartly dressed, sophisticated descendant of aristocrats. His hero and "big brother" from his first day in the classroom was now an ancient creature whose handsome face had been twisted into the permanent shape of complaint. His very ordinary striped shirt and wool pants and old-man's cardigan had been pulled on without making sure they were tidy. This was once the snappy dresser who had whisked them away from school every Friday afternoon in his little Triumph and driven them down to their table in the nearest pub. Though he'd arrived on the Coast only recently himself, he'd introduced Axel Thorstad to the roads and lakes and beaches of his own backyard.

Now he was a prisoner in this obviously safe, clean, uncluttered, orderly environment—as removed from the world as Mrs. Montana's imagined resident cruise ship. No turmoil or frenzy could survive here. You could see that someone had barred the gates against every form of anarchy.

The musical trio had reached a difficult part, perhaps a phrase they hadn't sufficiently practised. The pianist—a young woman with blue-and-magenta hair—appeared to be more than a little worried. Perhaps she foresaw getting lost or falling apart before they'd reached an end. The cellist was a short, rather pudgy lad who had not been convinced to keep his elbows high and his feet flat on the floor. His slashing glances around the room appeared to blame the dozing audience for his own shortcomings. Thorstad wondered if Audrey Montana had remembered to have his strings replaced.

"Well," Topolski said, perhaps recognizing in Thorstad something of a former version, "he . . . can take us . . . back . . . to that, pulp, pulp town."

Before Thorstad could explain that he'd been driven through the town just recently, had even passed by the school where the three of them had taught, Topolski laughed. "We'll . . . put on . . . p-play? That's . . . you're here, for?"

"What are you talking about?" Oonagh said. "It was a joke! Most of the cast are dead! Now we're old ourselves. Have you forgotten?"

She got up and walked away a few feet and stood with her arms folded to observe the trio, who had stopped to consult one another before going on. Going on, it turned out, meant starting a few bars back and taking another run at the passage that had resisted them.

"Well!" Oonagh said. "I'll leave you two to arm-wrestle or whatever men do when women are not in the room. I usually pay a short visit to Minnie Odegaard." The look she gave Thorstad clearly meant *Don't panic, I'll be back.*

But he *was* about to panic! His palms were damp. His stomach had developed a sort of tic. His body obviously did not want to be left.

"So," Topolski eventually said, while Thorstad stirred his spoon around in his pudding. "Here for . . . my money?"

Thorstad was uncertain how to react to this. "Oonagh suggested a visit, since I happen to be in the city."

"Not even . . . sh . . . she . . . gets all."

"I don't know anything about that, Top. I wasn't even sure I'd get to see Oonagh while I was here."

The eyes narrowed fiercely, the whole face working hard to get this out. "This . . . isn't that . . . play! Where . . . nice, guy . . . getsssss-uh . . . girl. She won't . . . abandon, now."

"I'm sure she won't," Thorstad said. He was beginning to feel ill. "Of course she won't."

"So-o-o-o . . ." Whatever he wanted to say next was causing him greater-than-usual difficulty. His face grew red from the effort. His hands clenched the arms of his chair. Then, suddenly, he relaxed and leaned forward. "Welcome to . . . club."

"What club is that, Top?"

"Dumped! Here! She . . . brought you. Samesss . . . me! Now . . . shhhhhe's . . . gone!" His face twisted into an awkward sort of grin—possibly malicious.

Oonagh spoke from the doorway. "So poor Minnie has gone and died on us, Top."

"Minnie?" Topolski said.

She took a deep breath and came in to the suddenly quiet room and sat down at her place at the table. "The nurses thought I'd been told."

None of them had eaten dessert. The coffee had gone cold. The trio had begun to pack up their instruments. Schubert had defeated them, at least in this setting. It was impossible to know whether the pianist was about to burst into tears or wallop the cellist with his own instrument.

Without the music, Thorstad realized there was not just quiet here but absolute silence. The thick rug and heavy drapes and perhaps the ceiling as well absorbed all ordinary sound. People sometimes spoke of the silence of the grave as an imagined absolute, but how could they know of such total silence unless they had been in this room? Such pure soundlessness could scare you half to death. He breathed in this terrible quiet and could not think of a thing to say to Andrzej Topolski, who had assumed they were members of the same club.

"Thorstad is down here helping a young actor with his exams. Isn't that something? Has he been telling you that?"

This was met with a steely indifferent look. "Just . . . sitting. A lump."

Oonagh put her hands on the table and began to rise from her chair. "Well, we don't want to bore you with people who sit like lumps. It's time we hit the road."

"Don't! . . . You came . . . to take!"

But Oonagh was standing now, and had pushed her chair in to the table. "You'll be taken back to your room soon."

Topolski stiffened against the back of his chair. "Damn . . . you!" His voice cracked in the midst of this, and, incredibly, he appeared to be, like the pianist, fighting to control the muscles in his face. "Oo-nagh! God's . . . sake!"

Oonagh's voice remained cheerful. "We have to go, my darling. We've a long drive ahead of us."

"No!" A fist struck the tabletop. "No! No! No!"

"I'm sorry," Thorstad began, intending this for Topolski. Or for the person Topolski had been. Or for the attendant who was hurrying across the dining room to do something about this angry old man who was pounding his table.

"Just come," Oonagh said to Thorstad. "I go through this

every time." She grasped his arm and guided him towards the open doorway to the hall.

She said nothing more until they had gone down to the foyer and were about to exit through the glass doors. She paused to let Thorstad open the door for her, and then went through and into the harsh sunlight. "I should have thought of this. He blamed you, you see. He believed she married you only because he had already married me! And that was your fault for throwing us together—or so he claimed. In fact it had nothing to do with you. He can be such a hateful bastard! I suspected at the time that you'd inflated the whole business into some great personal sacrifice, but it didn't have anything to do with you. I'm sorry, but it really didn't."

Thorstad said nothing all the way across the patterned tiles and past the largest of the splashing fountains, vaguely aware that something important in his life had changed. Then, in the parking lot, with his hand on the car door, he said, "He thought you'd brought me here to leave me behind, as you'd done with him."

She laughed, and got in behind the wheel. "Well there you are—one more reminder that you put your life in my hands the minute you get in my car."

Once they were both in the Mercedes they sat in silence for a while, looking out between the narrow eucalyptus trunks at the silent ocean. There seemed to be nothing to say. Thorstad, at least, could think of nothing. He fought the impulse to go back inside and apologize to Topolski. But for what? What he was feeling now was not so much guilt as horror. He should apologize for the horror, and for his pity. He would not, however, confess this small, uncomfortable, and unforgivable survivor's satisfaction— this *relief* that he hadn't, himself, reached so bad a state as poor Topolski—the man he'd once admired and known he could never equal, now gone far beyond any cause for envy. He felt as though he might put his face in his hands and cry.

"I always have to sit here for a few minutes afterwards," Oonagh said. "The ocean calms me a little."

"It's always as awkward as this?"

When she eventually spoke again, it was not to answer his question. "Someone should have told us long ago how fast it would all go by! We should have been warned."

It seemed, in the silence that followed, that some sort of response was expected, but he could think of none. Oonagh may have been talking to herself.

"Haven't you ever thought that? That someone should have told us life would go by so fast it would seem, looking back, to have lasted only a few months? Of course it could all be just a dream, couldn't it?"

"And what good would it have done if we'd been told this at the beginning?" Thorstad asked. "It's like saying, You might as well jump off a roof and get it over with, since your life will eventually feel as if it lasted no longer than your father's."

"It is not saying that!" Her open hand tapped the dashboard to the rhythm of her words. "It is saying, Whatever you want to do with your life, don't put it off, get busy and do it *now*!"

"Which you did! And I did! Do you have anything wise to say about when you *have* done what you wanted to do and then are pushed aside?"

She tossed her hair and started the engine. "Well!" The famous smile reappeared, though perhaps a little forced. Crows' feet shot out. Teeth gleamed. "It isn't over yet! It isn't bloody over till it's over! And for all we know it may not be over even then. I intend to stagger onto any stage or TV show that will have me until they have to drag my corpse out of their way to go on. I imagine you will do whatever you have to do to keep on going too. I don't think either one of us is the sort to sit down in front of a train." She laughed, probably thinking of the inconvenience they might cause the engineer who noticed the two determined septuagenarians camped on the tracks.

17

To Axel Thorstad their famous PCH appeared to be ribbon binding stitched to the frayed edge of the continent, a sinuous low-level border between the endless ocean and the precipitous hills, interrupted occasionally where roads disappeared mysteriously into wedged-in canyons. It was into one of these canyons that Oonagh had promised to take them today. Thorstad sat at an angle to keep his knees off the dusty dashboard, aware that behind him Travis crouched amongst the spare tires, oil cans, and several old coats. For the occasion, Oonagh had borrowed Skyler Shreve's ancient, dirt-crusted, open-air Bronco with Alberta licence plates.

"We're leaving it all behind," Oonagh said. "We are not neglecting our duties. We *have* no duties." For leaving it all behind she'd pulled her hair back tight to her skull and clipped it together with a silver brooch at the back of her neck. "Fortunately I love to drive—almost as much as being on stage—but you may have noticed I'm not especially good at it! Topolski once turned me in to the police—begged them to take my licence away. For the public's safety, as well as his own." She laughed so hard at this memory that she put her face right down on the steering wheel.

"Oonagh! My God!"

She jerked upright and got them back onto their own side of the road in time to avoid colliding with an orange Hummer. The child driver gave them the finger.

"Jeeeeez," Travis said.

"The police thought he was just another husband who wanted to punish his wife after a fight, but he really was terrified when I got behind the wheel." She briefly put a hand on Thorstad's thigh. "Poor man, taking your life in your hands when you'd rather be cramming *knowledge* into one young actor's head."

Cramming knowledge had never been his goal. It was *teaching* Thorstad regretted losing. But it was more than that. It was also the sort of comradeship that sometimes developed, where teacher and student might set off together in pursuit of something— experience, discovery, knowledge, and wonder.

"So this is what it's like to be a star?" Travis leaned forward to shout this. "Racing up and down the highway in someone's filthy truck!"

"And to think I turned down a chance to teach school for forty years." Oonagh raised both hands above her head. Her laughter was loud, teeth bared to the sky. But she took hold of the wheel in time to avoid mowing down a row of cyclists along the side of the road.

Eventually they turned inland off the highway and travelled for several minutes through deciduous woods where rough pavement gave way to gravel and dusty trees. "No ocean, no beach, no highway," Oonagh said. "No sound stages, no cameras." To Travis, who would not be needed at the studio till early afternoon, she'd promised he could "study your *Beowulf* or whatever on the terrace of a burnt-down house."

She had explained that the house had been a victim of a wildfire down off the Santa Monica range, the property later becoming a state-owned park. According to Oonagh, the site of the burnt house was so far up the canyon there'd be little danger of interruptions. Not even the Forces Dedicated to Defeating Axel Thorstad were likely to find them. As they stepped down onto the parking lot, she informed them there'd once been giraffes and camels and buffalo roaming here, a private zoo, though they wouldn't find any such creatures here now. "But keep an eye open for rattlesnakes and poison oak."

"Just what I need," Travis said, leaning forward to shake his knapsack a little higher up his back. "A hike through a dusty snakepit."

Before setting off up the trail, Oonagh removed a felt hat from the Bronco and used both hands to place it on her head at a tilt. It was the sort of fedora that had been worn by Humphrey Bogart in *Casablanca*.

Taking hold of the staff that Camilla Evans had pressed upon him, Thorstad set out to follow Oonagh along a rough track worn into the earth by thousands of hikers before him, the long dry grass crackling against his ankles. This was, he supposed, worth a try. He'd suggested to Travis that he record in his notebook anything related to his course in Geography—anything, that is, to do with characteristics of the earth's surface, including dirt, rocks, plants, trees, water, and any evidences of Nature's ravages upon itself: floods, droughts, forest fires, or slides. "If you pay attention to the ground at your feet and the landscape around you, I expect the terms *chaparral* and *oak woodlands* to enter our conversation. Also, maybe, *ridgeline*. Compare all this with home."

Oonagh led them up the narrow trail with long strides, a man's white dress shirt flapping its tails about her hips, and multicoloured bracelets flashing at her wrists. After all these years, he was on another hiking expedition with the radiant Oonagh Farrell. Topolski wasn't here to lead them, and Barry Foster wasn't here to complain, but Axel Thorstad was traipsing through unfamiliar bush with the present-day Oonagh Farrell, loud and seductive as ever.

Though it was Oonagh who led the way, Travis made it clear he knew who was responsible for this excursion. "I figure all teachers must take a course on, you know, how to use other people to get what they want themselves."

Thorstad said "Could be," but added nothing about the satisfaction he felt in knowing he was in charge of matters at last, at least for this morning. He was responsible for the shallow stream they followed for a while, and the stone cottage half hidden behind a leafy tree. He might even have conjured up the sign instructing hikers to yield to bikers, and bikers to yield to riders on horseback.

"Like we'd argue with a horse!" said Travis, who'd expressed serious doubts about this excursion. He hadn't come to California for a walkathon.

Thorstad tried to keep in mind that no one was especially interested in preventing him from doing his job; it was just that they didn't think his job was important. What was important was the TV series. What was important was Travis being in top form while the cameras were rolling, and co-operating with the magazine reporters. What was important was the money he could eventually earn if Old Man Thorstad did not get in his way with *Hamlet* or the causes of the Second World War.

"It'll be your fault if I'm bit by a rattlesnake," Travis said.

Oonagh responded without breaking her stride. "There's an old well up here we can drop you down if we need to. We'll tell them you ran away."

Nothing remained of the house but its foundation: three successive levels of paved terrace and marble floor in the shade of overhanging trees. A brick barbecue sat at the end closest to a small stream that tumbled down a rocky bank and into a pool before wandering off amongst the overhanging bushes. Off the opposite end of the terraces, a concrete box the size of a caboose was half buried in fallen limbs and other debris, a gaping doorway revealing only darkness inside. Thorstad wondered if, in the event of a wildfire, you would take shelter inside that box or run as fast as you could for the ocean.

Travis dropped his knapsack to the ground and ran ahead to leap, with arms flung wide, onto the lowest terrace. He turned and aimed his voice at the treetops: "Friends, Romans, Countrymen—lend me your chaparrals!" A mock Mark Antony or Marlon Brando in baggy blue shorts and a white *Forgotten River* T-shirt. He jumped up to the next terrace, then off to dusty earth, a set-loose child, and stepped onto a boulder in the creek's quiet pool. He balanced, arms out, from stone to stone, and then climbed, quickly, from one boulder to another up the face of the little waterfall. At the top he squatted, and dangled his arms off his knees. "You want me to cram for exams, *kemo sabe*? Come and get me!" He unravelled the black wire from his pocket and plugged the blunt end into his ear.

Oonagh shrugged out of her backpack and laid it on the lowest marble floor, and dragged Thorstad's bag over beside it. "Unless you have ambitions to be a monkey like your friend we can sit here till Curious George gets bored enough to join us."

Travis bounded down the waterfall as though he cared little whether he fell into the stream or broke his neck. It seemed ridiculous to Thorstad that he must rein in such energy for the sake of exams.

But Oonagh was unwilling after all to wait for Curious George to get bored. She raised her voice. "Come let me hear something from your next scene. Your *tutor* tells me you're pretty good but I want to see this for myself."

Travis unplugged his ear and stepped out of the creek, clearly alarmed. "Here?"

Thorstad had decided not to warn him of this, but had made sure he knew who she was.

"I won't allow a minute of History till I've seen you do your stuff," Oonagh announced. "Just give me your longest speech. Anyone can say 'Thanks' or 'I'll be back in a minute' and sound like they mean it. It's when you get two or three sentences in a row that we can tell if you're an actor." When Travis hesitated, she added, "I'm the one supplying lunch, so you can humour me, for goodness' sake! I'm in need of entertainment."

Thorstad felt his own version of stage fright on behalf of the young actor—required, now, to perform for the expert. *Go easy on him*, he was tempted to say.

Travis crossed the length of the highest terrace, one hand pushing his hair back, then letting it fall before pushing it back again. Colour had risen in his cheeks. He scratched at one bare knee. He paused long enough to glance at Thorstad and frown, as though asking for some assurance that this woman deserved the effort. Then, once Thorstad had nodded, he stepped down onto the middle level and worked his legs as though he were preparing for a race.

Oonagh stood up and removed her hat and stepped back to become his audience. "Any idea how much the crew is paid for every minute you stand there trying to remember who you are?" When Thorstad moved to stand beside her she put a hand on his shoulder as though to suggest he brace himself.

"Okay," Travis said. He began to pace again, possibly getting into character. He turned, suddenly, and directed a furious glare at something behind Thorstad, his fists clenched. "Don't you ever *think*?" He shouted this. Perhaps an imaginary person behind Thorstad had turned to walk away. He shook his fist. "You know what kind of danger you're dragging us into? *All of us!*" He turned, apparently to address a second invisible person. "You're an idiot! They'll come down on us now like a pack of bloody Storm Troopers!"

"Oh my darling boy," Oonagh said, both hands on top of her head. "Get down off that stage. You're doing this for television, not for someone on the far side of those hills."

Thorstad's muscles tightened. Had he brought Travis out here to be humiliated? This was not what she had promised.

With his eyebrows pulled into a fierce scowl, Travis leapt down onto the sparse dry grass and again paced for a moment before stopping to shout his accusations again at the guilty parties—one and then the other.

Oonagh turned away and studied the treetops for a moment. "Did you actually audition before getting this job, or did you save the producer's daughter from a fate worse than death?"

Travis shot Thorstad a glance that blamed him for this. Thorstad was himself indignant, and might have spoken up but Oonagh barrelled on. "You're only a yard or so away but I can tell you've been trained for an auditorium full of *old* people in chairs. Old *deaf* people in chairs. Old deaf people in *faraway* chairs. Too many high school plays, I think!" She closed her eyes and ran a hand down over her face, perhaps choosing her next words with care. "And you seem to believe you have to be *doing* something all the time. The camera will make you look like some kind of dope addict. All that twitching and turning will make you look shifty and guilty or maybe just plain stupid."

Travis appeared to be shaken by this. "You want me to stand here poker-faced when I'm supposed to be furious?"

Thorstad considered calling this off. There was little pleasure or satisfaction in observing the boy's discomfort. At the very least, if this continued, he should walk away and pretend he wasn't observing.

Oonagh walked up to Travis and put a hand on either side of his face. "Bear with me, my dear." Then kissed his forehead and stood back. "Imagine the camera is a person. I'm sure someone told you this your first day here but you were too impressed with yourself to take it in. The camera is looking at you from the same distance as someone you could be talking to. It's *close*! It picks up every muscle twitch and tiny movement of your eyes. So—don't show anger. Instead, try *not* to show your anger."

"What if I'm so good at it they can't tell I'm royally pissed?"

"If you act as though you're trying to *hide* something from the camera you'll communicate that very thing to the people at home. Instead of acting furious, try to keep the camera from knowing you're furious. Now run through that again. I'm the camera. Forget our friend Thorstad for a moment, he's just a stepladder for the lighting crew."

She turned to Thorstad and smiled. In case he'd taken offence? He supposed there were worse things to be than a stepladder.

Travis walked away the length of the terrace and then came back. This time he looked directly at Thorstad to say the first part of his speech with his voice so low he could barely be heard. He said the rest to someone beyond him as though he had trouble opening his mouth for the words.

Oonagh applauded "A little better."

"Why didn't Paolo tell me this?"

"Maybe you weren't listening. Or maybe 'Paolo' had other things on his mind. It's even possible that Paolo doesn't care if you're kicked off the show. He knows there's plenty of others waiting to take your place. Do it again. Don't let me see how furious you are. This is television. Say it to yourself. *This is television.* I had to learn this myself after a life on the stage." She was speaking to both of them now. "You think it's hard for you? Imagine if you came to TV in your sixties! I could introduce you to directors who pulled out all their hair implants before I finally caught on. Now listen. Think: *The audience is three feet away. They can see my every thought—especially in crucial moments. They can smell my breath.*"

"Yow!" Travis pulled a face and shook one hand to rid himself of something foul.

"Well, it helps if you think so. They're close enough to see it in your eyes. Will they see *I'm an actor pretending to be furious* or *I'm so furious I don't want anyone to see how bloody mad I am*? Let's hear it one or two more times. Then we'll see who's earned their lunch. The camera, remember, is embedded between my eyes."

Once Oonagh had handed out her packaged sandwiches and cans of ginger ale, Travis kicked off his sandals and sat at the edge of the stream with his feet in the water. Thorstad, joining Oonagh in the porous shade of a eucalyptus, felt compelled to defend the boy. "I think this is the first time he's had more than a few lines to learn. Until now he's been just a minor face in a crowd."

Her glittering bracelets dismissed this. "He couldn't be that bad and still have his job. The bugger was just humouring me."

"Well, he's a male, so he'll be as bad as it takes to get your attention." Thorstad imagined he'd been much the same himself, long ago. "As soon as he's finished wolfing down that sandwich he's going to ask if he can try again. It may not be quite so terrible this time but it will be bad enough to keep you watching for as long as you're willing—out here in this place where nature went mad and drove humans into the sea."

Oonagh was about to bite into her sandwich but paused long enough to growl: "I'm sure it drove them no farther than their insurance office."

She fell silent, then, and for a few moments appeared lost in thought. Then she laid a hand on Thorstad's forearm and slid it down to take hold of his hand, which she raised to her lips. "Axel Thorstad in California!" She laughed. "I loved your big hands— do your remember that?"

"I remember a good deal."

"I bet you do. Do you remember our little beach hut? We were so young!"

"We were. But I didn't think so at the time."

"I know you didn't. But for all my noise I seemed to be saddled with an ability to look at myself from some future time. It meant I was bloody sensible for someone so young. Spoiled the fun sometimes. But it also prevented mistakes." She paused, then smiled, and put a hand on Thorstad's arm and lightly squeezed. "I'm glad you looked me up. I wouldn't have been surprised if you'd despised me all these years."

"Company," Thorstad said. A middle-aged man and woman wearing khaki shorts, high laced boots, and sun hats had come into sight on the trail, each of them using a hiker's sturdy staff. Low bushes were examined, and then compared to something in the woman's book. Binoculars were raised to the crown of an evergreen, and handed from one to the other.

"Lovely morning," the man said, when he'd spotted those who'd got here before them.

Axel Thorstad nodded his agreement.

The woman said, "What a perfect spot for a home! It must have broken their hearts to leave it."

"Well, you would never feel the same about it again, would you?" the man said. "Not after escaping with the flames licking at your heels."

"You would still resent it, of course."

There was a sort of singsong quality to the couple's speech, as though they meant only to remind one another of an earlier conversation.

"You hearing this?" Oonagh said to Travis. "Your assignment is to explain how you can tell they're saying this for *us*. Also why they'd make fairly awful actors."

The man's attention was drawn to the concrete bunker at the far end of the terraces. "Sweetheart—the bomb shelter!"

It was clearly a hoped-for find. Both quickened their pace, perhaps to be first at the doorway. The man won, though neither went inside. Heads were thrust in the doorway, but quickly withdrawn. "Oh dear. Not very big."

"Still," the woman said, "you would be glad to be safe from the fallout."

Her head was again thrust in through the doorway, though shoulders-to-feet stayed safely in the outside world. "There must have been only the two of them." The head reappeared, speaking again for the watchers on the naked terrace. "We'd have needed this much space for just the food our hungry tribe would need."

This time the man addressed the Listeners directly: "How quickly we forget these shelters! You believed it was your only hope of surviving. How many backyards were dug up for one of these?"

When the couple had completed their examination and climbed over the remains of the house to set off beyond the water-fall, Travis went over to peer in through the door to the concrete box. Thorstad joined him, never having seen a bomb shelter himself. But there was little inside it to see. Rotted leaves. A fallen two-by-six, presumably from the concrete forms. The smell was musty, almost damp despite the dry warm air outside. There was no sign that humans had ever spent a single night in it. It may have been only a cellar to keep the vegetables cool.

"We know a few people who'd be happy to camp in this," Travis said, stepping inside.

Thorstad knew who Travis had in mind. He was reluctant to take the boy away from this bit of concrete history, if indeed that was what it was, but they had come here for more than one purpose. "I suppose we should take the opportunity, with this *thing* in our midst, to spend a few minutes on the Cold War?"

Travis protested from within. "We did the Cold War last week in school!"

"Well, it isn't the only war you need to know about." Thorstad removed exam papers from his bag and carried them up from one terrace to the next and onto the flat concrete roof of the bunker where he brushed rotted leaves and twigs aside to sit on the front edge with his legs dangling above the doorway.

Perhaps curious to see if the old man had taken leave of his senses, Travis came out of the concrete box and climbed up to sit beside him. "You planning to jump or what?"

"Only if you drive me to it."

Travis lowered his voice. "Man, I had you figured wrong. We've only been here a few days and already you've got yourself in with this big-time *actress*? You didn't tell me you were a ladies' man."

When Thorstad did not response to this, Travis sighed. "Okay, boss, you've got what you wanted. No Elliot Evans in sight. I dare you to teach me something."

Thorstad removed his reading glasses from his shirt pocket and put them on, then opened the exam on his lap. "Here's the sort of thing that could show up in either History or English. Two lessons for the price of one. And . . . to add to your listening pleasure"—he raised his voice—"we will now have a reading by one of the world's most highly regarded and honoured-with-statuettes actors."

Because the highly regarded and much-honoured actor had not been warned, she hesitated before taking the exam from his hand. She held it at arm's length and frowned hard. "*In Time of 'The Breaking of Nations.'* This what you want?" When he nodded, she let her gaze go down the page. "Am I reading this for television or for the stage?"

"For your friends and admirers on the roof of a bomb shelter," Thorstad said.

She repeated the title then, and, in her deepest voice, read the first stanza.

> *"Only a man harrowing clods*
> *In a slow silent walk*
> *With an old horse that stumbles and nods*
> *Half asleep as they walk."*

Travis wrinkled his nose. "A poem?"

"A poem," Thorstad said. "Poems are written in the midst of history. Sometimes poems are *about* history. Occasionally they can even *be* history. It's only schools that like to keep them separate."

"Man, you must have driven your principal *nuts*!"

"Just listen."

Oonagh read the first stanza again, and then the two that followed:

"Only thin smoke without flame
From the heaps of couch-grass:
Yet this will go onward the same
Though Dynasties pass.

"Yonder a maid and her wight
Come whispering by:
War's annals will cloud into night
Ere their story die."

When her audience had applauded, Oonagh bowed deeply and passed the exam up to Thorstad, who allowed some silence to follow—a few quiet moments in which he recognized that what he felt here, now, was something very close to joy. He was happy to be teaching again. He was happy to be teaching with Oonagh's help.

Oonagh broke the silence. "First question is from *me*. Does the fellow know what he's talking about? Do love and love stories really last longer than the effects of war? Hands up everyone who can't even remember the name of their first love!"

She raised her own hand. Thorstad did not. To Travis he said, "Because the examiners assume you're illiterate, they explain below that 'Ere' means 'before,' 'annals' are stories, and a 'wight' is a youth. We can look at all their tricky best-answer questions later. First we're going to consider everything you know about this as a poem, and then everything you know about the war that Thomas Hardy was aware of—within hearing distance, by the way, across a narrow strait."

When it appeared that Oonagh intended to wander farther into the woods above the little falls, Thorstad thanked her for her help. "Starting soon, this young man will want to send half his salary to the charity of your choice."

"He can start writing cheques any minute," she said, carefully arranging her Humphrey Bogart hat at a slant across her forehead.

"Ladies Too Old for the Stage need all the help they can get."

Once she was out of sight they considered the possible essay topics the English examiners might assign, based on this poem, and the possible topics they could imagine from the examiners of History, who would likely accompany this poem with a few short opinion pieces from others. "Let's gather everything you know for each, and then we'll see how we'd organize them."

Travis tapped his elbow lightly against Thorstad's arm. "You think she's got the hots for you? Coming out to this stupid place to do you a favour."

Thorstad lowered his head to look at Travis across the top of his glasses.

"Just wondered!" Travis laughed. His face was, for a moment, the face of a mischievous boy, maturity a long way off—a sharp reminder that Thorstad had been charged with the welfare and education of his parents' only child.

Thorstad shook the exam pages to draw Travis's attention to where it belonged. "Now, listen—they're not likely to use this poem again, so it's the process we're about to go through that matters, especially when you sit down to show them what you can do."

By the time Oonagh returned they had filled several pages with scribbled notes, at first random, then re-organized and numbered for both English and History, with supporting examples indicated briefly in the margins. They had talked about the nature and importance of *focus* in an essay, whatever its subject might be. Thorstad kept to himself his satisfaction in seeing how this time in the wooded canyon had demonstrated what could be done when they were beyond the interference of Elliot Evans's world.

At the foot of the waterfall Oonagh said, "Who remembers when we're expected back?"

Thorstad's entire body reacted. *Expected back* was an electric shock. Travis, too, had scrambled to his feet, looking at his watch. "*Crap!* It's nearly two-thirty!" He pulled his cellphone from a pocket. "I turned it off! I was supposed to be back at two!"

"Check for a message?" Oonagh said.

"No point now. Let's go!"

Oonagh snatched up her backpack from the floor of the dis-appeared house. "I'll have to drive so fast we'll be there before we leave *here*. Pray for no cops on the PCH."

Once she'd dropped them off at the gate to Evans's courtyard, Oonagh and the Bronco could not have reached the bottom of the hill before Elliot Evans was at the guest-house door. "So you decided to return." His face was flushed, his lips tight, his first scowl was for Travis. "I asked Paolo to re-schedule. Who do you think you're working for, anyway?"

Thorstad hoped the man could be reasonable. "Surely an hour or so—"

"I turned my phone off this morning," Travis said, "thinking I—"

"Don't!" Evans was evidently not in the mood for excuses. He stepped inside, his eyes blinking rapidly behind the rectangu-lar glasses. To Thorstad he said, "Just stay where you are and let me take this boy to the studio, where something might be sal-vaged from the day."

Seeing Travis's frightened face, and flushed with sudden sym-pathy, Thorstad assumed the blame. "It was my decision to take him out where he could study undisturbed. He has those exams to pass."

Elliot Evans crossed the room and turned to address them from behind the table and the vase of eucalyptus boughs. Perhaps he'd been an actor once himself. "He has a job to do! A job he is paid to do. He also has a contract that hasn't been renewed. I should have kept him in his trailer even when he isn't needed, just so I'd know where he is. Obviously you can't be trusted."

Travis tried. "Oonagh Farrell was helping me with my lines."

Evans, it seemed, was fighting hard against a temptation to explode. "You have a director. We have coaches if they're needed. We expected you to handle this role on your own!"

Thorstad was surprised at how quickly regret and guilt could become a surge of anger, an interior physical clench as though he was prepared to launch into a fist fight or a free-for-all. No one had ever accused him of being untrustworthy. His body didn't seem to know that physical violence was out of the question. The tendons in his throat felt tightened to the point of snapping. "Are we supposed to believe your work is more important than ours, just because there's so much money involved?"

Evans leaned forward, as though to address a thick-skulled child. "It's a simple matter of doing the job he's paid to do if he doesn't want someone else to do it instead. If he wants to work, he has to take it seriously."

"Please!" Travis said, moving to stand in the open doorway. "Let's just go!"

But Evans hadn't finished with the accused. He came out from behind the table as though to head for the door, but stopped too close to Thorstad. "You bloody teachers, you're so used to thinking your classroom is your kingdom you imagine your job more important than the *work* the rest of us do."

For a moment, Thorstad wasn't even sure it was himself who'd shouted *Stop!* though he was aware that he'd raised an arm, an open hand. "I won't have you bully him! I won't have you bully *me* with your sneer."

"I'm going," Travis said, already outside and hurrying down the steps. "I'll be in the car!"

Evans's forearm struck Thorstad's raised hand aside. "I thought his *mother* was a pain in the ass—but you! We've taken you into our home, we've put up with you at the studio, I would have thought you might be a little grateful."

Thorstad hauled in a deep breath and laced the fingers of both hands together, to prevent them from acting on their own. "It was a mistake," he said, as calmly as he could manage. "We lost track of the time. People sometimes do."

Evans exhaled impatiently and walked to the door. "Just remember why he's here."

From the deck Thorstad watched the BMW snake its way down the hill towards the highway, where heavy traffic raced in both directions. There was no traffic on the ocean's surface, and nothing at all on the horizon. By the time he recognized her voice she had been speaking, it seemed, for some time, from some distant corner of his mind. "I had decided I had nothing more to say to you, my darling, and the time had come to leave you to your own devices, but I cannot allow you to turn away from this conversation feeling that you are in the right and he in the wrong, because surely you of all people shouldn't need to be told that you are hardly the servant of love when you let your drive to succeed overtake your compassion and empathy and, of course, humility, since you've always insisted that teaching is less about drilling information into heads and more about passing on values and attitudes and habits—so I wonder when you began to forget this and started to—"

He said "No!" to this, and went back inside the guest house where he turned on the bathroom taps, he flushed the toilet, he switched on the little bedside radio, gathering up as much noise around him as he could. He knew what she would say and he did not want to hear. That the teacher and the executive producer were closer to being two of a kind than he'd imagined. He said "No!" to this at the empty centre of the guest house, refusing to believe this even when it came from somewhere within himself.

18

When it came to choosing a costume for his role in the ballroom scene, Thorstad could not bring himself to dress as Geoffrey Chaucer, which would have seemed presumptuous even to himself. From the rack of costumes Camilla Evans had arranged to have wheeled over to her husband's office, he selected an outfit that was, he supposed, generically medieval. In a brown tunic, brown leggings, a hooded cape, and with a purse at his belt, he was no one of importance, neither a wine merchant, a scribbler, nor a servant to a prince. The leggings and sleeves were too short, of course, but it was likely that the occasional citizen in Chaucer's time had worn hand-me-downs that left wrists and ankles exposed.

He was still surprised that Evans had not prevented him from taking part. By the time he'd telephoned Oonagh to report the confrontation that had taken place, he was convinced he could not stay on here any longer. "I shouted at him. I called him a bully! I raised my hand as though to hit him!"

Oonagh did not seem to take this seriously. "Elliot Evans has been called a bully before. I'm sure he let you ride in his car today, didn't he? In to the studio?"

"He did."

"And the boy?"

"Dead silence last night. Dead silence at breakfast. Dead silence in Evans's car. I'll be a chaperone now and little else, I suppose—make sure he gets enough sleep and keeps his distance from 'evil influences'—including helpful actresses.".

When Camilla learned of Thorstad's friendship with Oonagh, she'd insisted her husband put his anger behind him and offer the actress a visitor's pass to the studio for the shooting of the costume ball sequence. "She was so wonderful in *The Trip to Bountiful*, I swear I could hear her *think*!" But Oonagh would be in front of cameras herself for much of the day, and could promise only to stop by in the evening "in order to catch Axel Thorstad playing dress-up."

Because he'd struggled into his medieval outfit in the washroom next to Evans's office, Thorstad was given the opportunity to view scenes shot the day before outside a "dressed" hotel in the city. Evans and Paolo needed to examine these outdoor scenes before shooting today's interiors, but made it clear that the opinion of onlookers would not be welcome.

Camilla Evans was dressed as Marie Antoinette, her friend Louise as a diminutive Annie Oakley. Louise's husband was occupied elsewhere, presumably in his costume as a cosmetic surgeon for the stars. When Thorstad asked about Harold and Lyle he was told they'd gone back to Texas, taking with them the disappointing news that there was no appetite for another law-firm series at the moment, even one where all the lawyers were gay.

In the opening sequence they were looking at the front of an upscale hotel with a carpet running out to the drop-off bay. Police stood warily by at either end of the block, keeping an eye on the crowd of shabbily dressed men and women who'd formed a human cordon across the front of the building. As a stream of costumed people stepped out of cars and approached the front door, the human chain broke apart to let them go in to their fundraising ball, one couple at a time. Bouncing placards challenged the guests' sincerity—"Hypocrisy Wears a Friendly Face"—and questioned where the money would go—"Into Whose Pockets? Not Ours"—but no one was denied entry. An ostrich was followed by a grinning white-faced mime and a pair of clowns.

The camera lingered on Travis for a moment. "We want him to be recognized later," Evans explained. Travis hadn't told Thorstad about his role in the ballroom scene. "We'll want to cut in a close-up of Craig somewhere around here so we're not surprised when we see him later. He should have been closer to the entrance."

Paolo jotted in a tiny notebook while Evans explained to the watchers that the next sequence would appear in the midst of what they would shoot this afternoon. "Here comes Dolores."

A long black limousine glided into the picture. When it had stopped, the driver came around to help a stout elderly woman get out from the back seat, dressed in layers of pink net decorated with sparkling stars, and holding a wand. "Queen of the Fairies," Paolo said.

"She must have loved this," Evans said. "A grand entrance."

Paolo laughed. "Remembering the old days. An Oscar waiting behind that door."

Thorstad thought of her small chubby hand in his. *"You thought this old dame had died off years ago—admit it."* But she was still here, still working, long years after swooning in the arms of Gregory Peck.

Light exploded from press cameras. A reporter pushed a microphone at the wealthy woman and asked if the money raised would go towards converting her derelict building into a proper homeless shelter. "Will the Fairy Queen become a Fairy Godmother and give these people somewhere safe to sleep?"

But the Fairy Queen did not acknowledge anyone, even those who refused to allow her to reach the hotel door. When the Riverboat Gambler pushed Travis aside, Travis pushed back. The other protesters roared.

"We'll look at this again," Evans said, "once we have the interior sequences to work with. It's time to go to work."

The briefing room for the Extras was in Stage 7, only a few minutes' walk across the lot. Here Thorstad, along with Camilla and Louise and more than fifty others in costume, was herded into a large unfurnished and undecorated room where they were addressed by a woman with a clipboard. Glasses hung on beads against her chest. The dancers, she said, were members of an actual ballroom-dancing class hired for the occasion, and were being briefed elsewhere. Speaking from one side of her mouth— a tough *hombre*—she instructed the Extras to act as though they had been dancing only moments before but were currently taking a break. Some—"You, you, everyone to my left"—were instructed to pick up drinks on their way into the ballroom, and to hold them throughout the shoot as though they had just come back from the bar. Her chained glasses were raised to her eyes, the clipboard consulted. "There will be chairs against one wall, and this group, over here to my right, will sit on them throughout." The remaining Extras, including Thorstad, were to engage in muted conversations while watching the dance. They might flirt, or admire costumes, or simply discuss the weather, so long as their words could not be heard. "And don't *do* anything to draw attention to yourself! Imagine you are a background mural— barely capable of animation." The scene they were about to be part of, she explained, had already been rehearsed several times with the ballroom dancers and the actors' stand-ins.

While they were being led across the lane to another building, Louise promised Camilla and Thorstad there was no way she would sit on her butt once the riot had started. "I intend to get in a few good licks! What can they do about it then?"

Inside the sound stage, a fleet of assistant directors led them onto a polished hardwood floor and distributed them along the length of two white walls, where vertical mirrors alternated with tall sprays of crimson gladioli and velvet-cushioned chairs. A small orchestra had already assembled on the raised stage. A revolving chandelier hung from the raw undecorated beams, above which were stacks of lumber, sheets of plywood, and various pieces of stored furniture. Cameras looked down from a gallery above the third wall.

Not long ago he could have found a way to bring this experience into his classroom. An insider's glimpse of the television world might have been useful before showing a televised *Macbeth*. He might have assigned a writing exercise in which you were to recount an experience where you felt like a mere "extra" in the drama of someone else's life. As it was, he felt a bit unnecessary. It didn't help that he could not avoid standing out above the others. He should have exchanged places with the unhappily sitting Louise.

Beyond the rim of the hardwood floor, crew members were busy with cables attached to a large camera mounted on a trolley. But once another group in costume had filed in and taken up their positions as couples poised to dance, the several standing lights came on, flooding the entire room. Now Thorstad, instead of looking in from the shadows, was inside the effulgent world of excessive light this time, where everything and everyone was brighter than life. Crew and onlookers were invisible out there in what he knew was the chilled dusky world of an oversized storage shed.

Once the now-familiar words had been shouted from out in that dark, and the hired dance class began to whirl about the floor to music by some member of the Strauss family, the trolley moved down the length of the open wall carrying the seated cameraman with it. The Mother Superior confided to Thorstad that she felt as if she were in a Jane Austen movie. "I dare you," she said, and nudged him with a black-clad elbow, "to dance with a Mother Superior out on that floor with the rest."

He laughed. "Do you think no one would notice? I'm a guest of the executive producer. I'd be tossed out on my ear and made to sleep under a bridge."

Annie Oakley scowled out from her chair against the wall, waiting for the fireworks to begin. He hoped not to get in her way.

The afternoon stretched well into the evening, with breaks to visit the canteen for coffee and pizza or slabs of chocolate cake. Most of it was a matter of waiting for half an hour of camera-shifting and heated discussions in order to shoot for three or four minutes. Thorstad moved as unobtrusively as he could amongst the crowd, to keep his legs from tiring. When Oonagh appeared in a corner of the gallery amongst a small group of observers, he imagined how uninteresting this must be for someone used to being the centre of attention. You couldn't see Oonagh as an "Extra" in anyone's show any more than you could see her as an "Extra" in anyone's life.

Once the Queen of the Fairies had entered the ballroom with her husband and family in tow, she had little time to enjoy the applause before Craig Conroy and Travis burst in through the door behind her, followed by several additional protesters from the crowd outside. Conroy stood firm to shout: he wanted a chance to address the assembly, to explain. But even a society charity ball must have bouncers, and naturally a costume ball would have bouncers in costume. Two, three, four green elves with impressive shoulders attempted to persuade and then push and finally drag Conroy and Travis and the others back out through the door.

But they poured in again, with still more of the protesters behind them, and spread out amongst the alarmed dancers, knocking people out of their way. It wasn't long before Louise had abandoned her velvet-cushioned chair and thrown herself into the brawl.

Again they were instructed to freeze. For a moment Thorstad thought this might be so that Annie Oakley could be sent home, but it became clear that this was so a camera could be moved to where it would shoot a scene in which elves and other costumed folks pursued Craig Conroy up a zigzag staircase to the gallery. It was obvious now that they were called Extras not only because they were expendable and easily replaced, but because they were compelled to be as passive as a field of cattle or a stand of Douglas fir while others were living the story. It was not all that different, now that he was confronted with it, from a forced or unprepared-for retirement from a beloved career.

During his life in the classroom he had considered his role to be a facilitator working from the margins rather than an instructor pontificating from centre-front, but this had certainly not made his role extraneous. If anything, it had made him more actively involved in the individual student's work. That he'd refused to be preacher, professor, or hectoring boss man did not confine him to the role of mere overseer. He had never been, in other words, an Extra.

He was an Extra now. All fights resumed. Conroy stood behind the balcony railing and shouted again for attention, but no one paid attention, just as they'd been instructed. Eventually defeated, Conroy stepped back and came down the stairs to the dance floor where his double waited, wearing identical clothing. Once Paolo had spoken to both men and returned to his monitor in the darkened outer world, the double ran up to the top of the steps and climbed over the railing, where he bent his knees and launched into a jump, plunging to the floor where he rolled forward once and leapt again to his feet. After doing this jump three more times, he then threw himself into the crowd to set about freeing Travis and another protester from the elves.

After what seemed like several hours of shooting and re-shooting, Thorstad joined the crowd of dismissed Extras at the canteen truck parked outside the main door to the building. Here a long table had been set up with pizzas, coffee urn, soft drinks, and a large box of packaged snacks. A happy Annie Oakley reported that she'd got in a few good blows with the butts of her pistols. "There's some will notice bruises in the shower tomorrow."

When Thorstad recognized Craig Conroy's double amongst those at the table, he waited until the man was alone for a moment, eating his triangle of pizza from one hand while holding a coffee in the other. When he stepped up to express his pleasure at once again watching him at work, the man thanked him but looked puzzled, perhaps by "again."

"A few days ago you told me your grandfather had been a stuntman as well."

It seemed to take a moment for him to bring this previous conversation to the surface. Perhaps it was the medieval costume. "Oh. Sorry." He shook his head, blinking away his confusion. "Yes. He was pretty good in fights. You know—barroom brawls in the Old West? I remember one time he brought me into the studio to watch. He would've loved it here tonight, mixing it up with this crowd. Once he stunted for Randolph Scott. You heard of him?"

"I remember seeing Randolph Scott on the screen. I wonder if you asked your grandfather about Tomas Thorstad."

"Yeah-yeah." He nodded twice, in time with his words. "Your old man—right? My granddad says he heard about a Thorstad who fell off of a roof but he never knew him."

The stuntman tossed his coffee cup in the garbage can and turned as though to leave.

"Did he know how it happened? The accident?"

The man turned back, but appeared impatient to move on. "Sorry. He assumed the man just slipped. Miscalculated." He held out his hands, palms up, as though to deny responsibility. "I did a bit of asking around—just out of, you know, curiosity. I found out he was hurt pretty bad. Walked afterwards with a cane."

"No-no." Thorstad shook his head, disappointed in this man. It had been a mistake to trust him. The grandfather had remembered the wrong person. "My father was killed."

"So you told me." The stuntman looked down to study his own boots while he spoke. "Once he was back on his feet he helped out a bit, a sort of assistant to the new stuntmen at Centurion." After a brief pause, he looked up to study Axel Thorstad's face for a few long seconds. "My grandfather remembers him—says he must've lived for another twenty, thirty years."

Thorstad returned his coffee cup to the table with shaking hands. "He knew it was *Tomas Thorstad* you were asking about? You mentioned the dates, everything?"

The man nodded, obviously anxious to put this conversation behind him. "He remembered seeing him on the lot, running errands with one of those little motorized carts—y'know?"

But this could not be true. This could not be true. Yet Thorstad could not think what he might do about it. He felt rooted to the spot, and saw himself turning this way and that, looking for escape.

Perhaps the stuntman could imagine the shock. "Listen, if your mother left, she knew what she was doing. My gran was a nervous wreck by the time my grandfather retired. Some women aren't cut out for the life."

"Well!" It seemed that Oonagh had been close behind him for long enough to hear some of this. She took firm hold of his elbow. "It seems the past is not the past after all. It's a good thing we don't build our lives on what we've only been *told*! Let's get out of here, Thorstad. Let's get you out of that silly costume and leave."

There was no need to look for Travis. Travis would be attending a party tonight in Beverly Hills—a "housewarming" party for someone named Robbie Ford. It had all been arranged. Axel Thorstad had been coolly informed.

He allowed Oonagh to guide him, a hand on his arm, talking all the while though he could not quite register what she was saying. What he could hear was an inner voice, telling him that he had been lied to all his life, suggesting he'd been a fool, so easily convinced of a falsehood, so eagerly misled. He had been deprived of a father when he needn't have been. He had mourned for a man who had not only lived but hadn't bothered to look for his son. He supposed he ought to be happy for someone who'd survived a terrible fall, but felt he might throw up into one of these animal shrubs.

Once he had turned his costume over to Camilla at her husband's office and they had driven off the lot in Oonagh's old Mercedes, instead of taking him back to the Evanses' guest house she drove to what she claimed was one of her favourite restaurants, not far from the studio. "I'm starving," she said, as she guided him in through the door. The host who led them to a table near the back seemed to know who she was. He seemed to know, too, exactly what she wanted: a giant bowl of seafood chowder. "Bread for two! A pot of tea and a coffee."

"Tea?" Thorstad said.

"Don't you remember? Do you remember anything at all about me?"

"I remember how wilful you could be. And loud. And beautiful."

"For an old codger, your memory's pretty good. Now, where is that chowder? Let's eat."

Their steaming bowls arrived immediately. "Don't talk," she said when he tried. "Eat. Concentrate on each lovely mouthful. You can talk later, when your belly is full and you're overwhelmed with gratitude." She laughed at her own nonsense. A waiter near the front of the restaurant also laughed. Perhaps she ate here often.

"Oh, Thorstad! Axel! I'm sorry if I'm acting the fool, but I'll be damned if I'll let you brood like a bloody teenager. You like scallops? These are delicious. Do you make chowder up there on your island? We can talk about your mother later."

"My mother?"

"Eat. You haven't tried the bread. Your mother is the one to start with. She's the one who raised you to be who you are. The bread, Thorstad—try it! She's the one who created the myth."

"You mean, she lied."

"It doesn't change anything," she said when they were in her car again. "Your father was not around to be your father, just as you've always known. It is *his* story that got changed tonight, not yours."

His father had been alive when Axel Thorstad left home for university, possibly still alive during his first few years of teaching, but had avoided him. Had apparently not been curious. His mother had invented the man's terrible end. Those annual Christmas cards from a grateful Derek Morris had not been for an unfortunate death but for something else. If the actor had been home when Topolski drove them up to his gate, would he have told the truth, would he have explained how his father might be found?

Perhaps his body had not experienced real anger recently. It seemed unable to handle this. His stomach was in revolt, his hands were aching fists, his limbs had become shafts of knotted muscle, braced perhaps to strike out—at the news-bearing stuntman, at his father, at his mother, all safely beyond his reach. And at himself, the betrayed and disappointed fool.

Once she had driven to the nearest beach access they set out in the starry dark to walk, carrying their shoes, as close as possible to the foaming surf where the sand was not so loose underfoot. The beach curved ahead for several miles, it seemed, with lights here and there in houses along the beach and up across the face of the cliffs.

His father hadn't in all those years contacted his wife. He would have known where she'd come from, where she must have gone with their child. Had he not cared, or had she forbidden it? It was even possible he had come up for a look at his son but hadn't announced himself.

"Faster," Oonagh said. "You're dragging your feet."

Though the sea breeze was cool against his face, he could feel hot sweat inside his shirt. He realized he'd bared his teeth for this forced walk, like someone enduring intense pain, or braced for worse.

Had his mother lied to his grandmother as well? Or had the two women looked knowingly at one another whenever he'd asked to see his father's movie, when he'd spoken (so innocently) of the man's willingness to risk his life so that talented actors might not be harmed? He could not imagine why she hadn't burned the film, why she had encouraged him to admire the man who had not been killed after leaping from that roof.

"Come on," Oonagh said, taking hold of his hand. "We've got to wear you *out*!"

But he was already worn out. When they came to a low out-cropping of angular stone that protruded several metres across the sand, he broke free and found a rocky perch to rest on. Gasping, panting, he sat facing the darkened sea, bent forward over his folded arms, shutting out all of the world but his two large naked feet.

By the time they had finally driven up the zigzag face of the cliff to the Evanses' home it was after one o'clock. Lights were still on in the house and Elliot Evans was outside, about to get into his car.

"It's Travis," he said. "Somebody phoned from the party and asked us to come and get him."

Thorstad had stepped out of the Mercedes but hadn't yet shut the door. "What's happened?"

"Didn't say. Maybe he's done something stupid. More likely they got scared about having a minor at their party. Or got wind of a raid. Who knows?"

"My motor's running," Oonagh said. "Go back to bed. Tell me how to find him and we'll have the silly bugger home before he knows what hit him."

"But first," she added once they'd started down the hill, "we'll hold his head under water for about an hour, the little shit, and pull out most of his teeth." She was silent all the way down the snaking hillside road until, as they were about to pull out onto the highway, she added, "Where the hell do you think his chaperone was while this boy was getting himself in trouble? Out trudging through the sand, Your Worship, slave to a beautiful temptress. Who could blame him for that?" When Thorstad had still said nothing by the time they had passed by most of the shoulder-to-shoulder houses with their backs to the road, she said, "I'm sorry, Thorstad." She reached across and took his hand in hers. "Axel. Close your eyes and tell yourself that at least we're having more fun than poor ol' Andrzej Topolski."

Had she dismissed his news so easily, then? Did she think that he had already put it behind him? He doubted he would ever put it behind him, a mystery that in being solved had become even more of a mystery. Why had the man allowed himself to be deserted by wife and child, and never care enough to follow them? Why had there never been letters that began with *Dear Son . . . ?*

The party house was a white stucco art deco box in a grove of hairy evergreens at the top of a hill. There was no need to check the address since the front door was open at the head of a long curved flight of concrete steps, loud music thumping in the warm night air. A young man with a bald head came out and stood on the top step to smoke but stayed only long enough for two or three puffs before going back in.

No one met Thorstad at the door. No one welcomed him, or challenged him, no one even seemed to notice he was there. There was music somewhere, but it was obscured by the solid din of countless conversations happening all at once. To move at all required passing through a human jungle, where shouted isolated words seemed to have no specific origin. Bodies were pressed so close together that pale pink silk and brown leather and indigo jeans seemed to belong to everyone all at once.

This was a house designed for entertaining and little else. Thorstad found it hard to believe that anyone actually lived here. The large living room was obviously made for parties, but in his wandering through the rest of the house in search of Travis he saw nothing resembling a kitchen. He saw, through one open doorway, a large four-poster bed draped with sheer curtains, appropriate for a movie set in a Memphis whorehouse. And yet there were seven bathrooms along a single hallway—the row of doors opening and closing as he passed by, providing glimpses of mirrors and sinks and young women in party dresses straightening their bra straps and touching up their makeup before the mirrors. It was hard to imagine any one house needing seven bathrooms, even if parties were large and a good deal of booze was consumed.

One of the bathroom doors opened to allow two, three, four, five young women to emerge—all pretty, all blond—one after another, two of them unselfconsciously passing a finger beneath their nostrils and sniffing conclusively.

Perhaps there was more to worry about here than he'd imagined. "Travis Montana?" he said to a man who seemed to be the oldest one here, thirty-five at most. Possibly older, if Louise's husband and his instruments had had their way with him. Someone had certainly added the fullness to that upper lip. The man, in any case, shrugged, obviously uninterested in the question.

A young woman in a transparent broad-rimmed lacy hat smiled and passed by, the space so narrow that she put a hand against Axel Thorstad's chest to keep from being crushed. Perhaps to thank him for his assistance, she threw him a kiss before disappearing into the crowd.

Even within the crammed-together forest of bodies, people had formed smaller groves. Conversations took place in tight standing circles or amongst those who'd claimed the few seats, with faces pushed in close to one another. Undergrowth doing its best in the shadow of surrounding timber.

A fat man in red suspenders stood in front of Thorstad as though to challenge his right to be there. "You lost, Big Man?" This might be someone he'd met at the studio—a member of the crew or one of the writers, or possibly one of the Extras.

"I'm looking for Travis Montana?"

The man in red suspenders jerked his head to the left. "The pool. He got a little rowdy so they threw him in "

So they had had good reason to call for him to be taken home.

Beyond an open doorway to the outside, a long rectangular pool shimmered under floodlights mounted in the trees. Half a dozen people splashed about in the water while one clamped-together couple at the far end was taking advantage of the fact that the water there came as high as their waists. The young woman who surfaced to hurry along the tiles was naked. So was the young man who'd tried to catch her ankle but gave up and leapt onto the tiles to follow.

Apparently Travis had decided that he would stay in the pool and spend time with a slim young woman leaning back against the ladder, both arms angled behind its rungs. When Thorstad had caught his eye he frowned and looked away before looking back again, obviously puzzled. Then he climbed out of the pool, his jeans and T-shirt shedding water. "What are you doing here, man?" Frowning. Obviously not sure how he felt about this. He came closer, but stopped below Thorstad on his step. "Something wrong?"

"We were asked to come and get you."

Travis threw his head back and to the side as though he'd been slapped. "But the party's hardly started." He folded down to sit at the edge of the pool, his feet in the water.

Thorstad went down onto the wet green tiles, where the air was warm and clammy against his skin. "Someone here is worried you're underage." Because he and Travis had barely spoken since the angry exchange with Evans, it wasn't easy to know what tone to take with him now.

Travis stared at his own knee in silence for a moment, as though thinking this over, then pushed his hips forward to lower himself, legs first, into the water. He scooped up a handful to toss into the face of the young woman, who shrieked but appeared to welcome the attention. This was Rosie, hair plastered to her scalp, head tilted back, smiling or sneering—it was impossible to tell which.

Thorstad crouched on his heels. "You can't expect me to stand around and wait."

He meant that he didn't appreciate having to speak to Travis's back. Nor did he need another desertion tonight. Another betrayal, it felt like. He had barely enough patience to make himself sound civil.

"Get yourself a drink." This was shouted by a bobbing head out in the middle of the pool. "See Steve and he'll give you some shit. Relax, man. Join the party."

When Travis could see that Axel Thorstad appeared determined to stay where he was, he thrashed his way back to clutch at the edge of the pool. "What's the matter? You want a study session this time of night?" He seemed to think this was funny. "Causes of the Korean War?"

"You think I'd come here for that?"

"Why not? Everything is about you, isn't it? All that matters is what you want. Another feather in your cap. Another *medal*."

Thorstad stepped back, as though from a blow. "Travis?"

"You nearly wrecked everything." Then it seemed he'd changed his mind. "Well, you wanted to turn me into a scholar or something for my parents, but you nearly wrecked everything else."

Thorstad could not afford to take this seriously. The boy was annoyed, his party had been interrupted. "Let's just get you out of here."

"I'm not stupid, y'know."

Not stupid, maybe, but stubborn, self-centred, capable of causing hurt. "You're not stupid but you're a minor in a party house. Someone phoned and asked for you to be taken out of here."

There was alarm, now, in his face. "Who phoned?"

"We don't know who it was." Thorstad stood up. "C'mon. We need to get you dried off and out of here."

"Who says?"

"You sound like a five-year-old. *'You're not the boss of me!'* It's your producer who *says*. It's Elliot Evans who sent us and he *is* the boss of you! As you've both made clear. If you don't want to ruin your chances with him I think you'd better come."

Travis studied Thorstad as though for signs of deceit. "Evans sent you?"

"He's the one who got the phone call. Oonagh's waiting outside."

"Then you better join her." This was someone who had appeared suddenly at Axel Thorstad's side, a broad-shouldered man with his shirt unbuttoned down to his waist. He put a hand on Thorstad's upper arm and gripped tightly enough to hurt. His other hand clamped the back of his neck and propelled him forward up the steps to the crowded living room. This was obviously not the person who had phoned for someone to come and take Travis away.

The sight of someone being escorted from a party was probably a welcome distraction—an old man especially so. Maybe it was tradition to assist when it came to unwanted guests. At any rate, there were other young men willing to help him along—shoving, poking a fist at him. Young women in filmy dresses screamed insults.

"You're at the wrong party, Grampaw!"

"Try ballroom dancing!"

Reynolds Green, leaning against a wall, lowered his gaze to the floor.

At the top of the long flight of steps that curved down around a large outcropping of rock, Thorstad knew that if they gave him a shove he would not reach the bottom on his own feet, nor land unhurt. He knew too that Oonagh, opening her door to get out of the car, would not reach him in time to stop something bad from happening.

But he was escorted gently down the staircase, as though his handlers believed he was too drunk or stoned to make it on his own. Or too old to be manhandled without causing injury. The surprising thing was that he was aware of Travis immediately behind him, being escorted down the steps by his own pair of bouncers. This was all so well organized, so polite. At the bottom of the staircase, both were abruptly abandoned while their escorts returned to their party.

Even now, Travis was unwilling to go. He sat on the bottom step with his fists beneath his chin. "I can't stand this," he said.

Elliot Evans had known what he was doing when he allowed Thorstad to deal with this, becoming the villain in his stead. Caught between Elliot Evans and Axel Thorstad, who would *not* want to cry out "I can't stand this!" from a bottom step?

Thorstad put a hand on Travis's back. "It's late. We're keeping Oonagh from going home."

Travis shook the hand off. "Leave me alone."

"Oh, for heaven's sake, grow up!" Oonagh was with them now. "You think this is how you make your way in this town?"

"I'm going back in," Travis said. He stood and turned to start up the long staircase.

Thorstad put a hand around Travis's arm and held tight enough to stop him. "Evans is expecting you."

Unfair of course—to remind Travis who was pulling the strings around here. Not wanting to be the villain himself.

At first it seemed the voices had nothing to do with them— youthful voices somewhere in the shadows beneath the trees on the far side of the street. Shouting had broken out. Car doors slammed and figures emerged into the artificial light. Three, four, five youths approached, yelling, probably working up their courage to crash the party. Perhaps the escorts had vanished so quickly because they had seen the car in the shadows and wanted to lock the doors.

Now Thorstad was aware of the arrival of an Audi sport convertible crammed with too many youths, some of them standing up, most of them spilling over the sides and even the windshield, screeching to a halt too close to Thorstad and Travis. Most of them pushed by and rushed up the steps to the house, but some apparently felt a compulsion to deal with the abusive old man, pulling him away from the youth he'd been bullying at the foot of the stairs. None of these youths had visible features, their faces hidden within the dark caves of their hoodies. "Get your hands off him, you fucking swine!"

There was a time when he'd imagined or dreamt or feared a whole class rising up out of their seats and attacking him—not only refusing to do what they'd been asked to do but determined to show him how powerless he really was. But this had never happened. He'd been a reasonable man. He'd had a sense of humour. He'd made it clear how much he'd enjoyed the students even when they misbehaved, though he'd been visibly disappointed as well. It helped that he'd been tall and obviously strong.

It was necessary not to be impressed, or appear afraid. "All right," he said, now, holding both arms out wide as though to welcome these youths rather than fight, to demonstrate his willingness to talk, even to laugh at himself. To acknowledge that he was outnumbered but not intimidated. "We'll get out of your way. This is no place to solve differences. If you want an explanation we can—"

But this was not his classroom. A stubby boy leapt high enough to throw his arms around Thorstad's neck, to press his wedge-shaped beery face and weasel eyes to Thorstad's face, to plant his feet against Thorstad's shins and bash his forehead against

Thorstad's forehead—pulling him forward, bending him forward to collapse to the ground, and rolling him onto the brick walkway.

These youths—children, really—were shouting for the sake of shouting. Thorstad might have been an escaped animal they must capture, or a friend who'd betrayed them. He might have been in the midst of a schoolyard brawl. He was pulled by his arm in one direction, by the neck in another, and dragged by arms around his waist into the dark garden shadows behind an evergreen shrub.

He could hear Travis shouting for help, though he seemed to be still at the steps. The steady honking of a horn would be Oonagh raising the alarm.

Perhaps these youths, these children smelling of booze, believed Thorstad was someone else. But it was no good trying to protest, he could not be heard. They were wild hunters beating the bushes. Yanking at his limbs, pulling at his clothes. His glasses flew out from his shirt pocket and disappeared into the dark. He had found himself at the centre of that terrifying scene in *The Lord of the Flies*, the novel he'd been required to teach so often he'd eventually hated it enough to show the movie instead, just to get it over with. Was an old man, evicted from a party, automatically a despicable creature, an outcast, and a taller version of poor doomed Piggy? *D'you want to die, old man?* The youth at the ferry dock had warned him of this.

It would end badly, he knew that. From somewhere behind the yowling rabble he could hear Oonagh's horn still honking for help. If he was not to be stabbed, like Piggy, with pointed sticks, then certainly he would be beaten and left to die. It would have been better if his gentle civilized escorts had pushed him from the top of the stairs, as he'd expected, sending him flailing and stumbling down the concrete steps to suffer something as simple as a broken leg and some bruises.

As he was dragged away from the steps he had the impression that Travis, thrashing about, was being held back by one or two of the juvenile goons. But the mob, or what felt like a mob, let go—having dragged Thorstad away from the street and the lights onto grass—and stepped back to form a circle around him. They had all, evidently, been forced to read *The Lord of the Flies* in school and were about to punish him for it. The damn book may have been meant as a call for maturity, order, and compassion, but it succeeded only in putting ideas into certain heads. The only thing they knew to do with it was imitate.

One of the boys tossed Thorstad's wallet to the ground, and counted the bills in his hand. Held his credit card high, perhaps in search of light enough to read.

"Empty your pockets," someone shouted.

Thorstad turned out his pockets and let his folded white handkerchief fall to the ground. There was nothing else. A black comb.

"C'mon, c'mon, where you got it?"

He saw that the one who had raided his wallet was now pointing a handgun at him. Of course it could have been a toy. Did fourteen- or fifteen-year-old boys carry real guns? Did fourteen-year-old boys drive Audis? Apparently they did. Maybe this one with the gun, the smallest and therefore the cruellest, was actually a stunted adult.

"Nobody comes out of that house without something on them," he said. His face was unclear in the dark, but Thorstad could tell it was narrow and pointed.

"I have nothing on me. I've just come to take someone home."

Why would they expect a seventy-seven-year-old man to have drugs on him?

Because no one came out of that house without something on them, as the boy said. And presumably that must include the elderly. Perhaps they had watched here, night after night. Perhaps this was not a housewarming party at all, but a nightly debauch in a party house. And maybe they knew that at a certain time of night—when the danger of a police raid was greatest—someone old and respectable looking was sent out of the house with all of the unconsumed pills and capsules and powders, transporting them to wherever the party would move next. How could he have anticipated such a thing?

But he should not expect it to make sense. They had attacked him simply because he was there, and because he was old. And so they thought they might as well take anything he might have on him.

It might have been better if he'd had something besides his wallet to give them. They now had their disappointment as a reason to beat him. And indeed the little wedge-face with the handgun rushed at him, swinging the weapon, and cracked it against his head.

19

The cast on Axel Thorstad's arm was his first since 1939, when he'd lost control of Johnny Dixon's blue CCM bike and steered into a telephone pole. He'd forgotten what a nuisance it was to have a clumsy weight on his arm, though this plastic contraption was lighter than the remembered plaster. He dreaded the mirror and what it would tell him about the bruises on his face, the large bandage on his forehead. If a man his age must have wounds they should be hidden from public view.

Of course the cast and the bandage were not the whole of it. There were aches and pains throughout his body, some of them visible bruises. Those wild youths had made sure that every inch of him carried a reminder of their power and brutal contempt. He was not about to make any sudden moves.

Travis had not been in the guest house when he'd wakened this morning. He had gone with Camilla to meet Carl at the airport. Father and son were planning to accompany Evans while he visited a vineyard where they would shoot "on location" Monday morning. There was no real need for them to go but it was a way for Travis to keep his distance.

Soon after arriving, Carl had knocked on the guest-house door and come in slapping a brown envelope against his pant leg as though urging himself on, as he might a reluctant horse. Looking at Thorstad with an awkwardness he probably wished to keep hidden, he'd resisted what must have been a temptation to comment on yet another bandage to Thorstad's forehead. He regretted the assault, he said, but saw no reason for Thorstad to fly home when he could stay on and finish the job. "It's not like you to throw in the towel at the first setback. It's not like what I remember of you anyway."

Thorstad's aching wounds did not encourage him to be careful. "Meaning, you don't want to lose patients by staying here yourself?"

Carl was dressed today as he dressed for work, in grey wool slacks and a white dress shirt open at the collar. He shrugged off Thorstad's rude suggestion. "The young dentist we've brought in can take care of my appointments, but I'd really rather you didn't quit." He spoke with his back to Thorstad while looking out through the glass towards the ocean. "I guess I saw you as inexhaustible, with enough resources to keep any young actor riveted to the books. I remember how we'd miss basketball games in order to trail after you to some amateur play in a community hall." He turned back, smiling. "We'd be late for Math because we were up the hillside reading the Romantics."

"I was younger then. And didn't have to compete with a television studio."

Because he felt foolish talking with a former student who stood over him while he was sitting up in bed with his legs straight out before him, Thorstad insisted that Carl sit on a chair. "This is not what I'd call a mere setback, as you put it. It seems more like a wake-up call, a bonk on the head to convince me I'd taken on more than I can handle. Maybe I'm too old. I should have known I'd be no match for your son's real masters."

Carl sat at the front edge of his chair, obviously anxious to get away, yet he had assembled all the facial requirements to suggest sincerity. "It may have been a wake-up call for Travis, too. He feels bad about this, and promises to try harder."

Axel Thorstad had little patience for this. "He doesn't have the liberty to try harder. We've both been put in a position where what you ask is impossible."

Carl stood again. "I'm keeping the others waiting. All I ask is that you reconsider. I understand you'll be up and about in a day or so. Any help you can give is better than no help at all." On his way to the door, he tossed the envelope onto the bed. "Your mail."

Lisa Svetic had scrawled the Montanas' address in turquoise ink.

When he'd torn the large envelope open, a smaller blue-lined envelope fell onto the bedspread. A flower fell out as well, dried up and pressed flat by its journey—some kind of aster, he imagined, disintegrating into yellow powder.

There was also a pair of lined pages torn from the sort of school notebooks Lisa Svetic sold in her store, folded over once. Opened up, they seemed to be covered with the too-careful handwriting of a child, and yet, at the bottom of the second page was the postmistress's signature—sprawled wide and decorated with flourishes, looking as important as any prime minister's name on a legal document. No doubt she saw the forwarding of other people's letters as an opportunity to scold him about something, or bring him up to date on some local event he was meant to regret missing.

The return address on the blue-lined envelope was a village a few miles north of the school where he'd taught. The handwriting suggested haste, or someone who did not write often.

Dear Mr. Thorstad,

I was in your English class the year you invited that so-called "famous" poet to visit us and he was so drunk he could barely stand up straight. Sat on the corner of your desk but slipped off and fell to the floor. You scowled at us when we laughed. He read us one of his so-called poems. Filthy stuff. I never seen you looking so uncomfortable. The boys loved it, especially the descriptions of his first seduction of a Grade Nine classmate when he was fourteen. That may be the only thing I remember from my time in school.

How could he forget Rudyard McKenzie's visit! Not too long afterwards the man had published a long poem that bluntly outlined the charms of specific girls in Thorstad's class, detailing the fantasies they'd inspired in him, and ended by mocking the notion that a mere high school teacher could possibly have the talent, insights, and sensitivity to teach poetry to adolescents. The poem did the rounds of the staff room of course. Miss Mavis Hinds was apoplectic. The principal suggested Thorstad choose his guests with more care. Of course the poem did not mention that MacKenzie had kept Axel and Elena Thorstad up late into the night tolerating his stories of fellow poets he'd knocked senseless and the women he'd bedded. He would be the last classroom visitor to sleep in the guest bedroom.

Anyway somebody heard about an ad you put in the paper and found out you're living up on Estevan Island, enjoying your hefty teacher pension.

I got four children now, between the ages of 11 and 17. The second is named Axel but we call him Marty. You probably remember Con McGahan, always in trouble, brought his shotgun to school once to throw a scare into Pete Boyle who wanted to date me. As if! Well, he went and left us a year ago and hasn't sent a single penny or even a letter since. I've had to move us all to a low-rent shack miles up Caspar Road near the dump but can't always afford gas for the rusty old Honda Civic to get us in and out to shop for groceries. Not that I have much to shop with. Three of the four kids got something desperate wrong with them I can't afford to get fixed. (One with crossed eyes—in this day and age!) So I'm swallowing my pride to ask if you could help me out by

"Oh no!" He didn't know whether he should read on and have to deal with the request or act as though the letter had never arrived. When correspondents boasted of swallowing their pride, it was usually a reason to proceed with caution. The letter was signed "Taffy McGahan nee Tupper" two pages later—two pages that appeared at a glance to be filled with disasters. The phrases "house fire" and "overturned truck" and "multiple fractures" stood out, each of these underlined with three obviously violent strokes. Taffy Tupper had become pregnant during Grade Eleven, he recalled. It appeared her life had not improved much since.

The question was: How to help Taffy Tupper—or her poor children at least—without giving the impression he was an easy mark who could be bullied with further appeals? It made more sense to alert the social welfare people once he got home, though surely she would have done that already herself.

Strange, how it was possible to worry about a faraway hypothetical mess even while in the midst of a disaster of his own. He could imagine Oonagh's laughter if she were to learn that he had not dismissed this letter out of hand. But Oonagh was flying to New York today, to present someone with an award she'd won herself twenty years ago. "I suppose I'm to represent Living History—a shock for those who thought I'd gone to my ultimate reward!" She would be there for ten days—there were several shows to take in, many old friends to look up—before going home to her architect in Toronto.

She had accompanied Thorstad to the hospital, and, not surprisingly, attempted to keep him distracted with her mockery. "My God, Thorstad, do all your dates end up this way? Has every woman in your life had to stand by and watch you tossed out of parties?" Of course she laughed and wheezed and showed all her perfect teeth. She said she'd never known a man so quick to make enemies. "What the hell did you *do* in that house? Can't we take you anywhere?"

She'd rescued his wallet from the grass once his attackers had scattered, and had later reported the theft of his credit card to the company. Other cards were still in their tight leather slots.

Because he was a man "of a certain age" with a head wound, they'd kept him in for observation through the following day. Oonagh had visited again, and again had tried to distract him from the memory of the beating if not its wounds. She may have guessed that he now believed he'd been escorted down the coast-line in order to meet his death in Beverly Hills. Even while he lay on the dark grass outside the party house, with Oonagh and Travis crouched over him, he'd been convinced that the flowering oleander crushed by his face would be the last scent he smelled on this earth.

Instead of dying he had been burdened with the humiliating trappings of a boy who'd fallen from a bike. Anxious that he not take the beating personally, Oonagh had assured him that while he was being pushed around, the rest of the barbarians had rushed up the stairs to tear the party house apart. "*Trashed* it, as they say down here. Probably just for the fun of it. Others were hurt as well."

She'd called this morning before boarding her plane—to remind him she was leaving and, she said, to reassure herself that he hadn't died of self-pity. "And, if Evans doesn't fire the boy, and the boy's parents don't fire you, and if you come down again at a time when I'm here—well, we never did get to the Hunting-ton. And there's the gorgeous Getty museum. And, who knows, I may drag you off to a classier restaurant next time where you can see faces you almost recognize while you discover just how ordi-nary we really are down here."

Confident he would never see her world "down here" again, he had not responded to this but stumbled over words to thank her for the time she'd spent with him. "I'm just not sure what to say."

Of course she'd laughed. "My darling Thorstad, all you have to say is: 'That's all right, Ludie. I've had my trip.'"

Axel Thorstad had had no idea what she was talking about. Something he'd forgotten? Kicked out of his head by one of those brutes? "What's that supposed to mean?"

"It means what it says. Just *say* it! 'I've had my trip.' Carrie Watts at the end of *The Trip to Bountiful*—my favourite role."

"I read somewhere that Saint Joan was your favourite role."

"If you've kept tabs on me you should know that Antigone was my favourite for a while. And the Madwoman of Chaillot. And, most recently, Carrie Watts. Just say it. Say, 'That's all right, Ludie. I've had my trip!'"

He'd said it then, because she had asked, and because he supposed it was true in some way she'd wanted it to be.

"One more thing and then I have to run," she'd said. "Before you bite off Travis's head, ask him to show you what I found while you were lazing in that hospital bed." She did not explain this. "I'm sorry I won't be there to do it myself."

There were no birds outside at this time of day. The only sound through his open window was the muted roar of the surf far below. The air was filled with the rich scent off the desert flowers, though occasionally a light breeze carried the slightly medicinal scent from the eucalyptus trees inside. He might as well read Lisa Svetic's letter.

Dear Mr. Thorstad,

I'm putting this letter in with my own in a bigger envelope because Gwendolyn S asked me to send this flower. In case you don't recognize it, it's hairy arnica. She's pregnant again. Nobody knows whose this one is, any more than we know where any of the others came from. Anyway, she's sure this one will be a boy and intends to name him Hairy Arnica (my fault, I told her what you told me once). She says this'll probably be the last one because she suspects menopause is just around the corner. Too bad. I was hoping she'd eventually repopulate the island but I guess that's going to be up to someone else. Not me.

It's a good thing they didn't have a real funeral for Bo Ham-
mond because he's turned up alive in Haiti—they took him in
for questioning the minute he walked up out of the water. No, he
didn't swim all that distance, he's been living down there with
the woman he calls his wife and just went in for a dip that day
when the police showed up. He wrote all of this to someone at the
commune—big joke, I guess. He expects to spend some time in
jail. Just think, if you'd taken over his "books" you could be down
there in the Caribbean yourself by now, maybe sharing his cell.

So Hammond wasn't lost in the waters of Georgia Strait after
all! He'd simply engineered his own escape from Estevan. Thorstad felt a flush of joy at this. The commune people could dismantle their funeral pyre, though they probably shouldn't expect
Bo to return any time soon in order to continue trafficking in
clandestine books.

The way these letters keep coming in, it makes me wonder,
What has taken them so long? And, who keeps a single copy of
a stupid newspaper this long before noticing one ad on one page
amongst five or six pages of ads? Have you been sending out
more letters I don't know about?
You're not likely to get a better offer than the one you took, is
my guess. Hollywood! I'll tell Normie not to expect to see you
again, he's wasting his time down there patching things up and
digging around in your garden.
I hope you're impressed with my grammar. I got Alvin White
to check it for me yesterday morning and then spent all of today
copying it out again, word after painful word. My fingers ache!
Yours truly (whatever that's supposed to mean),
Lisa S

When Travis entered the guest house he did not look like
someone who had as much right to be here as the old man with

the fractured arm. To Thorstad he looked like someone intruding where he believed he wasn't wanted. Also where he would rather not be. He went into his own bedroom alcove and came out again, went out onto the deck and came back in, his hands twisting about one another and then running back over his hair and then twisting about one another again. He had dressed in jeans and his chequered runners and a shirt Thorstad hadn't seen before. Possibly sent down by his mother.

"If it's only what your father wants you to say he's already said it for himself."

"It's got nothing to do with him." He sat in the chair his father had sat in earlier. "I feel like crap—okay? I didn't mean for any of that to happen."

"You mean someone tied you up and forced something down your throat? Was it Rosie? Or her friend. I remember seeing him there."

"Reynolds Green was there?" He appeared to be genuinely surprised. Alarmed as well.

"He seems to have been everywhere. Waiting."

"Damn!"

There was silence between them for a while. Thorstad did not feel it was up to him to make conversation. He was the one in pain. Let the boy work at this a little.

"Elliot hasn't mentioned dumping me yet. Well, he wouldn't fire me off this episode, but he could refuse to renew my contract for next year's show."

And so Rosie and her friend may have got what they wanted. What was Axel Thorstad doing in a world where young people competed viciously for a place in the spotlight and a chance for astronomical wealth? He had spent his life amongst teens whose competitions were for a place on the basketball team, for acceptance into a university, for a job at a local hardware store. On Estevan, the pressures experienced by Travis and Rosie and her friend Reynolds would be met with blank stares or dismissive laughter.

Travis got to his feet and pulled one foot up behind his thigh, then returned it to the floor and pulled up the other. Somewhere in the distance an electric lawn mower was at work. "Maybe Reynolds will get to replace me and maybe he won't. I still got a couple of big scenes coming up." He crossed to the door and put his hand on the knob but did not open it. "Maybe you could help me with them?"

Thorstad allowed the silence to put some space between them.

"Or are you going to make me beg?"

Thorstad decided to ignore both questions. "You were right, of course. Or partly right. I've had the time to think about it now."

"About what?" Travis removed his hand from the door.

"What you said about me at the party." A second mower had started, somewhere higher up the hill. Perhaps a movie crew had moved into the neighbourhood and hadn't yet offered bribes. "With all these obstacles and frustrations, I can see where you might have got the wrong impression. I've been remembering how I felt about teaching at the beginning—little older than you are now. I can see your dedication is as genuine and important to you as my own was to me."

Travis bit his bottom lip and kept his gaze on the floor. The world outside had become busy with the sound of countless mowers.

By turning his head just a little, Thorstad could see a triangular portion of Pacific Ocean through the glass barrier on the deck. Lines on the surface converged towards something beyond his vision. "Of course we could both be wrong. Maybe that blow to my head was meant to wake me up to something. Maybe I tried too hard to live up to some idea I have of myself, or maybe my selfish drive to do my job made me as bullheaded as your Elliot Evans." He'd had plenty of time to think about this. He was careful not to look at Travis now. "Or just possibly, possibly, I was the nagging determined pest simply because I believed your best interests coincided with my own."

Lawn mowers were, one after the other, turned off. Some movie company had come through with the hush money. Travis crossed the floor to drop into the chair and put his face down into his hands. When he looked up again, it was clear he was having a good deal of trouble with this conversation. "So are we still a team or not? Will you, like, stay and help out when you can?" He hauled in a shuddering breath. "*If* I can just get around to saying what I dragged my sorry ass in here to say?"

"Well . . . maybe while you're trying to find the words you could tell me what Oonagh meant when she said you have something to show me?"

Apparently Camilla had already agreed to lend Travis her family-sized van for this. As soon as Axel Thorstad was able to get around with only a small amount of wincing and groaning, Travis drove him down onto what Thorstad had already begun to think of as the PCH and turned to the right, away from the city, to pass by several miles of gated estates and houses perched on cliffs and even beyond the entrance to the canyon of the burnt-down house until, eventually, he pulled in to the parking lot of a sprawling U-shaped strip mall. "Oonagh said she'd noticed this place before but didn't know what it was."

"This place" was at the centre-back of the mall, three tall narrow brick storefronts, one of them four storeys high, looking strangely foreign amidst all these low-slung pink stucco shops. Travis parked directly in front of the wide black doorway into the tallest building—red clay bricks, three rows of tall narrow windows, a rusted fire escape. Centurion Restaurant and Museum.

"Museum?" Thorstad said. Though Travis hadn't explained what this was about, the brick building and the name of the place had planted an anxious expectation in his gut. Had he not already discovered more than anyone needed in this city?

"She said she'd offered to look into it for you—right?"

"Did she check out this place, or did she only *find* it?"

"C'mon." Travis pushed open his door. "She's an old friend. You gotta, like, trust her."

The manager had obviously been informed they were coming. He met them inside the door and shook hands with them both, introducing himself as "Phil." Then he led them to a corner table with a *"Reserved"* sign on it. "Bruno will bring you coffee and a basket of bread." He pulled out a chair for himself.

He was probably Axel Thorstad's age, a slight man with a thin beak nose, and a cheap dark wig on his head—possibly a retiree who couldn't stay away from the business, anxious to keep an eye on his employees. The small room contained fewer than a dozen tables, prepared for a lunch crowd that had not yet arrived.

"Miss Farrell told me you have family connections to Centurion Pictures," he said. His tongue explored a gap in his upper front teeth. "I worked for them as a set designer for a few years— long ago, just before they went out of business. When developers started to tear it all down I bought these building fronts and opened up this restaurant behind them."

"Mr. Thorstad has come thousands of miles to see this place," Travis said, "even though he didn't know it existed."

Mr. Thorstad had not yet decided whether he wanted to be here. He could walk out any moment. He could walk out on the father who had walked out, so to speak, on him. He could walk all the way back to the Evanses' guest house if he had to.

"Ah yes," the proprietor said, his slightly Asiatic eyes examining the bandage above Thorstad's eye. "I explained to Miss Farrell that I knew your father when he was, well, quite a bit older than I was. Middle-aged? Limping a little?" He paused, perhaps thinking this over, and lowered his gaze to his own bony hands on the tablecloth. "He'd worked for Centurion long before I did, and seemed pleased I'd bought these building fronts. In fact, he was the one who suggested I add the museum." He spread his fingers and appeared to be studying his nails for a moment.

Axel Thorstad realized he'd been holding his breath. He closed his eyes and breathed again, and waited for this man to finish his story. There was the smell of fresh bread in the air.

"Well, it might not have been his idea, it just came out of our conversation." He looked up at Thorstad again and shrugged. "He'd learned I'd bought up a lot of other Centurion stuff as well—equipment, sets I'd designed—without any idea what I would do with it."

He left the table briefly to investigate a muttered exchange at the doorway to the kitchen. Enough time for Thorstad and Travis to raise eyebrows at one another but not enough time to sort out an old man's tangled thoughts. He was, he supposed, a little frightened of what he might hear. Yet told himself it didn't matter. He had already heard what mattered. Anything this man could say would not alter that.

When the proprietor returned, he brought a tray of coffees and a basket of bread for the table. Then he sat back in his chair and folded his arms while he examined his guests.

"Are you sure we're talking about the same man?" Thorstad said. His throat had gone tight and dry. "I would have thought he'd hate the sight of the place." He sipped from the coffee and chose the smallest piece of bread—a courtesy, he supposed. Had this all been invented for Oonagh's sake, or for Oonagh's sad old wounded friend? "How did you even know who Miss Farrell was asking about?"

"How many stuntmen named Thorstad have I known in my life?" He appeared to find this amusing. "He'd come in and order a glass of beer and a sandwich, but it was obvious this was just an excuse to have a look around. I remember one time he brought me that photograph over there. Pointed out himself." He nodded in the direction of the end wall, overspread with framed black-and-white photos. "He's with a group of young fellows. Hired as an assistant for a few years, he said—probably Centurion's way of making sure he didn't sue."

He led them over to the wall and pointed out the photograph. Yellowed, warped, and probably brittle—it had no doubt been clipped from a newspaper or a trade magazine. Thorstad put on his glasses and leaned in close. Six young men had been arranged around a Pony Express coach, two of them up on the driver's seat, the others standing on the ground. All wore moustaches and cowboy hats. There could be little doubt which of them was the deserter Tomas Thorstad. Looking as though he wasn't sure he belonged in the picture, the man farthest to the left was long-backed and slim and certainly over six feet tall. The prominent brow, too, was familiar. This was the man his mother had wanted him to believe was already dead before his son had been born.

"Did he ever mention . . ." A catch in his throat required a pause. He was not a child! And he must not be a sentimental old man. He bought time by examining the photo more closely. His father wore a checkered shirt very much like his own left behind in the shack. "Did he ever say anything about a family?" He meant a second family. The man wasn't likely to have mentioned a run-away wife and child he'd never bothered to pursue.

The proprietor shook his head. "Not a word about his private life. It was as if he existed only once he'd come in through that door."

Thorstad placed a careful fingertip against the glass. Once he'd walked out that door and left this city he would be half a continent away from this photo. He'd have only the printed frame from a film, only the back of a mysterious man in a police uniform. "Is it possible to have a copy made?"

He was fairly certain it would not be a daily invitation to renewed resentment, but rather a reminder of a question to be pondered at length. At any rate, he could not imagine going home without it.

The proprietor nodded several times while thinking this over, then agreed to have a copy made. "And lunch on me when you come to get it, so long as you call ahead. Tomas Thorstad's son!"

He shook his head, as though not quite believing what had just transpired. "You can visit the museum then, if you like. Unless you want to see it now."

Through the open doorway Thorstad could see more photos on the wall, as well as a number of props on display: a human skeleton, a stuffed horse, a diorama depicting a brawl on the veranda of a Western saloon. An arrow pointing up a staircase promised a *"Star Cinema."* Of course he was interested in visiting the museum, but he did not feel up to that today—too weak, or perhaps too confused by what he'd just been given.

Outside, before returning to Camilla's van, he laid the palm of his hand against the red clay bricks beside the door—sun-warmed and gritty. If he were capable of standing on someone's shoulders and then climbing the fire escape, rust would no doubt flake off in his hands. The whole thing would likely pull away from the building. One more Thorstad would fall.

A few bricks were missing, he noticed, others beginning to crumble. The glass in one of the upper windows was cracked, and part of the ledge along the roofline had broken away. This old face was even more worn than his own.

It was hardly Thomas á Becket's shrine—not something to set pilgrims in motion. But it had set him in motion, in a way, though he hadn't known it was here. Did he understand why? Did he understand, for that matter, what he had found? That his father had survived but hadn't bothered to look up his family. That, even crippled, his father—who might have become an angry self-pitying charity case—had apparently found something to do with the rest of his life, something that must have required humility in a man who'd trained as an actor first and then as a stunt double: a stand-in for others who were doing what he had been trained to do himself. And then only an *assistant* to the able-bodied stand-ins. His fall not only hadn't killed him, it hadn't even stopped him.

Of course there were more questions he wanted to ask, but they would have to wait until he returned for the photograph—

which he would frame and hang, eventually, with Cliff Lyons and Susan Hayward on the back wall of his Estevan Island shack.

20

By the time he'd boarded the little passenger ferry it was already loaded with machine parts, crates of vegetables, and stacks of fragrant lumber, as well as a few strangers and a small group of returning shoppers, most of them already reading their books or folding back the pages of a newspaper. Estevan Island was a ragged dark green reef far out in the strait, sharply etched by the afternoon sun at his back. The smell of diesel, the throbbing of the engine beneath his feet, and the tremor at the pit of his stomach told him he was nearly home.

Possibly. He wasn't sure. Unfortunately, *Maestro* Eugen von Schiller-Holst was aboard as well, his broad face flushed with obvious satisfaction when he saw that Thorstad had joined them. "Just as I predicted—hah? I know music, you see. You had little choice in the matter." He claimed that Axel Thorstad had had as little choice as the families of killer whales that returned every year for a reunion out in the strait. "K Pod is out there now, returned like yourself from California, or maybe Alaska, feasting with their aunts and cousins." He thumped the wooden deck with his staff. "Let us hope they don't bring crowds of tourists down upon us."

The *maestro* seemed to find it necessary to express hostility towards the tourists. Although the island's population had always grown a little during summers, most visitors arrived in their own boats and left them tied up at their private docks, leaving their cabins only when supplies were needed from Lisa Svetic's Store. "But now! They're coming by foot and bicycle—because they can stay overnight in that damn B&B they've opened in the only commune building that might not collapse on their heads!" He didn't seem to mind that the few strangers amongst them could hear his rant. He nodded sadly towards the cello case that Thorstad had leaned into a corner. "So—you have brought the unfortunate instrument home with you?"

Thorstad did not feel any need to discuss the cello. Though Mrs. Montana had had the instrument re-strung, it still belonged, like so many things, to a past that seemed to have receded beyond his reach. Only gradually, while Travis was in school, had it recovered a few more fragments of its memory.

The *maestro* went inside for a seat but Thorstad stayed out on the narrow deck to smell the familiar salty air of mid-July and watch the little wooded island grow larger as they drew near. Tiny buildings here and there along the coastline looked like toys wedged in beneath the dark and crowded timber that dwarfed them. Eventually, he was able to pick out the Free Exchange, whose old bleached planks and cedar shakes appeared to have been overlaid with silver by the lowering sun. Once they'd entered the little harbour, he could see that the rusted pickups and old sedans of weekly commuters were parked as haphazardly as they had always been, abandoned where they'd got to when the drivers saw the ferry was about to leave without them—some without doors, one without glass in the windows, but none without a few substantial dents and a coating of mud.

Though Travis's little Tercel was nearly as battered as these, it had almost matched his mother's Jaguar for speed. After dropping Thorstad off at the dock, Travis had honked his horn as he pulled away from the parking lot, in a hurry to visit an uncle on an ostrich farm a half-hour to the north. His last words: "You really sure you want to go back? Raccoons could be living in your house." He then reminded Thorstad of his cellphone number. "In case you change your mind. I can pick you up on my way back."

Travis might not have been so cheerful if the shooting hadn't gone as well as it had for the remainder of their time in L.A. Once they'd returned to the Montana home for the run-up to final exams, Travis had been willing to apply himself to his courses, while taking one afternoon of each week for them both to volunteer at the drop-in centre—where Angus Walker had not been seen, apparently, since their one encounter. No doubt Travis's good spirits today had something to do with his conviction he had "aced" his exams, though it was more likely he had simply "passed." Confirmation had not yet arrived on government letterhead paper.

Although he had not been "dumped" from the show, or even demoted to his original minor role, Travis had reluctantly agreed to attend the local university for the first-year program in Arts and Science to satisfy his parents. He would continue to fly to L.A. for specific episodes, but it hadn't yet been decided whether Thorstad would be needed with him.

Mrs. Montana had made it clear that Axel Thorstad would be welcome to return in September, not only to work with Travis but also to help her niece from Prince Rupert struggle through Grade Twelve. "Not a good student at all, but her parents have offered to pay you well if we provide the guest house." He had not made any promises.

His trunk would be delivered later in the week. Today he had only his luggage to drag past Lisa's Store and down his trail through the woods, dirt and twigs collecting around the tiny plastic wheels. One of the feral sheep bleated somewhere to the south. Summer heat had drawn out the strong acid scent of needles from the Douglas firs. Here and there in small grassy clearings the foxgloves, some of them as tall as he was, were near the end of their bloom, all but the top few flowers having lost their colour and fallen to the ground.

Yet something was not as it should be. His silent army of painted stumps stood about in the yard outside his shack like students who'd been rushed outside for fire drill, wondering why the bell-to-come-back-in had not yet rung. Their circle eyes waited for Thorstad to do something about this. His desk, too, was out in the weather.

The grass between his shack and the retaining wall was littered with items of girl clothes and glittering costume jewellery. The horizontal arbutus trunk was in use as a clothesline—a row of socks and brassieres lay drying on it now. His property was every bit as messy as the rocky beach below it, where the retreated tide had abandoned heaps of kelp and scattered planks of yellow lumber amongst the stones and tide pools and irregular islands of sand.

Gwendolyn Something made it clear she saw no reason to leave. "Losers-weepers, eh?" she said from his doorway. "It was a waste of a decent roof. I moved the older girls into Townsends'. This place is too small for us all." She seemed to be suggesting he'd failed her in this regard.

Not once in all those summers had he and Elena arrived to find someone living in their shack. He removed the cello from his back and set it against the cabin wall, reminding himself to be patient, there must have been a misunderstanding here. But there was no mistaking the internal flare of anger. "I have a deed of sale somewhere." It was probably with the rest of his possession in that heap beneath the blue tarp.

"You ever hear of squatters' rights?" Gwendolyn stood with one hip cocked defiantly to the side. Pregnant now with Hairy Arnica. "Use it or lose it. It's a universal law." Despite the body language, she was quite cheerful about this. She was, he thought, an attractive woman. It was not altogether surprising that she'd spawned so many children from so many men. What was puzzling was why none of the men had stayed—unless, of course, she hadn't wanted them to.

He never felt so clumsy and *oversized* as when he was confounded by the unexpected—thrashing about for the right words. "I hope you didn't put my books out in the weather."

"You kidding? When they burn so nice in the stove?"

Perhaps she saw something dangerous in his face. "Don't worry!" She laughed. "We haven't needed them for firewood yet—but we wouldn't know what else to do with them. You can have them if you want."

He didn't ask about the letters he had tucked between the books. He moved up to stand where he could place a hand against the weathered corner post of his shack. "There are abandoned houses all over this island. Deserted trailers as well."

"Not with this nice view there aren't," she said. "I never knew you could sit on your doorstep and watch the sun go down behind the mountains over there." She sat on the doorstep now, perhaps to demonstrate in case he had never thought of it himself. "You walked out and let it go to waste." She raised her voice: *"Girls!"*

Girls popped up from below the retaining wall. Girls in shorts ran out from the woods behind the shack. Two girls swung down from branch to branch of the hollow cedar, and dropped to the ground. A towhead ran inside and came back out with his shotgun, which she let hang at her side while she waited to see how this conversation turned out.

"This gentleman wants us to move into some old farmhouse swarming with rats and stinking of raccoon poo, which everyone knows is hazardous to your health. You think he's being fair?"

The indigenous flowers hissed. The girl on the step stuck out her tongue.

"I would rather not call the police," he said.

Of course she would recognize an idle threat. To invite police onto the island was to encourage them to investigate every rumour that had reached them in the previous year. They would comb the woods for grow ops the helicopters hadn't spotted from above. They would check out every shack for fugitives from the law, and certainly find a few. The person who'd called them over would be ostracized for life.

Gwendolyn explained that a room had been reserved for him in the Commune B&B. Another guest house! "Every room comes with its own reconditioned bicycle for getting around."

His shock and indignation must have made a boiled cabbage of his brain. He couldn't think of what to do. He hadn't raised his voice in front of youngsters since his first year of teaching, when he'd learned that it did little good and left him with a headache for the rest of the day. And showing his indignation had always made him look a fool. Students had taught him that, too. If he left here in a huff, the girls would imitate him behind his back. Yet how could he turn away from his own home?

Perhaps Gwendolyn understood his problem. "Go on to the Commune now and check in," she said, almost sympathetically. "If you come back in time for breakfast tomorrow, the girls will whip you up one of their mushroom omelettes."

On the gravel outside the front step to Svetic's Store, a bright red motor scooter stood at an angle, a shiny helmet hanging from the handlebar. When he'd stepped into the familiar scent of cinnamon, he saw that a bearded giant in black leather pants and vest had installed himself in Lisa's chair to read the weekend coloured comics. Though Lisa saw him enter, she dusted shelves all the way down the aisle to the end before coming up to stand behind her counter with the undershirt-duster still in her hand. "Yes?" She spoke to Axel Thorstad as though to a stranger who wasn't particularly welcome. "You remind me of someone I used to know, but he went off to live in Disneyland. You can't be him, because he would have warned me he was coming before I heard it from others." She bent to scribble on a pad of paper. "The trouble with summer is you never know who's on the island. Anyone can sneak their boat into a bay and take over a deserted shack—free holiday!"

She'd chopped her hair off just below her ears. Perhaps she'd despaired of anyone finding glamour in her topknot, or had grown tired of having it come down around her head every time she laughed. She wasn't laughing now.

"Gwendolyn has no intention of budging from my shack. The best I can expect is an omelette if I return in the morning—made by her daughters."

Lisa's laughter set her flesh in motion. No hairpins dropped to the floor but all chins trembled. She hauled in a deep breath, placed the tips of her fingers on the counter, and leaned in close. "Avoid the omelette, whatever you do! Those girls would lace it with poison mushrooms and never bat an eye." A small pair of crossed swords had been added beneath the thistle tattoo on her neck.

The bearded man in the red-leather chair shook the comics vigorously, perhaps to protest the distraction.

Lisa lowered her voice. "How's anyone supposed to recognize you in those city clothes? How long you think they'll last once you start prowling the bushes for junk? Or are you just a *visitor*?" She pronounced "visitor" as though it possessed a foul taste.

Thorstad looked down past the two perfect creases in his dress pants to his polished size 13 shoes, and laughed. They had already accumulated a rim of mud. "I've been a traveller in a strange land, Lisa—where streets are paved, though not with gold, and my baggy corduroys might have got me arrested. And, as I've just explained, there's a tribe of females living in my shack, where I'd expected to change my clothes!"

She turned to fetch a stack of magazines from his mail slot. "So are you back or are you not?" She grabbed a bag of salted peanuts from the candy shelf to place on top of the magazines. "Can I count on making a profit off of you again, is what I mean.

I've got oatmeal that's gonna be crawling with weevils soon if you don't take it off my hands."

Eventually she agreed to have a talk with Gwendolyn. "But I may have to make some promises *you* will have to keep."

"Such as?"

"Well. Such as maybe you could fix up one of them other shacks for her. Lord knows there's plenty around."

She didn't seem to see what a preposterous demand this was. "I'm to become a construction engineer at *my* age just to win the right to live in the building I already own?"

Rather than acknowledge this complaint, she reminded him that some of the buildings were off limits. The Radcliffes still came over now and then to camp in their old farmhouse. The Holloways liked to check up on their trailer, though never stayed overnight. "You want to stay clear of the old Salter shack though, down at the head of Deeper Bay. Kerry Holmes seen smoke—saw smoke—from the chimney when he was beachcombing yesterday and the Salters haven't been on the island for twenty years. Somebody's using that hidden place to distribute drugs, I bet you anything. You don't want to run into them guys without an army at your back."

It was up to him to think of something that would appeal to Gwendolyn, she said. "Nothing is simple with her. I used to figure she told me every thought that went through her head— except the names of the girls' fathers." Her gaze shifted to the figure behind the comics but darted as quickly away. "But never mind, I'll go down tonight for a chat. She's a little scared of me, I think—I don't know why."

She refused his money for the peanuts. "The Free Exchange will be glad to have you back. They're running low on junk. You can start by turning in them spiffy clothes." At the sound of an approaching engine running on just a few of its cylinders she stood up on her toes to peer through the window. "Here comes your hope for a ride."

His hope for a ride was a GMC pickup from the 1950s, without muffler, fenders, or much remaining paint. It pulled up on the wet gravel in front of the store, brakes squealing, the motor continuing to hum and cough and sound as though it were running backwards even after it had been shut off and the driver had got out and slammed his door. This was Alvin White, who must have rescued one more wreck from across the strait but hadn't restored it yet to health.

It was always a shock to see how thin Alvin was when he was upright, his white beard hanging to his belt. According to Lisa, he was on his way to work. "Real work for a change—isn't that right, Alvin? Not just fooling around with motors."

Alvin shut the screen door behind him and admitted that he was now a paid employee of the Commune Bed and Breakfast. "Handyman. Cook's helper. Waiter."

"It was that hospital shirt got him the job," Lisa said. But when the fellow in the leather chair looked out from behind the comics and cleared his throat, she lowered her voice. "Anyone who can keep himself that clean while messing with motors is good enough to work in a kitchen, even if he don't know a thing about food."

Alvin dipped his head to acknowledge the compliment. As usual he was indeed wearing one of his stolen baby-blue smocks. He reached to shake Thorstad's hand without quite looking into his face, then turned to Lisa. "I forgot to get myself some smokes yesterday."

"Forgetting's normal here," Lisa said, reaching for a package of the only brand she carried. "Mr. Thorstad forgot he'd deserted us and accidentally wandered back. Now he's just another tourist looking for a place to sleep. Maybe you can make sure Rainbow gives him a room? We don't want him sleeping under wheelbarrows, scaring kids and wildlife half to death."

Only when Thorstad was about to follow Alvin out the door did she remember, or pretend to remember, that one more letter had arrived. "From Calgary," she said. "I put it aside to send on."

As soon as he'd put his luggage and the cello in the truck bed and climbed into the cab, he asked Alvin if he knew the fellow in Lisa's chair. Alvin chuckled as he rammed the gearshift into first. "No one knows who he is. Appeared a couple weeks ago and made himself at home. I heard a rumour Lisa went across the water to post an ad on the Internet. 'Looking for love,' or something. Then this guy shows up, I guess for a trial run. Handling your letters must've give her ideas, eh?"

They were soon rattling down the road, slowing to skirt some of the narrower puddles and gearing down to plough through those that spanned the road and lasted for twenty or thirty metres. On the seat between them was a copy of *Under the Volcano*. "In case it's a slow night," Alvin explained, tapping two pink fingernails on the front cover. "I been working my way through some that Hammond left behind. This one's got me beat."

The commune was no longer quite the "filthy pigsty mess" that Lisa had warned him of. Though Bo Hammond's pyramid of logs and car tires and scraps of lumber remained, the dirt yard had been tidied up a little—rusted machinery hauled out of sight and some scotch broom cut back. The building's slab-wood walls had been given a half-hearted coat of battleship grey, but one window was still boarded up and several shingles had come loose to slide partway down the roof. Thorstad resented the reasons that put him here but he was curious to see what the commune folks had made of this place.

A potent bouquet of unpleasant smells was his first impression. His room reeked of the red paint that had been applied to the rough plywood walls, but this was mixed with the smell from saucers of scented wood shavings set down on the bedside table, bookshelf, and chest of drawers. There was even a scented candle burning on the windowsill. Where a proper hotel might have hung a framed print of a landscape, the managers of this B&B had tacked up a tie-dyed shirt, arms splayed so that every colour of the rainbow could be admired.

After a brief knock, Alvin opened the door just long enough to say, "Supper in half an hour. Tonight there's chili." When he had almost closed the door, he opened it again. "Vegetarian." His beard was crammed inside a hairnet attached to his ears.

Thorstad blew out the scented candle and gathered up the saucers of potpourri to set them outside the window. He stood on the chair to remove the thumbtacks from the tie-dyed shirt, and rolled up the shirt to push it beneath the bed. He had tolerated scented candles in his classroom when it seemed appropriate for lessons on the poetry of Woodstock, and had looked out at tie-dyed shirts for longer than he wanted to think, but he did not intend to spend the night surrounded by these trappings now.

How could he be certain that he wasn't as captive here as Topolski in his nursing home? The possibility, however unlikely, raised goosebumps on his arms. This could be precisely how it happened: you got old and one day appeared confused and unable to understand how someone else was living in your house, so people who thought they knew what was good for you tricked you into a building where your meals were cooked for you and your bed was made by strangers but you were not allowed to leave. Leaving would be difficult if the institution were on a small island with a passenger ferry that crossed the strait only two or three times a day, and a captain like Danny Joseph who could be instructed not to allow you to board.

Well, this was no time to let his imagination make a fool of him. He could have a fight on his hands just to recover his shack and should not allow himself to be distracted by what-ifs.

If he were indeed in an Assisted-Living Home for *senior-seniors*, he was one of very few residents. In the dining room, two elderly women in khaki shorts looked up from their meal and nodded pleasantly. He had his choice of table from the five that were still unoccupied. There was no trio attempting Schubert here. No nurses stood by to watch, though Alvin White stood in the kitchen doorway.

Once he was seated at his own table, one of the women looked up to ask if he supposed that pyramid of logs was the remains of a previous civilization. The smile invited Thorstad to join in the joke.

"Yes it is," he said. "Previous to the B&B, that is. This spring, in fact. A funeral pyre."

Smiles faded. "But it hasn't—"

"It hasn't been lit because the body was never found."

The woman with tight yellow curls nodded. "A monument, then. For the dead."

"The dead is no longer dead, and has resurfaced in a Haitian jail. Or so I've been told. I suppose they may burn it on Hallowe'en."

"Extraordinary!" The women returned to their meal, though they did not look convinced.

His bowl of vegetable chili was a stewed mixture of lima beans and chickpeas and colourful peppers and tomatoes, but smelled deliciously of fennel and celery and cilantro. He wished he'd brought a book to read, as he'd always done whenever he'd had to eat alone in public. It was often necessary to read those pages again, later, but at the time a book provided an occupation. If you had nothing to do but watch others you could be challenged by offended strangers, and yet if you did nothing but look down at your food you were little different from a cow at its manger, or a dog with its muzzle in a dish.

Of course, there was the still-unopened letter from Calgary in his pocket.

But it was not from Calgary as the envelope promised. According to the top of the letter itself, it had come from an unpronounceable location in Thailand. The signature at the bottom of the second page raised an immediate image of someone familiar, cast into doubt by a sudden dizzy spell. Maybe he'd experienced some sort of premonition, a warning against reading this thing.

Perhaps he was to receive letters from former students for the rest of his life—some thanking him, some delivering unhappy updates. This one was from Cindy Miller, the girl who'd looked out through a narrow inverted V in her long hair and slipped ambiguous love poems behind the windshield wipers of his car. He wasn't sure he had the courage to read it, but he would try.

Dear Mr. Thorstad,

I suspect you don't get many letters from former students awaiting execution. The Thai police intend to shoot me, which is what they do to people accused of bringing drugs into their country. To protest my innocence means nothing here, and there seems to be no way of proving that someone else stashed the cocaine in my luggage—though I haven't yet entirely given up hope.

A little breathless suddenly, Thorstad lowered the page to his lap. Was this a gimmick to catch his attention where the windshield-wiper-poems had not? He would prefer to think so, but feared it was genuine. At any rate, she had certainly made sure that he would read on.

Before it is too late, and in case I never see home again, I am using my time in jail to write a few letters of appreciation I should have written long ago but put off in favour of the demands of daily life and the excitement of too much travel.

I want to thank you for all you did on my behalf when I was the dreamy half-suicidal poet in the front row, no doubt driving you crazy with my imitative adolescent scribbling. You were always kind, and encouraging, though I realize now that it was not the poet you were encouraging but the unhappy teen. I suspect you knew that I had a terrible crush on you—how could you not? You were single, and rather good-looking, and only a few years older than I was. Yet you treated me with a distanced respect that somehow avoided hurting my feelings or making me feel rejected. I believe I would have killed myself if you had rejected me cruelly, yet I know very well that if you had taken advantage it would have been a disaster for us both. You may find it amusing that many years later, two of my poems were published in an obscure Alberta magazine—Yippee!—but that was both the beginning and the end of my literary career.

You may also find it amusing that I received my punishment by giving birth to a daughter who was, as a teen, as dreamy, moody, and "poetic" as I was myself. She eventually grew out of that, thank goodness, and is a lawyer in Calgary now, with children of her own, and is doing what she can to convince the Ottawa government to apply pressure on Thailand to give me a fair trial. It is a desperate hope, I realize, but we must do what we can.

(If you wish to contribute to my defence, either with money or by adding your name to my daughter's petitions, you will find her address on this envelope, for I will send all my thank-you letters to her and give her or her secretary the task of digging up addresses for the people I'm writing to. There is little else you can do—unless, of course, you are inclined to pray.)

Naturally the minute I'd written that last sentence I thought how awful it would be if every student you'd taught in your life were to write and ask for your prayers in an effort to help them clean up the mess they have made of their lives. I expect most would, if they thought of it. Even so, I would be inclined to claim the right to be first in line!

I have no idea where you are living now, or even if you are still alive, but I trust my daughter to seek you out and deliver these long-overdue words of appreciation.
Blessings on you, kind Sir!
Cindy (Miller) Wright

Axel Thorstad looked up to reassure himself he was still in the commune's dining room, that his vegetable chili was still half-eaten in the bowl before him, the large spoon leaning against the side. Obviously some of his pupils had gone out into a far more dangerous world than he had. How many teachers had received thank-you letters from former students about to face a firing squad?

Cindy Miller assumed that all former students had made a mess of their lives. Was she simply projecting her own failures onto others in order not to see herself as worse than the rest, or was this something for him to take seriously? Must he accept that whatever strengths you helped others achieve, whatever feelings of success you encouraged, you should assume they would all go on to make a mess of things? Perhaps it would be better to disbelieve in endings altogether. Carter Stone might live to love again. Cindy Miller might yet be freed. Hundreds could be praying, and the federal government could be already at work on her behalf.

Had he actually believed that if he nudged the young towards success and happiness this would last for the rest of their lives? If his father hadn't fallen on his first day in front of cameras, would he have continued to believe he was providing safety, happiness, and the opportunity for success to all those actors he was required to impersonate, or would he have decided eventually that his job had no real lasting moral importance at all?

21

Once the two elderly women had finished their breakfast, placed their suitcases in the bed of Alvin's truck, and left to catch the morning ferry, Thorstad removed the cello from its case and sat outside the front door on a short bench fashioned from rough lumber. Normie Fenton had set up a chopping block down along the side of the main building and was splitting stove-wood lengths of alder. *Thump! Crack! Thump! Crack!* Bo Hammond's pyramid glistened a little from the night's rain.

It seemed appropriate, though he wasn't sure why, that in this place, with the instrument between his thighs, he should offer up as many bars of Dvořák's Cello Concerto in B Minor as the Sinfonica would allow. And today it seemed his hands and fingers took over the task on their own, releasing him from any conscious effort and leading him effortlessly through such exquisite familiar sounds that a wistful sadness welled up to make him think of unhappy Topolski trapped in his Home for *senior-seniors*, of Cindy Miller confined to a jail in Thailand, and of his own beloved, lost, and recently silent Elena.

Yet it heartened him to think that Elena would consider this a sign that God had begun to speak to him in longer sentences. Or, more likely, that her husband had finally begun to listen. At any rate, the cello's small miracle this morning encouraged him to believe in the possible liberation of his expropriated shack. The rebuilt bicycle, which had obviously been intended for someone with shorter legs that didn't interfere with the handlebars, sent him abruptly from one side of the road to the other, and tried to toss him into the bush. But he eventually got the hang of it and pedalled, with knees wide apart, out the dirt road past abandoned fields and sagging barns and through dark stands of fir. Water fell on his neck from the laden trees and he had no choice but to splash through what were possibly the world's largest mud puddles as he sped south beside the open coastline towards the cluster of buildings above the ferry dock. A deer looked up from grazing in the field to his left, his five-spike rack of antlers ridiculously large for his dainty head. Farther along, a cock-pheasant exploded out of the ditch and flew upward across his prow, the surprise causing him to lose control of his handlebars for a moment so that he had to wrestle the whole rusty contraption back into obedience. Nothing stirred in the overgrown hayfield that had become the eventual resting place for Alvin's reconditioned vehicles. Hauled in and dumped at random, they'd been sewn to earth by the young alders and Himalaya blackberries that had grown up through their windows and doors and rusted-out holes.

From the gravel parking lot where trucks sat waiting at random angles for their drivers to return from night-shift work across the strait, he could see the little ferry ploughing its way through the water in this direction. Alvin's truck was nowhere in sight, but the two elderly guests of the B&B were standing down on the dock. Lisa's leather-clad friend was down on the dock as well, his motorbike beside him.

Lisa stood at the top of the ramp. "I'm here for the mail," she said, in case he thought otherwise.

"Your friend is leaving?"

"A fellow from Alberta's coming next week. Says he made a fortune working in the tar sands but likes the idea of helping run a store on a friendly island." She chuckled for a moment and studied the approaching ferry. "Think of all them letters you wrote and all the stamps you bought when you could've gone across and used the Internet. You must be getting old."

When the ferry had scraped against the dock, drifted briefly away, and was pulled back to be roped to the bollards, Lisa went down the cleated ramp to fetch the mail. Then, holding the canvas bag by the throat like a strangled goose, she followed several of the disembarking passengers up the ramp. While Thorstad walked his bike over towards the entrance to the Free Exchange, two men with lunch buckets under their arms hurried past in the direction of the waiting trucks. A third passenger had reached the top of the ramp before he realized who it was.

"I decided I couldn't go home without having a look at this place." His red maple-leaf knapsack hung off one shoulder.

Thorstad could not deny the pleasure he felt in this surprise—Travis in his shorts and T-shirt, grinning wide. He was probably grinning wide himself. "You can see most of it from where you stand. Welcome to downtown Estevan."

Travis appeared to think this was a trick of some sort. "This is it?" Mouth open, he turned full circle in case there was more.

"This is it." Thorstad pointed out the highlights: the dock, the Free Exchange, the parking lot, the Store and Post Office up the slope, and Alvin's machine shed beyond the giant maple. "It's possible to see everything worth seeing and get back on the same ferry you got off—if that's what you had in mind."

"I'm not leaving till I've seen your hangout. Where is it from here?"

Unwilling to be specific, Thorstad tilted his head in a vaguely southern direction. "Along that coastline there. Quite a ways along, past two or three bays and Sogawa Point."

At the top of the ramp, Lisa narrowed her eyes to study the newcomer. "So, what crimes did our friend commit while he was off where I couldn't keep an eye on him?"

Travis grinned. "Some bullying, a lot of nagging, and one noisy showdown, but we both survived. I just wanted to see what *this* place has that my parents' mansion don't."

"Doesn't," Lisa said. "Didn't he teach you anything?"

"I'll follow you up to the Store for some licorice all-sorts," Thorstad said to Lisa, once he'd done the introductions. "A few chocolate bars as well. If everything they serve at the B&B is as healthy as what I've had so far, my system may go into shock."

"You never said you live in a B&B," Travis said.

"That reminds me," Thorstad said to them both. "Make sure I come back to the Free Exchange. I need to look for something to use as a chamber pot."

Lisa crowed. "You refuse to use the commune toilet?"

"The commune toilet is for ladies only. Last night I got lost trying to find the men's privy—down a long hallway with a burnt-out light, turn left, find a door with your blind-man's hands, then outside across a pitch-black stretch of gravel till you come to the smell. I gave up and peed into a bush."

"Thank you for sharing that," Lisa said. Her breathing was heavy as she led the way to her Store, though there was obviously little in the mailbag at her side. Over her shoulder she announced that Normie Fenton had agreed to help fix up a place for Gwendolyn and her girls. "He adores you, Mr. Thorstad. I'm not sure why. He'd be glad to help you with any job it if means he'll get to hear you thank him for it. He'll even do all the work while you sit with your nose in a book and look up now and then with advice. As for Gwendolyn—"

Thorstad interrupted: "We can talk about that woman another time."

But Lisa had decided not to hear. "I scared her the best I know how. You'll have to wait and see if it worked. Tomorrow or maybe the next day you might get to live in your shack again. Or maybe not."

"Raccoons!" Travis crowed.

They were standing now on the coarse gravel Alvin had dumped in front of Lisa's Store to fill the large mud hole that swallowed a truckload of gravel every year.

Lisa laughed but did not turn back. "A whole tribe of females are living in his house. *Is* living in his house?" Her eyes shifted briefly to Thorstad, then back to Travis. "The place is draped with panties and fancy stockings. A couple of training bras too."

"Looks like I got here just in time," Travis said, walking again. "I've been dragged kicking and screaming out of squats often enough to know how it's done."

"Calm down," Thorstad said. "These are mostly little girls."

"Which doesn't mean you want to tangle with them," Lisa said. She paused for a rest before her doorstep. "We probably don't want Gwendolyn to get a good look at you, either. You may never be seen again—like a lot of other men and boys that wandered onto this island and disappeared." She grimaced. "Though not before leaving their mark, I guess you'd have to say."

Alvin's GMC pickup pulled off the road beside them. Brakes still squealed. Tailgate still rattled. Alvin had been neglecting his Mission in Life while he waited on tables. He sat behind the wheel with his window rolled down and his arm down the outside of his door, his fingers tapping at the crusted metal. His beard had been laid back over his shoulder. "You seen anyone go past just now?"

"Road's deserted," Lisa said, "except for you and these two refugees from California."

A passenger on the far side of the cab leaned across to explain. "We got a call from someone." Thorstad had never seen this man before, but that didn't mean he hadn't lived here all his life, down some overgrown trail. His chin was naked but his white moustache hung down past both sides of his mouth like twin beards pointing to the open neck of his shirt. Maybe this was Alvin's brother, visiting. Or maybe Alvin had advertised for a roommate during Thorstad's absence. "Said they left a man behind in one of them shacks at Deeper Bay."

"I figured they'd have to come by here for the ferry," Alvin said, "but if you never seen them they musta been leaving by their own boat. Shoot! Drug people, not wanting a sick man to slow them down." He spat on the ground. "Sorry, Leece."

"Said their pal was in pretty bad shape," the other man said. "They seemed to think they were doing him a favour, calling someone to get him. You sure you never seen strangers coming up the road?"

"I don't miss nothing goes by here." Lisa was clearly offended, as though both her word and her vigilance had been doubted. The aged building behind her was all the proof she needed of both her authority and her ideal post for surveillance. Everything and everyone dependent on road or ferry had to pass by here.

Alvin slammed his palm against the door. "Definitely calling from their boat on the far side. Big hurry to get away and didn't want to deal with their pal."

"Or," Lisa suggested, "someone stumbled on them that they had to shoot before they could leave." Perhaps she read the more violent sort of comics.

"This is island life?" Travis said, once the truck had roared up the muddy road and they'd followed Lisa inside.

"You must wonder how I could bear to leave with so much excitement going on!" Thorstad said. "Now tell me how long you'll stay. There're rooms at the B&B but we'll need to get you your own chamber pot first, unless you want to use the Women's Room."

Travis closed his eyes. "I have to catch the next ferry back—in two hours. I've got a rehearsal tonight." To Lisa he explained, "I'm Prince Charming."

Lisa snorted. "No kidding."

"A real test of an actor," Travis said. "Think of how you'd feel if two hundred kids walked out because they refuse to believe you are handsome and rich, with royal blood in your veins."

Inside the Store, once he had his chocolate bars and a can of processed meat to keep a balanced diet, Thorstad admitted he was inclined to risk Travis's life and virtue in order to check up on Gwendolyn again, "Just in case she's packed up and taken off."

Lisa said, "You could leave Prince Charming here with me."

"I don't think so," Thorstad said. "You need to get ready for your tar-sands fellow, who could arrive here any minute."

Lisa tilted down her head and stared at her countertop for some serious thinking. "Well." She looked up and turned her hardest gaze on Axel Thorstad. "Promise me, if she gets that look in her eye—you know the one I mean—you'll get this fellow outa there fast. We don't want any more young men missing!" To Travis she said, "We haven't found where she buries them."

Rather than taking the trail through the woods, Thorstad left the bicycle against the wall of the Store and led Travis down onto the beach to follow the shoreline—a chance for Travis to get a sense of his life on the edge of the sea. Any number of treasures might have been washed ashore and abandoned while the island's salvage-master was away.

Travis showed little interest in the washed-in children's toys or the unusual shapes of driftwood stumps. He saw only the potential souvenirs—conjoined oyster shells and patterned rocks, things to show off to friends or mount on display in his upstairs rooms. He admired the colours in a stone worn smooth by the tides; he could imagine that bright orange starfish hanging on his wall; he saw any number of purposes for a rusted oarlock off someone's boat. But Thorstad explained that collecting rocks and shells and dead animals was frowned upon here. "You should have brought a camera."

"You mean I can't keep this one mussel shell?" He opened his hand to show where the dark blue shell lay cradled comfortably in his palm.

Thorstad shook his head. "You could take that rusted oarlock up to the Free Exchange."

The mussel shell would look less interesting once Travis had got it home, of course, even if he slipped it under his shirt while Thorstad wasn't looking.

It was more difficult for Travis to obey the local rules when they came to the long bay of volcanic stone fashioned by time and tides into a broad staircase leading down into the waves. Here Thorstad pointed out the fragments of oyster shells embedded in the stone. "Eighty million years. Maybe more."

Apparently the number was so astonishing that it required repetition. "Eighty million years!" Travis bent low to study the eighty-million-year-old bits of shell. He stood up and looked one way and then the other. "If you'd turn the other way for a minute I could pry up a small piece. I promise I'd keep it safe."

"It's safe enough where it is. Let's go."

Gwendolyn Something sat on a log in front of Thorstad's shack, the skirt of her flowered dress pushed down between her thighs, her bare feet curled over the smaller log below, her gaze out to sea while a cigarette burned between her fingers. Though she could not have been unaware of their gravel-crunching approach, she did not turn to look. She raised the cigarette to her mouth, drew in deeply, and then exhaled the smoke. "Too soon," she said. "She said I had till tomorrow."

Her older girls were working in pairs to carry the painted stumps back into his shack. That the blue tarpaulin was unmoved since yesterday suggested they'd just begun.

"We're moving down to Townsends'—scrunched together even worse than here. We'll steal your tarp and string it up for a lean-to, so we can take turns going outside to breathe, even in rain." She said this to a small boat passing by. "Lisa said you 'n Normie'll add more sleeping space at the back."

"Unless we find something better." Farther away, he meant. "Is the coffee pot on the stove?"

"It is, but I'll pour it. I don't want you in there till we've cleaned things *up*!"

When she'd returned with two steaming mugs and Thorstad had introduced Travis—"a student"—Gwendolyn looked the boy over from his close-cropped hair down to his chequered shoes. "Hooker's Willow's daddy was a student. Said his specialty was the sex life of trees—whatever that's supposed to mean. Trees on this island mustn't have much sex, because he was here and gone in a day. Poor old Hooker's Willow nearly wasn't." She drew on her cigarette and looked again out to sea. "Wait a minute." While releasing shreds of smoke from her lungs she added, "I got it wrong. He wasn't Willow's dad, he was Rosy Pussytoes's. Which may explain why Rosy is such a quick little thing."

She stood up then, smoothed down her skirt while looking straight at Travis, and winked. Then she turned away and went up into Axel Thorstad's shack and came out again, this time with a pile of clothing over one arm, and started down the trail towards Townsends' little house. Travis watched her out of sight, then turned to scan the rocks and gravel and kelp and bits of driftwood down on the beach, looking no doubt for something to put in his pocket in case he had lost his chance for an eighty-million-year-old oyster shell. Yesterday's scattered lumber had been taken away by tides, and a birdcage had arrived from someone else's beach.

Sitting on the top log of Normie's retaining wall, they drank their coffee—which Gwendolyn had obviously made from his supply of Kicking Horse—while chattering girls went in and out behind them. Thorstad didn't want to see the inside of his shack before all of Gwendolyn's belongings had been removed. He knew the three photos would not be in their right places on the wall, the painted stumps arranged without any plan. The spines of his books would no longer be perfectly in line, some would be nearly falling off the shelf.

"You've agreed to go somewhere else in September, haven't you." Travis delivered this accusation without removing his gaze from the chain of mountains opposite. Sun shone down on the stony peak and timbered slopes, and no doubt on the hidden valleys with their wild animals and hermits, as well as on the glittering waves of the strait directly in front of them.

"If you keep your eyes peeled you might see a pod of killer whales out there."

Travis tore slivers off the log they were sitting on and tossed them, one after the other, down onto gravel. "You avoided my mother's invitation to tutor my cousin in the fall. I figure you decided against it. You've probably already signed on for somewhere else."

A pair of red kayaks appeared from behind the trees to the south and stroked by, perfectly abreast, the murmuring voices of the two rowers suddenly breaking into laughter for a moment. Thorstad waited until they had passed before responding to Travis's accusation—if that was what it was. "There's plenty of time to think about what's next—six more weeks of summer."

"Think about it now. Come back in the fall and help me survive my year of university. Come to L.A. again when I go. University is bound to be tough for a guy like me. It hit me while I was at my uncle's—I should've got a commitment out of you before I ever let you on that boat."

Thorstad leaned forward for a good look at Travis's face. How much importance should he give to this appeal? "Do your parents know you've made this little side trip?"

"My parents want you back to tutor my stupid cousin, you know that. You might as well nag at us both. Bring a piece of an eighty-million-year-old shell with you and you'll be the hero of my first-year science class. We won't have to stay at the Evanses' again. We could find a place of our own. My mother'll be so glad to have you keeping an eye on me I bet she'll pay for any sort of luxury we demand."

Travis hauled his knapsack onto his lap and ripped open a Velcro flap. "I wonder if a B&B without a toilet would have a DVD player. I found this in a store near my uncle's." He brought out a cream-coloured paperback and opened the back to display a disc inside. "Just because you're old don't mean you can't, you know, keep yourself up to date with what's cool! What do you think? *The Rap Canterbury Tales.*"

The next morning, Axel Thorstad rode the reconditioned bicycle down the trail to his shack to begin the task of putting things back where they belonged. This meant wrestling his desk from one wall to another, straightening out the books, and rearranging the wall photographs: Cliff Lyons on the U.S. Mail coach, Susan Hayward riding horseback with John Wayne. He removed the picture of his father in the moment before the fall, and laid it beside the Centurion Museum photograph of his still-alive father on top of the bookcase, uncertain where they belonged. Then he shifted the various stumps into positions that felt more familiar, most of them with their red circle eyes facing more or less in the direction of his chair, his desk, the window, and the view of the strait outside.

When the shack was once more his own, he went out onto the beach, stripped down to cross the gravel and sand and barnacle-crusted rocks, and walked into the water to set out for a swim. It was cold, but the water here was always cold except where it had just come in over rocks the summer sun had been warming for hours. It was the same body of water he'd swum in daily off the Montanas' place, and the same he'd seen from the Evanses' place but had swum in only the last few days before leaving, in a pair of Elliot Evans's trunks. He had been a swimmer all his life. If he'd been raised in California, his father might have encouraged him to become a stunt double for actors afraid of the water.

Until he was walking up the beach to fetch his clothes he hadn't noticed that Lisa Svetic stood beside the double-trunked arbutus waving her arms. Her bicycle leaned into a bush of oceanspray. "My lord! You should wear a bell around your neck when you're naked so people will know to keep away. Birds are dropping out of trees. The killer whales are probably halfway to Alaska by now, mothers covering the eyes of their calves."

She turned her back and spoke to the woods. "They sent me down to get you but they never told me I'd be stricken blind."

He had left his clothing folded neatly across the top of a drift-wood log half buried in gravel and worn smooth by decades of shifting tide. She waited till Thorstad had had time to pull his undershorts on before turning to face him again. "I'm surprised Hollywood let you come home, they could've used you for a lamppost now and then."

It wasn't easy to pull clothes on over wet flesh.

"This fella that was left behind in Deeper Bay? They brought him in and laid him out in the Free Exchange but he won't let them take him across to a doc. He's a terrible mess, but he wants you—Goodness knows why. He groans and moans and doesn't talk very clear but he knows how to get across what he wants. He's already made life hell for the guys that rescued him!"

Thorstad supposed this would eventually make sense. "You saw him?"

"Of course I saw him. Bloody. Filthy. At death's door but fighting the guys that try to help. They should've left him where they found him."

"He say who he is?"

"He said your name. Wouldn't say his."

With his corduroy pants pulled up, he carried his shirt and socks and shoes up the slope to the retaining wall and then up the steps to the grass. A distinct sense of foreboding had lodged somewhere inside him. He had come home from the world, for a while at least, but that didn't mean the world wasn't capable of following. "Did he say what he wants me for?"

"He wants us to bring him down to your shack, but I figured you'd want to have a look at him first."

"And he's in pretty bad shape, you say?"

"I could hardly force myself to look. Imagine a sick-and-dying man beaten to a pulp by a healthy gorilla. If he was mine I'd be bracing myself for the worst. A former *student*? He said a lot of things while they were bringing him in but most of it didn't make sense. One thing they caught—he knows you been looking for him. Asking up and down the streets if anyone knew where he was. You can take my bike if you want."

"You take it. Tell them I'm on my way." If he walked he'd have a little more time to think. And to gain control of this tremor in his hands, the confusion in his head. "You sure you heard right? He said I'd been looking for him up and down the streets?"

Lisa dropped a foot to the ground and turned back. "Looked pretty pleased with himself for a man breathing his last. Like he figured he was bringing you a great big gift you never thought to ask for!"

Acknowledgements

The quotations in Chapter 1 are from Geoffrey Chaucer's poem *Troilus and Cressida* and Earle Birney's poem "Bushed," from *Ghost in the Wheels, Selected Poems*, McClelland and Stewart, Toronto.

The quotations in Chapters 4 and 12 are from Geoffrey Chaucer's poem *The Canterbury Tales*.

The quotation in Chapter 8 is from Baba Brinkman's *The Rap Canterbury Tales*, Talonbooks, Vancouver.

The plot of the fictitious play *Returning to Troy* is very loosely modelled on the Lena Grove story in William Faulkner's *Light in August*, as well as Horton Foote's *Travelling Lady*, in *Collected Plays, Vol. II*, A Smith and Kraus Book, Contemporary Playwrights Series (later a movie titled *Baby the Rain Must Fall*). Oonagh's sentence "It's all right, Ludie. I've had my trip" is from Horton Foote's play *The Trip to Bountiful*.

The quotation in Chapter 13 is from Edgar Lee Masters's poem "Lucinda Matlock," in *The Spoon River Anthology*, The Macmillan Company.

The review of Matthew Schneider's *The Long and Winding Road from Blake to the Beatles* was written by Dr. Kim Blank for the *Victoria Times-Colonist*.

"In Time of *The Breaking of Nations*" by Thomas Hardy was composed in 1915 and published in *Collected Poems of Thomas Hardy*, Macmillan, London, 1932.

Estevan Island is a fiction and should not be identified with a real island.

The television network producing *Forgotten River* is also a fiction and not to be mistaken for a real network studio.

For advice, support, and other forms of assistance, I am grateful to Curtis Gillespie, Bill New, Shannon Hodgins, my agent, John Pearce, and my editor, Patrick Crean. I am enormously grateful to Brigitte and Hart Hanson and the generous actors, writers, producers, and crew members working on the Fox television series *Bones*. And again, as always, to Dianne.